THE
SECRET
ADMIRER

THE SECRET ADMIRER

CAROL WYER

Bookouture

Published by Bookouture in 2020

An imprint of Storyfire Ltd.
Carmelite House
50 Victoria Embankment
London EC4Y 0DZ

www.bookouture.com

ISBN: 978-1-83888-254-9
eBook ISBN: 978-1-83888-253-2

PROLOGUE

Dear Gemma,

  Hi!

  I wanted to tell you that I think you're incredible.

  I saw you in town today with your mother. I stopped and stared at you. I wasn't being rude. In fact, quite the opposite. I was hypnotised by you: the way you walk, the way you hold your head to one side when you are listening intently to somebody, and your smile. It is... perfect.

  Anyway, now you know how I feel and I'll pick the right moment to make myself known to you.

  I'm excited and nervous to find out how you will react when I speak to you.

  I hope you will smile at me.

  An Admirer

CHAPTER ONE

Nineteen-year-old Gemma Barnes threw her head forward and deftly raked her fingers through her long, ash-blond hair, pulled the elastic band from between her teeth and wound it around the locks, securing them into a ponytail before lifting her head again. She didn't bother checking her reflection in the darkened and smeared glass of the bus window. She knew she looked good.

The bus was travelling through the sprawling university campus and slowed to allow a group of students to race across the road. Gemma stared at the office-block buildings with several storeys of glass windows that made up the science department. She'd never been inside any of them, but according to one of her housemates, Lennox, there were laboratories and classrooms on every level, and on the top floor, a research area that was out of bounds to all students. They drew level with the car park. Lennox's distinguishable battered red Saab was parked directly outside the chemistry block. Although Gemma would have liked the freedom associated with owning a vehicle, she was happy enough to take public transport. Cars cost money to run and she didn't have a lot to spare.

She stretched out her legs under the seat in front of her and flexed her feet in their thick-soled boots, ideal for wet weather but less practical for a lengthy day of tutorials and lectures until seven o'clock in hot stuffy rooms. The day wasn't over yet. She had a tricky translation to complete for the following week, but she also had to finish reading the original version of *The Tin Drum* by Günter Grass in German for a seminar presentation on Monday. She stifled a yawn and lifted her canvas bag, containing her notes, books and laptop, from the well-worn seat next to her and stood up. She'd agreed to work shifts at Chancer's Bar on both Saturday and Sunday nights, which meant she'd really have to knuckle down tonight. The university library would provide fewer distractions than the house, where some of the students would be in a more party mood. It was Friday evening and she should have been joining them, playing music in her room and getting ready to head off to the students' union, or one of the many pubs in the area, for some time off. She bit back a laugh. She hadn't been out on a weekend in months, not since she'd started working at the same bar as her mum.

She thumbed the bell on the handrail to alert the driver. She was minutes away from Samford University library, located in what was once a grand manor house with three storeys of galleried landings, sweeping staircases and silence. She preferred working in her own homely bedroom, cluttered with familiar objects, but it was too easy to be sidetracked and nip downstairs to get a snack, or take a break to watch some television, then get chatting to somebody. The student house was home to five of them: twenty-year-olds Lennox, Fran and Ryan, and a mature student, Hattie. Gemma had only been living there since late August but got on with all the housemates, especially divorcée Hattie, who at twenty-six was the matriarch of the house and arranged all the cleaning rotas. Without Hattie, the two bathrooms, the kitchen and the large communal sitting room would be chaotically filthy.

Living with her mum, Sasha, while at university had never been an option. Gemma needed freedom to come and go as she fancied, keep irregular hours to suit her workload, and not have Sasha fuss over her and worry over little things – such as if Gemma was eating regular meals, or overdoing it – or ask about her life all the time. Besides, her mother needed to move on too. Sasha was only thirty-five herself, and because she had fallen pregnant with Gemma while still at school and chosen to bring up her daughter alone, she'd missed out on many opportunities, including romantic ones. It was time for her to find a new path too. They were close – closer than most mothers and daughters – but living apart was healthier for them both. It gave each of them the opportunity to become independent.

Gemma's phone buzzed and she looked down. It was Sasha. The bus lurched to a halt and she glanced at the message.

Finished this outfit today. Want your opinion.

The photo was of her mother, wearing impossibly large hooped earrings and her mane of white-blond hair piled high on her head. She was in a baby-blue jumpsuit that flattered her curvaceous figure. With her flawless complexion and naturally plump lips, she looked the same age as her daughter. Gemma smiled at the image. Her mother had no idea how beautiful she was. The doors swished open and Gemma bounced down the steps, thumbing a reply.

You look amazing. I love the jumpsuit. XX

She shouldered the heavy bag and slid the phone into her pocket, mind on Sasha. Some days, she didn't know who was the adult in their relationship. In many ways they were more best friends than mother and daughter.

It had been drizzling heavily for hours, and puddles had formed on the cracked pavement, shimmering under the lamplight like tiny black lakes. She splashed through them. The library loomed up ahead of her, dark and uninviting. She could still get back on the bus and make a return trip to Eastview Avenue, work at home, maybe even in her bed, snuggled under a duvet instead of sitting at a large table on a hard chair. Behind her, the bus pulled away with a fatigued hiss and she sighed; the work had to be done. She stuffed her hands in the pockets of her coat, wishing she'd worn gloves. It was a full-blown, miserable wintry evening.

The stone steps to the library were in front of her. Her phone buzzed again. She withdrew it and read:

Love you.

In a couple of hours, her mum would be at the bar in town. With Gemma no longer living at home, talented seamstress Sasha had begun to pursue a new career. Encouraged by her daughter, she'd saved some seed money to start up a new business, and the jumpsuit was a sign she was taking it all seriously and getting together a collection to show off her talents.

Engrossed in her thoughts, Gemma didn't hear the low cough or the gentle pop of a lid being unscrewed. She wasn't aware of the shuffling of feet. She didn't look up or notice any movement until a figure broke free of the shadows at the side of the huge building and rushed towards her. She looked up in surprise at the sound and motion, stared briefly at the raised hand, but her brain didn't register the jar of liquid being thrown until it hit her face. As pain seared across her nerves, and she clawed first her cheeks and then her eyes, she understood what was happening with sudden clarity. Someone had thrown acid into her face. Fear coiled around her heart and she screamed for all she was worth.

CHAPTER TWO

The dried mug squeaked a faint protest as the tea towel continued to revolve around and around its surface. DI Natalie Ward repeated the action as she stared out of the kitchen window onto the road beyond. Even at this late hour traffic rolled past, an incessant hum that could be heard inside the flat. Samford HQ was only a few minutes' drive up the same road, which was one of the reasons she'd chosen to live here. Work! She hadn't been in since August. Three horrendous, agonising months of purgatory, during which time she'd shed more tears than she'd ever imagined possible. It was only eight o'clock and far too early for bed. Even when she did finally give in and try to sleep, she knew what to expect: nightmares in which she'd relive the hours leading up to her daughter's murder, hours that couldn't ever be turned back and consequences that could never be changed.

She wiped the inside of the mug one last time then replaced it on the kitchen top, fingers sticking to the porcelain handle as she fought the guilt that billowed around her: an invisible, slow-moving fog that, as usual, started at her feet and rose up her body until it reached her throat, and she had to force herself to draw deep breaths, or she'd suffocate. *Count!* The psychiatrist had taught her the method to calm herself. She counted slowly on each intake of breath until she reached twenty. The imaginary haze subsided. This time, tears didn't sting at the backs of her eyes. She was making progress. She needed to. Her seventeen-year-old son, Josh, had texted her earlier to ask if he could stay over the following weekend. At the moment, he was still living in their old house with her estranged husband, David, but the place was up for sale and soon it – along with all the memories of Leigh living there – would be consigned to the past.

She ran her clammy palms under the cold tap and patted them dry on the tea towel, which she hung on the plastic hook next to the sink. The flat was functional and not at all homely but it served a purpose. It provided a roof over her head and enabled her to stay away from the family home in Castergate – a place filled with haunting memories. It gave her the space she needed to grieve alone and to help her come to terms with reality. Natalie's marriage to David had been in tatters long before Leigh and her best friend, Zoe, had been murdered, but afterwards, it had collapsed completely and David had turned his back on her. His contempt for her no longer hurt her. In some ways, she could expect nothing less; after all, her intention had been to leave him for Mike Sullivan – David's best friend and head of Forensics at Samford HQ, but then Leigh had been murdered and all Natalie's plans had been thrown out the window. David's crimes of lying and gambling seemed to pale into insignificance compared to hers. She had failed to save Leigh or Zoe, and that was unforgivable.

The hardest part of it all had been the effect on Josh, who'd initially taken his father's side and held her responsible for the family breakdown and for not preventing the murders. It had been raw and incredibly painful to have him retreat from her and her love. Having parents split up was a lot for any child to take on board, but to have it happen at the same time as losing a sibling was far worse, and he ought not to have been punished. He had surprised her though. He might have withdrawn from them both yet he'd still held down his summer job at McDonald's and started college as planned in early September. On the surface, he was coping better than her and David, and Natalie suspected it was in part down to the new friends he'd made and to his girlfriend, Pippa, who he'd met in August while on holiday with Leigh, their grandfather, Eric, and his girlfriend, Pam.

Over the weeks, Josh's attitude had changed and he no longer blamed her for the break-up or for his sister's death, but Eric, David's father, was struggling with the situation, and David himself still refused to have any dealings with her. Zoe's parents – Rowena and Patrick Keighley – wouldn't talk to her either. She had been ostracised. Had it not been for the support of her work colleagues and Mike, she would have gone under.

There was a pattering against the window, a faltering rhythm of large raindrops that slid down the glass and distorted the shapes of the vehicles below. Canned laughter rose from behind her. She'd left the television in the sitting room on for company but had no idea what was being aired. Every programme was a blur these days, exactly like her life. Initially, there'd been much to organise and she'd been kept busy with all the media fallout and endless arrangements: the funeral, dealing with relatives and friends and authorities; then afterwards, when Leigh and Zoe had been laid side by side in Castergate cemetery, she'd had to deal with Leigh's belongings. With the house up for sale, neither she nor David had wanted strangers to set eyes on their daughter's personal possessions. They'd become important – the only reminders of their beautiful daughter's life. They'd packed everything precious to Leigh into boxes to be brought out at a later date when they had moved on emotionally and physically. There'd been such a lot to deal with – the tidying up of one person's life was time-consuming and heart-breaking and had sucked from her every ounce of emotional energy.

She glanced at the silver circle frame – engraved with Leigh's name, and from which dangled a silver heart, inset with a large crystal – that stood on the kitchen window ledge. She didn't need a crystal heart to remind her of her daughter. Leigh would be locked forever in her own heart and soul. A single tear squeezed its way through her lashes and trickled down her cheek, and she let it fall, tickling its way down her face. She eventually brushed it from her chin and concluded she couldn't keep tormenting herself. Three months had passed since Leigh's murder, and Natalie could continue taking compassionate leave or she could return to work. She weighed up the choices again, thought about Josh, who was getting on with his life, reminded herself of who she was before all of this, and decided she couldn't remain in this limbo forever.

She reached for her mobile and rang Superintendent Dan Tasker on his private number. He was not upset at the intrusion into his evening. His voice was low and concerned.

'Hi, Natalie. How are you?'

'I'm fine, thanks. I only rang to say I'm ready to return to work.'

Dan didn't reply immediately and she could imagine his strong face, brows drawn together as he considered her words. They'd got off to a rocky start when he'd taken over from Aileen Melody earlier that year, but she'd proven her mettle, and she knew he wouldn't question her or attempt to dissuade her. He'd already discovered how determined she could be. 'Okay. Good. I know you've been missed.'

Dan had attended Leigh's funeral and visited her at the flat on a couple of occasions to offer support. It was unlikely they'd become close friends but he appeared to have respect for her and that would suffice for now.

'How soon do you want to return?' he asked.

'As soon as I'm needed.'

'Noted. I'll expect you Monday morning then.'

'Sir.'

She hung up and stared out of the window again. The rain had desisted and the picture outside was now clearer. She watched red taillights disappear into the distance. It was done. She'd followed

Josh's example and was getting her life back on track. Work would help her do that. She'd missed the camaraderie and her team: each individual who she'd come to know well, the challenges they faced together and the banter between them. Going back now was the right thing to do.

Her phone buzzed. It was Josh.

'Hi, Mum.'

'Hi.'

'I know I said I wanted to stay over next weekend but can I come tomorrow?'

'Sure you can. Want me to pick you up?'

'No, I'm working tomorrow. I'll catch the bus. I'll see you about six.'

'Okay. Six it is. Josh, is everything okay?'

His reluctance to respond was answer enough. Something was bothering him.

'Want to talk about it?'

'Maybe tomorrow.'

'Okay.' She knew better than to push her son. He'd matured rapidly over the last few months, and if he had issues he wished to discuss with her, he'd do that when he was ready.

'See you,' he said.

'Love you,' she replied with sincerity. She was proud of him and wanted him to know how much he meant to her. She wished she could tell Leigh the same: that she loved her with every fibre of her being. The phone screen went blank, leaving her lost for a second, then she placed it on the table and went to prepare the small spare room for Josh. It would keep her busy.

An hour later, she'd cleaned the room, made up the sofa bed and showered. She was once more at a loose end, unable to settle to watch television and not tired enough to go to sleep. It was only coming up nine fifteen but she took a novel to bed and opened it. She was stuck on the first chapter, and although she'd read the first few paragraphs over and over again, she still didn't know what they said. After a few attempts, she gave up and returned it to the bedside table, lay back against the pillow and stared at the water mark on the ceiling. It was the same most nights. She'd always had difficulties sleeping but now it was almost impossible to doze off. However, she wasn't going to rely on medication to help her. She wasn't going to become dependent on anything or anyone. *What about Mike?* With their relationship on hold, they'd had little chance to explore how they truly felt about each other. For now, Mike was a very good friend.

She reached out and extinguished the light, then settled back once more. She'd rest her eyelids and hope she'd relax eventually. The trick was to make her mind go blank long enough to fool her brain into sleep. She imagined a dark tunnel and mentally plodded towards it. She concentrated on the darkness, moved deeper into the tunnel where there was nothing but blackness and no room for any other thoughts. Deeper and deeper she went, her limbs beginning to feel heavy and relaxed. She was drifting... then the ringing of her phone yanked her immediately back into full consciousness. She reached for the mobile and squinted at the screen. It was Dan Tasker.

'Natalie, are you able to come back to work immediately?'

'Sure.' She was already halfway out of bed, waiting for instructions.

'There's been an acid attack on a young woman outside Samford University library.'

'How bad is it?'

'She died on-site. We're not sure how exactly. Might have been a heart attack or shock, or the effect of the burns. We'll have to see what the pathologist says. How do you feel about leading the investigation?'

'I'm up to it.'

'Then if you could meet me here outside the library, I'll make sure your team are contacted and know what's happening.'

'I'll be there in ten minutes.'

She threw the phone onto the bed and rummaged in the wardrobe for appropriate clothes. Once she was dressed, she paused by the front door to her flat. Was it too soon to return to work? Was she capable of leading this investigation? She shook off the doubts. This was what she needed. It was what she was good at. *But not always good enough.* She hushed the nagging voice in her head and raced outside.

CHAPTER THREE

FRIDAY, 16 NOVEMBER – LATE EVENING

Blue flashing lights bounced off the brown brick walls of the substantial building at one end of a pedestrian zone, now cordoned off. Police had moved away any onlookers, and the area was clear of anyone who wasn't associated with the emergency services. Natalie explained who she was, and received a polite, 'Ma'am.' His eyes said more. She was well known – her face had been plastered across the newspapers along with dramatic headlines: LEADING DETECTIVE'S DAUGHTER MURDERED! She ducked under the police cordon. A tent and lights had been erected close to the library, and forensic staff were already sweeping the area near it. She spotted Dan in conversation with Mike at the foot of the library steps, and headed directly towards them.

Mike gave her a small smile. 'I heard you're back in the saddle.'

She nodded. There was no irritation in his voice that she hadn't told him of her decision. He already knew she'd been considering returning and had been all for it…

She lifts the glass of wine to her lips. It's the first glass she's drunk in three months and it tastes sour to her palate. The pub is quiet and Mike has brought her out to remind her that the world is still turning and that she continues to hold a place in it. His eyes are trained on her – bright, keen eyes that ooze empathy and understanding. He has a five-year-old daughter who he loves with all his heart and who he only gets to see now and again. He comprehends some of the pain she's been experiencing and has been her rock the last few weeks. He places his pint glass on the stained cardboard beer mat advertising a Christmas special beer, and speaks.

'It's been the shittiest time for you but if you don't get back to work soon, you'll forget who you are.'

'What do you mean?'

He sighs. 'I don't want to be rude but you're changing, withdrawing into yourself a little more, day by day. I'm worried that if you don't go back soon, you'll not be able to.'

She looks down. He's hit the nail on the head. She's fully aware that she's been putting off the return to work. Dan told her to take as much time as she required, and to start with she'd needed it, but now she's finding herself wasting time, walking around shops, staring at clothes that Leigh would have loved, or spending time at the cemetery, simply sitting by her grave. She knows why, too. If she'd worked out who'd been behind the Blossom Twins abductions and murders earlier, she would have saved her daughter's life. The killer had been under her nose all the time.

Mike reads her mind. 'It wasn't your fault. Even Tasker read him wrong. He fooled us all.' He knows better than to mention the man who killed her daughter and Zoe by name. She never wants to hear it spoken again. The killer is behind bars, but in her book that isn't punishment enough for the pain he's inflicted on them all, and on all the other families whose children he murdered before Leigh and Zoe. He slaughtered nine girls in total – nine youngsters whose lives were cut short and whose families would forever live with the loss.

'I was leading the investigation.'

'If it hadn't been for your observational skills, we might never have found him.'

'By then, it was too late, Mike.'

'*I know. You paid too hefty a price, but you did absolutely nothing wrong. You worked the facts and got the result, in record time. You are a brilliant detective. If you are having doubts about that, put them aside immediately.*'

She offers him a faint smile. '*You know me too well.*'

'*No, I'm only beginning to know you well. Give me time.*'

'*I'm not sure I'm up to heading another murder investigation, Mike. I'm scared I'll screw up again.*'

'*You didn't screw up, so you can forget that argument.*'

'*I've lost my self-belief. Maybe it's time for me to hang up my hat and try my hand at something else.*'

'*Like what?*'

'*I don't know.*'

'*Natalie, you've only ever been in policing. You have made your way up the ranks. You work at one of the most prestigious headquarters in the UK, and you are there because you are one of the best. If you weren't any good at your job, you'd have been asked to step down. The psychiatrist has passed you fit for duty. Tasker wants you back. Your team want you back and you… well, you need to get involved in another case. Get your teeth into something that gives you a feeling of self-worth. It's the only way.*'

She raises the glass to her lips again, sips the wine, and then lifts her beer mat up, bringing with it a particular smell of malt or stale beer. '*If this mat lands picture up I'll retire and look for something else to do. If it lands brand name up, I'll go back to HQ. The universe can decide.*' *She balances the mat on its side and spins it. It turns on its axis and falls. The beer logo is visible.* '*Looks like you and the beer mat have spoken.*'

The corners of his eyes crease charmingly as he smiles. '*I think you'll benefit from returning, and besides, the universe is always right.*'

'*I'll give it a little more thought then ring Dan.*'

Her hand is on the table and he folds his own over it, squeezing it gently. '*That's my girl,*' *he says.*

*

'Good to have you back.' Dan's soft Welsh accent dripped like melted honey and he gave her a smile.

She wasn't fooled by his warmth. It could be turned off in an instant when things didn't go his way. She acknowledged him with a respectful, 'Sir,' and waited for further information.

'The victim is nineteen-year-old Gemma Barnes. According to the ID found in her bag, she was a language student here at the university. Nobody appears to have witnessed the attack; however, we can assume it happened sometime around seven thirty when her body was discovered.' He handed a plastic evidence bag containing the girl's university pass to her. The headshot showed Gemma to be a blue-eyed, fair-haired beauty with high cheekbones, full lips and a happy smile.

'Who found her?' Natalie asked.

'One of the lecturers – Dr Alex Fletcher, a scientist. She usually cycles this route home. She alerted the emergency services. She is positive Gemma was alive when she came across her, but by the time the paramedics arrived, she had died.'

'Have her parents been informed?' Natalie wasn't sure she was ready to break such dreadful news to a parent. That might be one step too far too soon.

'That's all in hand. Your team have been notified and are on their way, and Pinkney Watson is inside the tent, examining the victim. I'll leave you to it, but if you need to run anything past me or talk to me at any time, you only have to give me a ring or pop upstairs.'

'Thank you, sir.'

Dan gave a swift nod and then departed, leaving her with Mike.

'Well done,' he said.

'What for?'

'Making the right decision.'

'Thanks for helping me choose it. I'm still not sure though. Only time will tell if it was the right one or not. This feels… well, you understand.'

'It's bound to feel strange. You'll soon find your feet again. You need this, Nat, and it is the right decision.'

She held his gaze, drawing on his strength. She hadn't understood how much she needed his friendship and support until that moment. Being here reminded her of the last time they'd been together at a crime scene – her daughter's. She swallowed hard. 'Okay, what can you tell me?'

'Victim was found lying curled up on her right side here, though her bag, containing books, laptop and notes, was over there,' he said, pointing to a marker about a metre from the tent. 'There are scuff marks on the knees of her jeans and particles of what appears to be sand, which are also on the back of her coat.'

'And the woman who found her?'

'Dr Fletcher. She's inside the library with an officer. She saw Gemma on the ground and stopped to ask if she was all right. She immediately realised what had happened and threw the remains of her bottle of water over Gemma's face to wash off the acid before checking for a pulse. She rang emergency services as she raced into the library for more water and to get help. By the time she returned, it was too late. Gemma had died.'

Acid attacks were becoming increasingly common in the UK but this was the first Natalie had dealt with. 'Were there were no witnesses to the attack?'

'None, and there's no CCTV footage because the camera is out. It's been broken for about a month and they're waiting for it to be repaired. Apparently, there's a lack of funds for such work. Even though it can be accessed by members of the public, the library is on university land.'

Natalie stared at the imposing building. There were several windows overlooking the area. 'Nobody inside saw a thing?'

'No one's spoken up yet, although we've taken all their names and contact details for you to try them again. I've been inside; the windows are quite high and workstations are positioned in the middle or far end of each room. It's unlikely anybody would have noticed a fracas outside.'

'But surely they would have heard screams?'

'It's an old building with thick walls, and surprisingly sound-proof.'

'Damn! What about any evidence out here?'

'Nothing much to help us. Apart from Gemma's bag we haven't got a lot else. We also haven't found the container the acid was in. It's possible the assailant took it with them.'

'Or dumped it nearby.'

'We'll certainly be searching for it.'

Natalie looked about. The nearest car park was to the rear of the building. 'How did she get here? Drive? Walk?'

'I assume she doesn't own a vehicle because there were no car keys in her bag or driving licence in her purse. Chances are she walked, got a lift or caught the bus that passes through campus.'

'I'll check that out. Anything else?'

'We've sent her laptop and mobile to the lab. There was a message on it that she answered at seven fifteen. Her mother sent it. There doesn't seem to be an entry for "Dad", if that helps.'

'Single-parent family, then?'

'Seems that way.'

Natalie nodded. 'I'm ready to see her.'

'Are you sure? She's not a pretty sight.'

'I've seen victims before.'

His face grew even more serious. 'It's only been three months. I want you to be absolutely certain you are fine about this. There are other cases, other people. What I'm saying is, you don't have to take on this investigation if you're not ready to.'

'I understand you're trying to protect me. I have to do this. It's my job.' She inhaled deeply, squared her shoulders and prepared to move away.

He quickly squeezed her hand. 'I need to warn you… it's bad. Her skin has melted in parts and some of her cheekbone has dissolved.'

'It's okay, Mike. I can do this.' *Can you?*

'We've yet to identify the acid. Could be sulphuric, nitric or hydrochloric.'

'And all are readily available. Have you any thoughts on who might have carried out the attack?'

He shrugged. 'Too many options. It could have been executed for any number of reasons: anger at being sexually rejected, jealousy, personal conflict.'

It would only be by learning about the girl that Natalie would be able to work out why she'd been harmed this way. As she studied the area again, she caught sight of two members of her team – DS Murray Anderson and DS Lucy Carmichael. They were close friends and colleagues, having known each other for years, way before they both joined the force and ended up together at Samford. Murray was married to Lucy's best friend, Yolande, and had even donated sperm in order that Lucy and her partner, Bethany, could become parents. Baby Aurora had been born two months earlier. Natalie had not yet managed to visit the child, who had come into the world at a time when Natalie was struggling with the fact her own daughter had left it.

Her heartbeat sped up and for a moment, she didn't know how to act or what to say. Murray had been on leave in Australia when Leigh had been murdered, but he had returned for the funeral. She'd hardly spoken to him since then, and even though both Murray and Lucy knew she was now living close to headquarters, they hadn't dropped by to visit her, although they'd rung her on occasion. She hoped this wouldn't be awkward. She was in charge of this investigation and had to be seen to be strong and efficient. *You can do this. Deep breath.* She prepared to greet them as she would have done had she not been absent the last few months. She needn't have worried. They'd obviously decided the same.

'Hi, Natalie. Good to be working with you again,' said Murray in a matter-of-fact manner that was accompanied by a warm smile.

'Thanks, Murray.'

Lucy, only slightly shorter than her colleague, who was over six foot and wide-shouldered, gave her a nod and said, 'Me too. I'm really glad you're back. We know how hard it's been for you—'

Natalie stopped her with a small shake of her head. She didn't want to make this difficult for her team. They'd suffered alongside her and understood the depth of her despair, but now she was their boss again and had to show she could still command with clear-headed thinking. 'Thank you.' She paused, wondering if she should say more, then decided it would be superfluous and they were all here to focus on the investigation. 'We have an acid attack victim, Gemma Barnes, a student here at the university. At the moment we don't know why she was attacked. Murray, would you talk to Dr Alex Fletcher? She found Gemma and is waiting inside the library. And find out which officer took statements from everyone who was in the library at the time of the attack. We'll want to talk to those people again, even if they think they saw or heard nothing. I'm about to take a look at Gemma.'

'I'll join you,' said Lucy. Natalie was glad of her company. The last body she'd looked at had been her child's. *You can do this. Deep breath.* Lucy lifted the tent flap and followed Natalie into the small space.

Pinkney Watson, the pathologist, was on his knees replacing his instruments into his case. Natalie spotted flecks of grey in his hair that caught the light and was sure she hadn't noticed any before. He released a sad sigh as he patted the dead girl's hand. It was one of the main reasons she liked Pinkney. Not only was he a top pathologist, he treated all the victims as if they were patients.

'Absolutely horrible,' he said to no one in particular, eyes still on the victim.

Pinkney was unmarried and in his late fifties. He shared his Victorian, three-storey house in Samford with a pair of Aegean cats and had a love of walking and nature that saw him travel frequently in his bright-green 1960s VW campervan called Mabel. Ordinarily he and Lucy shared banter though today there was nothing other than sorrow etched on his face.

'How one human being can inflict such cruel damage on another is totally incomprehensible to me,' he said. 'She'll have suffered enormously before she died. Can you imagine what it's like to feel your flesh burning, to lose the sight in your eyes and to feel as if your very ears are melting? And the smell! The poor girl!' It was unlike the man to become emotional, and Lucy placed a friendly hand on his shoulder. He sniffed. 'Sorry. An unprofessional outburst. It's been a long day.'

'There's no need to apologise,' said Natalie.

He noticed her properly for the first time, his piercing blue eyes searching her face. 'Ah, Natalie. I didn't expect to see you back yet.'

'I couldn't bear sitting at home another day. I missed you all,' she replied.

'We missed you too. I certainly did. I haven't been to visit you only because I wanted to give you space. You had enough to deal with without this bumbling old fool turning up on your doorstep.' Pinkney may not have visited her but he had sent her flowers on three separate occasions and a card, bearing a thoughtful message, that had touched her deeply and made her cry.

'You are neither bumbling nor a fool and you did more than enough. I appreciated your kindness.'

He brushed away the thanks. 'Least I could do. Anyway, this, I'm sorry to say, is Gemma Barnes.' He turned back to the body on the floor.

The girl in front of her did not resemble the confident young woman on her ID photograph at all. The acid had dissolved not only the flesh on her face but had melted her right ear and eye and burnt away much of her hair, leaving little other than a disfigured head. She was wearing a woollen coat but the collar had fused with the flesh on her neck, making her look hideously ghoulish. Natalie crouched down and searched for signs to remind her of who this person really was. Her eyes alighted on the girl's elegant fingers, neat nails, painted pale pink, and the silver ring on the forefinger of her right hand. Natalie closed her eyes and pictured the girl as she had been, then a vision of Leigh replaced the image and she stood up, panic rising in her chest. She blinked it away. *Deep breath*. It was no good, she couldn't look at this ruined shell any longer. 'I've seen enough,' she said and dived back outside. A shower of rain had begun to fall, sprinkling the pavement with tiny droplets. Her chest rose and fell as she inhaled and exhaled deliberately, calming her racing heart. Lucy and Pinkney exited the tent and stood beside her, apparently unaware of the sudden panic she'd experienced.

Pinkney cleared his throat. 'I believe she died of circulatory shock. Such an attack, as vicious as it was, would not have been sufficient to kill her. I imagine the shock of the attack caused her blood pressure to drop rapidly, leading to organ hypoperfusion, which in layman's terms means decreased blood flow through vital organs such as the brain. This in turn leads to cellular death and multiorgan failure. With nobody around to witness the attack and rush to her assistance, shock would have passed through several stages quite rapidly. Had there been somebody about, she might have been saved, although what state she would have been in afterwards is anyone's guess. She most definitely would have been blind and possibly deaf in one ear. Awful business. I'm finished here. I'll let them know she can be moved to the pathology lab.' He hastened away, leaving Lucy to comment on his unusually sombre mood.

'Not like him to be over sensitive,' she said.

'Some cases affect you more than others.' said Natalie before adding, 'And she looked such a mess.'

A person strode purposefully towards Natalie and Lucy. It was PC Ian Jarvis, the junior member of her team. He'd lost weight since Natalie had last seen him – a good stone or more – and his lean frame looked rangy, his face gaunt and drawn. He stood awkwardly in front of her and spoke quietly.

'I'm really pleased you came back to us. I've missed working alongside you.'

'Thanks.' She gave him a small smile of appreciation for his heartfelt words and he seemed to exhale.

'I wasn't sure what to say to you,' he replied. 'I didn't want it to be... you know... awkward.'

'You said the right thing.' She didn't dwell on it but continued with her thoughts and instructions as she addressed her team. 'Ian, find out what Gemma studied, where she lived and how she got to the library. She replied to a text message from her mother at seven fifteen this evening, and her body was found by Dr Alex Fletcher at half past seven, therefore we can assume the attack took place sometime in those intervening fifteen minutes. We clearly need to find out who would attack her in this way. Dig around, talk to boyfriends, present and ex-, friends, relatives and find out if she was a member of any political or religious groups. We'll begin with the usual checks and gather whatever information we can. I'd like to talk to her mother soon too. Do we know who broke the news to her?'

'I'll find out,' Lucy said and lifted her phone.

Mike was wandering back towards them, head lowered. Natalie understood the enormity of the task he faced. It was always harder to find evidence when crimes were committed outside in public spaces. Mike stopped by her side and watched with her as the paramedics came into view, carrying a stretcher and body bag.

Gemma would be driven only a short distance to the laboratory. 'You okay?'

'Yes. Thanks.' She dug her nails into the fleshy part of her palm and tried not to let her mind drift back to August.

The library was at the edge of campus, some distance from the thoroughfare and other university buildings, in this quiet, pedestrian area. Had the attacker known Gemma would be coming here this evening, or had they stalked her, or was she the victim of a random attack? Her gut told her it was a deliberate attack and somebody bore Gemma Barnes a grudge. It was her duty to find out who and why, and bring them to justice.

Mike gave her a look that she interpreted as concern and she reassured him with a half-smile. She could handle this. This wasn't the work of a serial killer hell-bent on abducting children. This, she could manage. She hoped.

CHAPTER FOUR

FRIDAY, 16 NOVEMBER – NIGHT

Dear Gemma,

I feel really stupid. I'm not used to anyone smiling at me, let alone somebody like you. You took me by surprise, and when you caught my eye briefly and smiled in my direction, I could only return an ungrateful scowl, afraid you would see how I truly felt – in awe of you.

People like me never hit anybody's radar. We're shunned or, worse than that, ridiculed, so we end up skulking in the shadows – Billy no mates. We're riddled with insecurities and sadness. Not that somebody as popular as you would understand.

I blew my chance – my one chance to win you over, smile back at you and maybe capture your attention – and now I sit and watch and wish you would notice me again, really see me, not look through me, like everyone else does.

Are you like everybody else, or are you better than that?

An Admirer

*

A large picture of Gemma was stuck on the whiteboard in the office.

'She was nice-looking, wasn't she?' said Ian.

'Looked a lot like her mother. This is Sasha Barnes.' Lucy passed Murray the photograph she'd taken from the printer only moments earlier.

Murray whistled softly. 'Mother?'

'Thirty-five,' Lucy replied.

'Get out of here!'

'No. True. She had Gemma when she was only a schoolkid herself.'

'Wow! She could be Gemma's twin sister.' Murray's eyebrows lifted high on his forehead as he spoke.

'Maybe that's why this happened,' Ian offered. 'Somebody was jealous of Gemma?'

'There are lots of girls who are good-looking. They don't all get acid chucked in their faces – thankfully. Besides, her mother is the real stunner,' said Murray.

Natalie had been going through what they'd accumulated thus far and chose that moment to stand up and take control of the meeting.

'We're going to have to look at every possible angle on this and can't focus solely on the theory that Gemma was attacked because of her looks. She was in her second year of studying Russian and German. Obviously, we need to talk to her fellow students and those tutors who taught her. She also worked part-time at Chancer's Bar – same place as her mother – and we need to check it out as well. In the first instance, we should try to establish if she was assaulted by somebody she knew, possibly a lover or boyfriend, or if this was a random attack. That person might frequent Chancer's Bar or be a student. We'll consider other options later, but for now, start with her housemates at 53 Eastview Avenue. It's one of several houses dotted about Samford that are owned and rented out by the university. Murray, you and I will talk to Sasha. Lucy and Ian, talk to her housemates.'

'Reckon they'll still be up at this time?' asked Ian.

'It's eleven thirty on a Friday night and they're students. What do you reckon, you muppet?' said Murray.

'Oh... yeah... I wasn't thinking straight.' Ian flushed deeply.

Murray grinned at the junior officer's discomfort then suddenly grabbed either side of the man's face and planted a loud kiss on his forehead. 'Jeez, I've missed working with you.'

Natalie was surprised. 'You weren't working together?'

'Super split us up. I was moved to Narcotics and Lucy and Ian went to Vice. This is the first time we've been in the same team since...'

Natalie faltered for a second then quickly regained her composure. 'Since I took leave.'

'Yes.'

'Then it's definitely a good thing I returned. Wouldn't want to be held responsible for breaking up such a beautiful bromance.' It wasn't a particularly funny comment but it had the desired effect. Any leftover tension evaporated. 'Right, let's find out which bastard did this to Gemma.'

The showers had given way to proper rain that was being dumped from the sky and had already begun to flood the area outside the front door. Black branches that overhung the car park creaked and trembled as gusts of wind howled ominously and shook them.

'Flipping heck!' said Murray, as he and Natalie exited headquarters. 'Where are you parked?'

'Far end,' said Natalie.

'Shall we take my car? It's only over there.'

The Jeep Renegade was a few metres away and she didn't fancy a soaking. 'Makes sense.'

Murray blipped the key fob and the vehicle chirped as it unlocked. They both sprinted for the car, feet splashing through puddles that had quickly formed. She launched herself into the passenger seat, slammed the door shut and rubbed her calves to remove the water stains on her tights. In the brief moments the door had been open, rain had splashed inside, and droplets, like snail trails, trickled down the plastic dashboard. She inhaled the scent of freshly picked berries emitted by a jelly-bean-shaped air freshener that dangled from the rear-view mirror, the smell evoking dim memories of brighter days of summers past.

'Bloody weather!' She pulled down the vanity mirror to tidy herself up before visiting Sasha Barnes and was startled by her reflection. In the less flattering light of the car she saw what others must have seen: a woman scarred and broken by life. She'd seen the same hollow-eyed and sunken-cheek look on victims, aged prematurely by whatever misfortune had befallen them, never imagining she would suffer a similar fate. She'd never been one for preening or spending hours enhancing her appearance, but it was evident she'd neglected herself. She needed to rectify that. She couldn't be a strong leader if she looked downtrodden.

Murray started the vehicle and headed out of the car park, the windscreen wipers, even on quick-wipe, unable to cope with the volume of water that streamed down the glass, impeding his vision. He squinted hard and she noticed he'd put on a pair of spectacles.

'When did you start wearing glasses?' she asked.

'Couple of months back. I'm limiting their usage at the moment and only putting them on when I have to. Old age is creeping up on me.' Murray was only in his mid-thirties.

'Old age, my arse!'

Her response made him chuckle – a deep, relaxed sound that made her smile inwardly. She reached in her bag for a lipstick to smarten up her appearance, found one and slicked on some bright red. The result wasn't great but it would have to do.

'Where are we headed?' he asked.

'Juniper Road.' Sasha lived at the far side of Samford on the way to Stone and Stoke. It was about a fifteen-minute journey through town at this time of night.

'How far away is that from Chancer's Bar?'

Natalie returned the lipstick to the muddle in her bag and checked Google Maps on her mobile. 'About ten minutes by car. It would have taken Gemma a lot longer to get there from the university or Eastview Avenue, especially if she used public transport.'

'You'd think she'd get a job closer to the university,' said Murray as he drew up to traffic lights. The rain drummed against the roof, almost drowning out his voice. 'There must be loads of bar jobs about in Samford.'

'Maybe she already had the job before she went to uni and liked working there. We'll find out when we talk to Sasha. You need to take a right here,' she added.

He flicked the indicator switch and turned off the main road. They were now passing terraced houses fronted by uneven pavements. None of the houses had garages, and cars were sandwiched in one behind the other on both sides of the road, narrowing it and making driving difficult. Murray slowed to allow a van approaching from the opposite direction to pass safely. Natalie fell silent. The closer they got to Juniper Close, the more reality sank in. She was, as Mike had said, 'back in the saddle' and about to confront a woman who had lost her only daughter. She had to distance herself emotionally and that was going to be difficult.

Murray said something that was lost in the noise of the engine and driving rain. They were minutes away. Natalie counted slowly on each inhalation, calming herself, preparing herself. They took another turning; the bright lights of a 24/7 supermarket illuminated one side of the road, and opposite it stood ugly concrete blocks of flats, windows like black eyes peering out into the gloom. Another couple of turns and they were onto a quiet street. Here, semi-detached houses with driveways were set back from the road. Grey wheelie bins and tied-up black bin bags stood at the end of each property, forming a haphazard line along the pavement. Murray slowed the car and began searching for Sasha's house. They soon found it: it was the only house with all its lights on, a cosy glow falling over the small frontage. He drew up close to it. The rain had eased off, and although it was still tumbling, it no longer hammered noisily above them. The tempo of her heart increased and she took a moment to open the car door, before jumping down lightly. *Deep breath*. She could do this.

Sasha was planted in the middle of a pastel green settee, a large dark green cushion covered in blue hummingbirds clutched to her chest. Her face and eyelids were puffed and distorted from crying, and when she spoke, her voice was thick with phlegm.

'Why would somebody do such an evil thing?' she stuttered.

Natalie couldn't answer Sasha, merely empathise with her. Three months ago, she'd asked similar questions about the monster who had taken her own flesh and blood from her. She'd sat dazed and shattered, her life destroyed. She wouldn't be able to repair this unfortunate woman's life but in time, she would give her answers to some of her questions.

'When did you last see Gemma?' she asked.

'Two days ago, when I dropped her off a new hot water bottle. Hers had sprung a leak and it's cold in that old house at this time of year.'

'Did you often visit her?'

'Only now and again, to make sure she was okay, but we chatted every day on the phone.'

'And I expect you saw each other at work at Chancer's Bar?'

'Yes. Mostly on weekends. She did shift work there whenever she could find time.'

'Had she been working there long?'

'Over two years. She started while she was doing A-levels. She wanted to save up for university. I couldn't give her much money and fees are expensive.'

Natalie was puzzled by the fact the girl attended a local university yet still chose to pay for student accommodation rather than live at home. 'Why did Gemma leave home? You were obviously close.'

'That's exactly why she left. I didn't want her to. She believed it was the right time for her to leave, even though she'd have saved money by living here. She spent the first year in halls of residence. I had hoped she'd come back for her second year, but she chose to go into university accommodation – a house on Eastview Avenue.' She looked wistfully at a photograph of Gemma on a small table beside her. 'I think what she really meant was it was time for me to let go. Children have to find their own feet in the end, don't they? Do you have any children?'

Natalie had been dreading her asking the question, but Murray filled the brief silence with a quiet, 'No.'

'I fell pregnant with Gemma when I was still at school. I left before I took any exams. I don't regret it. I never regretted it.' She paused again, mind flitting through her backlog of memories, her voice wistful. 'Gemma was bright – really clever – and I was very proud of her. Me, I'm no good at all that academic stuff – writing and languages – not like her.' Her voice cracked again and she buried her face in the cushion, her shoulders shaking. Natalie couldn't bear to watch and crossed over to her, sat beside her and draped an arm over her shoulders. The simple gesture of kindness seemed to help. Sasha gradually calmed and all the while Natalie fought the pain in her own heart. She understood what this woman was going through.

She glanced at Murray and asked, 'Could you get Sasha a glass of water?' While he was gone she squeezed the woman's arm in solidarity. When the sobs abated and Sasha had sipped the water, she was able to answer their questions. Although she took her arm off Sasha's shoulder, Natalie didn't move from the settee.

Sasha tried again. 'I'm quite good at sewing, and Gemma persuaded me to start up a small bespoke clothing business. We made a deal: she'd get her degree and I'd take up the challenge to make a collection of outfits. She wanted me to use her bedroom as a sewing room while she wasn't there.' She stopped again, searched Natalie's face for a sign of comfort and received an encouraging nod. 'I sent her a photo of one of my outfits earlier. She loved it. I… I don't think I can manage without being able to speak to her ever again.' Her face shifted as if something broke inside her.

Natalie spoke gently, trying to tease the information from Sasha. She wanted to know who might have thrown the acid but she couldn't ask that directly. 'Do you have a boyfriend or partner?'

'No. There's been nobody serious for a long time.'

'Nobody since Gemma left home?'

'Nobody.'

'Was Gemma seeing anybody?'

Sasha rubbed at her red nose and shook her head. 'Her course was very demanding and any free time was taken up with bar work. She went out with Ryan for a while, but she ditched him.'

'Ryan? Do you know his surname?'

'No, but he lives in the same house as her. They got together at the beginning of September.'

'Did she tell you why she ended their relationship?'

The eyes filled again and Sasha stammered, 'She… told me… everything. There were no secrets between us.'

'What happened between her and Ryan?' asked Natalie.

'Gemma wasn't looking for anything heavy and he got too serious, too quickly.'

'In what way was he serious?'

'He was always texting or ringing her and wanted to make their relationship official and for them to be a proper "couple", but she didn't. She liked him a lot but she also enjoyed going out with other friends, and her job. He'd sulk or get argumentative if she took off on her own. After about a month, she dumped him.'

'Did she mention having any problems with him afterwards?'

'No. It was sticky for a while but they managed to remain good friends. Gemma had that effect on people.' She blinked back more tears and her voice wavered. 'There was no bad blood between them.'

'How about other housemates? Did she get along well with them?'

'She definitely got along with Lennox. He's very sweet. She was good friends with Hattie. Hattie's older than the others and used to live in a commune before she went back to college and got her qualifications to go to university, so she sorts out the housework rotas and is a bit like a mother figure to them. Gemma liked her a lot.'

'And the others in the house?'

'There's only Fran. Gemma didn't often mention Fran, but I bumped into her on a few of my visits and she seemed okay. Will I… will I be able to collect her personal belongings?' The thought clouded her face.

'The family liaison officer will go through what will happen next. They'll help and guide you. You won't be alone,' said Natalie, as Sasha's eyelids fluttered and her lips trembled again.

'Do you happen to know if Gemma was a member of any groups or societies?' she asked. It was an idea to find out who Gemma was likely to have mixed with and if any of them might have borne her a grudge.

'No. She wasn't in any that I know of.'

'She was studying languages, wasn't she?'

'Russian and German. Gemma was always gifted with languages.'

'Did she mention any of the other students taking the courses with her?'

Sasha ran a hand across her face. 'Only in passing. I don't remember their names.'

'Did she bring home any friends from university to meet you?'

'No. I met a few girls and boys when she was living in the halls
of residence. I don't remember all their names though. I'd only say
hi to them if I saw them on the stairs or in the flats. There were
lots of them.'

'Of course,' said Natalie with a nod.

'She didn't have any very close friends. She joked once, she
didn't need them because she had me.' She swallowed hard. 'We
had a very special relationship. Nobody could understand how
close we were.' Her lips quivered again and her eyes turned glassy
with tears. 'So special.'

Natalie put a hand on Sasha's. Faced with a woman who was
going through the same hell she had recently experienced was
proving tougher than she'd expected.

'You're doing really well. Is there somebody who can stay with
you tonight?'

'I can't think of anyone.'

'You have no friends or relatives?'

'I don't really see eye to eye with my mum and besides, she lives
in Bristol. There's my cousin, Gail, but I haven't seen her in years.
I can't burden myself on my neighbours because they've got young
children, and I can't ask any of my work colleagues. I don't really
have anyone other than Gemma,' she said, her words petering out
softly. There were three large photographs on the wall of her and
Gemma, black-and-white images taken by a professional of the pair
of them on a beach, laughing, hair blowing in the wind, holding
hands as they ran along the sand.

It was evident that Sasha depended on Gemma, and how she'd
cope without her daughter didn't bear considering. Natalie glanced
at Murray, who'd been sitting quietly during the remainder of the
interview, and he shook his head. He had nothing to add.

'Has a liaison officer been in touch with you?'

'Yes, there were two of them. They're coming back tomorrow.'
She reached for the cards bearing their names.

Natalie read them and knew the officers in question. One of them was quite young and still training. She thought of Tanya Granger, with whom she'd worked on numerous cases. Single mum Tanya would be a better fit for Sasha. 'I'm going to ask one of my colleagues to come across and keep you company for a while. She's a very experienced officer who'll understand exactly what you're going through.'

'Thank you. I'd like that.' Sasha reached for and clutched the cushion even more tightly. Such vulnerability and helplessness ripped at Natalie's heart.

'We'll do everything we can to find the person responsible,' said Natalie.

'Thank you, but… it won't change anything. She's gone.' Her words hit home. Natalie could never return this woman's daughter to her, any more than she could bring back Leigh and Zoe, yet that was all she could do: find the perpetrator and hope the justice system would handle the rest.

They returned to Murray's car, where Natalie slumped in her seat, arms folded tightly, thoughts on Sasha. Murray pulled away from the kerb and drove down the road.

Outside, the rain had petered out to a light drizzle. The town was quiet and people were in their homes for the night. Some would be snuggled in bed with their loved ones, others thinking about their long day at work. Their routines and lives took on a normality that only shifted when something unexpected occurred. Her life had been smashed to pieces and so had Sasha's.

*

Gemma,

I watched you and your mother today, your heads almost touching as you whispered behind hands, until you both broke away simultaneously and laughed until your eyes watered.

I'd have given anything to have laughed alongside you both and shared that moment.

You've never known what it is like to be unloved by the one person who should be by your side no matter what. Your mother watches over you, pride in her eyes. When she laughs with you, it's a sincere, proud, tinkling laugh, not a cold, disappointed bark. You have no idea what I would give to have a mother like yours.

I tried to talk to you today but you didn't see me. I edged ever closer to you, hoping you would speak first. When you didn't, I opened my mouth to talk, but you snubbed me and walked away. It wasn't wise to give me the brush-off, Gemma.

I can be a truly good friend but I also make the perfect enemy.

An Admirer

CHAPTER FIVE

Eastview Avenue, on the opposite side of Samford, consisted of three-storey Victorian houses in various states of disrepair. Numerous bicycles, their front wheels removed for added security, were chained against iron railings that fronted some of the tall buildings; Lucy guessed those were the houses occupied by students.

Ian couldn't find a parking space for the squad car so they double-parked outside number 53 and rushed towards the arched porch, where they shook off the water droplets stuck to their hair and coats. Rain gushed over a broken gutter and splashed down the side of the building like a small waterfall.

'Fucking shitty weather,' said Ian, rubbing his face dry. 'I hate it when it's like this. One day, I'm going to give this up and move somewhere hot and sunny like Australia.'

'Yeah, sure you will. You'd make a great beach bum – all suntanned and rippling muscles,' Lucy replied.

He smiled at the quip. 'I'd soon learn how to become one. It's got to be better than this.' Ian rang the doorbell and waited. When nobody appeared, he tried again and left his finger on it a little longer.

Lucy took a step back into the rain and looked up at the windows above her. 'There are lights on. Try again.'

Ian hammered on the door and pressed the bell once more. This time the door was opened by a woman in her mid-twenties, in a onesie, fluffy dressing gown and soft grey slipper-boots with furry tops. Her pale face, framed by deep-auburn hair, was devoid of make-up, and small creases appeared on her forehead at the sight of the officers. Lucy held up her ID card and introduced herself and Ian. 'Sorry to disturb you but could we come in and chat to you for a moment?'

The woman invited them into a hallway filled with the aroma of spicy food. The sound of laughter came from a room.

'We were just eating,' the woman explained.

'We need to talk to all of you. It's regarding one of your housemates.'

The woman hesitated before saying, 'Come through. There's only three of us here at the moment.'

Lucy and Ian followed her into the kitchen, where a young man with shoulder-length brown hair and a light beard, in jeans and a faded khaki sweater, and a girl with several facial piercings, wearing a baggy jumper, short corduroy skirt and thick striped tights, were sitting on plastic chairs and eating from aluminium foil takeaway trays. Dance music was coming from a black box on the kitchen top, which was cluttered with an array of cereal boxes, plastic bags of bread, jars, sauce bottles, mugs, glasses and dishes. The man placed his fork and tray on a scuffed wooden table.

'What's going on?' he asked.

Lucy and Ian introduced themselves again. 'Could you turn off the music, please?'

The girl with the piercings obliged and the room fell silent. 'I'm afraid we have some bad news regarding one of your housemates, Gemma Barnes.'

The woman who'd shown them in lifted a hand to her mouth and took a sharp breath. 'What's happened to her?'

'She was a victim of an acid attack outside the library earlier this evening.'

'No! Is she okay? Where is she? Is she in local hospital?' the young woman said in a rush.

Lucy glanced at the other pair, who seemed equally startled by the news. 'I'm sorry to tell you that Gemma died at the scene.'

The woman blinked furiously and said softly, 'No. No.'

'We understand this is difficult for you but we need to talk to you all urgently. You lived with Gemma and we need to find whoever did this to her as quickly as possible. We'd appreciate your help in finding who did this. I'd like to start by asking your names, please.'

Ian pulled out a notepad and prepared to write down details.

'I'm Hattie Caldwell.' The woman in the dressing gown moved silently across to the table, dropped down onto a blue chair and put her head in her hands.

'How did she die?' the young man asked.

'We aren't sure at the moment but we think it was as a result of the acid attack.'

'But an acid attack wouldn't kill her,' he replied, his heavy brows pulled together.

'Lennox knows because he studies chemistry and he's a bit of a boffin,' said the girl with the piercings. Her accent was broad Liverpudlian and she gave off a defiant air.

The young man scowled at her. 'Shut up! You're making me sound weird.'

'No. *You* make you sound weird,' she replied, pointing her fork at him. 'Fancy coming out with that shit. Gemma's dead and you talk about the unlikelihood of an acid attack actually killing her. She's dead, you cretin!'

Lennox drew a breath then started to speak again, but the girl stared insolently at Lucy and said, 'I'm Fran Ditton.'

'Thank you, Fran. Lennox, what's your full name?'

Lennox gave Fran a cool look then said, 'Lennox Walsh and I'm not weird. I don't understand how she could have died that way. I know about acid burns and they wouldn't kill her, not unless she was drenched in acid. Did she swallow any?'

'When we know for certain we might be able to tell you, but for now, I need to establish where you all were between seven and seven thirty this evening,' said Lucy.

'I was at a student council meeting at the students' union, to discuss entertainment for the coming year,' said Fran.

'What time was that?'

'Six until eight. It dragged on a bit longer than that and then we went to the students' union bar for a while. I got back about half an hour ago.'

'Lennox?'

'I was at the chemistry lab from six-ish until half eight or maybe a bit later.'

'Any witnesses to confirm that?'

'I was working alone on an experiment. One of the lab assistants might have spotted me although I don't remember seeing anyone. I was busy. Somebody will have seen my car. I own an old red Saab. It's quite recognisable and it was in the science car park all the time I was working there. We have to swipe our passes for access into the labs. You can probably check I was there with the science department staff. It'll be logged on a system somewhere.'

Ian made a note to check how far away the science department was from the library, to check the pass entry system and to establish if any CCTV cameras had picked up Lennox so they could confirm he was in the lab the whole time.

'Hattie, where were you?'

The young woman was miles away, her eyes unfocused. She didn't respond.

'Hattie, where were you earlier this evening?'

'Oh, sorry. I was here all evening. Gemma and I had a cup of tea and a chat before she went to the library.'

'What time was that?'

'Around quarter to six.'

'What time did she leave?'

'I don't know exactly. She was going to catch the bus into town and I think that goes every half an hour. We were in the kitchen at least fifteen to twenty minutes.'

Fran spoke up. 'The buses leave from the bus stop at the bottom of the road at ten past and twenty to the hour.' It meant Gemma would most likely have caught the bus that left at twenty to seven.

Hattie continued, 'Gemma asked me for a lift because I normally have a lecture at six on Fridays, but I couldn't take her. I was feeling lousy – I think I'm coming down with flu or something – and I skipped off.' She looked up with damp eyes. 'If I'd taken her, this wouldn't have happened.'

'I don't think you can blame yourself at all.'

'I should have driven her. This *is* my fault!' Hattie wrapped her arms around her thin body, hugging herself tightly, tears cascading down her face.

Fran leapt off her chair and crouched down in front of Hattie, putting hands on the woman's shoulders. 'Pack it in, Hattie. It isn't your fault. You didn't chuck acid at her.'

'I know, but—'

'There is no "but". You did nothing wrong.'

'But dead... she's dead.' Hattie looked away again. Her words were forced, one syllable at a time. 'I... need... to... leave.'

Lucy said, 'I understand how hard this is for you but we really do need to get as much information as we can. If you could just—'

Hattie shook her head and Fran jumped up and faced Lucy; her jet-black eyes were like flinty rocks.

'You can see how upset she is. She can't help you. Let her go to her room.'

Lucy acquiesced. 'Okay. Hattie, do you want somebody to go with you?'

Hattie shook her head, lips tightly pressed together.

'I'll come and talk to you in a minute in your room. Would that be better for you?' said Lucy.

Hattie managed a brief nod then got to her feet and swayed slightly; she steadied herself by putting one hand on the table.

'You sure you're all right?' asked Lucy.

'Yes.' Her voice, thick with emotion, belied the truth.

'I'll go with you,' said Fran, who put an arm around the woman's waist.

Lucy watched as they left the room, Hattie's head bowed low and Fran murmuring reassurances to her. After they left, Lucy turned to Lennox. 'Who else shares the house with you?' she asked.

Lennox ran a hand through his thick mop of hair. 'Only Ryan Hausmann. He's out at the moment.'

'Any idea where he might be?'

'No idea at all.'

'Have you got a phone number for him?'

Lennox nodded. 'I'll ring him.' He scrolled through his contact list, touched the screen and held the mobile to his ear. After a moment he said, 'He's not answering. Do you want his number?'

'Yes, please.'

Lennox read out Ryan's number for Ian, who jotted it down.

Fran reappeared, slid onto a chair and folded her arms.

'Do you know where we might find Ryan?' The question was aimed at Fran, who looked puzzled.

'Sorry, no.'

Lucy picked up on the shift in attitude. Now that the news had sunk in, both students were more docile; even prickly Fran had the grace to tone down her attitude. Lennox plucked at his beard absent-mindedly, possibly still trying to work out how Gemma had died from an acid attack.

'Was Gemma in a relationship?' Lucy asked Fran.

'I didn't talk to her very often. I don't know if she was or wasn't.'

'How does that work, then? You all live in the same house but don't know anything about each other?' asked Ian. He was met with blank looks.

Fran answered with, 'We didn't choose to live with each other. The university authorities allocated rooms to us. In fact, my best mate lives in a different house altogether. We're a random selection of students of all ages, studying different subjects, who might bump into each other in the kitchen or sitting room. Sometimes, like this evening, if there's a few of us about, we'll order a takeaway or watch telly together, but apart from that we lead separate lives. This is only somewhere we sleep and work.'

'I see. You didn't talk much to Gemma?'

'No. We didn't avoid each other or anything, but I'm taking French and she's reading German and Russian. Apart from both studying languages, we didn't have a lot else in common.' Fran's dark eyes flashed.

'Did she mention being concerned about anyone following her?' asked Lucy.

'No,' said Fran.

Lennox shook his head.

'Did she get along with everyone here?'

'Yes,' said Fran without any hesitation.

Lennox agreed, 'Definitely.'

'Did she have any friends – male or female – that came back to the house?'

Lennox spoke. 'I never saw anyone with her apart from her mum.'

'Sasha was nearly always around here: in the kitchen, in Gemma's room, waiting in the sitting room for her to come back from lectures,' explained Fran. 'She was here so frequently, I used to wonder why Gemma ever left home.' Lucy detected a bitterness in the girl's voice even though it appeared to be a throwaway comment. Fran rolled up the sleeves on her jumper to reveal heavily tattooed arms and continued talking. 'Gemma got on well with Hattie. Hattie might know more than us.'

'Did either of you see Gemma today?'

'No.' There were more shakes of heads.

Lucy decided to end it there and talk to Hattie. 'Which room is Hattie in?'

'First floor. Second room on the left.'

'And Gemma's?'

'Next to Hattie's,' said Lennox. 'Her name is on the door.'

'I'd like to take a look at Gemma's room.'

'Sure, but it's probably locked. We all have individual keys to our bedrooms.'

'Do you have any spare keys?'

'No.'

'Okay, well, if it's locked, we'll come back and take a look later.'

Lennox reached for his tray of food, prodded at it with the fork then pushed it away and stood up. 'I'm going upstairs. I'll show you Gemma's room.'

They ascended the stairs to the first floor, and after pointing out Gemma's name on her door, he disappeared up a narrow staircase. Below them the music had started up again. Ian tried the door handle. The room was locked.

Hattie's room, next to Gemma's, was barely large enough for the furniture in it. A cluttered, oversized desk was under the window, and a floor-to-ceiling bookcase filled with textbooks and folders stood against one wall. A collage of photos of Hattie and her friends covered the space over the single bed that was rammed against the opposite wall. Hattie was resting against pillows, still wearing her dressing gown, her slender arms wrapped around her knees. Her thin face was streaked with tears. 'I can't believe it.'

'You were good friends with Gemma?' Lucy asked.

'She was a lovely girl. We got on well.'

'Do you know her mum too?'

'Sasha? She's fab too.' She let out a long groan then said, 'Does she know about Gemma?'

'Yes.'

'They were very close. This will kill her.'

Lucy glanced at the titles of the books on the shelves: *Sociology of Personal Life, Key Concepts in Family Studies, The Sociology of Health and Illness*. 'We're trying to find out if Gemma brought anyone back here at all.'

'Only Sasha.'

'Has she had any run-ins with anyone in the house recently?'

'No. She got on with everyone although there was a bit of an argument going on this morning between her and Lennox. They were having words in the kitchen but they shut up as soon as I went in. I asked if everything was okay and they said it was. I don't think it was anything serious. I heard Sasha's name mentioned a couple of times but I didn't hear what they were arguing about. It was probably something and nothing. They get along fine normally. In fact, I thought they were starting to get it on together but Gemma laughed at that idea and said she wasn't his type.'

'Can you think of anyone at all who would want to harm her?'

'No one at all.'

'Did she talk about the other people on her course?'

'Not really. She was very sociable but she didn't seem to hang out with anyone in particular – she was more a social butterfly, never settling with one group or person.'

'What did you and Gemma talk about?'

'Life, the future, the environment, television, travel, friendships, families, boys – all sorts.'

'You're studying sociology?'

'That's right. I'm in my final year.'

'What will you do when you get your degree?'

'Work abroad with the VSO. Do something to help fight poverty. My dad's a vicar in Little Beansfield. He worked in Africa years ago. I'd like to do something similar.' Little Beansfield was a small village about fifteen miles from Samford, surrounded by agricultural land; a quiet place whose inhabitants were generally elderly farmers.

'What about Gemma? Did she have any plans?'

'Nothing fixed, although she wanted to travel, especially to Russia to learn about her family's origins. She'd get really excited when she talked about that and now… she won't be able to go. This is… shit!' She hugged her knees tightly.

'We'd like to see inside Gemma's room but it's locked. Do you have a key, by any chance?' Lucy asked. She was met with a shake of the head. Hattie was crying silent tears again. The key might well be on Gemma's person. They'd have to get it from Forensics and come back.

'Is there nothing you can think of that might help us? Anything she said – a concern about somebody, an awkward customer at work, somebody being bitchy about her? Anything?'

Hattie hiccoughed, struggling to fight the tears that now tumbled freely. 'I… can't think of… anyone. She was nice. To everyone.'

With the girl now in floods of tears, there was little more they could glean from Hattie. As they stood on the landing, Lucy said, 'I think we should try Lennox again to see why he and Gemma were arguing.' They ascended to the top floor and, not knowing which one was Lennox's, tapped at both bedroom doors, but got no reply. They turned around at the sound of a voice.

'He left a few minutes ago.' It was Fran on the stairs, a glass of water in her hand.

'Any idea where he went?'

'He said he was going out for a drink. I think he's pretty shaken up about Gemma.'

'Which room is yours?'

'Same floor as Hattie and Gemma. Mine's opposite Gemma's and next to the bathroom.'

'Okay, thanks. We'll catch up with Lennox later.'

Outside the house, Lucy pulled a face. 'What did you make of them all?'

'An odd mix. Makes me glad I wasn't ever a student. I'd find it hard sharing with people who weren't into the same things as me.'

'Yeah, me too. It reminded me of living in foster care – none of us really got on. We simply made do.'

'I'm mindful of the need to catch this perpetrator but I don't think much more can be achieved tonight, or rather, this morning,' said Natalie, glancing her watch and noting it was almost one o'clock. 'We have two clear directions to take: the housemates – especially Ryan Hausmann and Lennox Walsh, whose alibis need examining in more detail – and Chancer's Bar. I want to know if anyone working at or visiting that bar had an issue with Gemma. Somebody targeted this girl for a reason and knew she was going to the library. Who?'

'Hattie knew Gemma was going to the library. She would have given her a lift if she hadn't felt ill,' said Ian.

'Then let's make sure we know exactly where Hattie was at the time of the attack, and find out who was on that six forty bus at the same time as Gemma. Unless she was a random victim, someone knew her movements or followed her. Okay, see you bright and early,' said Natalie.

Murray and Lucy left but Ian, sorting through notes, didn't follow them. Natalie returned to her desk. She had no immediate plans to go back to her empty flat and a night of torment. Ian looked up and said casually, 'I'm not in any hurry to go home. I'd rather go through the databases and pull together whatever I can on the housemates.'

'If you feel up to it. I'm hanging back for a while to go through CCTV footage and see if we can confirm Lennox's whereabouts.'

He took that as confirmation and moved to the back of the office, where he logged on to the computer and the general police database. Natalie sat in front of her own terminal and watched the footage that had been sent over from the university. Lennox's pass had been swiped outside one of the laboratories at five past six, as he'd claimed, although it didn't necessarily mean he'd been the person who'd swiped it, and until they could prove he'd actually been in the lab, he would remain under suspicion.

The science departments were housed over several floors in one large, glass-fronted building, in the middle of campus next to a car park, and accessed by two entrances, only one of which had an active CCTV camera. She checked the main entrance, where the camera was trained on the path leading from the car park and would reveal any comings and goings. The footage showed nothing but a grey image of the empty pathway. Minute after minute nobody came or left, but Natalie watched intently. If Lennox Walsh had left the building and walked along this path to his car, she would spot him on this footage. It would make their lives a lot easier if she could find him, but she knew life was never easy. This was going to be a long, difficult process.

CHAPTER SIX

SATURDAY, 17 NOVEMBER – MORNING

Natalie grabbed a quick shower at headquarters and changed into a blouse and underwear she'd thrown into a sports bag and left in her car. She didn't feel especially tired even though she'd been up all night, combing through footage. She was more irritated by the fact she'd been unable to locate Lennox until he left the department at six minutes past eight that evening and strolled towards the car park. She had reasoned he might have left by the back entrance, and had tried footage taken from other CCTV cameras attached to various buildings trained on the footpath leading to the library, but not spotted him anywhere. If he had left the laboratory and attacked Gemma, he certainly hadn't been caught on university CCTV. That nobody had yet vouched for his presence in the laboratory still left a question mark over whether or not he'd been there, but for now, she had to look elsewhere, and she'd start with the other housemates and then go to Chancer's Bar.

Ian had stayed for almost two hours, and after gathering as much information as possible on the students living in the house on Eastview Avenue and going through statements from those who'd been inside the library at the time of the attack, he had finally left to snatch some sleep. He'd reappeared bang on seven and had been silently working since.

Natalie hadn't wanted to ask about his personal circumstances. His girlfriend had left him several months earlier and taken their baby girl with her. After wrestling with the option of quitting the force to win her back, he'd eventually decided to stay. Since then, he had appeared to throw himself ever deeper into his job, and judging by his appearance, it was taking its toll. However, looking at her own face in the mirror, she couldn't comment. She was looking decidedly old, tired and worn herself. She adjusted her outfit, ensured she looked respectable for the day ahead and headed upstairs, where Ian had finally unearthed something of interest about Lennox.

'Hattie said he and Gemma were arguing yesterday morning and Sasha's name came up, so I've been looking at his social media accounts and he not only follows Sasha on Insta, but he's liked every single one of her photos and left comments on most of them.'

'Does he follow Gemma as well?'

'Yes, but he hasn't liked any of her pictures.'

'Show me.'

Ian pulled up Sasha's Instagram page. The photos were mainly of her and Gemma and various outfits, but more recent ones were of Sasha wearing clothes she'd made as part of her new project.

Natalie read through the comments and said, 'They're not outlandish but I'd say Lennox definitely fancies Sasha: "Looks terrific on you." "You look stunning in blue." "Very sexy!" I think we need to talk to Lennox again. What do we know about him?'

'His mother is Jocelyn Walsh, a top interior designer for the rich and famous. She divorced Roderick Walsh, a property developer, before Lennox was born. Roderick moved to Perth, Australia, in 1999. I don't have any more information on him. It looks like Jocelyn employed nannies to look after Lennox when he was younger then sent him to boarding school when he was eight.'

'Eight!' She refrained from making any further comment. Her own job had made it nigh on impossible to look after her own children, but she'd been fortunate and had David and Eric, her father-in-law, to help her out when she couldn't be there for them. She speculated as to why Lennox would be keen on Sasha, but it wasn't difficult to reason – the woman was gorgeous. 'I'm not sure why he'd target the daughter of a woman he had the hots for, but given he argued with Gemma yesterday morning and later that day she was attacked, we'll definitely pursue this angle.'

Lucy appeared with takeaway coffee for everyone. 'Ian said you were in. Figured you could do with a caffeine pick-me-up. Murray's on his way. He stopped off at the bus station.'

Natalie thanked her and took the offered cup. It felt strange having people look after her needs. 'Thought we'd try the university again. Can you and Murray get together a list of all the students on Gemma's course and talk to them and the lecturers who taught her?'

'Sure.'

'Ian, you and I will try the housemates.' She looked up at the approaching figure.

Murray strode down the corridor, shoulders swinging, like a gladiator about to take on a fight. 'Morning, all. Did you get me a skinny soya latte?' he asked Lucy.

'Like fuck I did. You get your usual full-fat milk, three sugars, treble shot, heart-attack special.'

'Excellent!' He grabbed the cup she indicated, took a large swig then smacked his lips noisily before saying, 'I spoke to the bus driver who was on duty last night. He remembers Gemma. She was the only person to get off at the stop near the library.'

'Looks like we can rule out anyone on that bus then,' said Natalie.

'Yep. Which leaves us looking for someone who knew she was headed for the library, or a random attacker,' Murray replied.

'Could be either although Lennox's alibi is still a little hazy and we discovered he was arguing with Gemma yesterday morning.

We're going to tackle him about that.' Natalie replaced the lid on her cup and made ready to leave.

Lucy jangled her car keys at Murray. 'Come on. Get that drink down you. We're interviewing students.'

'We'll catch up later,' said Natalie as she headed out of the office, Ian hot on her heels. Three paces along the corridor and her phone buzzed. It was her son. She spoke as she walked briskly.

'Hi, Josh.'

'Checking it's still okay for tonight.'

'Absolutely. Listen, I'm working an investigation and I'm not sure what time I'll get in.'

There a was a lengthy pause followed by a wary, 'Are you sure you're okay to go back, Mum?'

'I'm fine. I needed to return.'

'Well… If you're sure.'

'I'm sure. However, it means I might be out when you come over.'

'It's okay, I've got a spare key.'

'I'll try not to be too late.'

'Sure. No probs.'

'See you later. Love you.'

'Yeah. Back atcha.'

His response warmed her heart. It had been a long time since he'd shown any affection. No matter what was going on in this investigation, she wasn't going to push him aside. She'd lost one child. She wasn't going to lose another.

Lennox wiped sleep from his eyes and sat on the edge of his bed. The room smelt of sweat and stale clothes. *Like the laundry basket in the bathroom back home*, thought Natalie. The young man's room was surprisingly tidy with a laptop, folders and pens neatly laid out on an angular table with plastic red trays instead of conventional drawers underneath its laminated surface. There were no posters on his walls, only a cork message board to which he'd attached his timetable and a list of assignments to be completed.

He rubbed at his face and yawned again before speaking. 'It wasn't really an argument. Gemma was pissed off with me, that's all.'

'Why?' said Natalie.

He shrugged lightly. 'Her mum. Gemma said I was showing too much interest in her.'

'And were you?'

'Not really. I follow her on Instagram and I've chatted to her a few times when she's come by.'

'Why do you follow Sasha on Instagram?'

'You've seen her,' he said, opening his palms and shrugging again.

'Because you find her attractive?' Natalie asked.

'Yes. She's very fit.'

'I can't understand why Gemma would be upset about that. She knew her mother was good-looking and I'm sure she knew she had plenty of admirers. Is there something you're not telling us? Because if there is, it might be better if you spit it out now rather than me finding out and having to come back.'

He rested his hands on his pyjamaed knees. 'She was annoyed because I went to Chancer's Bar a couple of times and talked to Sasha. She said I shouldn't try it on with her mum.'

'Again, I don't see why that caused an argument.'

He sighed heavily. 'She said I was stalking Sasha.'

'And were you?'

'No!'

'She must have had good reason to accuse you of that.'

'Gemma overreacted and had a go at me.' He glanced across at the bedside locker, where his mobile lay, and Natalie wondered why he was suddenly rubbing his knees nervously.

'If I asked you to hand over your mobile, would that be a problem?'

'No.' His face said otherwise.

'Is there anything on your mobile that you wouldn't want us to see?'

'Okay. I took a few pictures of Sasha when she was here in the house. She's beautiful and she's really nice and easy to talk to. There was no harm in it.'

'Did you talk to her often?'

He hung his head. 'Pretty much every time she came by. If I heard her voice, I'd pop downstairs and have a few words with her.'

'Show me the photos.'

He reached for the phone, flicked through the camera roll and passed it across. He'd taken at least fifty of Sasha, in the house, talking at the table, walking down the path, getting into her car, working behind the bar, smiling, laughing; in most, if not all, of them, she was completely unaware he'd taken them.

'Are these photos the reason Gemma got cross?'

'Sort of. Those and going to the bar. She made it out to be something it wasn't.'

'That's a yes, then?'

'I wasn't stalking Sasha.'

'I'm going to hang on to this phone for a while. Get it looked at.'

'Why? There's nothing else on it.'

'Then you won't mind our technical team examining it, will you?'

'No. I suppose not. When can I get it back?'

'When they're done.' She passed the phone to Ian, who put it in a plastic bag. 'Would you say you were slightly obsessed with Sasha?' she asked.

'Not obsessed. I fancied her. That's all. It's not unusual, is it?'

'But Gemma obviously thought it was an obsession,' said Natalie.

He nodded. 'She blew it out of all proportion and told me to back off or she'd tell the police I was harassing Sasha.'

'But you weren't?'

'No way! Gemma was being overprotective. *She* had the problem, not me.'

'And you were arguing about this yesterday morning?'

'Yes.'

'Did you and Gemma often fall out?'

'No. That was the only time. We were sound before that.'

'Did you like Gemma?'

'What are you suggesting? I didn't hurt her. I was in the chemistry lab all evening until shortly after eight.'

'We're looking into that. What were you doing in there?'

'I was working on an experiment.'

'What experiment?'

'To develop green reactions using an applied magnetic field that can contribute to a sustainable chemical future,' he replied. His answer was way beyond Natalie's understanding of chemistry but she noted it anyway. His tutor would confirm it. The young man ran a hand through his bushy brown hair, and spoke again. 'Honestly. I didn't attack Gemma.'

'We'll have to talk to Sasha, and then if we have any further questions, we'll be back,' said Natalie. This wasn't over yet. The boy clearly had a crush on Sasha and had managed to upset Gemma enough that she'd threatened to report him to the police.

'I'd like to ask you where you went last night, after my officers spoke to you.'

'Only into town for a drink. It was a massive shock hearing about Gemma, and Hattie was bawling her eyes out in her room, and I couldn't face staying here. How is Sasha?'

'As you'd expect.'

'I thought about going to see her.'

'I would leave it a while.'

He rubbed at his whiskery beard that made him appear older than he was. His eyes were downcast. 'Yes, probably best.'

'Where did you go for a drink?'

'Only into town – the Three Kings pub. I met Ryan and a few other students I know there and told them about Gemma. I had a few shots and chatted for a while then went for a kebab. I got back late, probably after one o'clock.'

'Ryan's room's opposite yours, isn't it?'

'Yeah, the other side of the bathroom. I'm sure he's in. I heard him showering a short while ago.'

They left the boy's room and ducked out onto the landing. It was pokier on this floor, with much less headroom than the floor below, and the threadbare carpet didn't prevent the floorboards from creaking noisily as they crossed to Ryan's door and knocked. Natalie felt in her pocket for the key to Gemma's room that she'd collected from Forensics before leaving HQ. She was putting off looking in the dead girl's room until she'd spoken to Ryan Hausmann, who'd been involved with her.

Ryan, dressed in jeans and a crisp blue shirt, emerged from the bathroom, bringing with him the scent of cinnamon and citrus. He drew to a halt in front of them. Broad-shouldered, with an expressionless face and straw-coloured hair cut very short, he reminded Natalie of an action figure. They showed him their IDs and he nodded politely. 'I'm Ryan. Lennox bumped into me in town last night and broke the terrible news about Gemma.' His accent wasn't English; a mixture of Dutch and something else Natalie couldn't identify.

'We were hoping you could tell us more about her.'

Ryan made no move to invite them into his room but kept his eyes fixed on Natalie. 'I don't have much to say other than she was a really nice girl. Really nice. I guess you heard we were an item for a while.'

'Why did you split up?'

'Gemma wanted to concentrate on her studies.'

'Her mother told us you were serious about Gemma,' said Natalie.

'Serious? I liked her a lot but not *serious.*'

'And after you split up, you got along okay?'

'Sure we did, although I didn't see a whole lot of her on account of our timetables clashing. We would cross paths in the hallway as one of us was going out and the other was coming in.' The accent was beginning to sound more familiar and Natalie identified it as Afrikaans.

'Did you know what her plans were for yesterday evening?'

'She was going to the library to catch up on some work. She was way behind on some assignment or other.'

'When did she tell you this?'

'Yesterday morning, when Hattie asked who was going to be in later that evening. She was trying to organise a takeaway night. We sometimes do that. We pool our cash and buy in some food and share it.'

'Who else was there when Hattie asked who'd be in?'

'Fran and Lennox.'

'And Gemma announced she was going to be out.'

'That's right. She said she probably wouldn't be back until after the library shut at ten.'

'What about Lennox? Did he say what he was doing?'

'He was up for it and said he'd be back in time. Fran too, although she had some meeting or other first. I dipped out. I'd already made plans to go into town with friends.'

'Where did you go last night?'

'Pub crawl around Samford until late. I can give you the names of the guys I was with.'

'You look pretty fresh for someone who was on a pub crawl last night.'

'Strong constitution. I can take my drink,' he said.

'Where did you go?'

'White Hart, Stolen Pig... I don't know the names of all of them.'

'We'll need to talk to your friends. Can you give me their names?'

'Stuart Button and William Ingles. They only live three doors from here, towards the main road.' He hesitated briefly before asking quietly, 'Did she suffer?'

'I really can't discuss that.'

'It's absolutely disgusting what happened to her. Acid! She didn't deserve that. What bastard would do that to her?' It was the first time he'd shown any emotion. He visibly struggled to compose himself, then, before she knew it, his features had rearranged themselves once more and his face was blank. He asked if he could help any more.

'We'll be in touch if we need to speak to you again,' she replied.

They left him where he'd been standing, descended the few stairs to the first-floor landing and stopped outside Gemma's room. Natalie fished out the key, slotted it into the lock and twisted it. The door opened with a soft groan. The curtains were drawn and Natalie had to lean across the sofa bed, piled high in cushions, to open them. Turning back around, the first thing she spotted on the table against the wall was a silver frame with a photograph of Gemma with her arms around her mother, both smiling for the camera. A lump caught in her throat.

Ian began searching through the fitted wardrobe and drawers. Natalie let her eyes wander over the striped blue, silver and white cover – with coordinating cushions in a mixture of plain blue and patterned – that was neatly doubled on the foldaway bed to create the impression of a sofa. Three silver plant holders filled with artificial lavender stood on the window ledge, and pale blue and white storage boxes filled with personal belongings – make-up bags, clothes and books – sat between the bed and table. Natalie spotted a turquoise water bottle next to a matching teddy bear and was reminded again of Sasha. She read through notes and glanced through the girl's work. Her handwriting was the tidiest

Natalie had ever seen. She was well-organised, and an A5 diary, covered with blue butterflies, that lay on her desk was filled only with coursework due dates and shift times at Chancer's Bar. There were several pieces of paper slipped into the back of the diary – an out-of-date flyer for a free drinks night at the students' union, a receipt for coursework books, a letter inviting her to apply for a credit card at a special student rate and a folded piece of A4 paper. Natalie unfolded it. It was a typed note, signed 'An Admirer'.

'She had a fan. Listen to this, Ian. "Dear Gemma, Hi! I wanted to tell you that I think you're incredible.

'"I saw you in town today with your mother. I stopped and stared at you. I wasn't being rude. In fact, quite the opposite. I was hypnotised by you: the way you walk, the way you hold your head to one side when you are listening intently to somebody, and your smile. It is… perfect.

'"Anyway, now you know how I feel and I'll pick the right moment to make myself known to you. I'm excited and nervous to find out how you will react when I speak to you. I hope you will smile at me. An Admirer."' She studied the note again. There was no date on it, no envelope, and it was difficult to tell when Gemma might have received it. The flyer was for an event taking place on 28 September, and the book receipt and credit card letter were dated 18 and 19 September respectively. There was a chance the note from her admirer was delivered at around the same time rather than more recently. 'We'll take it around the students here and see if they know anything about it.' She slid it into a plastic evidence bag and continued searching for more notes, but there were none, and nothing else shouted out at Natalie.

'I can't see anything untoward,' said Ian, shutting the bottom drawer he'd been examining.

'No. She was exactly as everyone described – a nice girl.'

'Maybe that's exactly why she was targeted,' said Ian.

Natalie looked again at the photograph of Gemma and Sasha. She wasn't as glamorous or as striking as her mother, but she had a freshness and vitality that was arguably attractive. Somebody had wanted to destroy that. 'You could be right,' she said.

*

Gemma,

I'm used to insults. I've heard them all, but I thought better of you. You may think you were whispering quietly, but I overheard the comments you and your mother made about me. There seems little point in trying to befriend you. I don't care if you are popular and pretty and everyone likes you. You're as bad as all the other girls I have met: a cruel bitch. In some ways you are worse than them because you trick everyone with your false smile and fake interest in them. You can fool them but you don't fool me!

If I were as popular as you are, I'd be genuinely nice to everyone and not make snide comments about others behind their backs.

If you could spend one day in my shoes, you'd understand how I feel, and you would never have treated me in such a way. I wish I could show you how hurtful it is to be mocked.

An Admirer

CHAPTER SEVEN

SATURDAY, 17 NOVEMBER – MORNING

Natalie and Ian passed the note around the housemates but none of them recognised it or had any idea who might have sent it. Gemma hadn't mentioned it to any of them. The only person they couldn't ask was Hattie, who didn't answer her door; there was no sound from inside her room. Trying the door handle, they discovered it locked.

For a moment, Ian was nonplussed. 'I expected her to be here. She was really upset about Gemma last night… and she said she didn't go to her six o'clock lecture yesterday because she felt run-down.'

Natalie registered his concerns. 'She might have nipped out for any number of reasons; however, double-check that she really was here yesterday evening, and see if you can find out how much of a friend she really was to Gemma.'

'Her father's a vicar,' Ian said vacantly then pulled himself up short with, 'Yes… I know. That means nothing. I think what I'm actually trying to say is she came across as genuine. She wants to help fight poverty abroad.'

'That's highly commendable but we both know appearances can be deceptive and people lie. Vicar's daughter or not, let's make sure she was actually at home when she said she was, shall we?'

'She owns a grey Nissan Micra. I'll check the route between the house and the library and see if it passed by any cameras between six and seven.'

'That's a good starting point, although even if she was responsible for the attack, she might not have used her car – maybe she caught a bus or taxi into town instead, or even got a lift with somebody.'

'And reached the library before Gemma did?'

Natalie knew it was only a shot in the dark but she had to pursue it regardless. 'There's a chance Hattie went on ahead and attacked Gemma. I'm not sure how likely that is, but given we can't yet confirm she was at home when Gemma was attacked, we need to explore that possibility. Right, let's try Ryan's mates. Which house do they live in?'

'Number 59.'

As they walked along Eastview Avenue, they checked for Hattie's Nissan Micra but there was no sign of it parked in between the numerous vehicles squeezed into impossibly small spaces. The street was strangely silent, absent of traffic noise at this time of the day. It was far quieter than the main road outside Natalie's flat, where the constant hum was a permanent background noise. Eastview Avenue was a place that, without the vehicles, was stuck in a time warp, with grand edifices, bicycles against wrought-iron railings and aged trees, empty of foliage, their roots twisting and bulging beneath the cracked asphalt. She stepped over one such section of raised pavement in front of their destination and turned into a narrow, leaf-covered path. The house bore similar outward signs of disrepair and neglect as the one they'd just visited: paint peeled from window ledges, and the windowpanes were so thick with grime she could make out three smiley faces that somebody had traced on the inside of the one downstairs.

The doorbell pealed faintly, and within seconds a plump girl with a closely shaven head that revealed glimpses of a pink scalp opened the door. She glanced swiftly at their identity cards. 'Have you come to ask about Gemma? We've heard what happened to her. Bloody awful or what?' Her accent was thicker than Dan Tasker's but unmistakably Welsh. She continued chattering at high speed as she showed them into a gloomy hallway, where a couple of grubby bicycles with mud embedded in their tyres were propped against a wooden staircase to their left. It might once have been a grand Victorian residence, but to Natalie it felt abandoned and unloved. The cream walls had been scraped and dirtied in places, and apart from a notice of 'dos and don'ts' there was nothing on the walls. Directly ahead of her, the kitchen door opened onto a shambolic mess of unwashed pans and crockery piled next to a sink, and a table littered with tins, boxes and condiments that hadn't been replaced in cupboards. The air smelt of stale cigarette smoke. It was far less organised here than in the house where Gemma had lived.

'My friend Fran lives in the same house as her. I can't get my head around it. I only saw Gemma yesterday.'

'We were hoping you might be able to tell us a bit more about her. What's your name?' Natalie asked.

'Me? I'm Rhiannon Williams. I live here with three others but one of them, Libby, is away at the moment, in Cornwall. She takes geology, see? And she's on a field trip until next Wednesday, and I don't suppose she's heard about Gemma yet.' Her voice rattled like an express train.

'How well did you know Gemma?'

Her stencilled eyebrows pulled together. 'Fran shared the house with her and I used to go around a fair bit, cos Fran and I are best friends, and we spend a lot of time together there. Their house is much nicer than this one, see? I prefer to go around there, rather than Fran come here because they have nicer stuff in it and their sitting room is friendlier.'

'Did you talk to her much?'

'I talked to her. You can't exactly ignore somebody if they're sitting watching the same programme as you, can you? But I wouldn't say we talked about anything serious. It was all about whatever we were watching or university stuff.'

'You weren't friends as such?'

The girl's pale amber eyes screwed up and she shrugged. 'Not like I am with Fran. She was really nice but she was studying different languages than me and we weren't in any of the same lectures or classes. Apart from when I bumped into her at the house, I didn't really get many opportunities to chat to her, alone like.'

There it was again. That same word: *nice*. 'Fran didn't discuss her with you? Mention seeing her with anyone – a boyfriend maybe?'

She blinked as she thought, thick fake eyelashes that swept up and down like tiny brooms. 'Oh, yes, Gemma went out with Ryan for a short while but Fran and I didn't talk about her. Why would we? I barely knew her and Fran didn't exactly hang about with her. Gemma was usually with her mother.' Rhiannon's lip curled slightly after she spoke. For Natalie, it was a recognisable sign of disgust. The girl was not one of Sasha's fans.

'You speak to Sasha at all?'

'Uh-huh. She tried to get in with us, if you get my meaning. She's one of those mums who copies their kid, which is pretty sad, isn't it? I mean, if my mum started wearing the same clothes as me, I'd go off on one at her. It was a bit awkward sometimes.'

'Can you explain?'

She paused to collect her thoughts then the words tumbled out. 'It's always the same when you talk to adults, or other people's parents. They don't know what to say to you so they stick to stuff like: "What are you studying? Are you going to travel as part of your course?" They pretend to be really interested in you, when really they're not, but they want their kids to think they are. Gemma's mother's like that, sort of OTT about everything. For instance, Fran told Sasha she was thinking of applying to the Foreign Office to be an interpreter, and Sasha nearly fainted with excitement. She sat with her mouth open like Fran was some sort of celebrity.'

'But Gemma was close to her mum.'

Rhiannon's lips twitched again. 'Yes, she was. That was strange too. My mum and I argue all the time. They were like best mates.' She stared directly at Natalie and shook her head. 'It's horrible, though, what's happened to her. Really horrible.'

'What about Hattie, how did she get on with Gemma?'

'Good, I think. Hattie's very… hippy. She loves everyone.'

'Who else lives here with you?'

'William, Stuart and Libby.'

'Are any of them in?'

'The boys might be, but like I said, Libby's away on a field trip in Cornwall and won't be back until mid-week.'

'When did she go?'

'Last Wednesday.'

Natalie pulled out the note she'd retrieved from Gemma's diary. 'I don't suppose you know anything about this, do you?' she asked.

Rhiannon read it through and looked blankly at Natalie. 'No. I haven't seen it before.'

'And Gemma never mentioned having an admirer to you?'

'Never. I expect she had plenty of admirers though. She was very pretty.'

Natalie asked if they could speak to the young men who'd been out with Ryan on the pub crawl, and Rhiannon raced upstairs to fetch them. The first to descend was a skinny youth, over six feet tall and dressed in slippers, fleece loungewear and a patterned beanie hat. He rubbed at the stubble on his face and told them he was called Stuart. His breath smelt of alcohol and his eyes were bleary.

'We're following up on a few details regarding the death of Gemma Barnes. Did you know her?'

'Only to say hello to. We saw Lennox last night and he told us she'd been in an acid attack and died. Fucking awful.'

'What time was that?'

'I haven't a clue.'

'Where did he meet you?'

'Might have been the Three Kings. Yeah, I think it was. It was late by then, but the Three Kings stays open until midnight on Fridays.' He'd confirmed what they'd been told: Lennox had gone to the Three Kings pub.

'Ryan says you were with him last night.'

'That's right.'

'All night?'

'Pretty much.'

'Can you tell us your exact movements?'

The boy winced as if the effort was too great, and with eyes screwed up he said, 'We met in the students' union bar about half past six, had a couple of pints, then headed into town and hit a few pubs. Started at the White Hart.'

Upstairs Rhiannon's voice yelled, 'Will! Wake up. Police!' and there was further banging as she attempted to rouse the boy from his bed.

'Can you tell us exactly where you went?' asked Natalie.

The boy rubbed at his chin as he thought. 'White Hart… Stolen Pig… Swan and then… Three Kings.'

Ian wrote down the names of all the pubs. Above them, floorboards squeaked loudly and footsteps thudded across the ceiling. There was a quick exchange of words, followed by the sound of somebody descending the wooden stairs, and a barelegged youth with curly black hair and dressed in a short blue dressing gown appeared in the hallway. Stuart turned to him and said, 'Will, the police are trying to sort out where we all were last night. Where did we go after the Three Kings?'

'Tumbledown Dick.'

'Oh, yes. That's it.'

'William Ingles?' asked Natalie. He was one of the names on the list.

'That's me. We were together all night – me, Stuart, Ryan… and Lennox, but he didn't join us until later. We got an Uber home at about one-ish.' William hesitated briefly then asked, 'What exactly happened to Gemma? Lennox told us somebody threw acid in her face and she died.'

'That's correct,' said Natalie. The boy grimaced. 'Did you know her well?'

'Only vaguely. She and Ryan were getting it on for a while, but she never came out with us. He used to speak about her all the time, but it was mostly about what a babe she was and how great their relationship was. He was majorly cut up last night when he found out about what had happened to her. He went straight home.'

'Did he go out with her for long?'

'They were together for a while at the start of this term, till she mugged him off.'

'What happened?'

'Don't really know for certain, but Ryan was definitely pissed off about it for a while. He skived a few lectures and wouldn't even come out for a drink.' He turned to Stuart for confirmation, who nodded in agreement.

'Stuart?' Natalie said. The boy wasn't much more forthcoming.

'He was into her and she wasn't into him. That's all I know. Ryan isn't big on talking about feelings and shit like that.'

She reached again for the note and showed it to them. 'Do either of you recognise this?'

Stuart shook his head.

'William?'

'Never seen it before.'

'Neither of you wrote this?'

Stuart snorted slightly. 'No way! I didn't fancy Gemma. I've already got a girlfriend, Kaitlin. She's a student here. Gemma wasn't my type.'

'Mine neither,' said William, quickly. 'I'm seeing somebody too. She's back home but we've been together since I left for uni.'

'Do you think Ryan might have sent it?'

Stuart's brow lowered. 'Absolutely not. That doesn't sound like him at all.'

William agreed. 'He wouldn't write anything like that. He says what he thinks and he's not at all shy.'

She put the letter away again. They'd established Ryan's whereabouts, and regardless of what had happened between him and Gemma, if he'd been with the boys at the time of the attack, he had a cast-iron alibi – although Natalie was also aware he could have been responsible and involved somebody else to throw the acid. Nothing could be discounted at this stage. They'd finished here.

'I'll ring around the pubs and see if they have any CCTV footage that might confirm Ryan definitely was on the pub crawl,' said Ian as they climbed back into the squad car.

Natalie nodded. She was in favour of thoroughly checking every detail, and to that end she wanted to make sure Hattie hadn't left the house after her chat in the kitchen with Gemma. 'We'll try Chancer's Bar next. And I'd like to get hold of Hattie. Have you got contact details for her?'

'I put them in the file.'

She twisted around, pulled the manila folder from the back seat and hunted for what she needed. Traffic into town was building with shoppers heading towards the retail park, and they had to traverse the centre to reach the bar. Natalie dialled the number. It went to answerphone.

'Oh, bugger!' she said with a lengthy sigh. She could have done with getting hold of Hattie and having a quick chat without adding it to the to-do pile.

'Maybe she's gone to visit her dad.'

'I'm not chasing about after her. We'll get hold of her later.' She picked up the communications unit handset to contact Murray.

'Receiving,' he said.

'Anything to report?'

'Nothing yet.'

'While you're talking to students, find out what you can about Hattie Caldwell. See if she's friendly with any other girls and if she and Gemma were close.'

'Will do.'

She hung up and eased back against the seat.

A vintage, bright-orange Citroen beer truck emblazoned with the bar's name was parked on the forecourt of the former garage turned bar. Ian drew up behind a drinks lorry that was being offloaded and they followed the delivery driver into the establishment, where they were met with an explosion of rainbow colours against brick walls, the result of a wild paint-throwing party or uncontrollable toddlers let loose with cans of paint. The effect was made worse by the bright sunlight streaming through the skylights, which made the colours all the more garish and the furniture look cheap and tacky. Natalie's gaze fell upon oil drums now upcycled into stools that stood in front of the bar – another nod to the place's heritage – and to the man who squatted on one, hunched over a copy of the *Sun*.

'Morning, sir. Do you own this place?'

The man's head snapped up and he pushed back his reading glasses on top of his wiry black hair. The paper remained open at the sporting news for the day. 'Er, no. I only work here.'

'And what's your name?' Natalie asked.

'Joe Yanick.'

'We're here regarding the death of one of the bar's employees, Gemma Barnes.'

'She's dead?'

'I'm afraid so.'

The man dragged his wide hand across both cheeks and it crackled over his bristled chin; a scraping sound like sandpaper gently rubbing a surface. 'What happened to her?'

'She was involved in an attack.'

'A knife attack?'

'Acid.'

His face contorted and he sucked in air through clenched teeth, then said, 'Oh my God! Her face?'

'Yes.'

This time he released the air, his teeth still clenched. 'Poor... poor Gemma... but why? Everyone liked her. Why would somebody do that?'

'That's why we're here – to try and find out as much as we can to help us find the person responsible. Can you recall seeing anyone hanging about when she was on duty, maybe talking to her, showing more interest in her than any of the other bar staff?'

'She got attention all the time – not from one person, from lots of people. Some of the men, and the ladies, only come here to be served by her and Sasha. Naturals, both of them. They made more tips on a Saturday than the rest of us made in a week.'

'Did they pool their tips?' Natalie asked, wondering if their popularity might be a reason for somebody to be jealous of them.

He made a sucking noise through his teeth and shook his head as he processed once more what he'd learnt only a moment ago. 'All the money goes into the gratuity jar, and each week we divide the contents among us all. Yes, they shared their tips.'

'Did you talk to Gemma much?'

'If we had a quiet few minutes, but that was rare. This place is pretty heaving weekends, and that's when she usually worked.'

'How would you describe her?'

'Easy-going and likeable. She always asked about my family too. Nice that. Not everyone is interested in you. She and Sasha are people's people, you know what I mean? They're interested in everyone and listen, not talk over them all the time like some people do.'

'She didn't mention having an admirer, did she?'

'She didn't talk about anyone in particular, but like I said, she got plenty of attention.'

'You don't recognise this note?'

He squinted at it. 'Sorry, never seen it before.'

'When did you last see Gemma?'

'A fortnight ago, before I went on holiday. I only got back last night.'

'What time did your flight land?'

'Twenty past nine. Got home close to eleven. Luggage took forever to come through.'

There was no way this man could have been behind the attack, and judging by the tone that had crept into his voice, he wouldn't have wished her any harm.

'Would you say, then, that Gemma got along with everyone here?'

'I most definitely would. Lovely girl.'

'And you didn't notice anybody acting strangely in her presence – customers or staff?' Natalie asked again.

He nodded to himself as if trying hard to shake his thoughts into order. 'There was one lad. Big guy with blond hair and a waxy, smooth face. He's been coming in a fair bit recently.'

The person sounded like Ryan. Natalie spoke up. 'Did he have an accent?'

'Yes, there was an accent but I don't know what it was. I'm no good with accents.'

Ian hunted through the file he'd brought along of all the housemates' details and passed over the picture of the young man in question.

'That's the fella,' said Joe.

'Did he hassle Gemma?' asked Natalie.

'Oh, no, he usually sat over there,' he said, pointing at a group of seats against the wall, which was adorned with metal posters of old adverts for various beers. 'He drank on his own, but he'd stare at her a lot. I noticed him doing it a few times while I was out there collecting glasses.'

'Did she complain about him?'

'To be honest, I don't think she was aware of it happening. She was always chatting to customers or pouring them drinks. I probably wouldn't have noticed if I hadn't been glass-collecting at the time – and he did have a weird face. Like a puppet.'

'Can you recall when you last saw him?'

'Again, it was soon before I went away… maybe the day before although I can't be sure. I asked if he'd finished with his empty glass and he passed me it without a word and carried on sitting there, like he was waiting for somebody.' It was certainly suspicious behaviour and needed investigating even if Ryan had an alibi for the time of the attack on Gemma.

'Did anyone join him?'

'No.'

'Is there anything else you can think of that might help us?'

He shook his head. 'Sorry.'

The delivery driver pushed another handcart piled with crates across the tiled floor, causing the glass bottles to perform a tinkling, jangling symphony that reached a full-blown clattering crescendo by an open door behind the bar, before they disappeared tunelessly into the void beyond.

Natalie waited for the noise to cease before asking, 'Are there any other staff members here today?'

'They'll be in later, before opening time. We don't open until six. I'm only here to keep an eye on the deliveries.'

'We'd like to speak to everyone who works here. Do you have a list of employees' details?'

'I don't have that information. You need to ask the owner, Phil Chancer. He's in Spain at the minute but he'll still be able to help you out.' He lifted an old Nokia, screen smeared with thumbprints. A child's face appeared and Natalie's heart jumped in her chest. But it wasn't Leigh she saw on the screensaver. This girl was about thirteen, her dark hair plaited in cornrows and a hint of a smile on her heart-shaped face as if she knew a secret. Natalie didn't ask but it was most likely the man's daughter. The face vanished and Joe hunted for his boss's contact details, reading them out for Ian, who jotted them down.

Natalie pulled out a business card, which she slid across the bar. 'Thank you for your time, and if you can think of anything else, please contact us.'

By the time they emerged from the bar, the sun had reached its zenith, casting shadows across the car park that flickered unsteadily as light clouds flitted overhead. Natalie pulled her jacket tighter, unsure if the cold fingers running down her spine were due to the cool temperatures or seeing the girl on the phone. She slid back into the suffocating air of the squad car, which had heated up in the direct sunshine, and lowered the window.

'Back to Eastview Avenue?' said Ian.

'Yes. Might come across Hattie while we're there.' She fumbled for the air-con switch and put it on, turning up the fan as well to direct cooler air onto her face.

Ian twisted around in his seat to reverse the car back onto the main road. 'I know Ryan was with Stuart and William last night but that doesn't mean he can't be behind the attack on Gemma,' he said.

Before she could agree, Murray's voice came over the communications unit. She answered, 'Receiving.'

'Nothing to report yet, only that Hattie Caldwell is extremely well liked and the other students on her course only have good things to say about her.'

'You haven't come across her at all today, have you?'

'No. No one we've spoken to has seen her today.'

'Anything on Gemma?'

'She was a likeable student who worked very hard. We've drawn nothing but a load of blanks. We've got a couple of Gemma's language lecturers to interview next.'

'Will you also talk to Lennox Walsh's chemistry tutor to confirm he was working on an experiment to do with... Hang on...' She flicked through her notebook and read out loud, 'To develop green reactions using an applied magnetic field that can contribute to a sustainable chemical future.'

There was a pause and then, 'Using an applied what?'

She repeated the sentence more slowly so he could write it down.

'Okay, I've got all that,' said Murray.

'Find out how students access the chemicals. I'm guessing they need signing out and I'd like to know if he's removed or requested any acid although I can't imagine he would. It wouldn't be the brightest move to make, and he would surely guess we'd check on him. We're returning to the student house to talk to Ryan again, and then we're heading back to the station.'

'We'll get onto it and keep you posted.'

Natalie shut her eyes to help her consider the facts. This type of attack was rarely random. Assailants were invariably those who wanted to maim and disfigure an individual who they were jealous of or who had hurt them in some way. It was likely to be somebody who knew Gemma who'd carried out the acid attack. If Ryan had been dumped, as he admitted, but was still crazy about Gemma, he had a motive, yet he also had an alibi as to his whereabouts at the time of the attack. Once more she lifted the file that Ian had compiled and searched for information on the student, noting he had come from Johannesburg and been sent to a private school in the north of the UK for the last two years of his education before applying to do politics at Samford. She rang HQ to request information on his past and see if he had ever been in trouble with the police in South Africa.

Drawing up once again outside the house where Gemma had lived, Natalie released her seat belt and prepared to clamber out of the vehicle. She cast about but there was still no sign of Hattie's grey Nissan Micra. 'I hope he's still in,' she grumbled. 'I'm getting fed up with all this toing and froing.'

'He's there!' said Ian suddenly, and sprang out of the car. Ryan was striding out along the path, wheeling a bicycle. 'Ryan!'

The young man stopped in his tracks. He was now dressed in a tracksuit and had a backpack over his shoulder.

'We'd like a few more minutes of your time,' said Natalie.

'I'm on my way to the gym for a workout,' he replied.

'It'll have to wait. Can you come back inside, please?'

'Why?' he asked, his cool gaze on Natalie. There was something unnerving about his expressionless face.

'We've uncovered some information that needs looking into. We've been to Chancer's Bar and we need to talk again.'

He lifted the bike effortlessly and marched back to the house, where he fumbled for his keys and let himself in. He propped the bike up against the wall and then faced them. 'What do you want to know?'

'I'd rather do this in your room.'

'I'd rather not,' he replied.

'Why is that? Do you have something to hide?'

'No.'

'Okay, we'll do it your way. You were seen on several occasions at the bar, sitting alone and staring at Gemma. The most recent was only a couple of weeks ago.'

'That's not true.'

'You have been identified by a member of staff and we can request CCTV footage to confirm if you were there or not. Shall I ask you again?'

There was no scowl or defiance only a sullen response. 'I might have gone to the bar.'

'Might or did?'

'Did.'

'Why were you sat there, staring at Gemma?'

'I wasn't aware I was staring at her. I was probably miles away, in my head.'

'Do you often go into bars and stare into space?' Natalie said, hoping to provoke a response, but all she got in return was a blank look. 'You told us earlier that Gemma ended your relationship.'

'That's correct. She did.'

'And that you weren't "serious" about her. Sitting alone in a bar, staring at an ex-girlfriend, suggests otherwise. It suggests you were still hung up on her.'

He shifted from one foot to the other and Natalie had to keep her head slightly tilted backwards to maintain steady eye contact with him. 'Do you want to continue this conversation in your room or at the station?'

He gave a curt nod and led the way upstairs. As Natalie entered the room, she realised why he'd been reluctant to let them in initially. A large photo of Gemma was on his bookcase in front of his textbooks and another by his bed. He dropped his keys onto the duvet and sat down, palms on wide thighs. 'It's not what it looks like. I wasn't spying on her as such. I needed to know if there was anybody in her life.'

'I asked you about this note I found in Gemma's room,' she said, holding it out. 'I'm asking you again. Did you write it?'

'No. I don't do subterfuge. I asked Gemma out the day after she moved in here. I prefer to be direct.'

'And she never spoke about this letter or about having an admirer?'

'Not once. I don't know who sent that but I haven't seen anyone hanging about her. I'd have known if there was anyone.'

'You'd have known?'

'Yes.'

'Because you were keeping an eye on her?'

'In a way, yes.'

Natalie didn't push for an explanation. Ryan adjusted his position, preparing to speak, and her silence was more effective than questions.

'I fancied her from the off. She arrived on the Saturday before term began, same day as me, and we kept passing each other on the stairs. I asked her out for a drink the next day, and the following week we began going out together. Then I screwed up. We went to a party at the beginning of October and I drank way more than I ought to have and told her I was falling for her. It was such a fucking dumb-arse thing to have come out with, because she broke up with me over it. Said she couldn't deal with that sort of shit. She completely overreacted and was even going to request a move to other accommodation. The only way I could convince her to stay in the house was to assure her I'd only said it because I was drunk and that I was completely chill about her splitting up with me, which was bollocks, but it was better to have her close by than not to see her at all. I actually hoped she'd change her mind in time and we'd get back together again. The thing is, I haven't been able to get over her since we broke up. I invited her out a few times for a friendly drink but she refused every time, and I got it into my head she'd found somebody else. I went to the bar to make certain she wasn't cracking on with any of the guys there.'

'Were you jealous of the men she served?'

'Not jealous as such. I wanted to be reassured she wasn't seeing somebody else.'

'Was she?'

'Not to my knowledge.'

'Are you saying you never watched her flirt or engage with any other men at the bar?'

'She didn't *flirt*. She was naturally friendly – really easy to get on with.'

Natalie gave him a curious look but he shrugged it off.

'How do you feel now you know what's happened to Gemma?'

'I feel sick. Sick to the very bottom of my stomach.'

Ian threw the young man a quick look and commented, 'You don't look too distressed about it.'

'I don't do emotion.'

Ian snapped back with, 'Gemma had acid thrown in her face and as a consequence died. This is the same girl you couldn't "get over", who you sat and observed regularly while she was working at the bar to make sure she wasn't seeing another bloke. What does "I don't do emotion" mean, exactly? Because it sounds like a load of bullshit to me. If you feel strongly about someone, you can't help but react.'

'You can if you come from where I do. You learn to toughen up from a very early age,' Ryan replied.

Ian was having none of it. 'You can't admit to falling for somebody and in the next sentence say you "don't do emotion".'

Ryan responded by looking at his hands curled lightly on his knees.

Natalie sensed the tension rising between the pair and took over. 'Do you have any idea at all who might have attacked her?'

'No.'

'Did you notice her talking to any customers in particular? Somebody who seemed keen on her?'

'No. There wasn't anyone who stood out.' Then there was a flicker of eyelids and, 'Maybe you should look online.'

Ian replied, 'We've examined her social media accounts. There's no suspicious activity. Do you know something that we don't?'

'I don't know how relevant it is but Fran and Rhiannon were slagging Gemma off a while ago on Facebook in a private conversation. Fran got pissed one night and showed it to me. She thought I'd find it amusing but I didn't.'

His hands balled into fists and Natalie took it as a sign that what he was saying was very relevant. These girls had angered him. 'Tell us more.'

'I can't remember exactly what was said. I read some of the conversation and told Fran to grow up and stop being a stupid bitch.' The fists had clenched tighter and he continued, 'The fact is, Gemma was a class act and way better than those nasty bitches.'

'Who else was part of the group?'

'I don't know.'

'We might need to talk to you again.'

'Okay. Can I go to the gym now?'

'Yes.'

'Are you going to talk to Fran and Rhiannon about this?'

'We are and I would appreciate it if you don't mention what we've discussed with anyone. This is an ongoing investigation.'

'I won't say anything,' he replied. With that, he pushed himself to his feet and stood in front of them, his large frame blocking the light streaming in through his window.

Natalie noticed how spartan his room appeared to be with no personal effects, other than the photos of Gemma, on display. It was like the young man himself, giving no clue to his true identity or to his past life. She couldn't imagine what his life had been like before he'd come to the UK, but it must have been difficult if it had driven him to hide behind a perpetual, controlled mask. The question of whether Ryan was responsible for the attack on Gemma hadn't really been answered, and although they had another direction to investigate, she wasn't ready to discount him yet.

CHAPTER EIGHT

SATURDAY, 17 NOVEMBER – AFTERNOON

Fran wasn't in her room, and unable to raise her or Hattie on their mobiles, Natalie and Ian returned to headquarters to delve into Fran's Facebook account. Natalie headed to Forensics to see where they were with the investigation and found Darshan Singh and his wife, Naomi, in the lab. Both renowned in their fields, Naomi Singh was a top forensic anthropologist while Darshan was a specialist in forensic odontology.

'Hi, Natalie,' said Naomi, lifting her dark eyes momentarily from the damaged, yellowed skull she was examining. Slender as a child and only five foot three, it often surprised those who met her that she was a leading authority on her subject and had travelled the world to lecture on it. Darshan, equally slim but much taller at almost six foot, was visible through a window that separated this lab from the actual autopsy room, where modular steel cabinets and countertops spanned the back wall. He had his back to them and was studying some X-rays on a backlit screen. The body of a young man lay on a trolley beside which was a row of shining tools laid out on a pristine white cloth. As a forensic odontologist, it often fell to him to help identify a John or Jane Doe.

'Mike around?' asked Natalie.

'He's been called out,' replied Naomi, pushing herself and the wheeled stool away from the bench into the centre of the room, where she got up and crossed the sparkling clean floor to Natalie and took the woman's hands in both of her own. Her palms were cool and dry but her eyes were liquid and warm. 'How are you, really? I don't want to hear the brave face version.' The action and gentle words caused Natalie's throat to constrict but she managed to nod.

'You know.'

Naomi squeezed her hands slightly – a gesture of kindness and concern. 'I'm very pleased to see you've come back to work, and if ever you want a chat or a coffee or anything, you only have to pop upstairs or ring me.'

'Thank you.'

Naomi had a no-nonsense approach to everything but this show of empathy was sincere, and etched on her forehead were lines of concern. She studied Natalie's face carefully and offered a small smile. 'You need to look after yourself. You've lost too much weight.' She released Natalie's hands. 'Why not come around for dinner tonight? Darshan is cooking one of his specialities later.'

'That's really kind of you but Josh is staying with me tonight. I thought I'd pick up a takeaway on my way home.'

Naomi gave another smile and, lightly rubbing Natalie's upper arm, said, 'Another time then. Make sure you order plenty – extra-large dishes. You need to keep up your strength.' The focus shifted back to work. 'What can I do for you?'

'I wondered if you could examine this note and check it for fingerprints. I'd like to find whoever typed it.'

'Sure. I'll get somebody onto it immediately. As far as I know we've nothing new on Gemma Barnes. Wait a minute.' She buzzed the intercom that connected the main laboratory to the examination room, where her husband was working.

'Darshan, Natalie is here. Has Pinkney finished with Gemma?'

His voice was amplified through the speaker in the room. 'Hello, Natalie. Pinkney hasn't written up the official report yet but there is no doubt that Gemma died from a severe form of hypotension, most likely caused by the shock of the attack. You should receive it within the next hour. We've identified the acid as high-strength sulphuric. It melted a great deal of her flesh so either the attacker obtained pure sulphuric acid or removed the water from battery acid to make it stronger.'

'How would they do that?' Natalie asked.

'One of two ways: wait for it to evaporate naturally – but that would take several days or even longer – or use a borosilicate glass pan such as a Pyrex dish and boil it. That carries quite a risk, especially as the glass could shatter.'

'They'd need proper equipment for that, wouldn't they?'

'Definitely, and knowledge about what they were doing. The steam given off turns into white vapour, which is dangerous if inhaled.'

'Who am I looking for, Darshan? Somebody with a knowledge of chemistry?'

'Not necessarily. They might have purchased the acid online or even in stores. Some drain cleaner has a high enough percentage of sulphuric acid to cause this sort of damage to flesh.'

'Could be anyone then?'

'It could indeed.'

'What about the dust particles on her clothing?'

'It was the same polymeric sand used in the joints between the pavement slabs by the library.'

She thanked the man, who returned to his work.

Naomi was not done. 'It was an abhorrent and cruel act. Some people have very black hearts indeed.'

Natalie could only agree. They'd all seen and experienced cases that would haunt them for the rest of their days.

Naomi had said her piece, her attention back on Natalie. 'Have a good time with Josh. How's he getting along at college?'

'He's enjoying it. Says it's much better than being at school. I'm glad he's no longer attending Castergate too. It'd be yet another reminder of Leigh.' There, she'd said it out loud – her daughter's name.

'It's better that way. You know what they say, though: kids are resilient. He'll heal way quicker than you.'

'I'd be happy about that.'

'Give yourself a chance, Natalie. And make sure you eat properly tonight. You don't want to end up looking like that,' she said, indicating the skeletal remains on another bench.

She was rewarded with a tired smile from Natalie, who slipped back out into the corridor. It had been tricky keeping a lid on her emotions when she'd mentioned Leigh by name. She'd wanted to pour her heart out to Naomi but work wasn't the place for such an outburst. She could do with whatever mental armour Ryan used to protect himself from emotions. It seemed to work for him. She passed the vending machine on the landing and bought cups of tea and a chocolate bar each for her and Ian before returning to the office.

'Cheers,' said Ian, ripping off the wrapper. He snapped off a large section of chocolate, popped it into his mouth and chewed as he repeatedly clicked his mouse.

Natalie looked over his shoulder, a paper cup of warm tea in her hand. 'That Fran's Facebook account?'

Ian nodded.

'The techies got into that quickly.'

He swallowed the chocolate. 'Yes. It came a few minutes ago. I'm going through the conversation threads now. Nothing yet – they're mostly discussing lectures and work schedules at the moment.' He continued to scroll as he spoke. 'The tech team didn't find anything suspicious on Lennox's phone, and I contacted the pubs Ryan and his friends visited last night and their story checks out. There's footage of them all at four of the pubs – the White Hart, Stolen Pig, Swan and the Three Kings– and CCTV at the students' union bar shows they left there at seven forty-six. Ryan didn't join his friends at the fifth pub, the Tumbledown Dick, and I could only spot his friends on the pub's footage. I guess that supports his story that he went home.' As he spoke, his fingers repeatedly clicked the mouse, bringing more of the lengthy conversation into view.

A shrill ring interrupted them and Natalie answered the internal phone. 'Yep. Okay. Thanks for looking into it.' She put down the receiver and said, 'Ryan has no police record in South Africa. Never been in trouble.'

'He's a hard nut though, isn't he? His father's the CEO of a media company.'

'Yes, I read that in the file you prepared.'

'You see the bit about the family being attacked?'

'Uh-huh.'

Ian continued all the same. 'Yes, some gunmen broke into their complex and held the children and mother at gunpoint. Little wonder Ryan's as hard as he is, given he was there when it happened.' He lifted his cup with his free hand then froze.

Natalie, who'd been reading the screen at the same time as him, shouted, 'Stop!' but he already had, cursor hovering over the conversation between Fran and Rhiannon that Ryan had mentioned.

Fran: Totally pissed off with Gemma for flirting with Ryan even though she broke his heart

Rhiannon: Bitch

Fran: She's a total flirt. Apparently, she sits in the front row and makes eyes at Professor Younger every time he lectures them

Rhiannon: She's probably hoping to bed him to get a better grade

Fran: More than likely. She'll probably screw her way to a first-class degree

Rhiannon: She was hanging around the prof like a bad smell today. I had a lecture with him after hers and she was still in the lecture hall, standing all doe-eyed while he explained something to her

Fran: Did she flick her hair?

Rhiannon: Yeah

Fran: She does that all the time when she's talking to guys

Rhiannon: 'Oh, look at me… I'm really sexy… flick… pout… flick… pout…'

Fran: I swear, one day, I'll pull it out of her fucking head

Rhiannon: We should tie her down and shave her head. LOL

Fran: It'd only grow back

Rhiannon: Something else then?

Fran: Yeah, something that would fix her for good. I know people who'd sort her out once and for all

Rhiannon: Ooh, scary! What? Get a contract out on her? LOL

Fran: Not exactly. Just rearrange her face a little

Rhiannon: Fran, you wouldn't!

Fran: Wouldn't I?

Natalie broke off from the dialogue on the screen. She reached for the folder and read the few paragraphs about Fran who'd been brought up by her mother and stepfather in East Toxteth, one of the most deprived areas in the country. One of a family of six, Fran had got into trouble as a youngster and, along with other members of a small gang, had offended several times before being put into care at the age of twelve. A year later, she'd gone to live with her maternal grandparents in Childwall, Liverpool, and had not been in trouble since.

'Fran was at a meeting last night, wasn't she?'

'Something to do with the students' union social committee,' said Ian.

'Make sure she was there for the entire meeting, will you?' She left him working on it and rang Phil Chancer, the owner of Chancer's Bar, to find out who else worked there. No sooner had she obtained the list of names than Murray rang in with an update.

'Lennox's chemistry tutor says the lad was definitely working on that particular experiment. He reckons Lennox has been in the lab most nights over the last couple of weeks because his report on it is due in at the end of this coming week. We checked the lists and with the lab assistants, and Lennox hasn't signed out any acids at all this term. We've only got one more lecturer left to interview about Gemma – Professor Younger.'

It was the same lecturer whose name had cropped up in the Facebook conversation between the girls. Natalie explained what they'd uncovered.

'Okay, we'll grill him thoroughly. Maybe there was something going on between him and Gemma,' said Murray.

Ian waited until she ended her conversation with Murray before telling her what he'd discovered. 'I've been going through the rest of Fran's conversation with Rhiannon and there aren't any other references to Gemma. I think this was a one-off occurrence.'

'We can't discount the fact that Fran reckoned she knew people who would "sort out" Gemma and that she said she'd "rearrange" Gemma's face. Those might be throwaway comments and have no substance, but there are grounds to suspect she and the others were jealous of Gemma. Fran is good friends with Rhiannon. Do we know where Rhiannon was last night?'

'No. I'll find out.'

She got into the general database and hunted for information on Rhiannon Williams. She didn't notice Dan Tasker's arrival until he gave a soft knock on the glass door. Ian leapt up to let him in.

'I wondered how you were getting along with the Gemma Barnes investigation. We've arranged a conference with the media for this afternoon. It's been decided it is best to get the media on side for this one and put the word out. We don't want the public anxious that there is an attacker on the loose,' he said.

Natalie shook her head. 'Surely, if there is a random attacker, we do want the public to be extra vigilant.'

'Do you have reason to believe it was a random attack?'

'Not really, sir.'

'More often than not, these types of attacks are by people known to the victim.'

Natalie nodded. 'That's true. We don't have a great deal to follow up at the moment although we're looking into the possibility that one of her housemates or a fellow student was behind the attack. At present, we have little evidence other than an online conversation.'

'Tell me what you know.' Dan folded his arms and rested against the desk to listen.

She ran over what they'd ascertained, and when she'd finished he said, 'Given Fran's background and what was said online, I'd suggest you might have found your attacker.'

'Fran was in a meeting at the time of the attack on Gemma. Ian, you checked that, didn't you?'

'Yes. She didn't leave until it was over.'

'What time was that?' Dan asked.

'After eight o'clock, sir.'

'What about the other girl in this online conversation? Where was she at the time?' Dan kept a steely gaze on Ian, who didn't buckle.

'I'm still in the process of checking her out.'

'And why haven't you done that yet?'

Natalie stepped in. She wasn't going to allow Dan to goad her officer. Ian had already compiled detailed files on the students who had shared the house with Gemma. He hadn't had time to do the same for those who resided nearby, at 59 Eastview Avenue, or those who were on the same course as the girl. 'This online conversation has only recently come to light. Rhiannon doesn't live in the same house as Gemma, and we've been concentrating on those students who shared accommodation with the victim before casting the net further afield. Now we have reason to suspect Fran and maybe Rhiannon were involved in the attack, we are making the necessary enquiries.'

Dan answered with a curt nod. Riling people seemed to be his way of getting things done, but she didn't need goading. Her team was all over this, and they'd find out who was responsible. He shifted from his relaxed stance into a standing position and, ready to depart, said, 'I'll be informing members of the press that we're looking for an individual or individuals who are most probably known to the victim. If there is any suggestion that that is unlikely to be the case, then I shall require informing immediately.'

'Sir,' said Natalie.

Once Dan had left, Ian discharged a noisy breath. Natalie didn't comment. She was about to assist Ian, who was still finding out information on Rhiannon, when she received a call from an unknown number.

'DI Ward?'

'Yes, who am I speaking to?'

'It's Hattie Caldwell. I need to talk to you about Gemma.'

'Do you have some information for us?'

'I must speak to you alone.'

'Do you want to come to the station?'

'No… no. I'll meet you outside Chancer's Bar in half an hour.'

'It'd be better if you came here to the station. Hello? Hattie? Shit!'

Ian looked across. 'Problem?'

'No. She rang off. Hattie wants to speak to me alone in half an hour at Chancer's Bar. I'll leave you to continue with these checks. We need to gather as much information as we can find.'

'You think she might know who killed Gemma?'

Natalie thought about the breathless urgency in Hattie's voice. She was anxious. 'Yes. I think that's possible.' She hoped Hattie held the key to this and they'd be able to identify and arrest the attacker. It wasn't purely about a quick result. She wanted this for Sasha's sake so she could learn the truth, which in turn would help her find closure.

CHAPTER NINE

Lucy and Murray were in Murton-on-the-Water, a densely populated industrial town some thirty-five miles east of Samford, noted for its brewing industry. They parked on St Peter's Road outside Professor Younger's house, a nondescript semi with a bricked-over front drive on which were parked four cars.

Murray read out the information he'd received about the man. 'James is a fifty-one-year-old linguist specialising in German, Spanish and French. He has a first-class honours degree from Manchester University and a PhD in Applied Linguistics from Reading University. He worked at a university in Berlin from 1985 to 2005 and returned to the UK in 2006, where he took up his position at Samford University. Married to Anika Beck, a German woman who is a part-time lecturer in Health Studies at Murton-on-the-Water College. They've got a twenty-year-old son and a seven-year-old daughter,' said Murray.

Lucy rested her hands on the steering wheel and looked glumly ahead. 'It's doing my fucking head in. All day and not a sniff of anything untoward. If this guy wasn't involved with her, who do we try next?'

'We don't. We head back and see what Natalie says.'

Lucy sighed heavily. 'Okay.'

'Come on, Lucy. This isn't like you. What's up?'

'Nothing. Tired maybe. Aurora kept us up half the night again.'

'She teething?'

'No. It's too soon for teeth. She's grouchy.'

'Takes after you then,' he replied with a grin.

Lucy gave him a semi-sad smile. 'We both know that isn't possible.'

Murray threw her a concerned look but she spotted it and punched him gently on the arm. 'Before you say anything, I'm sound and I love her to bits and I wouldn't change a thing about her or being a parent. It's the best feeling.'

'But…'

She snorted gently then said, 'One day, Aurora will be out in the world on her own, and Bethany and I won't be able to look after her or protect her. It's a scary thought, especially when I see what's happened to Leigh and to Gemma.'

'I get that but you can't dwell on future possibilities. You'll drive yourself mad. Millions of kids go through life without any issues; we get to see the ones who don't, which means your perspective is skew-whiff.'

'I know. I'm being silly. We should have stopped for some lunch. I'm having a sugar dip,' she replied.

'We'll get this over with then stop off on our way back to the station.'

'You're on.' She threw open the door and once more prepared to interview somebody who had known Gemma. Murray was beside her when she pressed the doorbell, which created a soft musical melody that seemed to come from the rear of the property. The door opened and a handsome man with dark hair flecked with silver, who was wearing an apron over a cable-knit jumper and trousers, appeared. He waved a pair of tongs and said, 'Just sorting out a barbecue. Come through.' Catching the expression on Murray's face, he added, 'I know, sounds crazy, doesn't it? A barbecue in November.'

He ushered them through the sitting room into a decent-sized conservatory, where two women sat on wicker chairs, glasses of red wine in their hands. It was snug inside, even with the doors open onto the patio.

James was still talking. 'It's a little inclement to sit outside to eat but it's okay for cooking. The girls insisted on a barbecue.' He pointed to an enclosed trampoline, where a couple of young girls in woollen jumpers and trousers bounced. Meat sizzled enticingly on the round barbecue and the aroma of chargrilled meat wafting through the doors made Lucy's stomach rumble.

He nodded in the direction of the women and said, 'That's my wife, Anika.'

The thinner and taller of the women, with chestnut-brown hair, said hello.

'Anika, the police have come to ask about Gemma.'

'Ah, the poor girl.' She gave a sad shake of her head.

'Did you know her, Mrs Younger?' asked Lucy.

'No. I work in Murton-on-the-Water. I don't know any of James's students although he has spoken about her. She had much potential.'

'What about you?' she asked the other woman, who shook her head.

'That's Anika's friend, Debbie. She knows very little about my work. Now, how may I help?' James said to Lucy.

'Tell us whatever you can about Gemma.'

'To echo my wife, she was a fine student with potential. She took studying very seriously.'

'Is that surprising?'

'You don't often get students as advanced linguistically as she was or as determined to succeed… so, yes… it was a little unusual. Would you mind if I attend to the food? You're welcome to stay inside.'

'Go ahead.'

He moved immediately outside the conservatory and deftly grasped a blackening sausage, removing it from the centre of the grille and placing it closer to the edge where there was less intense heat.

'We understand she stayed behind after lectures.'

'There was only one occasion where I can recall that happening. I'd been lecturing on the changing face of Germany in film and text, and she hung back to ask me some questions about Heinrich Böll's novel *Das Brot der frühen Jahre*.' He flipped a burger with a practised hand.

'What sort of questions did she ask?'

'She was interested in the key concepts covered in the book, such as symbolism, religion and emotions, and keen to read more by the same author. She quizzed me on which novels she ought to read to help her understanding of the writer. I gave her a summary of each of his greatest works.'

'And was this unusual?'

'It was unusual to see such enthusiasm from a student, and refreshing.' He gave a smile that did not reach the corners of his eyes.

'Would you say she was gifted?'

'Enthusiastic and willing to put in the hard work to gain the rewards, rather than gifted in writing essays or doing critiques. Linguistically, however, she was gifted. Her grammatical knowledge was sound and her pronunciation very good indeed – impressively so, given she'd never visited the country.' He pushed the meat about the grille as he spoke.

'She told you she'd never been to Germany?' Murray asked.

'Yes.'

'During a lecture?'

'No, during a seminar. I'm a lecturer but I also host seminars on a variety of subjects. This term I'm offering a seminar on German history and culture. Gemma signed up for it.'

'How many other students are in that group?'

'One – Douglas McCrabe.'

'And how often do you hold these seminars?'

'I really don't see the relevance of your question,' said James, his eyes narrowing.

'We're trying to get a picture of Gemma's movements, who she had lectures with, who she sat with in seminars,' said Murray.

'She didn't really sit with anyone in particular,' said James. 'She invariably chose the front row and sat with whomever was around her.'

'How did she get on with Douglas?'

'Fine. They were matched intellectually and we had some excellent, lively discussions.'

'What can you tell us about Douglas?'

'He's also a very bright student. His mother is German and he's bilingual.' He turned a sausage that hissed and spat fat, causing him to jump back out of harm's way.

'Did Gemma ever talk to you outside of seminars or lectures?' asked Murray.

'Maybe a couple of times when we passed each other on campus.'

'Did you discuss anything other than university subjects?'

'Nothing else at all.'

The children had given up leaping up and down, clambered off the trampoline and were now running around, kicking up dead leaves and shrieking. Debbie caught Lucy's eye and smiled politely.

'She never mentioned her home life, mother, job, other students?'

'I can't see any reason why she would. I'm a lecturer not a university counsellor.'

'You ever go to Chancer's Bar in Samford?'

'Would you mind, one second?' he said, indicating the food.

'Go ahead.'

He slid a flat spatula under a burger, dropped it onto an open bun and repeated the action with a second, then, walking towards the table with them, called, 'Girls!' The squealing stopped instantly and both girls raced inside, eager hands outstretched. One of the children, with hair the same colour as Anika's, reached for the ketchup, but James swooped on the squeezy bottle and squirted a dollop onto the side of the paper plate for her.

'On the burger, Daddy!' she said plaintively.

He lifted the bun and poured the red sauce onto it. The girl took the plate, ran across to the women and dropped onto a large furry rug next to them, followed swiftly by her friend.

'You want anything to eat yet?' James said to Anika.

'We'll wait until you're ready,' said his wife.

'I'm sure the officers are finished with me, aren't you? I can't really tell you a great deal more.' He directed his words at Murray.

'Chancer's Bar, sir?' said Murray. 'Did you visit it?'

'No. Is it in Samford? I don't know where you mean.'

Murray studied his face, which remained impassive. 'Okay, that's everything, thank you,' he replied, then turned and asked Anika the same question.

'Do you know of a bar called Chancer's?'

'Sorry, no. I haven't heard of it.'

'If that's everything, I'd appreciate it if we could eat now,' said James to Lucy.

'Certainly, and thank you for your time, sir,' came the reply.

James led her and Murray back through the house to the front door, where Lucy asked, 'Do you ever see your students privately to discuss their grades?'

'Yes. I arrange meetings in my office at the university.'

'And did you make any such arrangements with Gemma?'

'Only for her last assessment in October.'

'Did she pass the assessment?'

'With an A,' he replied heavily. 'Such a tragic waste of an intelligent young woman with a bright future. Good day, officers.'

With that, he shut the door behind them, and Murray asked Lucy what was bothering her. She seemed lost in thought.

'I was wondering why he evaded the question about the bar. Or am I reading too much into it?'

'I don't know. We'll see if we can dig anything up on him, but to be honest, I didn't pick up on anything odd in his behaviour.'

'Good-looking bloke though, isn't he? I never trust a guy that good-looking, especially when his wife's friend can't take her eyes off him.'

'Debbie was staring at him?'

'The whole time we were talking.'

'She was probably trying to hear what we were saying.'

'There was more to it than that. She wasn't looking at us. She was staring directly at him.'

'Do you think he and Gemma had some sort of a relationship?'

'That's the million-dollar question and I don't have the answer. All I know is I don't trust him.'

*

Chancer's Bar's forecourt was empty when Natalie pulled onto it and parked facing the orange beer van. From there she looked onto the plain rendered building, which still resembled a garage with its flat roof and brick extension that had once been an office. The owners had left as much authenticity as possible and retained the original façade, although the large metal shutter had been replaced by a tinted glass window that reflected back her own vehicle.

She glanced at the display on her dashboard. It was almost quarter to five, twenty-five minutes since Hattie had rung her at the station, but there was no sign of the woman yet. A crow landed with an audible thump in front of her car and bumped and hopped ungainly across the tarmac in search of food. It appeared clumsy but its eyes were keen, and within seconds it took off and landed on a fence that cordoned off the skip and recycling bins, only to re-emerge seconds later with a titbit in its beak. Natalie turned her head left and right but couldn't spot a grey Nissan Micra. Why Hattie wanted to speak to Natalie alone and had chosen this spot, outside the very bar where Gemma had worked, was perplexing. Maybe this location held some relevance and Hattie knew who had attacked Gemma. It might even have been the woman herself or somebody they'd already interviewed.

A movement caught her eye. It was a tall figure in a coat with the hood up. Natalie squinted, but as the person passed the forecourt, it was obvious it wasn't Hattie. Natalie twisted around in her seat but could spot nobody else. The woman was now late. Five more minutes passed and she tried the mobile number Ian had given her for Hattie. It went immediately to answerphone. Five minutes stretched to ten and still nobody appeared. She rang Hattie again and left a message, saying she was waiting, and would Hattie ring her immediately, then she waited until ten past five before she gave up and drove off, annoyed at wasting time.

Back at headquarters she found her entire team gathered in the office and told them of her fruitless mission. 'Could somebody try and pinpoint a location for Hattie's phone?' she asked as she threw down her bag and prepared to tackle any new information. Lucy raised a hand in acknowledgement and set about the task.

'Do you reckon she was messing you about?' asked Murray.

'I don't think so, and I'll admit I'm concerned that she isn't answering her phone. If she has information regarding the attacker, she might be in danger.'

'There could be another reason she isn't responding,' said Murray. Natalie had already guessed what he was going to suggest but let him speak regardless. 'She's responsible for the attack on Gemma. She wanted to confess but got cold feet.'

She agreed with him and then said, 'We have to track her down. Meanwhile, let's talk to Fran Ditton and Rhiannon Williams again.'

'Transcript details and background information on both girls are all here,' Ian said, holding up printouts.

Murray gave a wry grin. 'You're very efficient today, Ian.'

'Every day, mate, every single day,' came the reply.

Lucy had spoken to the phone company and rejoined the conversation. 'Hattie's phone was last used in the vicinity of Eastview Avenue at around the time she rang you, Natalie. There's been no signal transmitted since then. I've asked for details of calls, contacts and messages.'

'What about her car?' asked Natalie. 'If we could get a trace on it, we might be able to locate it.'

Ian nodded. 'I'll put in a request to the traffic division to see if it has been picked up on any local cameras.'

Natalie thought for a second before speaking to both men. 'Would you also contact her father to see if she's shown up there? Find out where else she might be. Lucy and I will head back to Eastview Avenue and speak to Fran and Rhiannon. We'll check to see if she's there.' She glanced at the office clock. Josh would be arriving at her flat in about an hour. She didn't want to be too late getting home. She saw little enough of Josh and they needed this time together; however, her job had to take precedence. She'd message him if she was forced to and hope he'd be understanding.

The pathology report was in her inbox and she read it through quickly before she headed off again to Eastview Avenue. It made for grim reading. The acid had eaten away most of Gemma's face and blinded her in at least one eye. Even if she had survived the attack, she would have had to have undergone some extensive reconstructive surgery and would have been scarred for life. *Better that than dead*, she thought as she stood up once again and prepared to make the journey across town.

CHAPTER TEN

SATURDAY, 17 NOVEMBER – EARLY EVENING

Gemma,

It was stupid to turn your back on me after I'd made such an effort to engage you in conversation. You have no idea how much courage that took for me to sit near you in the students' union bar, especially as you were surrounded by others. To speak to you took even more nerves, and then to have you stare indifferently at me was, to be honest, an insult.

You belittled me.

You wounded me.

It was unnecessary. You could easily have answered me or acknowledged me instead of blanking me. How would you like it if you were snubbed that way?

You ought to be careful who you choose to alienate. Some of us take rejection very badly indeed.

An Ex-Admirer

*

Fran and Rhiannon were in the sitting room at Fran's house, a room only large enough for a threadbare settee, an armchair and a table that bore so many coffee-stain rings that Natalie briefly wondered if they were a deliberate design. Somebody had stuck up a poster of an Indian temple on the wall opposite a television, and the only other nod to furnishings, apart from some mismatched cushions and a faded orange beanbag on the floor, was a green Buddha positioned on a shelf behind a line of empty miniature bottles, the type purchased on board aircraft or in hotel minibars. Neither girl knew where Hattie was although Fran claimed the young woman had left to stay with a friend from school and would be back by Monday.

Fran screwed herself further into the corner of the settee and scowled at Natalie, wiry arms wrapped around herself protectively, her dark eyes flashing. 'You have no right to go through my social media accounts without my permission.'

'We do if they concern a murder investigation,' Natalie replied.

'It's an invasion of my privacy,' Fran continued.

'It's not up for discussion. What is, however, is the conversation you had with Rhiannon on Friday, November the second, two weeks before Gemma had acid thrown in her face.'

Rhiannon shook her head repeatedly and said, 'We had nothing whatsoever to do with that attack. You can't believe we'd do that. It doesn't matter what we said, we'd never do anything as terrible as that, would we?' Her cheeks deepened in colour and her eyes widened earnestly.

The silver studs in Fran's nose and eyebrows, and the two hoops that looked like staples on her bottom lip, glinted as she moved her head and they caught the evening sunlight that streamed into the room. She was wearing ripped jeans and a lemon vest and Natalie's eyes grazed the young woman's upper right arm, where a tattoo of a bird fleeing from captivity had been inked in black onto her flesh. Natalie glanced at the open door of the cage, the black thorny roses and the swallow that flew towards the young woman's collar bone, and she wondered if it was to represent Fran's own desire to escape something. Fran raised her eyes and said, 'I had nothing to do with what happened to Gemma.'

Natalie read from the sheet of dialogue. 'Can you explain, Fran, what you meant when you said, "Yeah, something that would fix

her for good. I know people who'd sort her out once and for all."
That seems quite threatening to me.'

'I didn't mean anything. It was only a dumb online conversation
that people have when they're angry. It wasn't serious at all.'

Rhiannon's face puckered and tears formed. She twisted a
strand of mauve and pink beads around her wrist that matched the
colour of the flowers on her patterned woollen dress and whispered
hoarsely, 'It was nothing serious, you see. We were messing, weren't
we, Fran?'

Natalie ignored the girl's discomfort and continued her questioning, looking directly at Fran. 'Then can you explain what you meant
when you replied to Rhiannon's comment, "What? Get a contract
out on her?" with, "Not exactly. Just rearrange her face a little."?'

Fran inhaled and exhaled noisily. 'I can't explain it. It was some
random shit I said. Sometimes, I say stuff I don't really mean. We
were coming out with fantasy scenarios. Neither of us were serious.
I can go off on one now and then, can't I, Rhiannon?'

Her friend ran a stubby finger under her eyes to remove
smudged mascara and sniffed back more tears before saying, 'Yeah,
Fran gets pissed off at times, but everyone who knows her knows
she doesn't mean it. She wouldn't do anything as wicked as this.
This was Fran blowing off, wasn't it? Gemma had been winding
her up again.'

'How so?'

'She'd been hanging about Ryan, even though she dumped him.'
Fran shot her a dark look. Rhiannon lowered her gaze for a second
then apologised. 'Sorry, Fran, but I don't want the police to think
you did anything wrong.'

Fran didn't respond, merely averted her eyes while Rhiannon
continued explaining to Natalie. 'Fran is keen on Ryan – has been
for quite a while. Gemma split up from him but she didn't want
him to move on, and whenever he and Fran were chatting in the
kitchen or in here, she'd appear and break up the conversation.'

'That true?' Natalie directed her question to Fran, who played with the fringed edges at one of the knee holes in her jeans.

'Yeah. I knew Ryan before she came on the scene. We had a bit of a thing last term and I kind of thought we'd start up something this year, but Gemma arrived and he fell for her bullshit then suddenly she split up with him and I thought we'd pick things back up. For the last month, he and I have been getting on well, and that day, when I let off steam on Facebook, I'd been having a pretty heavy conversation with Ryan when Gemma swooped in and hauled him off to her room. I let rip in that conversation. That's all I did. I meant none of it.'

'She *was* a flirt,' said Rhiannon with a nod to reaffirm what she was saying.

Natalie tried to weigh up the situation. Rhiannon was clearly mortified that they were being questioned about the attack and considered as suspects. Fran less so, although she claimed to be innocent. 'Fran, you ended the online conversation with a response to Rhiannon. Can you recall what you said?'

'No. I haven't looked back at what was said then. It was a spur-of-the-moment thing. It wasn't that big a deal at the time. You're making it out to be more serious than it was.'

'It might not have been serious, yet when Rhiannon said you wouldn't rearrange Gemma's face you replied, "Wouldn't I?"' Fran stared at Natalie.

'What can I say? I didn't hurt Gemma. I wrote some stuff on Facebook that, with hindsight, was stupid. I had no way of knowing that somebody would actually throw acid at Gemma. If I'd known that at the time, I'd never have made those comments. If I'd been responsible for what happened to her, I'd have deleted that conversation because it only makes me look guilty, and I'm not. I wasn't anywhere near the library at the time.'

'But you claim to know people who could have made the attack on your behalf.'

'That was a load of bullshit. I'm not a bad person!'

'Yet you made claims that suggest you would harm Gemma.'

Fran spoke slowly and loudly. 'I… did… not harm Gemma!'

'Then we need to prove that,' said Natalie. 'Rhiannon, where were you Friday evening between seven and eight?'

'At the students' union bar. I hung out with loads of different people. Somebody will be able to say they saw me there.'

'And Fran, what about you?'

The girl glowered but spoke all the same. 'I was there too. I went there after the meeting, before the band went onstage.'

'How long did you stay?'

'We both left after they packed up, around eleven.' Fran looked up at her, face stern. 'I didn't order a hit on Gemma. My mouth runs away with me sometimes.'

Natalie continued with, 'Which band was performing?'

'Hell For Ever. They're a local group.'

Natalie nodded. The girls had alibis for the evening; however, either of them might have slipped away unnoticed or might even have asked or paid somebody to disfigure Gemma. The technical team would have to search for evidence to find out if either girl had made contact with anybody inside or outside the university. 'I'd like you both to hand over your devices so we can check them,' said Natalie.

'You are kidding, aren't you?' said Fran, suddenly pushing herself into an upright position.'

'I'm not,' Natalie replied.

'Why?'

'We need to make sure you're telling the truth and you weren't somehow involved in the attack on Gemma.'

Fran stared indignantly at Natalie, her nostrils flaring and her lips pressed tightly together. She weighed up her options and then muttered to Rhiannon, 'Can you fucking believe this?'

Her friend's wide eyes were damp with tears. 'Mine too?' she asked Natalie.

'Yes, all your devices – laptops, iPads, mobiles. We'll return them as soon as we've examined them.'

'But… it was only a bit of online banter,' said Rhiannon.

Natalie's reply was terse. 'It sounded like more than "banter". You were conjuring up ways to humiliate and harm Gemma only a fortnight before a person actually threw acid in her face. We are taking this matter seriously.'

'This is utter crap, you know?' Fran grumbled, but she got to her feet all the same. 'Rhiannon, just do it. They'll see we have nothing to hide.' She stormed off upstairs.

Rhiannon sniffed again and whined, 'We were only messing about.'

'I'll come with you to collect your stuff,' said Lucy.

Rhiannon stood to join her but gave Natalie one more tearful plea. 'Please. We didn't mean any harm.' Her face puckered and tears spilt.

'Come on,' said Lucy.

Natalie used the time to gather her thoughts. Even if the pair hadn't been involved, they might have planted seeds in the attacker's mind. She'd have to follow up that possibility.

There was creaking from above then light footfalls and Fran reappeared. She only reached Natalie's shoulders, and with her slight, lean frame and shaven head, she could be mistaken for a youth. Natalie suspected her fierce appearance and attitude were mostly for show and detected a shift in the girl, who now stood with her head bowed, arms outstretched. Natalie took the Toshiba laptop covered in stickers from her.

Fran lifted her head and spoke more softly than she had up until this moment. 'I shouldn't have got involved in that bitching session. Neither of us should have said what we did, but that's all it was – a bitching session. I wish it hadn't happened; that none of this had and Gemma was still here. What's happened is horrible – worse than horrible.'

She handed over her mobile too and left the room. Natalie watched her retreating form and tried to work out if what she'd witnessed moments ago was a genuine display of regret. She'd like to believe it was but she'd long ago lost faith in people and their sincerity. She tucked the laptop under her arm. It might yield something that proved the contrary, and until she found out otherwise, Fran and Rhiannon were still suspects.

It was almost seven thirty by the time Natalie decided to wind up the investigation for the day. All the electronic devices had been sent to the laboratory and were undergoing examination, and her team couldn't pursue that angle any further until they had information to act on. They'd circulated Hattie's details around police stations with a request for the woman to be brought in for questioning. They'd also contacted various ex-schoolfriends of hers but drawn blanks as to her whereabouts. No one had seen Hattie. It had been a collective decision to intensify the search for her the following day.

They went their separate ways and Natalie headed back to the flat. Pulling up into her designated space outside the block, she stared up at the second floor where she now lived. It was only a temporary residence until she got half the proceeds from the sale of their family home. Losing the house in Castergate was similar to bereavement, she mused. The place was filled with memories of her children and stretched back to a time before they were born…

The house is waiting for them, the 'sold' board proudly displayed in the small front garden with a neatly mown lawn bordered by nodding daffodils and richly coloured polyanthus plants with crimson red, deep purple and vibrant yellow petals. The windows sparkle sunlight back at her, and to her mind, the place appears happy to see its new owners.

After she unlocks the front door with the key they received only an hour before this magical moment, David says, 'Hold up a second.'

'Why?'

'Because, PC Ward, we must do this properly,' he replies with a wide smile that makes his face even more handsome. She loves this man passionately. He has dragged her into the present from a solitary existence fixed in the past, and shown her that the world is a far happier and more pleasant place than she could ever have imagined.

After her parents died, she was in a limbo, working her way through each day, neglecting her well-being and suspicious of everyone who attempted to break down the mental armour that protected her emotions and heart. David has been her salvation, and the two years she's been with him have been the happiest of her sad life. Soon they'll be a proper family with a new life to look after.

He holds out his hands. His eyebrows perform a merry dance and she laughs at him. 'You're not going to attempt to lift me over the threshold?' she says, rubbing a hand across her swollen stomach. 'I weigh a tonne!'

He chastises her with gentle tutting, slips an arm behind her back and stoops slightly to scoop her up effortlessly. He kicks the door open and carries her into the empty hallway, her laughter echoing around the walls, then he lowers his face towards her, their lips brush gently and settle, and he kisses her deeply.

Natalie has never experienced such utter happiness. The house is only the start of their wonderful future.

Natalie squeezed her eyelids shut. Tears didn't come. An emptiness resided in her chest – a vacuum. Upstairs was all that remained of her precious world. Josh would be in her pathetically small sitting room, watching television and simultaneously texting or gaming on his mobile, waiting for her return. She squared her shoulders. There was still one valuable part of her life left, and nothing would ever take that away from her.

She climbed out into the cool air. Sparrows were settling in bushes in front of the block of flats, their excited chattering loudest as she approached the main entrance and unlocked the door with her code. The door swung open and she entered the airless space, taking the stairs to the right that led to her floor. She didn't know any of the people who lived in this block. She had no desire to learn about them or their lives, and more importantly, she didn't want them to become interested in hers. She valued her privacy. Her flat was close to the stairs and she slipped the key into the slot. There was no David to carry her over this threshold. That David was consigned to the past.

'Hey!' Josh called out as soon as she entered.

She chucked her keys into the pot on the table and went immediately into the sitting room, where she found him stretched out on the settee, television control in his hand. He sat up straight away.

'I brought a takeaway,' she said, holding up the paper bag of Chinese food she'd bought on the way home. 'Is Chinese food okay?'

'Great. You get any spring rolls?'

'And crispy aromatic duck.'

His face lit up and for a split second she was reminded of David. Josh had his father's smile and jawline and his dark hair. 'I already set the table,' he replied.

'Wow, you must have been hungry,' she joked and headed to the kitchen where knives and forks had been laid out on maroon placemats, along with glasses. 'You want anything to drink?'

'I'm okay, thanks, I took a can from the fridge.'

She busied herself putting out the foil trays. Josh slipped onto a chair and took the nearest one, teasing the foil away from the cardboard lid, releasing the aroma of five spices into the room. Natalie hunted for the soy sauce in the cupboard and then set out the pancakes and spring onion on a separate plate. As she did so, she asked casually, 'Everything okay?'

He paused, fork in mid-air. 'To be honest, no. I don't want to live with Dad any more. I want to live with you.'

This sudden revelation surprised her but she continued laying out the food, setting out the pot of hoisin sauce that came with the duck before joining him at the table and saying, 'You want to talk about it?'

Josh picked up a spring roll with his fingers and slid it around a tiny pool of soy sauce. 'It's Dad. He's hard to get along with.'

'This is quite sudden. Has something happened to make you decide you want to move out of the house?'

He sighed and put down his fork. His face was suddenly earnest, brows drawn together. 'He drinks, Mum. Every day. And you can't get through to him sometimes. He's either asleep, angry or miserable. He's changed a lot and we argue all the time. I can't seem to do anything right.'

'He's still hurting, Josh. It's natural to lash out at the people you love but it wouldn't be intentional. You mean everything to him… to us both.'

Josh shook his head sadly. 'You're hurting too, but you don't sit about the house in a foul mood all the time, or go out and come back in the early hours obviously drunk. You text me or ring me, or ask how I'm doing. Dad… well… it's like he wants nothing to do with me. I told him I was coming here and all he said was, "Fine." Nothing else.'

'No. That's not right. You are hugely important to him,' she said. She had no idea that David had become so difficult. *How could you know? You turned your back on them and ran away to lick your wounds.*

He shook his head. 'You don't know the half of it, Mum. He's like a completely different person – really angry at times. Now and then, I hear him yelling out and smashing about the kitchen. I went downstairs a couple of nights ago to see who he was shouting at but there was nobody there, only him, and he'd obviously broken a couple of plates. There were pieces on the floor and he was marching up and down, muttering to himself. He didn't see me and I went back upstairs. I think he's having some sort of breakdown. I can't be around him at the moment.'

She wanted to hug the boy fiercely and tell him it would be all right, that she would always be there for him, but he had only recently come back into her life. He wasn't ready for such a huge display of affection. She had to prove how much he meant to her, not merely say words that would rebound off his newly toughened exterior. Josh had been through hell the last few months, as indeed they all had. She marvelled at his strength that had seen him through.

'He's having a hard time adjusting. It's been a lot for him to take on board,' she said. The look on Josh's face said he was not convinced.

'I understand that but I can't put up with it. I can't go back to all that misery, night after night. It's starting to affect my studies. Is it okay if I move in here? It'll only be until I finish my A-levels and go to university.'

'You can stay as long as you like. You know that. You're always welcome to stay here or wherever I move to. It'll be your home too. Forever.' The relief was tangible and Josh's brow smoothed at the response. It had taken a lot for him to open up about this and she had renewed respect for her son.

'Cheers.' He picked up his spring roll, dipped it in some sauce and bit it.

'I'll have to explain how you feel to your father,' she said casually.

'I'm not going back to the house. It's not just Dad. I can't stand going past Leigh's room with her no longer there. We keep the door shut but it feels... wrong.'

She picked at some duck, her appetite suddenly waning. 'I understand. I'd feel the same way.'

'But you didn't stay, did you?' His words weren't accusatory, merely factual.

'You know why I couldn't stay.'

'Yes.' He separated a pancake from the others in tinfoil as he spoke. 'Will you never get back together?'

She finished her mouthful before addressing him. 'No, and it is not because of you or because of what happened to Leigh. It was over before all of that.'

Josh didn't reply. He added shredded duck to his pancake, drizzled sticky sauce onto it and rolled it up. He gave a swift nod before eating it. Some things didn't need to be said. Josh knew about David's gambling and that it was the catalyst for her leaving. What he didn't know – and she wasn't going to tell him yet – was that Mike was more than a family friend. That was unless David had said something. She studied his long eyelashes and again thought how much he reminded her of her estranged husband. She hoped he wasn't as weak-willed as his father.

'He said he taught the students together and never mentioned that Douglas had given up. Now why would he do that?'

'My immediate reaction is to say he kept silent to hide the fact that something had been going on between him and Gemma,' said Natalie.

'That's what we think. His wife and her friend were within earshot when we interviewed him so it'd be unlikely he'd confess to a liaison with a student in front of her. Lucy noticed something odd too: Anika's friend, Debbie, was staring at James the whole time we were speaking to him.'

'Like she had a crush on him,' said Lucy, 'or was worried he'd say something he shouldn't. It was an intense look, not casual.'

'Maybe they're screwing,' said Ian.

'That was my first thought,' Lucy replied.

Natalie was quick to decide on what course of action to pursue. 'Bring him into the station for further questioning. Let's see if him being separated from his wife during an interview yields more honest answers, and find out where he and Anika were on Friday evening. If Anika suspected him of sleeping with Gemma, she might have retaliated and attacked the girl. In fact, find out where that friend was too. If she is involved with him and the jealous type, she might not take kindly to him carrying on with a student behind her back. Any news on Hattie?'

Ian shook his head. 'She's still not answering her phone and there's nothing back yet from the phone providers. I spoke to her father, who hasn't seen her since last weekend but he's unconcerned and says she often goes visiting friends, especially over weekends when she has no lectures or little work to do.'

'Surely he's concerned about her not answering calls.'

'According to him, she often doesn't pick up when he rings her. He says she's a bit scatty and sometimes forgets to charge it or she leaves it behind altogether.'

Natalie found that hard to believe. Josh always had his phone to hand and a charger in his backpack. 'Really? I can't imagine

CHAPTER ELEVEN

SUNDAY, 18 NOVEMBER – MORNING

Josh had left for an early-morning shift. He'd planned to meet his girlfriend Pippa in Derby and was expected back at the flat that evening. They'd spoken about living arrangements and what she expected of him while he was staying with her, and he'd seemed more than happy to accept it all. She would have to try and find time to talk to David and she had no idea when she'd manage that.

The team was already assembled when she arrived in the office, and she interrupted a lively debate about one of Gemma's tutors – Professor James Younger.

'What's going on?' she asked.

Murray answered, 'As you know, Lucy and I spoke to James yesterday and he claimed Gemma and a lad called Douglas McCrabe attended one of his seminars. Ian's found out that Douglas transferred from Professor Younger's German history and culture seminar to one about culture and film about a month ago.'

'That means he'd have taught Gemma alone in that time,' said Natalie.

'Exactly, and he denied it.'

'He denied teaching Gemma alone?' Natalie reiterated.

she'd want to be without her phone. What about her mother? Have you tried her?'

'She passed away when Hattie was eleven. There's nobody but her father. I was going to try her housemates again to see if she's returned home.'

'Do that now. It's bothering me that she's gone to ground so soon after contacting me. We might have to get MisPers involved pretty soon. Try the house on Eastview Avenue in case she's returned. We confiscated Fran's and Lennox's phones. Try ringing Ryan's mobile unless there's a landline you can call.'

'No landline. I'll try him. There's been no sign of Hattie's car either,' Ian said.

'Nothing on any ANPR systems?'

'No,' he replied.

'What about cameras close to where she lives?'

'The technicians are still searching footage.'

Natalie's nostrils flared as she inhaled deeply. This didn't sit right with her. If Hattie had rung her to confess to the attack on Gemma, she would surely have handed herself in at the station. She was more certain than ever that Hattie knew who'd thrown acid at Gemma and had either gone into hiding or been taken hostage, or worse. 'We need that info. Get them to speed it up, Ian.'

He nodded, phone to his ear.

'Maybe she's keeping her head down,' said Lucy with little conviction.

'I hope that's the case but I rather think something has happened to her. All this bollocks about not charging phones or forgetting them... She rang me, arranged a meeting then disappeared. I'm concerned about her,' came Natalie's reply.

Murray spoke. 'We'll head off to fetch the professor and talk to his wife.'

Natalie added, 'If Anika has no solid alibi for Friday evening, bring her in as well.'

Lucy hesitated before saying, 'They've got a seven-year-old daughter. Might be awkward to arrange.'

'Do it. Find somebody from social services to look after the daughter if needs be.' Natalie wasn't in the mood to hang about on this. If she trod on toes, then so be it.

Lucy hastened after Murray.

Ian ended his phone call and gave Natalie the latest news. 'Ryan has knocked on Hattie's door and she's not in.'

'Not in or not answering? Get hold of the university and get somebody – a caretaker or housing officer – to unlock that door and check she isn't in there. Someone will have a master key.'

She bent over the desk, hunting through the notes to see what details they actually had on Hattie. All of a sudden, this young woman had become pivotal to their enquiries. She extracted the relevant sheet from Ian's file. Apart from Hattie's father, the only other person in her life was an ex-husband. Hattie had married somebody called Ocean Stone at eighteen, splitting up from him two years later. Further searches revealed the man to be a founder of an alternative eco-commune in Wales, one which chose to ignore modern-day trappings such as mobile phones and the Internet. There was a possibility Hattie had fled there.

Natalie put in a call to the Monmouthshire Police to see if Hattie had been in touch with her ex or was hiding out there. While she was speaking to them, Ian arranged for the university housing officer to head to Eastview Avenue. After she explained the situation to her colleague in Wales, who agreed to head to the commune to ask about Hattie, she set off, first collecting Lennox's mobile to return it to him.

Dan, waiting close to the front entrance, cut a dashing figure in his uniform: immaculate white shirt, trousers crisply creased and shoes so highly polished, they'd impress a regimental sergeant. His face was waxy smooth and not one follicle of his trimmed hair was out of place. He moved her out of earshot of the desk staff, and as he leant in to speak to her, she caught a whiff of expensive cologne. 'Anything to report, Natalie?'

'We're hunting for a missing housemate who might have valuable information about the attack on Gemma,' she said.

His eyebrows lifted. 'Sounds like you're closing in.'

'I wouldn't be overhasty, sir. I'm not sure why she contacted me and I don't know where she is.'

'Let's hope nothing's happened to her. The media were quite searching with their questions yesterday and I had trouble convincing them this was a one-off event. I want you to find her quickly.' He spotted his guest coming into the lobby and moved away to greet them, and Natalie left the building. She'd refrained from making any comment about the press conference. It didn't matter what she thought about her superior's handling of sensitive situations. He had his reasons for dealing with them the way he did while she had her own investigation to run, and right now, she had a niggling doubt about Hattie.

*

Professor Younger's house, like many others on St Peter's Road, showed no signs of life. Curtains remained pulled to and a pint of milk, a bottle of orange juice and a loaf of bread stood in an open plastic box on the front step. Murray glanced down at the provisions. 'I didn't know anyone made milk and juice deliveries these days.'

Lucy shook her head. 'None where we live. It's a quick milk trip to the supermarket if we run out.'

Murray attempted to rouse the family and they waited a while for someone to answer the door. It was opened at last by Anika, in her nightclothes, her hair uncombed.

'We'd like to ask you and your husband some further questions, please,' Murray told her.

Anika gave them both a searching look before granting them entry, and this time they found themselves not in the conservatory but in a kitchen out of a 1960s home catalogue, with antique cherry wood cabinets, yellow Formica tops over wooden base units, a free-standing larder and a retro fridge-freezer in bright yellow; it recaptured the days when bold colours were de rigueur. The effect was brought into line with a rug on the floor incorporating the same garish yellow but with the addition of clashing lime green, turquoise and pink – shades of which were also picked up in the trays, cooking utensils and pots that adorned the surfaces. Anika squatted onto one of the four chrome-legged chairs with white and turquoise padded seats next to a white table with matching legs, but didn't invite either officer to sit down.

'We'd like to talk to your husband too,' said Murray.

'He was asleep when I got up. Ask me what you need to first and then I'll wake him.'

'We'd like to know your whereabouts on Friday evening.'

'Do you have a specific time in mind?'

'Between seven and seven thirty.'

'I was at work.'

'Can anyone confirm that for you?'

She gave him a cool look and replied, 'About eighty students. I was lecturing at the time.'

'In Murton-on-the-Water?'

'Yes, officer. In Murton-on-the-Water, at the college where I work.'

'Do you often teach in the evening?'

'Only on Fridays during term time. I hold two lectures on a Friday evening.'

'What time did you leave?'

'The usual – immediately after my second lecture finished around eight. I came straight home. The babysitter can confirm that.'

'Your husband wasn't at home at the time?'

'He wasn't.'

'Have you any idea where he was?'

'Work, I assume.'

'But you don't know for sure.'

She stared at him unblinking, like a lioness studying its prey, before saying, 'No. I don't know for certain. Shall I tell him you wish to speak to him now?'

'If you wouldn't mind.'

She left the room and Lucy whispered, 'She's a cool character. Bit standoffish. Not much emotion at all.'

'She has a fairly cast-iron alibi for her whereabouts though.'

'She does. Maybe she made sure she had. You can't convict a person who has that number of witnesses. She could still be involved and hired somebody to do the dirty work.'

Lucy glanced about the room and puzzled over why it felt staged then it struck her: nothing was out of place and there was nothing to suggest a family lived here – no photos, no personalised mugs, no drawings, no children's clutter. She didn't get the chance to point it out to Murray because James appeared.

'Morning, sir. Apologies for the early visit but we have to follow up from yesterday.'

Anika's long, thin face came back into view behind her husband, and she took up her position again on the chair she'd vacated minutes earlier.

James scratched the back of his neck and responded with a weary, 'Go ahead.'

'No, sorry. We need you to come down to the station this time.'

Anika's voice was sharp. 'Can't he answer any questions you have here?'

'Yes, I have nothing to hide from my wife,' said James.

'It's concerning your whereabouts on Friday evening. Can you tell us your movements?'

'I attended a departmental meeting at five. That went on for over an hour, after which time I joined my colleagues and the chancellor for drinks and nibbles in the old hall. I was there until about seven thirty and then I returned to my office to finish marking some papers. I got home sometime between half past ten and eleven.' He looked keenly at Anika but she ignored him.

'Mrs Younger, can you confirm that?' asked Lucy.

Anika shook her head. 'I was asleep. I don't know what time he came in.'

'Surely, you must have heard me come to bed,' James said, his look imploring her to speak up on his behalf.

'I'd taken a sleeping pill,' she replied.

'Those bloody pills! I thought you'd stopped taking them.'

'I needed them.'

He raised his palms then let his hands drop with a slap against his thighs. 'What's the point? You never listen.' He turned his attention back to Murray and said smoothly, 'I'm sure my colleagues can vouch for me being at the meeting and the event. After that, there's nobody who can substantiate my claims, so you'll have to take my word.'

'I see. We shall have to confirm you were at the meeting and drinks as you claim but we'd also like to talk to you about Gemma again. Some new information has come to light.'

'What new information?' Anika looked sharply at her husband but he ignored her.

'That's what we'd like to discuss with your husband… preferably at the station. If you wouldn't mind getting dressed, sir, we'll continue this conversation in Samford.'

James complied, leaving his wife alone with Lucy and Murray.

'Do you have to take him away?' asked Anika.

'We need to substantiate his alibi for Friday evening and question him further, Mrs Younger. Once he's helped us with our enquiries, he'll be free to go.'

Anika's face gave nothing away but Lucy noticed her hands were trembling. Her stony-faced exterior was a mask to hide her true emotions.

'Is there anything you wish to tell us before we leave?' Lucy asked.

Anika opened her mouth and shut it before shaking her head again.

'Is he often out late?' Lucy asked.

'His job keeps him out late some nights.' Anika stood up and walked towards the corner of the room, where she turned on the kettle and kept her face hidden from them.

James was back quickly, in jeans and a blue top. His face was unshaven and his hair unruly. He ran a hand through it to tidy it, walked towards his wife and pecked her on the cheek. 'I won't be long.'

She didn't reply and Lucy noticed she stiffened as he placed a hand on her shoulder and said in a low voice, 'I've not done anything wrong.'

*

Hattie's room was empty and there was nothing in it to hint at where she might have disappeared to. She'd taken her mobile and laptop with her, as well as her toothbrush and toothpaste, suggesting she'd intended staying somewhere other than her room for at least a night. With the door locked once more and the university accommodation officer departed, Natalie spoke again to Fran, Lennox and Ryan, who were gathered in the sitting room.

'She said nothing to me about going away,' said Lennox. He rubbed fingers over the screen of his mobile that had been returned to him as if it were a long-lost toy.

Ryan, sprawled on the settee, shook his head. 'Nor me.'

Fran was sat cross-legged on the settee, a scowl on her face. 'She definitely mentioned a schoolfriend to me when I saw her in the kitchen late Saturday morning. She told me she'd been out to the shops for a mooch about and was at a loose end. She was still cut up about what had happened to Gemma and was thinking of spending a couple of nights at a friend's house rather than stay here. I assumed she'd decided to go because I didn't see her after that.'

'Did she mention this person by name?'

'No.' Fran looked hollow-eyed and, without her make-up, pale-faced and much younger than her actual age. For a brief moment Natalie didn't see Fran. It was Leigh sat on the settee, watching a soap opera. Her heart lurched and dropped in her chest and she had to bite back the stinging tears that wanted to fall. She pretended to have something in her eye and rubbed away the damp. *Deep breath.*

She cleared her throat and asked, 'Did she mention a place, a town name?'

'Sorry, she didn't and I didn't ask her. She often disappears for a night or two. She knows lots of people – alternative, like her. She's got a friend in Cornwall who she spent nearly all of the summer with. It might be her she visited.' She shrugged an apology.

'When did you last see Hattie?' She let her stare bounce over Lennox and Ryan.

Lennox was the first to respond. 'Not since Friday night.'

'What about you, Ryan?'

'Last spoke to her Friday morning when we talked about the takeaway. I didn't see her at all yesterday – not before I went to the gym or afterwards, and I was in all afternoon.'

'Did you come back here after your workout?'

'Uh-huh. I spent most of the afternoon working. I dozed off for a couple of hours after that. I went out at about nine.'

'Why are you trying to find her?' asked Fran.

'We need to talk to her, that's all.'

Ryan cocked his head to one side and lifted a finger in a knowing fashion, waving it at Natalie. 'No, it's more than that. You think Hattie had something to do with the acid attack on Gemma, don't you?'

Natalie didn't wish to engage in speculative talk with the young man with the intense glare and expressionless face. 'If you see or hear from Hattie, let me know immediately. In the meantime, I'd like you all to remain in Samford and not leave the area without letting us know.'

Ryan sat back against the cushions. 'You know, Hattie didn't like Gemma as much as she made out she did.'

'Ryan, shut up!' Fran was indignant but Lennox spoke up too. 'No. He's right. She didn't like Sasha much either and she bitched about Gemma behind her back.'

'Fran, did Hattie complain about Gemma?' asked Natalie.

'Maybe she had a few moments when she whinged about Gemma but it wasn't any more serious than my Facebook conversation with Rhiannon was.' She glared at Natalie, who didn't waver.

'Did Gemma ever mention Professor Younger to you?' asked Natalie.

'Sure. He's the hottest lecturer on campus. His name cropped up regularly. We've all had a crush on him at one time or another. Gemma did too,' said Fran.

'Did you overhear any of these conversations, Ryan?' Natalie asked, watching the boy shift on his cushion. He didn't reply immediately. A muscle in his jaw flexed several times before he spoke.

'No. I didn't hear any of that, but I think she and the prof actually had something going on.'

'An affair?'

'Maybe.'

Fran shook her head and gave a derisory snort. 'Idiot! She wasn't having an affair with him.'

Ryan's voice became icy. 'I say she was.'

'What makes you think she was?' Natalie asked Ryan.

Fran folded her arms and shook her head in dismay. 'Ignore him. Ryan's got Gemma issues. He got green-eyed every time he saw Gemma with another bloke. He's making this up. Professor Younger wouldn't screw a student... any student.'

Ryan didn't respond. Natalie forced him into giving an answer. 'Is that right, Ryan? You are only saying this because you were jealous of her lecturer? I haven't got time to be jerked about. Tell me the truth.'

'I *know* they were seeing each other.'

'You fuckwit! They weren't. Prof Younger is straight up,' said Fran.

'He definitely screws students he fancies,' muttered Lennox. 'That sort of thing goes on all the time. There are certain lecturers who'll change students' grades for *favours*.'

Fran opened her mouth to reply but Natalie was sick of the bickering. Her heart was heavy after the unexpected reminder of Leigh and her patience with the trio in front of her had waned. 'Pack it in! Do I need to remind you what this is about? One of your friends, your housemate, is dead. We're looking into a murder and we need to establish what happened to her. So, can you all cut out the crap and the childish asides, and act in a more adult manner! Now, have any of you got anything to say that might help us track down the person who assaulted her?'

Fran flushed deeply and lowered her head. Lennox stared intently at his blank mobile screen. The South African steepled his fingertips, pressed them momentarily to his lips and then spoke. 'A couple of weekends ago, I saw Professor Younger and Gemma together outside Chancer's. They were standing close to the fenced-off area in the car park. He was holding both her hands in his and talking to her quietly, and at one point he reached out and stroked her cheek.'

'Did they kiss?'

'Not that I saw but they seemed very intimate.'

'And this was a fortnight ago?'

'Yes. Saturday night.'

'Did you challenge either of them about it?'

'I spoke to Gemma, who said I was mistaken and they were only talking about university work. She'd been upset about a bad grade he'd given her. He'd been comforting her. Sounded total bullshit to me.' Ryan's admission not only put James and maybe even James's wife, Anika, in the frame, but also served to point the finger of blame further at himself. A bitter ex-lover might be capable of such a heinous act.

'Why didn't you tell me all this when I first asked you about Gemma being involved with anyone else?'

'You already thought I was obsessed with her. If I'd told you that at the time, you'd have been even more convinced I was the one who attacked her. I can see how it might go down – you thinking I was so angry and resentful about her relationship with the professor that I tried to hurt her.'

'Did you?'

'No, I didn't. She convinced me I was being pig-headed and getting worked up over nothing. I let it go. Now, I only want whoever killed her to be found.'

Ryan's reasoning was logical and his sincerity apparently genuine; however, he'd remain firmly on her radar even though it struck her as strange that the professor would discuss the subject of a poor grade outside a bar rather than during a seminar or in his office. Moreover, according to Lucy and Murray, James had told them he'd never visited the bar. Fran and Lennox had fallen silent, their gazes averted.

'Is there anything else any of you want to tell me? Because now is a good time.'

No one had anything new to add and she left the housemates under the impression that in spite of what good had been said about the dead girl, Gemma had still managed to raise hackles and fan flames of envy. No sooner had she left the house than she received a call from Monmouthshire Police, who'd had no luck at the commune in Wales. Hattie hadn't been back there. Was the young woman staying with a friend as Fran had suggested, or had something happened to her? Natalie wasn't wasting any more time. She'd get one of the team to talk to Hattie's ex-husband, Ocean

Stone, and see if he could think of anyone Hattie might be staying with. If they had no joy, they'd alert Missing Persons. She hoped they'd be able to locate her before it was too late. She couldn't bear it if the woman was harmed or killed because of Natalie's tardiness in working out her whereabouts. She already carried enough guilt without adding to it. The image of Leigh and Zoe flashed before her eyes, arms outstretched, holding hands in death, as they had in life. She couldn't fail again.

CHAPTER TWELVE

SUNDAY, 18 NOVEMBER – MID-MORNING

Professor James Younger adopted a practised pose, hands relaxed in his lap and one leg thrown casually over the other; the controlled image was betrayed by the mismatched socks on display in the gap between his trendy jeans and the top of his sturdy walking boots.

Natalie took a moment to study the man before speaking. Judging by the way he held his chin up and looked her in the eye, he certainly didn't lack confidence. 'I'd like to talk to you about your relationship with Gemma Barnes.' She passed across a copy of the note from the secret admirer. 'Do you recognise this?'

His brow lowered as he read through it, then he pushed it back with a shake of his head. 'I've not seen this before and I certainly didn't send it to her, if that is what you want to know, nor do I know anything about it.'

'You deny writing such a letter?'

'Absolutely. Before we go any further, I have a confession to make,' he said smoothly. 'I might have misled your officers yesterday when I failed to mention the fact that Douglas McCrabe transferred from my seminar last month. I was somewhat distracted and obviously upset about what had happened to Gemma, so when DS Anderson asked me about Douglas, I neglected to add that he'd changed seminars.' He nodded in Murray's direction and added, 'I apologise for that.'

Natalie wasn't impressed by this admission. 'You failed to disclose relevant information.'

'And I apologise for that omission. It wasn't deliberate.'

'I see. And had we not spoken to you today, would you have contacted us and told us this?' asked Natalie.

'Most certainly.' He gave a slight nod and a half-smile to indicate his sincerity.

'Since you're less distracted, maybe now you could tell us about your relationship with Gemma.'

The smile was replaced by a downturned mouth and a heavy sigh. 'Poor Gemma. She was, as I told your officers yesterday, a very bright young woman and had a gift for languages. She was keen to learn and that enthusiasm extended beyond the confines of the syllabus. On the occasions we spoke, it was invariably an animated discussion about German literature, culture or history. It is refreshing when one meets a student who is intellectually capable of conversing with their tutor.'

His pomposity and gushing monologue served to further annoy Natalie. 'I've no doubt she was a clever young woman but you are sidestepping the real question here. Were you and Gemma having sex?'

Her direct question caught him off guard and he shifted position before saying very quietly and slowly, 'No… we did *not* have sex.'

'Was there any physical relationship between you?'

'There was none.' He drove home his point by locking eyes with Natalie and repeating, 'None. Nothing happened between us. Our relationship didn't extend beyond the boundaries of tutor and student. I value my position at the university, my career and my reputation. I would never compromise any of those by having a fling or relationship with any student.'

Natalie noted he didn't say he valued his marriage or family. 'Then can you explain why you were spotted outside Chancer's Bar on Saturday, November the third, holding hands with Gemma?'

He shifted again in his seat and this time adopted a less relaxed pose, both feet now on the floor. He squeezed his nostrils between his forefinger and thumb then nodded as if only just recalling the occasion. 'Ah, yes. I remember now. I'd stopped off at the bar for a drink after work – I'd been preparing lectures, and Gemma was serving. She was upset about a grade I'd given her for an essay and asked if she could talk to me about it outside. I naturally agreed and when we were outside she began crying. She'd never had anything less than an A grade before and she couldn't understand why she'd only got a C. I explained that some of her arguments in the essay were flawed and that getting a C grade wouldn't influence her final grade for the year because she produced consistently high-standard work; that it was merely a blip.'

'You could have told her all that when you returned the essay to her.'

'Initially, she wasn't upset and accepted the grade and left my office with no comment to make. She reflected on it during the day, and by the time she saw me, she felt she should ask me why I had marked her down. It was no more than that.'

'And you felt you should hold her hands while you told her this?' Natalie said.

'She was upset. It was only a friendly gesture.'

'But one that could be misconstrued if observed and one that could damage your reputation if it got out you'd been spotted.'

'I was being understanding and sympathetic.'

'Do you often hold your students' hands when you give them bad grades?' asked Murray.

James bristled at the remark. 'I don't think that's a relevant question.'

'Go ahead. Answer it,' said Natalie.

'No, DS Anderson, I do not. Gemma was emotional and I had a soft spot for her – not in a sexual way, more in a paternal capacity. She wanted to excel, and when she didn't, she was very hard on herself. I demonstrated human kindness which extended to holding her hands briefly to make my point – that she had nothing to worry about.'

Murray continued to goad the man. 'You held her hands in an act of kindness?'

'Yes.'

'And stroked her cheek in the same act of kindness? Funny that. I don't normally stroke people's cheeks when I'm being nice to them.'

'It was a paternal gesture.'

'You see yourself in a fatherly role?' Murray said, resting his elbows on the table. Natalie sat back. Murray was good at intimidating suspects, which often resulted in them confessing to misdemeanours. A bead of sweat appeared on James's upper lip.

'I am an *educator* and, in that capacity, I build relationships with my students. I help them attain their educational goals and, like any parent, I am proud of their achievements. You could say there are similarities between what I do and the role of a parent.'

Murray clicked his tongue. 'Can you cut out all the high-brow, intellectual lingo and tell me why you stroked Gemma's cheek?'

'I was comforting her.'

'Comforting her?' Murray repeated, leaning closer.

'That's all.' James wiped a finger over his lips. 'Honestly.'

Murray said nothing for a moment then pushed himself back into an upright position, a sign for Natalie to continue.

'We've spoken to a few of your colleagues who were at the departmental meeting you attended on Friday evening. I understand you went to the old hall for drinks afterwards?'

'That's right. I'm sure they saw me there. I was speaking to the chancellor for a while and to quite a few people.'

'Funny you should say that because none of them remember seeing you after six thirty.'

'They probably lost sight of me. We were mingling in the dining hall close to the buffet and in the reception room. I must have been in a different room to them.'

Natalie let a pause hang before saying, 'That is possible; however, one of your colleagues said you excused yourself to take a phone call and disappeared shortly afterwards. He was going to the toilets and saw you leave by the side entrance at six fifteen.'

James's shoulders sagged.

'Where did you go?'

He rubbed at his lips again and then heaved a sigh before saying, 'To visit my lover.'

'Who, James?'

'This won't get back to Anika, will it? It's over. We've called it a day. I have my family to think of.'

'How very noble. Who is she?'

'Debbie Randle. She was at our house yesterday when you came by,' he said to Murray.

'Your wife's best friend?' Murray replied coolly.

'That's right.'

'And she'll be able to confirm this, will she?' Natalie asked.

'I don't want her involved in this. Her husband doesn't know about us and doesn't need to.'

'But we need to verify your whereabouts.'

'Can you ask her when her husband isn't about?'

'We'd like her contact details, please.'

'Only if you promise to be discreet.'

'This isn't a marketplace where you can haggle. We have to speak to her to confirm your whereabouts. Now we can do that immediately or we can leave it and let you stay in one of our cells until we manage to talk to her. What would you rather we do?'

He was beaten. He shut his eyes for a few seconds, long enough to consider his options, then opened them and said, 'I'll give you her details.'

'Before you do that, I'd like to return to the subject of Chancer's Bar. Why did you previously deny ever going to – or even knowing about – Chancer's Bar?'

'Because I didn't want my relationship with Debbie to become public knowledge. I didn't wish to draw attention to the fact I was there to meet her. If I'd admitted it, you would have questioned me further about my motives for being there, especially in light of the fact Gemma worked there. I ought to have come clean. It was… foolish of me. I see now it would have been better had I admitted it sooner.'

Natalie's eyes narrowed at the flimsy excuse. 'How often did you go there?'

'Only the once.'

'And that was on Saturday, November the third?'

'Yes.'

'I'm having difficulty working out why you chose to go there. You see, it wasn't on your way home. In fact, you'd have gone out of your way to get to it. Was it to see Gemma?'

His voice suddenly sounded tired. 'No. It was Debbie's idea to meet at the bar. I didn't even know Gemma worked there. By the time I spotted the girl, it was too late to walk away. She'd already clocked me and was waiting to serve me. I bought a small whisky and texted Debbie to tell her I'd meet her somewhere else. I quickly drank up and made to leave but Gemma was upset. That part was all true. She was due a break and asked if she could have a quick word with me outside, where she challenged me about the grade I'd given her. I told her what I've already told you, and I didn't hang about afterwards. I drove to the Grey Goose instead to meet Debbie. She'll back me up on that.'

'Would you mind waiting here while we look into this?'

His response was a weary, 'Fine, whatever, but please don't do this in front of her husband. I don't want to ruin her marriage.'

'And what about your marriage?'

'It's too late to save that,' he replied.

CHAPTER THIRTEEN

SUNDAY, 18 NOVEMBER – LATE MORNING

Debbie Randle's voice fell to slightly above a whisper when she discovered who was ringing her and was asked if she could confirm James's whereabouts for Friday. 'Wait a minute,' she said and the phone fell silent. Natalie hung on patiently for the woman to come back on the line. She imagined Debbie's husband had been present when she'd answered the phone and had not wanted him to overhear.

'Sorry, it was difficult to speak to you. I've come outside now,' Debbie said.

'We're trying to establish James Younger's movements on Friday evening, and he has claimed he met up with you.'

'That's right. We met outside the Bell Inn but we didn't go in. I got into his car and we drove to Samford Chase, where we walked for a while and then sat and talked. He wanted to end our relationship. Anika's become suspicious and he was concerned she'd find out what was going on and leave him. I was willing to give up my marriage for him but it turned out he wasn't prepared to ditch his family for me.'

'What time did you and he part company?'

'I'd say around quarter past ten.'

'James ended the relationship yet you still went to his house yesterday,' said Natalie.

'Anika invited me for lunch before Friday happened. I wasn't going to go but James said it would look suspicious if I suddenly pulled out, and that Anika would guess who he'd been seeing. My daughter is good friends with theirs and she'd been looking forward to going. It was hard for me but it is what it is,' she said. Sorrow had crept into her voice.

'I also need to ask you about a Saturday evening two weeks ago, on November the third, when you arranged to meet James in Chancer's Bar in Samford. Whose idea was it to meet at that bar?'

'Mine.'

'Can you tell me what happened?'

'He arrived ahead of me because I was running late. I was about five minutes away when he messaged me to say we needed to change the venue. One of his students was serving behind the bar and he didn't want her to see us together. We agreed to meet at the Grey Goose and I drove there. He arrived a quarter of an hour later. Apparently, the girl challenged him about a grade he'd given her that day and he'd had to have a few words with her before he could actually leave.'

'Did he mention the student by name?'

'No. He said she was a second-year student who had to learn that sometimes her work didn't deserve the A grade she believed it did.'

'Did he often talk about his students?'

'Not when he was with me.'

'Would you say he likes his job?'

'No, I'd say he loves his job, probably more than he loved me or his wife. It's everything to him.'

'How long have you and James been involved in a relationship?'

'Since March.' The sigh that followed was audible and lengthy.

'Did he ever mention Gemma Barnes to you?'

'In passing. She was one of his bright hopes.'

'He didn't tell you she was the student working at Chancer's Bar?'

'No, he didn't tell me that.'

'Okay. Then, that'll be all. Thank you for your time, Debbie.'

'I know why you're asking me these questions about James, but he wasn't involved in that attack on Gemma. James wouldn't have harmed her and certainly not by throwing acid at her. James hurts people differently. He breaks their hearts.'

With no grounds to detain James, Natalie and Murray returned to the interview room to tell him he was free to go. He had the grace to look shamefaced, and before he stood to leave he said, 'I'm not a bad person. I didn't mean for any of this to happen and I'm trying to rectify the situation and do right by my wife. Don't judge me.'

'It's not my place to. I'm only interested in catching the person responsible for killing Gemma.'

He gave a nod and the officer in the room with them accompanied him out. No sooner had the door closed than Murray let out an angry, 'Self-pitying prick! So much for being a father figure. He's only concerned about himself.'

The skin had tightened around Natalie's forehead and she pressed her fingers against it.

'I think we'll try Sasha. She might be able to remember something that will help us.'

'She didn't know anything the last time we spoke to her – only that Ryan was possessive,' said Murray.

'She was highly emotionally charged at the time. She'd just found out about Gemma. Since then, she's had a little time to come to terms with what's happened and she might think of somebody we haven't yet interviewed. It's worth a shot.'

It was afternoon by the time Natalie and Murray reached Sasha's house. A jumbled pile of textiles – jade silks, pastel cottons and paisley checks – covered the kitchen table. A photo album rested on top of it, open to a page showing a teenaged Sasha and a toddler, both barefoot, in matching blue-denim bib-dresses side by side on a brick wall, waving at the person behind the camera. Even as a child, Gemma had resembled her mother. *Two peas in a pod.* The place smelt sour; the culprit, an opened bottle of milk abandoned on the top next to a plate of limp, dark-green lettuce leaves and a half-eaten tomato.

'I'm sorry… I'm not making any sense today. My head really throbs,' said Sasha.

She placed the pills on her tongue, winced at the acrid taste, then gulped down the glass of cold water she'd run straight from the tap. Judging by her heavily swollen lids and pink sclera, Natalie assumed constant weeping had caused the headache. Natalie had been told that eyes become puffy through crying because emotional tears are less salty than ordinary tear secretions and eye tissue, so through the process of osmosis, water moves into the saltier ocular tissues, causing them to swell up. It was only a few months ago that, like Sasha, she'd experienced similar tension headaches and had sat immobile with inflamed eyes for days on end. Her heart went out to the woman, who was going through the same agonising emotional turmoil she'd experienced after Leigh had been murdered.

'Don't apologise. It's understandable,' she said, kindly.

'Would you like a cup of tea?' Murray asked.

Sasha shook her head. 'Tanya's made me lots of cups of tea during her visits. She's very kind but I'm a bit sick of tea now. I can't face anything to eat or drink.'

'You probably need to rest. Have you no one to come and stay with you?'

'My mum might come over from Bristol but her partner's not very well at the moment, and she and I don't have the best of relationships. There's my cousin, Gail, in Blackpool. I could ring her but we haven't spoken in such a long time that it would be… weird. There was only really me and Gemma. She wanted me to make more friends, and her moving out was part of that plan of hers. She didn't realise it's a lot more difficult for me than it was for her. Most people my age are in relationships and don't suddenly want a new friend tagging along.'

'Do you feel up to talking about Gemma again?'

'Not really but if it will help you find out who did this to her, I'll try and answer any questions. Did you talk to Ryan?' She sounded nasal, another result of crying.

'We did.'

'It wasn't him, was it, or you'd have charged him?'

'We're still investigating and it takes some time. We found an anonymous note to Gemma in her room. It was signed from "An Admirer". Did she talk to you about it?'

'Oh, yes. I remember that. It was hand-delivered to Eastview Avenue soon after she moved into the house. I was there when she opened it and read it. We couldn't guess who it was from.'

'What was written on the envelope?'

'Only her name.'

'What did she do with the envelope?'

'She threw it in the bin in her room.'

'But she kept the letter. Can you think why she'd keep it? It was in the back of her diary.'

'I don't know why she kept it. I don't think it was intentional. We were busy arranging her stuff in the room and I think she left it on her desk after reading it. Maybe it got swept up and slipped into the diary. She might have forgotten it was there.'

That seemed to make sense. The letter had been with other out-of-date items, but Natalie wanted to be sure that the letter wasn't significant. 'Did she get any other notes like it?'

'No. I asked her if she'd heard any more from her admirer a week or so afterwards, but she hadn't, and by then she'd begun going out with Ryan, and we thought the letter had come from someone who'd backed off when they'd found out she was seeing him. She definitely didn't get any others. She'd have told me if she had.'

It sounded logical, and without further notes from the admirer, the letter in the diary appeared to be a dead end. Gemma hadn't talked about it with or shown it to anyone else. It had simply been tidied away and forgotten in the back of the diary, out of sight.

Sasha plodded across to a chair and reached for a box of tissues, taking one and blowing her nose. Even with swollen eyelids and an uneven complexion, she was still striking. Nothing could detract from her platinum-blond hair, oval face, slim nose, smooth jawline and perfectly shaped bee-stung lips. She must have had admirers and boyfriends. They knew about Lennox, but was there somebody else who'd maybe been rebuffed by Sasha and targeted the person she loved the most?

'We spoke about anyone who might have had an interest in Gemma, but what about you? Is there anyone who's been pestering you recently?' asked Natalie.

Sasha pressed her fingertips to her temples and winced. 'I can't think clearly. I'm useless. I want to help you but…'

Natalie could sense the anxiety rising. 'Take your time. There's no pressure on you. What about somebody who asked you out? Maybe at the bar.'

There was a long pause and then Sasha lowered her fingers and said quietly, 'There was somebody – a recent regular. He's only been drinking at the bar about a month. He seemed really nice but low – depressed – and he always sat alone, but he was no trouble and he was nicely spoken. He looked like he was having a tough time. You can tell when people are going through bad times and he was one of those people. I made a bit of an effort when I served him, tried to find time to chat with him, be a little extra-nice and friendly.

'Then last Wednesday evening, he was waiting for me outside the bar when I finished work. It was obvious he'd been drinking because he was unsteady on his feet. First he complimented me on my outfit, then thanked me for being nice to him, and then he asked if I'd like to go out with him sometime. I told him I didn't date customers and he flipped from the nice, quiet gentleman to a complete prick. He asked what was wrong with me and said I'd given him the come-on every time he'd visited... but I hadn't. I'd only been pleasant because I felt sorry for him. He started shouting I was a prick-teaser and I got into my car and drove off before he could say or do anything else. Oh, my!'

Her eyes widened as she realised the significance of what she was about to reveal next. 'He knew Gemma too. He was in last Saturday night and I saw them talking. I didn't think anything of it at the time.'

Natalie kept up the momentum of the conversation. This was important. The stranger at the bar knew both Sasha and Gemma and had shown aggression towards Sasha after being knocked back. 'Did he threaten you?'

'No, but there's something else you should know. I think he was standing outside my house on Thursday evening before I went to work. I ran upstairs to double-check and maybe call the police, but when I looked out of the bedroom window, there was no sign of him and I thought I'd imagined it. I haven't seen him again since.'

Murray gave Natalie a quick look that said everything she was thinking. This could be a strong lead.

'Do you know the man's name?'

'Only his first name – David.'

'And can you describe him?' asked Natalie.

'In his late forties, glasses, dark hair, slim and I think he's a translator.'

Natalie's mouth went dry and she reached for her mobile phone, swiped several photographs and found one of David with Josh sitting together on a bench. She held it up for Sasha to see.

'That's the man. That's David.'

CHAPTER FOURTEEN

SUNDAY, 18 NOVEMBER – LATE MORNING

Fran ended the call and hurled the mobile at the wall. It hit with force but dropped onto the duvet and she joined it, falling onto her back and staring at the ceiling, face set. Thanks to the police confiscating her mobile, she'd had to borrow Ryan's to ring her mother. The call had started off okay but had rapidly deteriorated into the usual snide comments and then argument…

'So, you're too good for us all now to come home?'

'Why do you come out with such crap, Mum? I rang, didn't I?'

'I'm only stating the obvious.'

'I didn't come home this weekend cos I had work to do and it's fucking expensive to get back. I'm a student not a banker in case you've forgotten, and I've hardly got enough money to eat let alone travel back and forth to Liverpool.'

'You get a student discount for travel on the train.' Her mother's voice was peevish and Fran could picture her perched on the kitchen stool, thin lips pressed together in disapproval.

She'd never wanted Fran to go to university. She'd wanted her to leave college, where she'd been studying for A-levels, and bring some more money into the household, but Fran had stuck to her guns. Nanna had encouraged her to study for university, and even though the old lady was now ill with dementia, Fran wanted to do right by her. Her grandmother had believed in her and wanted better for her. However, had Fran not been granted a full student loan, she wouldn't be here.

The loan would be paid off in time, when she got a decent job with her degree. Far better than other options. Returning to East Toxteth wasn't one of them. For one, she hated Jerry. Her unemployed stepfather was lazy and demanding and liked booze too much, and her younger siblings were hard work. She would have to share a bedroom with ten- and twelve-year-old stepsisters, and her fourteen-year-old brother, Kyle, was a bag of trouble who would soon end up in prison. Fran would have returned if she could have continued to live with her grandmother in Childwall, as she had for several years in her teens – years that had kept her out of trouble and away from the influences of her old friends in East Toxteth, girls who now had two or three kids of their own, or were still hanging about with local tearaways and members of street gangs like sad groupies. But after Grandpa had died, Nanna had got ill, and only six weeks after Fran had taken her A-levels, the old lady had been admitted to a care home.

She stood a chance with a degree and was more likely to have a better future than if she'd remained in East Toxteth. There, she was far more likely to end up pregnant, on drugs or stabbed in some pointless yet vicious fight. She'd never learnt to keep a lid on her temper. At least in Samford she found herself in less volatile situations.

She wasn't keen on her housemates, other than Ryan, and much preferred Rhiannon's company to Hattie's, but the sodding university housing authorities had got their applications mixed up or lost, or some other bullshit, and instead of sharing a house as she and Rhiannon had both intended, they'd been separated. Fran didn't get along with many other girls at university. They were put off by her looks and attitude, which suited Fran. Rhiannon, however, hadn't been, and during their first year at university they'd forged a good relationship. It had been a different story with Gemma, who'd got right on Fran's tits from the off – partly because she'd been placed in the house and not Rhiannon. She was such a girly girl and so fucking nice to everyone. It wound Fran up even thinking about it. Gemma's mother was even worse. Fran hated all that bullshit. It had to be false, didn't it? Nobody she knew behaved that way. Watching Ryan fawn over Gemma had been sickening, more so because, up until then, she'd had hopes for a relationship with the South African. Gemma had put paid to that.

She sighed. It had been really fucking stupid to have put all that crap online about harming Gemma. She'd got carried away in the moment. She should have kept her opinions to herself. Her fiery temper was to blame. She couldn't control it at times. It was the same temper that had won her a fearsome reputation before she'd moved to Childwall. If anyone was going to lash out uncontrollably, it would be Fran. She'd broken a girl's nose and cheekbone during one such altercation and been lucky that charges hadn't been pressed.

She scowled at the stains on the ceiling where somebody before her had put up posters that had left behind marks shaped like fat love hearts, which had yellowed with age. Fat chance of her finding love any time soon! The sour mood wasn't entirely down to feeling unwanted. As usual, her mother had pissed her off. Fran hated ringing home at the best of times – her mum usually grumbled and complained the entire conversation – but it was her grandmother's birthday today, and Fran had been expected to return to East Toxteth and pay lip service to the old lady who probably didn't even remember who Fran was. Dementia had destroyed the one person who'd truly believed in Fran. A trip was out of the question. She'd plumped for a phone call rather than face the ordeal, in the knowledge there'd be an emotional fallout. Her mother wouldn't let her get away with it and would keeping pushing Fran's buttons until she felt so guilty she'd return home. Fucking families!

She checked the phone to see if the screen was damaged. It would be a swine if it was. She couldn't afford to repair it. That temper of hers. Her mother had always warned her it would get her into trouble one day. Fortunately, it was okay. She palmed it and dragged herself from the bed. She'd return it to Ryan and then she could do with a drink, something to take the edge off a shitty few days – but first she had to speak to somebody. It was a decision that would cost her dearly.

CHAPTER FIFTEEN

Now that it was fast approaching 4 p.m. and trading had almost ceased, the car park at Wolseley Bridge Garden Centre was rapidly emptying. Lucy remained in her car and observed the stragglers emerging from the exit, pushing trolleys laden with plants and bags of soil or fertiliser. She had little interest in their purchases. She and Bethany weren't big gardeners. Their back garden was set to lawn, a practical choice for a couple with a child. Even though Aurora was only a baby at the moment, it wouldn't be long before she'd be playing outside. Lucy could picture it all – a swing, trampoline and sand pit, and smiled at the prospect.

Ocean Stone had unexpectedly agreed to meet up with Lucy to talk about his ex-wife, Hattie. She wasn't sure what to expect. Her idea of a commune was probably outdated or based on television programmes she'd watched. She'd never been into an alternative lifestyle or understood the desire for anybody to shut themselves off from the world. A blue VW campervan, a little like the one Pinkney owned, pulled into view and a man descended from the driver's seat. He cast about the car park, eyes settling on the unmarked BMW squad car Lucy had driven. He raised a hand. It was Ocean.

Ocean was almost upon her before she'd stepped out of her vehicle, hand outstretched, and she was struck by his clean-cut looks. She'd expected a hippy, not somebody who looked like a businessman, dressed as he was in grey trousers, white shirt and a long, dark coat. His nut-brown eyes rested on her. 'I'm pleased to meet you, DS Carmichael. It's a shame it isn't under more pleasant circumstances.'

'It's good of you to come all this way, to talk to me face-to-face.'

'I confess it is not out of my way. It made sense to meet you here because I'm actually on my way to visit another commune, near Nottingham. Hence the last-minute phone call to you to arrange this.'

'Thank you all the same. As you know, we're concerned about Hattie and hoped you could help us.'

He gave a sad smile. 'Yes, the local police told me. I'm not sure how much of a help I can be. I haven't seen Hattie since she walked out six years ago.'

'Have you had any contact with her since then?'

'The only contact I had was via a solicitor as the divorce went through. As far as I knew she returned to her father in Little Beansfield.'

'It's imperative we talk to her. Is there any possibility she'd have contacted any of her friends at the commune?'

He shook his head. 'That's unlikely. Hattie wouldn't have been made welcome by anyone there.'

'Why is that?'

'She caused a lot of upset and grief before she left.'

'I'm still a bit in the dark as to why she actually left. Can you spell it out, please?'

Ocean gave a sigh. 'Let me explain in more detail and then maybe you'll understand the situation. I first met Hattie at a party. She was an eighteen-year-old, rebellious vicar's daughter who wanted to save the planet and everyone on it. She shared my beliefs and ideals and I was bowled over by her enthusiasm. I was in the process of building up the commune and had already invited a few like-minded people. We had a passionate and whirlwind romance and I believed I'd found my soulmate, somebody to be part of my life and who'd fit in perfectly in the commune. There's a saying: *Marry in haste and repent at leisure.* That was us. Within only a few months, Hattie was sick of life in the commune and griped about everything. She dragged everyone down, and obviously it reflected on me as their leader. Then, out of the blue, she accused me of sleeping around. She became obsessed with the idea and spread vicious rumours about some of the women and caused a lot of unrest. She even made moves herself on some of the men in the commune, in some pathetic attempt to make me jealous.'

'Were you having an affair behind her back?'

'Absolutely not, but she wouldn't take my word for it. In hindsight, I think she was blinded by jealousy. The larger the commune became, the more she resented me and my role as leader, until she couldn't stand it any more and left.'

Lucy nodded. 'I see. Well, we really need to find her. Can you think of anybody she might have gone to stay with?'

'I'm afraid not. I don't know any of the people she might now call friends. I can only reiterate that she hasn't been in touch with any of us and I would know if she had. I can tell you one thing though: don't be taken in by her. I was, and I doubt she's changed that much in the last six years.'

'What do you mean?'

'Hattie's very two-faced. She could turn from friend to foe, very quickly.'

'Did she turn on you?'

'Twice. The first time, she threatened to go to the press and tell them I was running a cult and screwing all the women in it, and the second time, she attacked me with a knife, threatening to cut off my balls.' He held up his right palm to show Lucy a thick, pale scar. 'She sliced me before she dropped the knife and ran off.'

'Why didn't you report her?'

'I don't know. I suppose I ought to have but I didn't want to involve the police. We live peacefully and given that one of the nurses at the commune fixed me up, I was fine.'

'But she attacked you!'

'And she left the commune that same day. She was out of my life. I didn't see the point in pursuing it.' He rubbed his palm absent-mindedly.

'What else can you tell me about her?'

'That's everything really, except I hope you find her and that she hasn't done anything stupid.' He looked across at the VW campervan. 'Is there anything else you want to ask me?'

'I can't think of anything.'

'Then I'd better get going. It was nice meeting you, DS Carmichael.'

Lucy watched as he made his way to the vehicle and clambered in. The calmly spoken Ocean had been a surprise but his revelations even more so. Hattie was not the loving, gentle person they'd initially believed her to be. Had she become jealous of Gemma and tried to hurt her? That now seemed a possibility.

*

'I don't care what my relationship with him is or was, he's a suspect, and as such, he has to be interviewed,' said Natalie to Dan Tasker.

'There's a conflict of interest and I can't have this investigation compromised,' Dan replied.

She glared at him. 'I refuse to give up this investigation. You assigned it to me because you knew I was the right person to head it. I will let nothing jeopardise this case, and I mean nothing at all. I shall treat David as I would anyone sitting opposite me in that interview room, and you know that, Dan! Besides, I am the best person to see through any lies. I'll know every tell-tale sign, every giveaway he makes when he's lying. I'll know if he's holding back on anything. Nobody knows David better than I do. I ought to be the one to interview him.'

He lifted his palms to appease her. 'Okay. I'll leave it with you but I want DS Anderson to sit in on all your interviews with him, and if he feels the investigation isn't being handled correctly, I'll have no option other than to remove you. I don't want to do that, Natalie. I'll give you the chance to show me you can handle this.'

'Thank you.' She took off again. Murray had already gone to Castergate to fetch her soon-to-be ex-husband. She read through the notes she'd made while talking to Sasha and ran a hand over her forehead, fingers brushing away light strands. This was madness. David was a gambler and he lied to protect himself, but to throw acid in a young woman's face? It didn't seem at all plausible, yet if he'd been drinking and felt rebuffed… who could tell how somebody who'd experienced the anguish of the last few months would act? Josh had left home because he couldn't bear to live with his father, and facts were facts. David had been frequenting Chancer's Bar and had verbally attacked Sasha. Would a drunken and rebuffed David retaliate in such a horrific way by harming the woman's daughter? Natalie had to remain impartial. That was the key to it all. She was not to let her feelings or her past relationship with the man influence her in any way.

The internal phone rang and the desk officer informed her that Murray and David had arrived and were in room A.

'Okay. Let Murray know I'm on my way down.'

She glanced at her watch. It was almost four thirty. Her stomach was in knots. David of all people! She'd told Dan she could handle this investigation but her sweaty palms and hammering heart suggested otherwise. She had to divorce herself from her personal relationship with David and get to the bottom of this. She swallowed hard. It was going to be difficult to look into David's eyes and not see the hurt and anger. It was going to be almost impossible not to think of Leigh. Should she hand over the investigation? No.

She rubbed her hands on her thighs and inhaled. *Deep breath. You can do this.*

David had lost weight. He had always been naturally slim but his old work jacket was two sizes too large for him and he seemed swamped by it. His neck had become craggy and grey whiskers poked out of a badly shaven chin. She caught her breath at the sight. The trauma of losing Leigh had aged her but it had destroyed David.

He shook his head sadly as if it weighed too much for him and said, 'Why am I here, Natalie?'

'We need to record the interview to keep this official and you will have to address me as DI Ward.'

'Hanging on to my surname then, are you? I thought you'd have dumped it along with everything else.'

Natalie didn't bite at the barbed comment. She nodded at Murray who set off the recorder and made necessary introductions. Once he'd finished, Natalie began. 'DS Anderson has explained why we'd like to talk to you. We have reason to believe you know Sasha and Gemma Barnes, and that you had several conversations with both of them at Chancer's Bar over the last month.'

He nodded wearily. 'I did.'

'Why did you start going to Chancer's? It's quite a way from where you live.'

'You want me to be honest?'

'I *need* you to be honest.'

He took a lengthy inhalation and released the air slowly, his chest and face deflating like a collapsing balloon. He stared at the table for a few moments then said, 'I've been struggling with coming to terms with Leigh's murder and the breakdown of my marriage. I began visiting bars in Samford because my estranged wife had left me and moved there. I got it into my head she would be out and about in the town, probably with her new boyfriend, and for some unfathomable reason I had to see that with my own eyes. What started as a thought consumed me and I *wanted* to see her living a new life, able to move on when I couldn't, because I convinced myself if I saw that, it would help *me* to move on too. I needed to see it, because I was imprisoned in some appalling limbo unable to find my way out.

'Anyway, I visited several bars and pubs but didn't spot her and gradually realised the idea was utterly stupid – it was the act of a desperate man who had lost his way. I gave up and had a drink at Chancer's Bar. The bar staff there were friendly and I found myself opening up a little to Sasha, who was kind to me. I appreciated that compassion and I returned on several occasions to drown my sorrows and to feel more human, more normal. Is that honest enough for you, DI Ward?'

In spite of his frosty words, she maintained her professional demeanour – her front. David had surprised her. She hadn't had him down as a bitter and jealous man who would hunt her down and spy on her. This was a side she hadn't seen before. Was David capable of turning jealousy into hate? Murray hadn't flinched at David's revelation that Natalie had a new man in her life, and she wondered how much he knew about her and Mike.

'Thank you. I need to discuss an incident that occurred last Wednesday, November the fourteenth, at ten thirty at night, when you accosted Sasha Barnes outside Chancer's Bar.'

His shoulders sagged and the iciness that had pervaded his earlier words disappeared in an instant. 'I can explain what happened. I made a fool of myself by asking Sasha out and reacting badly when she refused. I'm not proud of myself. I'd been drinking and I was bang out of order. As soon as she drove away, I felt nothing but shame.'

Natalie recognised the sorrow in his eyes. He was ashamed. She'd seen that very look on his face before: when he'd admitted to gambling and when he'd confessed his addiction a second time. What she couldn't be sure of was whether he was feeling guilty because of how he'd acted in front of Sasha, or because of what he'd done to Gemma.

'I expect you felt angry at being rejected,' she said.

'Don't put words into my mouth or try to lead me on this. I was upset at her reaction. I'd misunderstood the situation between us and was surprised and upset rather than angry.'

'According to Sasha you became angry.'

'It might have come across like that but I hadn't intended it that way. My pride was bruised. It's taken a right beating the last few months and it took a lot of effort to conjure up sufficient confidence to even ask her out for a drink. I was… *wounded* by her rejection.'

'So much so that you accused her of leading you on and shouted insults at her?'

'I'm embarrassed to admit I made some ungentlemanly comments, which I immediately regretted. They spurted out in the heat of the moment. I didn't mean them.'

'Sasha said she saw you outside her house on Thursday evening before she left for work. Were you there?'

He lowered his head and said, 'Yes.'

'Can I ask why you went to her house?'

'I wanted to apologise for my behaviour the day before but I chickened out and decided to avoid the bar instead. She clearly wasn't interested in me.' Natalie looked for any tells. David would often rub his head if he was anxious or hiding a secret, but he remained fixed to his seat, arms hanging limply by his sides – a defeated man.

'How did you know where she lived?'

His voice dropped. 'I followed her home one time.'

'Why? Why on earth did you do that?' Natalie couldn't keep the disbelief out of her voice. She no longer understood what made this man tick. He'd become a stranger to her.

'I was curious about her. I wondered if there was a man in her life.'

'Why didn't you simply ask her?'

His words were flat. 'I don't know. I don't know what I was thinking of at the time. My mind has been all over the place the last few months. I suppose it sounds stupid to you, but I wanted to know a little about her before I asked her out.'

'You followed her to her home. That isn't simply finding out about somebody. That's stalking.'

'I didn't stalk her. I only followed her to her house once. In hindsight it wasn't the wisest thing to have done but you have to understand I've been under a lot of pressure. I haven't been thinking straight.'

Natalie accepted what he was saying although she was staggered by this news. Stalking women, verbally abusing them. Who was this man? Nevertheless, she moved on. 'David, where were you Friday evening between six and eight?'

He blinked and studied his hands before answering. Natalie wondered why he was taking so long to respond. 'David?'

A sigh. 'I was asleep.'

'You were asleep at six in the evening?'

'I had nothing else to do. Josh was out at his girlfriend's house.'

She wanted to shake him and remind him he was still a father to Josh, who didn't deserve to come home to find his father in such a self-pitying state. He should be holding down a job and moving forward with his life, as difficult as it was, like she was doing. Instead she asked, 'Can anyone vouch for you?'

'I was alone.'

'What time did you wake up?'

'I don't know. Late.' He lowered his head. Natalie couldn't establish whether he was embarrassed by his confession or hiding something.

'Let's move on to Gemma. You spoke to her at the bar?'

'A couple of times.'

'What did you talk about?'

'She was studying languages and we got on to German and how difficult the grammar can be. She was interested in my job,' he said, then gave a bitter laugh. Natalie understood. Losing the job he'd loved as a translator for a law firm had been a terrible blow, one from which he'd never fully recovered. His efforts to try his hand as an online translator hadn't provided him with a decent enough income or challenge, and slowly but surely, every shred of self-belief had been eroded. He'd have seen Gemma as somebody who had a bright future. Maybe that had riled him.

'Did she discuss what she wanted to do after she left university?'

'She did. She had quite a few ideas; one was to work for a foreign embassy abroad in either Russia or Germany.'

'As a translator?'

'Yes, as a translator.' His face seemed to grow longer and leaner, almost melting with misery.

Natalie sensed his unhappiness and moved on. 'Did you ever see or meet Gemma outside of the bar?'

'Never.'

'You didn't arrange to meet her at all?'

'No.'

Even though the note from the secret admirer now appeared to bear little relevance to the case, she still had to ask the question. 'Did you ever write to Gemma?'

'Absolutely not. I'm not responsible for what happened to Gemma. Please believe me.'

She wanted to but the David she knew wouldn't have tailed a woman who was almost fifteen years his junior back to her house, or got drunk every day and neglected his son, or frequented bars or dozed off on an evening. That man wasn't the sorry specimen who now sat in front of her, and on top of it all, she had to follow procedure. David's whereabouts couldn't be confirmed, and although she doubted he'd be callous enough to inflict such harm on a young woman, she couldn't fully dismiss the idea. He'd been drinking even more than usual, and drunken people weren't always in control of their actions. She'd borne witness to his moods and to a violent anger that had erupted following the death of their daughter. He'd thrown her out of their home with such venom she'd wondered if he would harm her…

Josh races from the room, unable to share his feelings with his parents. His face is a mixture of shock and sorrow and sobs rack his body.

Natalie can hardly breathe but she makes after him only to be halted by David, whose voice drips poison.

'Leave him!'

'But he needs me.'

'No, he doesn't. He doesn't need you and neither do I. We needed you but you chose to leave us. We all needed you but you weren't around for us.'

She is aghast. 'I was. You know I was. Admittedly not all the time, but somebody had to—'

He interrupts her with, 'Work. Somebody had to work. Yes, I know. I've had it rammed down my throat ever since I made the mistake of gambling our savings. You never let me forget and you treated me with disdain afterwards. I probably deserved it but the children didn't and they needed you. The truth is that you really went to work because you loved your job more than being around here, around me and all this reality. You took on extra shifts not so much because we needed extra cash but because you wanted to, so you could be at work – closer to Mike.'

'That's not true! I only took them on because we had bills to pay. Mike wasn't the reason.'

He silences her with a look. 'We needed you here. Leigh needed you, especially after what happened earlier this year. Running away was her attempt to get us to fix things between us, but you didn't try.'

Tears tumble as she speaks. 'I did try.'

'Not hard enough!' he bellows. 'This is on your shoulders, Natalie. This is all your fault.'

She starts to speak but again he stops her, this time by raising his hand in the air. 'You wanted to leave, so go on. You've got the keys to your new life. Get out now before I kick you out of the door myself.'

'You're upset...'

'Too true I'm upset. Our daughter is dead and it's because some fucking crackpot had it in for you but chose instead to murder our daughter. I can't look at you. I can't be with you. Just go.'

'What about Josh?'

'I'll look after him.'

'David—'

'We're done. Get out.' He turns his back to her and stumbles out of the room.

There was a tap at the door and Murray left to answer it. David took the opportunity to address Natalie quietly. 'Help me, Natalie!' he pleaded.

She couldn't turn her back on him but what if he was guilty? Had she the strength to bring down her own husband?

Murray returned, grim-faced. Natalie read the note he'd been given, folded it in half and said, 'We will probably want to talk to you again but you can go for now. DS Anderson will arrange transport to take you home.'

With both men gone she read the note again and took a few seconds to digest what was written. A body identified by her student card as matching the description of Fran Ditton had been discovered in an abandoned doorway in Samford, under a pile of blankets. Natalie was probably no longer dealing with a one-off attack. She was hunting for a killer who might well have other victims in their sight.

CHAPTER SIXTEEN

SUNDAY, 18 NOVEMBER – EARLY EVENING

The pathologist, Pinkney Watson, returned the rectal thermometer to his medical bag and rose from the shop doorway where he'd been stooped.

'I can't determine exact cause of death,' he said. 'There are no ligature marks or defence wounds or any sign she was attacked. I have my suspicions but I need to examine her before I can be more certain.'

Natalie tore her eyes away from Fran Ditton's pale body and the tattoo of the escaping bird that seemed even darker against her white flesh. In the evening light, the girl's face had softened and Natalie saw the beauty that Fran had tried hard to disguise with her scowls and aggressive attitude. In death, she appeared much smaller, younger and more fragile than she had in life. She'd been discovered under a pile of frayed blankets, next to a stack of grubby belongings in tatty plastic bags. Their owner, one of the many homeless people in Samford, was sitting inside an ambulance, a blanket over his shoulders, deep in conversation with Murray and Lucy, who'd joined them from Wolseley Bridge where she'd been talking to Ocean. He'd come across Fran's body when he'd returned to his spot in the wide doorway of the abandoned shop.

'What are your thoughts, Pinkney?' Natalie wouldn't ordinarily press a pathologist because she understood the complexity of their occupation. Cause of death was not always apparent, but if Pinkney said he had suspicions, she knew he would share them with her. Pinkney hesitated before responding.

'There's no sign of staining or inflammation around the lips or mouth, or any obvious smell, but there is slight damage to the membranes in the oesophagus, which might have been caused by something she ingested.'

'Poison?'

'Maybe.'

'Do you think she took her own life?'

'It's possible.'

'Have you any idea of the time of death?'

'Rigor has only recently begun to take place in the smaller muscles in the face and neck, and her body temperature has lowered by three degrees. In all likelihood, she probably died only a couple of hours ago. Mike, what do you think?'

Natalie hadn't been aware of Mike, who was standing behind her. 'Sorry, I was miles away. I didn't register you were there.'

'Not surprising. I was taken aback too when we first arrived. There's no sign of a struggle or any indication she was dragged to this spot, so she either came here alone and died, or she died and was transported here. Had it not been for Evan returning to his pitch unexpectedly, she'd have remained undiscovered until much later tonight. Normally, he only sleeps here but today he felt unwell and returned. Got the shock of his life.'

'I can't imagine why she'd come here to this doorway and kill herself,' said Natalie.

'I'm not sure she did. We've taken away some empty bottles – vodka, gin and beer. Evan thinks they all belong to him but he isn't sure. We've sent them all for testing,' said Mike.

'Pinkney, have you anything else that might help us work out what's happened here?'

'I'm afraid not. There are no wounds, bruises or marks on her body. I'm hoping the post-mortem will yield an answer. Mike, have you finished? Can I take her back to the laboratory?'

'Sure.'

Natalie took a step back as the team was sent in to remove Fran. 'What the hell has happened here? First Gemma, then another housemate, Hattie, disappears, and now yet another housemate, Fran, is dead. Was there a suicide note on the body, Mike?'

'Nothing.'

'Then this might well be connected to Gemma's death. I can't see how, unless Fran was responsible for what happened to Gemma, and when Hattie threatened to expose her, she killed herself. That makes some sort of sense although it's only conjecture on my part.'

Mike agreed with her and added, 'At the moment, that's as good a theory as any because we've found nothing to suggest somebody killed her here. Let's see if there's anything on or in the bottles we sent for examination to support it. The crime scene photos were emailed directly to you and should be in your inbox.'

'Will you send someone to her room to check if she left a suicide note there?'

'Absolutely. I'll arrange that.' His eyes fixed on hers for a long moment and she found herself wishing they were somewhere else, somewhere private, where she could tell him that she was almost ready to move forwards. She gave a smile of thanks that was intended to say what she couldn't at present.

'Have you had a chance to look at that anonymous note from the secret admirer we found in Gemma's room?'

'We finished examining it a few minutes ago. We only found Gemma's and her mother's prints on it.'

'No other prints?'

'None.'

'Then whoever wrote it really wanted to keep their identity a secret.'

'Think it's relevant?'

'I really don't know. Sasha was certain there were no more letters, and in light of what has happened to Fran, it seems even less relevant, but would you please check in case there's a similar note in Fran's room?'

'I'll get an officer onto it and let you know the second we find anything.' He gave an imperceptible nod and let his eyes rest a few seconds on her face once more. She held his gaze and thanked him before turning away to observe as officers laid out a body bag on the pavement in front of the doorway ready to receive Fran's body. It was suddenly too much. Here was yet another young woman who would never see the sunshine again, who would never grow up to love, live and have a family of her own. Cold fingers curled around her heart. The sudden sadness that accompanied the thought drained her, and she fought it by focusing on her surroundings. This whole area was filled with vacant premises, relics of a vibrant high street that had closed down after the supermarkets and retail parks grew in popularity. It was one of the shabbiest streets in Samford, a ten-minute journey by car from where Fran had lived and five minutes from the university. Ripped posters advertising a funfair from 2017 sat cheek by jowl with flyers advertising pop-up carpet and garden furniture sales and lost pets. Lanky weeds grew through the cracked paving slabs, and discarded cigarette packets, squashed drinks cartons and balled takeaway packaging had collected in every doorway. Fran would soon be transported away, and once the police and forensic team moved off, there'd be nothing left to show she'd even been here. *Why did she come here to die?* She took one last look at the high cheekbones and pallid face and spun on her heel. It wasn't Fran she saw. It was Leigh.

Lucy and Murray were still taking a statement from a man who sat on the edge of an ambulance trolley. Somebody had given him a mug of tea, and steam curled up over his shaggy beard and mous-tache as he sipped. He stopped to cough – a long, hacking cough.

When he'd recovered, Lucy introduced him to Natalie. 'This is Evan Robertson. Evan, this is our boss, DI Ward.'

He lowered the drink and Natalie could see he was far younger than she'd initially taken him for. He was probably no more than thirty-five. 'I couldn't believe my eyes when I hauled back my blanket and found her. I didn't know what to do. I tried to put the blanket back exactly as I found it,' he said. His voice surprised her even more than the bright, azure eyes that looked intently at her. It was educated and pleasant to the ear although he sounded slightly breathless. He coughed again after speaking and took another sip of his drink.

'You hadn't seen her before?' Natalie asked.

'Never set eyes on her.'

'You came back to where you sleep because you felt unwell. Is that correct?'

'That's right. I'd been out on the streets since ten this morning. I spent most of the time hanging by the Grey Goose pub, but I felt really lousy. I've had this cough for ages and it's wearing me down. I thought a few hours' kip would do me good. I returned to my spot soon after four.'

'How long have you been sleeping there?'

'Only a few days. I couldn't get into the shelter. It was full.'

'Did nobody give you the names and addresses of other shelters to try?' asked Natalie.

'They did but I chose to go it alone for a while, although after this, I'll try one of the other places tonight.'

'Have you seen anyone suspicious around these parts?'

'No. I've been alone here every night. It's very quiet.'

'No gangs?'

'No.'

'What about during the day?'

'I don't know what goes on then. I usually leave my gear here and head into town to try and beg some food.' He took several sharp breaths and then cupped the mug even more tightly.

'What about volunteers? Do they come by?' Natalie knew a few organisations often distributed warm meals and blankets.

'Yes. The first night I spent here, a young woman came by. She gave me some soup, a blanket and this hat.' He tapped the plain black beanie on his head. 'She didn't come back.'

'What did this woman look like?'

'In her twenties. She was tall, willowy, very pale-faced.'

'Did she tell you her name?'

He shook his head.

'What colour hair did she have?'

'I don't know. She was wearing a woollen hat and a long, hippy-like skirt with a fringe and a shawl.'

His use of the word 'hippy' brought Hattie to mind. It was worth checking. 'Murray, will you ask Ian to send across a photo of Hattie? See if Evan recognises her.' With that she thanked the man and moved away from the ambulance, indicating Lucy follow her.

'He seems well-educated. How come he's on the streets?' she asked quietly.

'Bad luck. Wife divorced him, lost his job which meant he lost his flat, then got into drugs. He's clean now but still unemployed. The paramedics are taking him to hospital to get him checked out. They think he's got pneumonia.'

'I take it he didn't have much information for us,' said Natalie.

'Nothing terribly useful other than what he told you.'

'Mike said he removed some empty bottles that he thinks belonged to Evan.'

'That's right. Evan isn't a hundred per cent certain if all the bottles were his. He's been buying cheap booze from the off-licence a couple of streets away to keep him warm at night.'

'If Forensics come back with anything from the bottles, we'll check out that store. Can you ask Ian to check all of Fran's social media accounts to see if she left any farewell message or hinted she was suicidal?'

'Will do.'

'And get onto Merseyside Police. Somebody over there needs to notify her parents, then we'll talk to the students who live on Eastview Avenue again.'

Murray called Natalie's name. She strode back towards the ambulance. Evan was bent over, coughing again. The photo of Hattie was visible on Murray's mobile. Murray nodded. 'It was Hattie who came by.'

'Find out who she was volunteering with and if she was alone.'

Hattie again. They needed to find her urgently but where on earth was she? Lucy had established the woman could be volatile and had attacked Ocean, and although there was a chance Hattie might have attacked Gemma out of jealousy, Natalie couldn't work out why she'd kill Fran. Yet the body was in a doorway in an area where Hattie had been doing volunteer work. Hattie had to be found.

CHAPTER SEVENTEEN

SUNDAY, 18 NOVEMBER – EVENING

The vicarage at Little Beansfield was an individual, black-and-white, timber-framed cottage with a black-arched doorway, over which an untamed winter clematis climbed, its dangling tendrils like wafer-thin bunting, wafting in the breeze. Thick evergreen pyracantha covered much of the front of the house, and bunches of orange berries bounced gently on thin stems against the dark leaves. Natalie switched off the headlights and plunged the road and house into inky-black darkness. Here there were no street lights and even the star-studded sky did not illuminate the driveway. She pulled out a torch and flashed it in the direction of the house, the beam landing on the latched wooden gate, and climbed out of the car into the cool evening. The wind lifted her hair and cooled her neck, caressing it with feathery strokes. Lucy had lit her torch as well and shone it ahead of them, the light picking up tiny weeds growing between cobbled stones that led to the front door.

Natalie unhinged the gate, which groaned mournfully, like a weary soul in pain. The sound, amplified in the stillness of the night, was immediately seized upon by a hissing scream that halted her in her tracks. Trying to locate the direction from which the noise had come, she shone her torch over the leaf-covered grass until it came to rest in a corner of the garden, its light scattering over the lightly rippled water of a large pond. There was no one

visible yet she had the sense of somebody watching her. The beam
swung over the bushes and trees and, catching the rustle of crisp
leaves on a branch, she was in time to spot a large owl as it took
off from its perch in the shadows.

'Wow! That's huge,' said Lucy. 'Why did it make that noise?'

'Don't know. Probably defending its territory.'

Not living in the countryside, she was unused to such night-time
noises. The ones with which she was familiar were all man-made.
She rang the doorbell and almost immediately a light snapped
on upstairs. 'Coming!' shouted a muffled voice. More lights were
turned on, the door opened and a grey-bearded face peered out.

Natalie spoke. 'Mr Caldwell?'

'Yes.'

She lifted her ID card. 'I'm DI Natalie Ward, in charge of the
investigation into an attack on Gemma Barnes, and this is DS
Lucy Carmichael.'

He stepped back to allow both officers space to enter. The place
was welcoming, the pungent aroma of burnt wood from a recent
log fire filling the narrow, dark hallway, which was brightened by
numerous paintings of landscapes and a large standard lamp that
emitted a soft orange glow.

They followed him into a room – a study with wooden book-
cases and a green leather swivel armchair, a glass-topped table with
ornate legs and feet, and a matching leather settee with cushions
on which were embroidered ducks. The desk was pushed under a
net-curtained window – highly polished and clear of clutter with
a notebook open on it and an ornate lamp over it. It was the sort
of old-fashioned office Natalie would expect to see in the Houses
of Parliament or a grand house.

Mr Caldwell spoke calmly. 'How can I help you?'

'We're searching for Hattie. We're unable to locate her and we
think she might have valuable information she wished to share
regarding the attack on Gemma Barnes, but she failed to make

a pre-arranged meeting. Have you any idea at all as to what she might have wanted to tell me?'

He placed his hands behind his back, entwined his fingers and pondered the question. 'Sadly no. I can't think why she contacted you. She said nothing to me about any attack, but she's not very good at staying in touch. Or, should I say, we're not very good at staying in touch.'

'She never mentioned Gemma to you?'

'Only in passing. I know she's one of Hattie's housemates.'

'You didn't know about the attack on her?'

'Alas, I didn't. I'm a little behind with the news at the moment.'

'I'm afraid she died.'

'Oh. I'm very sorry to hear that.'

'Did you ever meet her?'

'No.'

'Did you ever visit Hattie at the house on Eastview Avenue?'

'Once when she first moved to it. We went out for lunch together and I stopped off for a cup of tea.'

'Did you meet any of her housemates?'

'They were all out at the time so no, I didn't.'

'You've not been back to the house since then?'

'Hattie's a grown woman. She doesn't want or need her septua-genarian father dropping by every week. Besides, it gets difficult to know what to talk about. She's a young sociology student and I'm an old fossil who spreads God's word.'

'You do see each other though, don't you?'

'Oh, yes, she comes by during the holidays. Her room here is always made up for her and she's always welcome, but to be perfectly frank, there's not much for a young woman in this quiet village, which is probably why she left in the first place.'

'To marry Ocean?'

'She fell head over heels in love with him. I was happy for them both even though she moved away to live in the eco-commune.'

'Did you visit them there?'

'A few times but I always felt a little awkward – an outsider – even though they were all welcoming enough.'

'Do you know why she left the commune?' Natalie asked, aware of what Lucy had told her.

'I do and it surprised me. It transpired Ocean was keen on multiple relationships with his female followers and Hattie wasn't the only woman he wanted to be with. She wasn't prepared to stand for that and upped and left. She divorced him soon after. It was a sad state of affairs. I'd really taken to the man but, well, Hattie's my daughter. Anyway, Hattie came back and wanted to get some qualifications. It wasn't easy for her, sitting A-levels at night school while holding down a job, but she did it and was accepted into Samford University to study sociology, and I'm very proud of her.' Mr Caldwell's story didn't really tally with Ocean's version and Natalie still had a muddled picture of Hattie.

'Can I ask, who funds Hattie's education?'

'Ah, that'd be me. I used a small inheritance I was bequeathed from an aunt a few years ago to pay for her accommodation and fees. I'm also able to give her a small allowance to live on, and she manages well. She's not silly with money.' His face brightened with pride.

Lucy had been listening quietly and now asked, 'Do you know any of her friends' names or where any of them live?'

The man shook his head. 'That's the thing… I don't.'

'She never told you anything about any of her friends?'

'I vaguely know first names like Charlotte or Yvonne, but I don't know who they are or anything much about them. Charlotte has a dog, I think, and Yvonne went to Edinburgh – to The Fringe – with Hattie, but I don't know any more than that. I'm very sorry.' He rubbed a shaking hand across his wispy hair and Natalie felt a pang of sorrow for the man. He knew very little about his daughter yet cared very deeply for her. The gap between them was wide and she hoped she'd never face such a void with Josh.

She steeled herself and said, 'This might seem an odd question but has Hattie ever lost her temper with you?'

'Hattie!' His face broke into a smile. 'She's the most mild-mannered person you could ever hope to meet.'

'She's never raised her voice or fallen out with you?' asked Lucy.

'No.' The smile was still there.

'Or complained about any of her housemates to you?'

The smile faltered. 'No. What are you suggesting?'

Natalie replied, 'We're trying to establish why Hattie might have gone off without telling anyone where she's gone, and why she isn't answering her phone.'

He sat back with a small chuckle. 'Because she's Hattie. That's her nature. She goes off on a whim and wanders back a few days later. She's a free spirit. Exactly like her mother.'

It was a good hour later, after talking to Mr Caldwell, that Natalie and Lucy stood outside 59 Eastview Avenue, the house three doors down from where Gemma and Fran had lived. They wanted to talk to the person who had known Fran the best and could maybe help them decide if she had committed suicide.

Rhiannon answered the door, a pair of huge round glasses balanced on her snub nose. She peered myopically at Natalie, Lucy and the university counsellor – a woman in her thirties called Katherine, who Natalie had requested accompany them – and invited them inside.

'There's nobody else here but me,' she said.

'It was you we wanted to talk to. Can we go into the sitting room?' Natalie asked kindly.

'Sure. I'm in the middle of writing an essay. It's due in tomorrow,' the girl burbled as she walked, obviously nervous about the intrusion. The singsong voice became hesitant and she asked, 'Have you found the person who attacked Gemma?'

Natalie refrained from answering and followed Rhiannon into the sitting room – much like the one in the house where Fran and Gemma had lived, but furnished even more sparsely, with a couple of beige beanbags strewn on the floor, a green armchair and three hardback chairs that were better suited to the kitchen. There was no television in this room, only a CD player, thick with dust.

'Sit down, Rhiannon,' she said, indicating the armchair and choosing one of the chairs for herself. Lucy and the counsellor did likewise, pulling up the wooden chairs with cushioned seats and forming a semicircle around the girl. Rhiannon flopped into the armchair and rested her hands on her thighs. Natalie noticed the recently applied false nails – long yellow talons, seemingly at odds with the grey sweatshirt that read *Girl with Curves*, long mustard cardigan, black leggings and fluffy boot slippers. Behind the lenses, her eyes were made up with cream and gold eyeshadow, her eyeliner on perfectly, eyebrows groomed and her foundation flawless. Rhiannon took care with her physical appearance but it struck Natalie as odd that she should make such an effort if she only intended working on an assignment. Maybe she rather liked one of her fellow housemates and hoped to impress them when they returned.

Natalie had waited until she'd heard that Fran's parents had been notified about their daughter's death before returning to Eastview Avenue, and she now had to learn what she could from Fran's closest friend. There could be no beating around the bush and no way to soften such a blow. 'I'm afraid that I have bad news. Fran is dead. I'm very sorry. I know you were close.'

The girl threw her hands up in front of her mouth and gasped loudly.

'Is there anything we can get for you, or anyone we can contact?'

'No… no.' Her eyes began to fill. 'This can't be happening. I saw her earlier. She was fine. I don't understand.'

Natalie tried to calm the girl by talking quietly. 'You've met DS Carmichael and this is Katherine Weber. She's one of the university counsellors and she'll stay with you for a while after we leave.'

The reply was a feeble, 'Okay.'

'If you feel up to it, I'd like to continue with a few questions. They won't take long.'

The tears had spilt over her lashes and she didn't stop them. 'I'll... try.'

'Thank you. Can you tell me when you last saw Fran?'

'This morning... about ten. I went to her place.'

'How long did you stay there?'

'Only a quarter of an hour. I had to get on with my work.'

'Did Fran say if she was going out?'

The girl blinked back more tears and swiped at her cheek. 'No. She wanted to finish reading one of her set texts and prepare for a tutorial. I've not spoken to her since then. I've had my head down, working on an essay.'

'I see. Tell me, was Fran unhappy at all?'

'Yes... no... I mean... sort of. She got a lot of grief from her ma about not visiting her grandmother often enough, but she didn't want to go back.'

'Was there any reason for that?'

'Her grandmother's got dementia and Fran couldn't bear seeing her in that state. She visited a few times last year but every time she went, she'd come back to Samford depressed, and I think her grandmother has got much worse since then. Fran had such a shitty time growing up and had so much trouble she had to move out and live with her gran. She hated going back to East Toxteth and being reminded of her old life.'

'What sort of life was that?'

'A rubbish one. She told me some pretty scary shit about what it was like living there. She knew if she went home, she'd be dragged back into all of it again – the gang culture, the drugs and watching her back all the time. We talked about renting a place together during the Christmas holidays when term ends. That way we could both stay in Samford. We were going to try and get jobs.' She pressed her fingertips against her forehead and Natalie coaxed her on.

'Did she seem depressed to you at all?'

'No! What? Are you saying she killed herself? She wouldn't do that.' Her voice rose in indignation.

'She never mentioned taking her own life?' Natalie asked again.

Rhiannon shook her head. 'Never.'

'Tell me what else you can about Fran.'

'She was a great friend.' Rhiannon's voice cracked and her voice became thick with emotion.

'I understand you were best friends and you'll want to be loyal to her memory, but if she was involved in anything we should know about, please tell me.'

'She wasn't involved in anything. Honestly. She only wanted to get a degree and move on.'

'What about her relationship with her housemates?'

'She got on well with them.'

'Really?'

'Yes.'

'Apart from Gemma.'

'She put up with Gemma. Gemma was full-on, if you know what I mean? Fran was actually quite introverted and backed off from people like that. She got along with Evie and Taylor and a couple of others on the same course as us, and Hattie.'

'About Hattie, have you heard from her?'

'No. Is she okay?'

'We're trying to locate her. She told Fran she was going to stay with an old schoolfriend.'

'I don't know anything about that. Hattie can be a bit… dreamy at times and does stuff like that. She'll suddenly go off to join a march or protest about a windfarm. She probably has gone to visit one of her hippy friends.'

'Do you know anything about Hattie helping a homeless charity?'

The girl snivelled again and replied miserably, 'Yes, we all helped out for a week. Hattie was raising awareness and roped us all in: me, Fran and Gemma. She's always supporting one good cause or another and none of us really wanted to do it but it was okay. Fran really got into it. She even considered signing up to help more often but she was already on the student social committee so it was a bit much, especially as we're both top of the list for jobs at the students' union bar… to earn money to rent together over the holidays.'

The girl started to cry harder. Natalie had to get her to refocus. 'You only did the volunteer work for a week?'

Rhiannon choked back the sobs and rubbed under her eyes where her make-up was running. 'Yes. Hattie does it regularly. Once a week, I think.'

'What's the name of the charity?'

'Samford Help for Homeless.'

Natalie would pass the name on to Murray if he hadn't already found out about it. There might be some connection between the girls and the charity, or the people they'd met while delivering food.

'You said Fran was quite shy.'

'She was.'

'Did she have any serious relationships during her time at Samford?'

'She really liked Ryan but no, there's been no one I know about.' She scrubbed her shaved head, grazing it with her nails. 'Though maybe there *was* somebody. A couple of weeks ago, I was chilling in her room and suggested we went out together later that day. She got all cagey and said she was meeting somebody else later. It wasn't like her to be secretive, so I messed about a bit and kept on at her and I asked, just as a joke mind you, if she was seeing a married man. Well, she totally lost it with me. I was shocked but I saw her the following day and everything was fine. She never mentioned it again and I didn't bring it up.'

'You have no idea who it might have been?'

'No. I didn't ask again. I didn't want to fall out with her. She was my best mate.' She stopped talking and looked miserably at Natalie.

'Has she had any run-ins with anybody recently?'

'I can't think of any.'

'She didn't mention any problems with any other students or any unwanted attention?'

Rhiannon's eyes had filled again and she struggled to reply. 'No.'

Lucy left the room to get some tissues for the girl.

'What about her housemates? Did she have disagreements with them?' Natalie asked.

'Nothing major, only about whose turn it was to clean the bathroom or kitchen.'

'Did she complain about any of them?'

'Only Gemma and only when she was annoyed with her. Fran wasn't mean at all. It's going to be dreadful without her. I don't have any other friends. None like her.'

Lucy reappeared, a toilet roll in her hand. 'I got this from the downstairs bathroom.' She passed it to Rhiannon, who took it, pulled off several strips and blew her nose.

'What time are you expecting the others to come home? We'd like to talk to them too.'

'I really don't know. I didn't speak to any of them today other than to say hi. I'm not especially friends with them. I talk to Libby sometimes but she's rarely here. She's nearly always on campus, working. That's why I went around to see Fran as often as I did.'

'You don't have contact details for them?'

'Not without my phone.' She shook her head and sniffed again. 'When can I have my phone back? I want to speak to my da.'

Natalie noted she hadn't said she was going to ring her mother. 'I'll see if the lab has finished with it, and if they have, we'll return it and your laptop later today.'

Katherine, who'd been silent throughout, now spoke quietly. 'You can use my phone, Rhiannon.' The girl nodded thanks.

Natalie was done for the moment. 'Thank you for talking to us.' She studied the girl's face, which was dropping in misery. Rhiannon dabbed under her eyes with fresh pieces from the toilet roll and raised her eyes to Natalie.

'I can't believe this; Gemma and Fran dead, and Hattie gone. What's happening?'

'We're getting to the bottom of it. I'd like you to stay here for the rest of the evening. We've contacted the university and Katherine will talk you through what'll happen regarding studies and counselling services. If you think of anything at all that you think is relevant, ring this number,' said Natalie, and she passed a business card to the girl. 'Have you any questions you want to ask us?'

'No.'

'If you think of any after we've gone, either ask Katherine or write them down and we'll answer them next time we come by. And one last thing, if any journalists contact you, please don't speak to them.'

They left Rhiannon with the counsellor and headed up the road to confront Lennox and Ryan once more. As they walked along the pavement, Natalie rang Mike.

'Has anyone had a chance to examine Fran's mobile yet?'

'It's on the table as we speak.'

'Her friend, Rhiannon, thinks Fran was seeing a man, possibly a married one. Would you let me know if there's anything on it to suggest who he was?'

'Certainly shall. I heard back from the officers I sent to Fran's room a short while ago. There's no sign of a farewell note or a letter from a secret admirer.'

'Nothing?'

'They checked her desk, bookcase and folders but didn't find anything.'

'Then we still don't know if she intended taking her life or if she was killed. Shit! Okay, thanks. I'll try the mobile provider for a list of contact numbers. I'll talk to you later.'

She hadn't intended to sound brusque but she knew Mike would understand. This was an investigation and there was no place for anything other than professionalism. She rang Ian and requested contact details from Fran's mobile provider.

'I've already asked for them. They came in five minutes ago and I'm working my way through them now. I've also been through her social media accounts and found nothing to hint she was considering taking her own life.'

'Rhiannon seems to think that's unlikely too.'

'Reckon Fran could have been murdered then?'

'It's looking increasingly like a possibility. Is Murray in the office?'

'Yes, I'll put him on.' There was a murmuring and the phone was passed across. Murray came onto the line.

'Natalie?'

'You might already know but we think Hattie was doing some volunteer work for Samford Help for Homeless.'

'That's right. I spoke to Julietta Michigan, who runs the charity. Hattie began volunteering a month ago. She started out helping every evening then cut it down to Wednesdays only, because of her studies. She delivered hot meals and clothes collected from the office at eight and then distributed them. She and Julietta worked together as a team, apart from last Wednesday. Julietta had a heavy cold and Hattie went alone. I said I'd talk to her later to get further details but she has no idea where Hattie is either, only that she's expecting her as usual this coming Wednesday.'

'No sightings of Hattie?'

'Nothing.'

'This is crazy. What about her car?'

'Nothing.'

'We need to step this up and involve MisPers. Sort it out for me, will you? I want her details sent to every station.'

'I'll arrange that. Wait a minute. Ian wants to talk to you again.'

Natalie couldn't make out the exchange between them but Ian's voice had altered and sounded wary. 'You're not going to like this.'

'Like what?'

'David's telephone number is on this call list. Fran contacted David several times over the last four weeks.'

CHAPTER EIGHTEEN

SUNDAY, 18 NOVEMBER – NIGHT

Natalie called her son from the car to warn him she would be home late but made no mention of David. Josh sounded upbeat and said in that case, he wouldn't head back to the flat until nine, but would hopefully catch her before he went to bed. Neither Lennox nor Ryan were at home, and she and Lucy were heading back to the station, where she'd await David's arrival for another interview. The idea he was involved in this case was preposterous, yet faced with facts, she couldn't ignore the possibility that he was; until she could clear his name, he was a suspect.

The Sunday evening traffic had eased with most folk back in their homes, preparing for the new week, and the squad car raced through green traffic lights, past the lit supermarket car park where a group of skateboarders, in traditional skateboarding uniform, including baseball caps with peaks facing the rear, used the disabled ramp and tarmac to show off their abilities. Natalie idly watched a lad pop his board away from him, kick and flip it 180 degrees before landing squarely on it. The movement was fast and slick and had clearly been practised numerous times. Josh had never shown any interest in the activity and she'd been glad. She hadn't wanted him to entertain anything that might result in broken bones. Her gloomy thoughts were interrupted by Pinkney, who rang her mobile. She put it on speakerphone so Lucy could hear what he had to say.

'I've not completed the full post-mortem yet but I think I know how Fran died,' he said. 'I believe she ingested a harmful substance, and my suspicions are based on three important discoveries. The first, acute oesophageal mucosal injury in the form of lesions and red spots undoubtedly caused by ingestion of an acid. The second, her stomach contains close to a litre of acid fluid which is dark in colour and contains blood clots, or what we call grume, which look like coffee grounds. Lastly, her kidneys are showing significant signs of renal failure. I can't be positive without a toxicology report, but I'd say these all point to one substance – oxalic acid.'

'What do you know about it?' Natalie asked.

'It's a tasteless white crystalline substance that dissolves in water to create a colourless solution. Less than a teaspoon of this stuff would kill an adult. It's also inherent in some foods such as broccoli, sprouts, spinach, peanuts, cucumbers and even potatoes and tea, although in such minor amounts as to not harm humans. It is, however, also present in slightly higher amounts in rhubarb leaves, which you may know are harmful to eat. Apparently, during the First World War, people ate the leaves as a vegetable and died of too much oxalic acid.'

'Could Fran have done the same? Eaten too much of it?'

'No. There was only liquid in her stomach. She hadn't eaten anything for at least four to five hours. I'd say she drank it.'

'Thank you, Pinkney. I'll let Mike know.'

'I already contacted him. They're examining the bottles they removed from the crime scene in case they contain any leftover oxalic acid crystals.'

She thanked him again. Lucy kept her focus on the road but added her thoughts. 'One victim dies of shock after sulphuric acid is thrown in her face and another dies through drinking oxalic acid. I'd say that wasn't a coincidence, even if we are dealing with different types of acid. Do you think Fran deliberately drank it?'

'There's a chance she did but why didn't she leave a farewell note or letter of explanation behind, and why on earth would she hide herself in an abandoned doorway under blankets? Why not stay inside her room where she wouldn't be discovered for a while until somebody unlocked her door? I can't help but feel somebody left her in that street.'

'I suppose there's an outside chance this was an accidental death and somebody panicked and moved her body.'

'Two accidental deaths in the space of two days and two young women who shared the same house. And... both cases involved acid. I don't buy that.'

'No, neither do I, really. I'm trying to make sense of it.'

'Can't do that without evidence and facts,' Natalie replied. She wondered how much David knew about oxalic acid.

David sat down in the same seat he'd used the last time Natalie had interviewed him, earlier that day. He was also wearing the same clothes and hadn't shaved. His eyes were dim and his breath smelt sour.

'I didn't attack Gemma,' he said as soon as he sat down. The duty lawyer who had been asked to sit in with him cautioned him to say nothing and to wait to be questioned.

'I'd like to talk to you about another student. Do you know this young woman?'

She slid Fran's picture across the table. David released a low moan.

'Do you know her?'

'Yes. Listen, Natalie—'

She held up her hand and said quietly, 'DI Ward.'

'Oh, for fuck's sake!' David pressed his hands to his face, covering it while he struggled for self-control. 'Could I have a glass of water?' he asked.

'Certainly.'

Murray headed outside and no sooner had he left than David leant across the table. 'Natalie, for the love of our children, will you please let this drop? I'm not guilty of anything. This is a fucking nightmare that I've somehow become entangled in, and I can't cope with it, especially on top of everything else – you, Leigh, Josh!' The stench of alcohol hit her full on. His mention of their children incensed her. How dare he bring them into this!

'Would you please advise your client he is to address me correctly and that we require his full cooperation.'

Her cold manner brought him back to his senses and he sat back. Murray entered with a plastic tumbler of water that David took with thanks and downed like a man parched in the desert.

'I repeat, do you know this young woman?'

'Yes.'

'How do you know her?'

'I stuck a card up on the university noticeboard offering help and extra tuition. I needed to earn some money and I thought if I could attract a few students to help them out with assignments or whatever, it would at least be something. Fran saw the card and got in touch with me. She wanted assistance with some work she had to hand in and we arranged to meet in a coffee shop in town. I met her twice. That's all – twice.'

'What was the name of this coffee shop?'

'It's the Costa on the high street.'

'When did you meet her?'

'I don't know for sure.'

Natalie said nothing but passed across the call list taken from Fran's phone with his number highlighted in blue.

'You made five calls to her last week. None of them lasted longer than thirty seconds. Why was that?'

He rolled his eyes. 'She didn't want to talk to me and eventually she blocked my number.'

'Why didn't she want to talk to you?'

'She was being unreasonable.' He hung his head.

'Unreasonable? How was she being unreasonable?'

'It doesn't matter. She just was.'

Murray looked up and said, quietly, 'Maybe she didn't like you pestering her, like you pestered Sasha?' He hit his mark.

'Shit, no! It wasn't like that at all.'

'Explain why she didn't want you to ring her then,' said Natalie.

'This is all pretty embarrassing for me.'

'Fran was found dead earlier today,' said Natalie and let the news sink in.

David shut his eyes tightly and shook his head. 'This is nuts. I had nothing whatsoever to do with her death.' He opened his eyes with a weary sigh. 'She owed me money. I chased her up for it but she refused to pay me. That's why I said she was unreasonable. She contacted me to help her with a tricky translation. She wanted to do well in the assignment and I coached her with it. Afterwards, when I asked for my fee, she simply wouldn't cough up the money.'

'You were doing students' work for them? You were helping them cheat.' Natalie kept the scorn out of her voice.

'No, I wasn't! I haven't fallen that low. I pointed her in the right direction.'

'But her tutor could have done that, or one of her friends on the same course.'

'Apparently, according to Fran, university staff are hard pressed to spend extra time with students, so much of the workload falls on the individuals themselves. Fran had had some guidance but she'd failed her last translation assignment, and if she'd failed again, she'd have been forced to retake that part of the course. I tackled the task in a different way, using techniques I've picked up over the years. There's a knack to translating that extends beyond a foreign language dictionary.'

Natalie accepted his explanation. David had an ability to think in three languages and speak them all fluently even though he'd been unable to use this talent in recent months. Work had simply dried up. Even her attempts to find him employment in courts or at the police station, acting as a translator, had come to nought. Although that part of his account was credible, there was still something troubling her. 'How come she gave you her phone number? If she intended ripping you off, I'd have thought she'd have been more careful about handing it over to you.'

'My phone number is on all the cards I put up in the university so students can contact me, which is what Fran did and as a result I had her number.'

'She didn't withhold the number?'

'No, and if she had, I'd have probably asked her for it for the sole purpose of making arrangements to meet up.'

Natalie tapped the call list. 'I see the first time she rang you was on Wednesday, October the twenty-fourth.'

'That would have been the day she rang to ask if I could help her. We arranged to meet the following day.'

'At the Costa?'

'That's right. She brought her translations with her and we went through the ones that had received fail marks. I spent well over an hour with her, going through them and helping her understand her errors. It went well and she asked if I could help her with the one she was currently tasked with. We arranged to meet that Friday but she rang the following day to change the day to Sunday.' He pointed at a second number. 'That was when she rang me to change the date.'

'You saw her again on Sunday the twenty-eighth?'

'Yes. We met at eleven at the same place.'

'She rang the following Tuesday. Was that for more help?'

'No, that was to say she was going home the following weekend and she'd pay me when she got back.'

'And then all these calls?' said Natalie, pointing at the received calls highlighted in blue from David's phone.

'That was me, phoning to ask when she was going to pay and getting the brush-off. At first, she claimed she was waiting for some money from her parents and then she didn't have it. I needed the money and kept ringing her but she threatened to report me for harassment and I decided I'd have to cut my losses.'

Natalie inhaled deeply. As likely as this sounded, she had to remain impartial. 'I'd like to know your exact movements for today.'

David stared at the ceiling and then made an unconscious gesture she recognised – he rubbed the back of his neck, a sure tell that he was hiding something. He'd performed it on occasions in the past when hiding the truth about his gambling addiction. 'Apart from earlier, when I was here, being interviewed?'

'Yes.'

'I was at home.'

'All day?'

'All day. I have nowhere in particular to go.' He rubbed the spot again then dropped his hand.

'And can anyone back you up?'

'No, Natalie, they can't.' His words dripped sadness and regret but she was not for swaying. With his movements before and after the interview unaccounted for, she still had to consider him a suspect.

'We'll need to take a DNA sample from you,' she said.

He nodded and uttered a jaded, 'Go ahead.'

She terminated the interview and left Murray to take the sample. Her head and gut both said David couldn't be involved in this, but there was a question mark over his whereabouts and the tell-tale sign he was hiding something. She would have to dig deeper if she was to find out what that was, and there was only one sure way she could prove his innocence – by finding the real murderer.

A surprised Mike rang her when she was halfway up the stairs to the office. 'I hear David's been brought in for interview again.'

'That's right.'

'Really? You think he's behind this?'

'He knew both the victims and can't account for his whereabouts on Friday evening, or before 4 p.m. today when Murray collected him to bring him to the station, or after 4.50 p.m. when he left the station. I had no option but to talk to him again.'

'But David?'

'I know. I ought to discount him immediately but something's changed in him and Josh said he's been having violent outbursts and heavy drinking sessions. You see such a lot in this job and you learn not to jump to conclusions about people.'

'True, but I find it hard to believe David would do such a thing.'

There was a heavy pause and she said, 'We've been duped before by people we thought we could trust, haven't we? If I'd seen through—'

He grasped the meaning of her words immediately. She had no need to mention her daughter's killer, who they'd known and had confidence in. He rushed in with, 'If you want a friendly ear, you know where I am. Don't let this eat into you.'

'Thanks. I'm surprisingly okay at the moment. This is an investigation like any other and David is a potential suspect like many we have had in the past. I'll follow the facts and evidence and eventually the truth will come out. It always does.'

'Offer's open if you need it.'

'And I'll take you up on it... soon. I promise.'

She'd reached the top of the stairs, where she halted for a second until she caught sight of Lucy standing in front of the office, signalling at her. She strode towards her, hoping she had some good news, but Lucy's face said otherwise.

'We've found Hattie's car. It's in Samford railway station car park, but there's no sign of her. We sent officers over to break into it. Her mobile was found switched off and in the glove box. It's being taken to the tech team for examination. Looks like she's caught a train.'

'Can we find out which one?'

'There's a problem with that because there are no active cameras and the ticket office closed down over six months ago and was replaced by a self-service machine.'

'What about the car park? Surely there are cameras there?' She moved into the office, lit by ceiling lights which brightened the room considerably in sharp contrast to the blind-free windows – large black rectangles that framed the dark November sky.

'There's a number plate reading camera that logs each car's registration when it enters and exits. Apart from that there's nothing.'

'Then we ought to be able to tell what date and time she arrived there and work out which trains were leaving around that time,' Natalie said.

'Only if we can get hold of the machine operators, which is what Ian's trying to do at the moment.'

Ian looked up at the mention of his name and shook his head. 'Can't reach anyone. All the numbers go to an automated service and no one is available until tomorrow morning.'

Natalie cursed and chewed over the options. Getting hold of timetables and guessing where Hattie had gone wasn't efficient policing and would result in too much speculation. They'd have to wait for the relevant information from the car park before they could begin to deduce her movements and contact trains for surveillance footage or question guards.

'Is there any way we can find out what tickets were purchased from the ticket machine at the station?'

'Again, we need to talk to the company that owns the machine and there's nobody available,' said Ian. 'Needless to say, she might not have bought a ticket from the machine. She might have purchased it online, and if she did, the tech team will be able to tell us, but we know how stretched they are and we might not get that info until tomorrow. If she didn't, we'll have to try the first option.'

Natalie was inclined to agree. 'If only we could pinpoint her movements. Why haven't we heard back from her mobile providers yet? Have you chased them up, Ian? I'd like to know where she went before she headed to that car park. It might give us an idea of where she is.'

'I did but I've run across the same problem I've got here – lack of staff on a Sunday and nobody could approve my request.'

'Then we'll have to do what the rest of the country seems to have done and call it a day. We're flogging a dead horse here.'

Murray meandered in and sat down heavily. The chair groaned in protest. 'What's up?'

'We can't move on and make any progress tonight. It's time to turn off the lights and go home,' said Natalie.

'Good. I could do with some sleep. I'm knackered,' he replied and rubbed a hand across his five o'clock shadow.

'Aren't we all, big man,' said Lucy, turning off her computer and reaching for her bag. 'Some of us haven't slept in days.' She clamped her mouth shut and cast a look at Natalie, who returned a smile to allay her fears.

'Aurora keeping you awake?' she asked.

'Yes. I didn't mean to—'

'She's a couple of months old, isn't she? Some babies start sleeping through the night from about four months. Josh did. You might get lucky,' said Natalie, preventing Lucy from apologising. There was no need to pussyfoot around her all the time. People had lives and children and shouldn't feel they couldn't talk about them because they'd trigger an emotional outburst or upset her. 'You got any photos of her?'

Ian had packed up and left with a 'good night'. Lucy pulled her phone out of her bag, unlocked it and handed it to Natalie. The screensaver was of a beaming Bethany holding a chubby-faced baby with large blue eyes who looked at peace with the world.

Natalie smiled at the sight, studied the dimpled cheeks for a moment before handing back the phone. 'She's absolutely beautiful.'

Lucy looked at the picture and replied, 'Yes, she is. Thank you.'

'Try and snatch some sleep before she wakes you up,' Natalie replied.

Murray and Lucy left her alone to pack away. She ambled to the window overlooking the empty streets below. She'd taken another major step forward and been able to hold it together while looking at the picture and talking about Lucy's baby girl, but now tears trickled over her cheeks and she struggled to compose herself. She had photos of Leigh as a baby – a happy, smiling baby. Her daughter had had a sweet nature and Natalie missed her with every fibre of her being, but she reminded herself that her other child was only a few minutes away in her flat, and she wiped her cheeks. His father may have lost direction for now, but she hadn't, and Josh needed some normality in his life. As she turned out the lights, she thought of Fran's mother and of Sasha, who'd be experiencing the same set of emotions as Natalie. Tomorrow, staff would be back in their offices and behind their desks, and tomorrow, she'd get the answers she needed.

*

Gemma,

You and I are similar. I hide behind a mask and nobody knows the real me.

You also wear a mask. One that hides your fakeness. See, Gemma, I know you're fake. I can see right through you because we are the same. We're not what the world sees.

You aren't as warm-hearted as you make out, are you, Gemma? You surround yourself with people who worship the bloody ground you walk on to give yourself a sense of importance.

Your mask actually conceals an inner ugliness.
Mine hides my anger.
Everyone loves Gemma… bloody wonderful Gemma.
Fuck you, Gemma!
An Ex-Admirer

CHAPTER NINETEEN

MONDAY, 19 NOVEMBER – MORNING

Natalie woke at seven, having slept through the night. She found Josh up and mooching about the kitchen, hunting for something to eat. He lifted up the bread bin lid and shut it again.

'Hi. Sorry I missed you last night,' she said.

'It's fine. I got on with some reading for today and went to bed quite early.' She took in his fuzzy chin and realised he'd grown up in front of her very eyes. It only seemed a month ago that he was a painfully shy teenager, embarrassed about wearing braces on his teeth. Her heart lurched with affection and love for this man/boy, in his jogging bottoms and dressing gown that was too small for him, who'd become the most stable of all three of them. She produced a clean cream bowl from the dishwasher that was yet to be emptied and opened the cupboard to reveal a box of his favourite cereal that she'd purchased for the days he wanted to overnight at the flat.

'How's Pippa?' she asked.

'Good. We went for a walk around the estate.'

Pippa's mother managed some holiday cottages on a large country estate set close to the Peak District in Derbyshire, and Josh seemed to have found solace in spending time there among nature, and in the company of the girl, who was also taking A-levels.

'I'll try and get back earlier tonight. Got a bit of a heavy case on at the moment.'

The cereal tinkled against the china bowl as he poured it from the packet. 'No probs. I have plenty to get on with.' He doused it with milk and sat down to spoon it into his mouth.

'I'm going to Castergate before work,' she said. She'd made the decision some point before she'd dropped off to sleep.

'To speak to Dad?' he mumbled through a mouthful of chocolate-flavoured granola.

'Yes. I wanted to check you're quite sure you want to live here, or wherever I end up, rather than go back.'

He swallowed before answering. 'Go back? No way. I'm deadly serious, Mum. Would you tell him I'll meet up if he wants now and again, but I don't want to stay in the house?'

'I'll speak to him. He might want to see you to talk about it.'

'Yeah. I suppose so, but I don't want to do it when he's in a shit mood. I'll ring him first and arrange a meet-up.'

'There's something else you need to know. We had to interview him as part of our investigation. He knew two of the victims. Has he mentioned seeing anyone to you?'

'What, like a girlfriend?'

'Just people he'd met recently and become friendly with.'

'He's barely managed to say hello to me the last three months, Mum, let alone tell me what he's been up to.' His spoon hovered over the bowl.

'Did you know he'd started advertising translation services at Samford University?'

'He didn't tell me about that but I know he had some cards printed to put up in the local shop windows. He asked me if I could stick them up in our window at work but it's against company policy.' Josh had unwittingly validated part of his father's story.

She turned on the kettle. It wasn't going to be easy to talk to David but it had to be done. It was yet another step she had to take on this difficult new path.

'You want a cup of tea?'

'No, thanks. I'll stick to orange juice. Is it okay if I grab a shower in a minute?'

'Help yourself. I'm done in the bathroom. Do you need a lift into college?'

'It's sorted. One of my friends will pick me up.'

It was odd to imagine Josh's friends old enough to drive. To her mind they were still schoolboys and yet they were all becoming young adults and discovering their independence. She tried not to think of her daughter, who would be forever young.

The morning was dark grey, as if life had been sucked from nature. Even the sea buckthorn bushes with their silver leaves and orange berries that normally filled a corner of St Mary's churchyard in Castergate were without colour. In the ensuing weeks after her daughter had been buried here, Natalie had visited every single day and stared silently at the white headstone bearing Leigh's name. She'd rearranged the flowers in vases and the trinkets and heart-shaped pots endlessly, fussing over them, adding to them, and all the while she'd forced herself to come to terms with the fact her daughter was buried in this cemetery, and wasn't at home, lying on the settee, laughing uncontrollably at some comedy film, or singing in the bathroom. Leigh had filled all their lives with her presence, and coming to terms with the fact she was no longer with them was nigh on impossible. So, Natalie had visited the graveyard, sometimes twice in the same day, and brought more flowers or soft toys, and piled them up on the mound of grass until the spot overflowed and she knew she was bordering on insanity. Over the last month, she'd cut her trips down to once a week. It was better to distance herself, but there was no way she could come to Castergate and not tend her child's grave.

She wandered along the narrow path, passing headstones that had been there for decades and were now pitted and weathered with age. The further along she walked, the newer and fresher the stones appeared to be, some in jet-black granite with gold lettering, others grey stone, or white marble. Some bore fresh flowers while others only had wilted stems or empty jugs or artificial posies that had faded to off-white. She could never let Leigh's or Zoe's graves become neglected.

Her heartbeat quickened as she approached the spot where her daughter had been laid to rest, adjacent to her best friend, Zoe, who'd been murdered with her. The freshly tied roses in water-filled gift bags that she carried, one for each of the girls, would last a couple of weeks. As she drew closer still, she spotted a familiar figure: Zoe's mother, Rowena. Before the terrible tragedy, they'd got along well, but ever since, Rowena had kept her distance. Rowena was hunched over Zoe's grave and hadn't seen or heard Natalie – who was about to leave and return later – when suddenly Rowena got to her feet, turned around and looked directly at her. Natalie was fixed to the spot, not sure what to expect. Rowena's eyes blazed and her fists clenched, then she spotted the flower gift bags in Natalie's hands and her shoulders sagged.

'It's you. You're the person who's been bringing Zoe flowers,' she said. When Natalie nodded, she continued with, 'I wondered who'd been leaving the flower bags. I thought it might have been a schoolfriend. I should have known.'

'I can never make it up to you, and if I could turn back the clock, I would in a heartbeat.'

Rowena stopped her with a slow shake of the head. 'I don't want this any more, Natalie. I don't want to hate you and I don't want to blame you. You've lost as much as I have. In some ways, you've lost far more than me. Look at you! I hardly recognised you. You look... different. I'm sorry.'

'No. I'm sorry. I'm truly sorry we couldn't save them.' She walked towards the woman and held out the gift bag with Zoe's name written on it.

Rowena took it, lifted it and admired the pale pink buds that would open over the coming days. 'They're lovely.' She crouched and put the offering close to the girl's headstone, murmuring as she did, 'These are from Leigh's mum. Aren't they beautiful? And your favourite colour. I have to go to work now. I'll be back later. Love you, baby girl.' She got to her feet once more and said, 'I'll see you again, Natalie. Thank you for the lovely gesture.' With that, she made her way up the path Natalie had followed, leaving her alone in the cemetery.

Her words were sufficient for Natalie to understand they'd overcome a hurdle. There was no more anger or bitterness from Zoe's mother and it gave Natalie a sense of relief. It was her turn to squat in front of a white marble stone that bore her child's name. She removed the flowers she'd brought last time she'd visited and replaced them with the fresh, moving a soft teddy bear in a pink bow to one side to make space for them. Then she stared in silence at Leigh's name engraved on the stone. The heartfelt words she had for her daughter were all in her head, and not spoken aloud.

David wasn't as forgiving as Rowena and kept Natalie standing on the doorstep. Her nose wrinkled at the miasma of stale alcohol and body odour that accompanied his words. 'You haven't come to arrest me, have you?' he asked.

'I've come to talk about Josh.'

He let out an irritated sound, a *pfft*, that was accompanied by a rolling of his eyes.

'He wants to stay with me for a while.'

'Fine.'

'Is that all you can say? Fine?'

'Not much point in saying anything else, is there?'

She studied his narrowed eyes and jutting chin and decided it wasn't worth trying to appeal to his better nature. At the moment, he wasn't exhibiting one.

'Then he'll stay with me for the foreseeable, and when the house sale goes through, I'll buy somewhere else to live together.'

'You done?'

'David, I don't know what's eating you but you are being incredibly disagreeable. We're talking about our son and his happiness. This isn't about us, it's about a young man whose life has been turned upside down.'

'All our lives have been turned upside down. You and he seem to be getting along fine. If he wants to live with you, I'm not going to stop him. In fact, it's probably better he does. As for the house, there's a viewing tomorrow. You might get your wish. Have you checked out my DNA yet?'

'I'm not here to discuss the investigation.'

'Then I don't have anything else to say to you.'

She'd never known him to act like this. 'Josh said he'll ring you and come and talk to you.'

'Whatever. He knows where to find me.' With that, he retreated into the house and slammed the door so it reverberated in the aged wooden frame.

Natalie was tempted to pound on it and tell him what she thought of him but that sort of negativity was counterproductive. He'd decided to be uncommunicative and cold-hearted. She was done with him!

'Morning, Natalie,' said Lucy.

'Morning. Get any rest?'

'Yes, Aurora slept right through until five, which really helped. I've been on to the authorities at Samford railway station and they're going through their logs to see what time Hattie's car entered the car park.'

'Excellent. That's a start. I was thinking about her phone. Why would she make a train journey without it?'

'I wondered if she'd headed to the eco-commune in spite of what Ocean told me. They are anti-technology there, and if she's in hiding, she'll have deliberately left it behind to make sure she can't be traced.'

Natalie let out a hiss of exasperation. 'I'll ask Monmouthshire police to try the commune again, maybe this time with a warrant. If she's hiding there, I want her dragged out. This is bloody ridiculous.' Although she was irritated by the fact Hattie might actually be at the commune, the fact her mobile had been left switched off in her car was also of concern. If something serious had befallen Hattie, it would turn the investigation on its head. She rang her Welsh colleague again and made it clear that she wanted Hattie Caldwell found.

Murray appeared with a phone in his hand. 'This belongs to Rhiannon. It's clean, no references to harming Gemma and nothing suspicious on it. Shall I get somebody to return it to her?'

'Yes, please. What's happened to Fran's phone?'

'Still upstairs. They've not finished examining it yet, or Hattie's.'

'Okay, while you're all here, let's have a quick run-through. As you know we're concentrating on locating Hattie. Fran claimed Hattie had gone to visit a friend and would be back today but something doesn't feel right about this, especially as she rang me on Saturday and didn't show up at the meeting. With regards to Gemma, who's been dealing with all the statements taken from the people inside the library at the time of the attack?'

'Me. I've been through them all and there were no witnesses,' said Ian.

'Oh, crap. I was hoping we'd missed something.'

'No, and I also took statements from everyone who was on the bus she took Friday evening, and not one of them noticed anything suspicious; a couple of people said she got off the bus at the library stop alone,' said Ian.

Natalie was perplexed. She had no firm suspects and several loose ends to sort through and, looking at the expression on Dan

Tasker's face as he marched in the direction of the office, another problem.

'Can I have a word with you, Natalie?'

She moved into the corridor to listen to what he had to say.

'There are reporters outside. Somebody has found out about the victims living in the same house and they want answers. I'd like you to join me and give them a few crumbs.'

'We don't have anything to offer.'

'Then we'll have to stick to a more general script.'

'Why do you want me there?' she asked.

He had the grace to look shamefaced for a moment. 'There'll be interest in the fact you're leading the investigation and that might buy us some time.'

'Because I am the detective at HQ whose daughter was tragically murdered on my watch?' she replied, her voice remaining calm in spite of her rising anger.

'You know how it works, Natalie. We need some space to operate efficiently. We won't get it if we have the media watching our every movement. It'll only be for a minute.'

'Let's get it over with,' she replied and headed towards the stairs. 'I'll do all the talking.'

'Good, because I have nothing to say to them.'

He stopped her at the foot of the stairs, a hand on her wrist. 'I understand how you feel but you can see I'm right about this. I wouldn't ask you to do this unless I felt it was the correct approach.'

'I know, sir.' She adjusted her blouse, ensuring it was tucked into her skirt. She wasn't as fastidious as Dan about her appearance but she wasn't going to appear on the front page as anything other than efficient and tidy. Side by side they exited the atrium, which was light even on this dull day, to popping flashbulbs and journalists, jostling for position and clamouring for her attention.

'Natalie, can you confirm that the victims are both students?'

'DI Ward, is it true the victims shared the same house?'

'Natalie—'

Dan lifted up a hand to silence them while Natalie stared over the heads of those in front of her. She maintained focus on the dark trunks of the sycamore trees at the far side of the car park and kept her arms folded behind her back to ensure nobody would spot her trembling hands.

Dan made his statement, succinct and to the point. 'Good morning. I can confirm that DI Natalie Ward is leading the investigation into the suspicious deaths of two students from Samford University. We are following a number of leads and hope to reach a swift outcome. We'll be happy to talk to you once we have further information. Thank you all for your time.'

Light bulbs flashed one after another and Natalie tried hard not to blink in the face of the blinding glares directed at her.

'DI Ward, can you confirm that both victims are female?' The journalist closest to her held up a recording device.

Dan responded, 'You'll appreciate at this stage we can't release much information, but when we are able to, we'll release a statement.'

He took a step backwards and prepared to depart when a voice Natalie recognised shouted, 'Having suffered such a recent tragic loss, does DI Ward feel she is sufficiently recovered to lead this sensitive investigation?' The speaker, Bev Gardner, journalist for a local paper, was wearing a leopard-print full-length coat, her hair tucked under a felt hat. Bev took as much care over her appearance as Dan did. Her face showed no sympathy and Natalie felt her pulse quicken. This woman had written about her private life too often in the past. Natalie bristled, ready to snap at the woman, but Dan took over. 'I can assure you DI Ward is *exactly* the right person to lead this investigation and she needs to return to it immediately. Thank you. That's all.'

The shouts followed them as they retreated into headquarters but Natalie strode confidently, willing herself to show no signs of weakness. The glass doors opened and sucked them inside, away from the baying journalists. They passed reception and moved deeper into the sanctuary of the building, past the stairs to the lifts that Natalie rarely took, where they halted.

'Thank you,' said Dan. The lift doors slid smoothly apart and he gestured for her to go in first. He pressed the button for the first floor and continued to speak as they ascended. 'That should appease them for a while. Have you located this potential witness yet?'

'No, sir. We've found her car and my team's looking into the possibility she caught a train to stay elsewhere for a few days. As soon as we have anything, we'll let you know.'

He stared hard at her. 'I meant it. You are the best person for this job.'

'Then I'd better get back to it and do something to warrant that praise.'

The lift came to a smooth stop, and as the gap in the doors widened, he waved in the direction of her office with the flourish of a head waiter indicating the way to a reserved table. 'I'll leave you to it.'

Natalie exited onto her floor and marched along the corridor, teeth clenched so hard her jaw began to ache. She hated fucking journalists!

'Did it go okay?' asked Murray, glancing at her face.

'As well as you'd expect. Any developments?'

'Oh, yes. Hattie's car entered the car park at seventeen minutes past ten on Saturday evening.'

Natalie slid onto her seat with ease and reached for the file containing information on Hattie. 'What trains left around that time?'

'There were seven trains between 10.25 p.m. and 11.21 p.m.,' said Lucy. 'Three of them, including the 10.25 p.m. train, were destined for Birmingham, and three were headed to Manchester. There was also a train to Crewe at 11.21 p.m.'

'Then it would appear she wasn't headed to this eco-commune in Wales, unless she planned to change trains,' said Natalie.

Lucy was quick to answer. 'You can change at Birmingham and again at Bristol to reach Cardiff.'

Natalie drummed her fingers on top of the file. That was quite late for her to travel, and would mean she'd have arrived well after midnight. In spite of his denial, had Hattie gone to visit her ex-husband? 'This isn't right. We should have traced her by now and where was she between the time she rang me at 4.20 p.m. and the time she arrived at Samford railway station? That's six hours unaccounted for.'

Lucy lifted her hands. 'We've no idea. MisPers haven't come up with anything and they haven't been able to locate her car on any other surveillance cameras or CCTV.'

'Her sudden disappearance is worrying me, especially as we now have two female victims from the same house. Okay, moving on, talk to Ryan and Lennox. Obviously, they're the only remaining housemates, and Lennox's alibi wasn't rock-solid for Friday evening. Then there's Ryan. Although he had witnesses to confirm his whereabouts on Friday night, he might still have ordered the attack on Gemma. We need to dig deeper. I can't work out why either of them would kill Gemma or Fran but we have to eliminate them, if nothing else.' She pressed her lips together and tried to think who else could be responsible. The only other person they had in mind also had no concrete alibi – David. She was determined to pinpoint the whereabouts of Lennox and Ryan, so why should she dismiss him so easily? She straightened her shoulders. Like it or not, David's claims that he was at home Friday evening and Sunday, before they interviewed him, needed looking into too. She rang his mobile provider. They'd be able to confirm if his phone had moved over the last forty-eight hours, and he'd better watch out if he'd been lying to her.

CHAPTER TWENTY

'Fran's dead?' Lennox looked like he was about to be sick.

'I'm very sorry,' said Natalie. They'd finally managed to track down both him and Ryan, and they were now in front of her and Murray in the sitting room at 53 Eastview Avenue.

'Did you see her yesterday?' Natalie asked.

Lennox shook his head. 'No. I didn't get up until mid-afternoon and then I went to the lab and after that, I went into town.'

Natalie turned her attention to Ryan. 'What about you? Did you speak to Fran?'

'I saw her late morning. She asked to borrow my mobile to ring her mother. You had confiscated hers and she needed to ring home because it was her grandmother's birthday. I loaned her it and she brought it back about twenty minutes later.'

'That was generous of you.' Murray fixed his eyes on Ryan, who merely shrugged.

'She had no phone. I didn't mind.'

'How did Fran seem?' Natalie asked.

'Low. Fran was always a bit aggressive, whatever the situation. It was her personality, but when she returned the phone she seemed deflated.'

'Did she say what she was going to do next?'

'She mumbled something about needing a stiff drink after the call and sorting out some shit, but didn't expand on it. I asked her if she was okay and she said she was fine. I didn't see her again and I went out soon afterwards. I play rugby for the university and we had an away match at Leeds. We went to their union bar afterwards and got hammered.'

'Can either of you think where Hattie might be?'

Natalie was met with head shakes. Lennox kept his head down the entire time.

'Lennox, is there anything you can add?'

The young man shook his head again but she noticed he was clutching his hands together so tightly his knuckles had turned white.

'Lennox?'

'Nothing. I don't know where she is.'

'Are you sure?'

'I don't have a clue. If I knew where Hattie was, I'd tell you. This is all really weird. First Gemma, then Fran and now Hattie has vanished. What's going on?'

Natalie had no answers for the young man. They were getting nowhere and time was of the essence. If Hattie was in danger, Natalie needed to locate her and quickly.

It had been a long, frustrating day for the team, with little progress made. They'd confirmed Ryan had been at Leeds with the Samford University rugby team, and once again Lennox's pass had been used to gain access to the science department. By three o'clock, Natalie was becoming concerned about the lack of breakthrough. She had to remind herself that not all cases could be resolved within hours or days; some took months and years. She headed outside for some fresh air and was glad when she saw Mike's car pull into the car park. He looked fresh and clean.

'How's it going?' he asked as soon as he was within speaking distance. He jammed his hands into his pockets and pulled out a packet of chewing gum. 'Want any?'

'No, thanks.'

'I'm trying to cut down on the fags,' he said, unwrapping a stick of gum, balling it and popping it into his mouth. Mike had been a smoker for years, and since he and his wife, Nicole, had split up, he'd more than doubled the number of cigarettes he smoked in a day. Although Natalie had also smoked, she'd given it up in 2016.

'Good for you. What's brought this on? You haven't been told off by Bean, have you?'

Bean was the nickname for the lanky medical examiner at HQ who, along with a part-time nurse, was responsible for the mental and physical well-being of all the staff.

'Nah, Bean knows I wouldn't listen to any advice he gave me. I decided it was time I made a conscious effort to cut down, or quit. I have good reason to now.' His look carried the weight of his meaning. He and Natalie were edging ever closer to a proper, full-time relationship. She caught the glint in his eye and gave him a smile.

'Yes, although it might be tricky with Josh around now.'

'We'll manage.'

'I spoke to David this morning. He's in a pretty shitty frame of mind about everything.'

'You don't still think he's involved in this investigation, do you?'

'I got hold of his phone provider earlier, and according to them, his mobile didn't leave Castergate on Friday evening or Saturday, even during the time we interviewed him at HQ.'

'Well, there you are. He was at home, like he said he was.'

'Or he left it behind on purpose. He didn't bring it to the station with him. David's certainly no fool. He knows mobiles emit a signal and can be traced. This isn't enough to prove his innocence.'

'What about his car? Have you tried tracing its whereabouts?'

'The technical team is working on that on the off-chance it passed a surveillance camera. See what I'm up against! We're chasing the smallest pointers and qualifying the tiniest pieces of information in the desperate hope it will lead us somewhere, and all the while, I feel we're missing something important – a clue, a vital sign, a suspect.'

'There's always the satnav. The techies might be able to pull data from it even if it hasn't been programmed with a destination. Satnavs are like having a tracking device in your car.'

'David's car's pretty old. I doubt the system is sophisticated enough for that.'

'Course it will be. Come on, Natalie, it's not like you to get wound up like this. You've had frustrating dry days before on other investigations but you keep plugging away until eventually something comes to light.'

'It isn't happening this time, and I don't know where to look next. I'm not feeling my way through the case like I usually do. What the fuck's wrong with me?'

He spoke firmly. 'This is because of what happened in August. You're worried you'll slip up, but you won't.'

'How can you be sure I won't? Even that sodding journalist, Bev Gardner, questioned the fact I was heading the investigation so soon after my "tragic loss". I understand it's partly because of… the last investigation… and yes, I'm paranoid about ignoring what might be under my nose, even to the point of being anal about following up on every sodding detail, but I have little evidence to work with. I can't point the finger at anyone. I have no witnesses, no suspects and no clues. I'm not making headway and it's really starting to piss me off.'

Mike's phone buzzed and he answered it with a series of affirmations, then placing his hand over the receiver, he said, 'We've identified some of the DNA on Fran's clothes and body. There are matches to all of her housemates and Rhiannon.' Natalie had ensured all the students had given DNA samples, including those who lived with Rhiannon. It was a start.

'Okay, thanks, Darshan. I'll be ten minutes.' Mike ended the call.

'Was there any other DNA?'

'Yes, three lots – one came from that homeless guy, Evan, whose blankets she was under. I assume it was transferred from them. The other two don't match any we have on record.'

'We sent a sample of David's DNA across to the lab. Can you prioritise it for me? The sooner I can eliminate him, the quicker I can get on with looking for the person responsible.'

'Then you do believe he's innocent?'

'Truthfully, I don't know.' A wind was getting up and whistled around the back of her knees. She needed to go back inside. Mike's jaw moved slowly as he worked his gum. He didn't move and neither did she. Did she think David was behind these deaths? He wasn't a killer. The man she had loved wouldn't murder or commit a barbaric acid attack, would he? Her gut gave her the answer, and if she was right and David wasn't anything to do with this, she would have to work out who else might have killed Fran and Gemma.

'Dinner,' he said for the second time.

'Sorry, I didn't hear you. I was miles away.'

'Dinner. Come around for dinner at the weekend. Saturday night. I'll cook for you, and Josh if he wants to join us. Not seen him for a while and it would be nice to find out how he's getting along.' Mike had known the children since they were born. Being David's best friend, he'd become part of the family long before he and Natalie had had their one-night stand back in 2016. Josh and Mike had always got along well. It might be a good idea.

'It's a date,' she replied, distracted by the angry buzzing of her phone in her skirt pocket. She fumbled to withdraw it, and at the same time, Mike's mobile rang.

She frowned and held it to her ear, turning her head away from Mike in order that they could both hear more clearly. Lucy sounded distant even though she was only upstairs.

'They've found a body on campus. It sounds like it might be Hattie.'

'Three victims, four days,' said Pinkney, then remarked, 'That sounds like the title of a horror movie.'

His weak attempt at light humour managed to counteract the sinking sensation in the pit of Natalie's stomach. The afternoon had turned into evening and darkness had fallen quickly. Dan Tasker had arrived at the scene and was on the phone, presumably to the media office at the station in readiness for the inevitable onslaught. Three female students in their late teens and twenties, all dead. She could already imagine the headlines. He strode backwards and forwards outside the cordoned area, efficiency leaching from him, and although his face was unreadable, Natalie guessed that behind his super-composed exterior was a man preparing for battle. It would arrive soon enough in the form of journalists and television cameras and presenters, all mad eager to report about the recent spate of murders taking place at Samford University.

She showed her pass to one of the officers standing close to the rear of what was called the Heraklion Centre – a drama studio that was now disused thanks to the more recently built, larger building that had been erected adjacent to the library, at the far end of campus. She ducked under the cordon and strode onwards. Pinkney followed her into a small concreted area enclosed by high panel fencing and accessed from the building by large double doors, or through the entrance she'd used – a shabby wooden gate. Floodlights had been erected and it was difficult to know what purpose the space served as it appeared to be a dumping ground for piles of broken plastic chairs, tatty stage props and decorated backdrops to sets.

Natalie studied one of the panels, a hand-painted woodland scene filled with pine trees. Pine cones had tumbled to the fern-covered ground and a red squirrel was caught in mid-dash up a tree trunk, a cone in its mouth. She glanced at the section propped next to it, where a woodpecker was searching for insects in the bark of a tree, then as her gaze descended, she spotted a pair of boots protruding from the bottom of a long, dark green skirt with a lace trim. Hattie was on the ground behind a row of white metal lockers, the type found in schools, but with handles either side of them and on castors for easy manoeuvrability around a stage. She moved towards the body, taking in the green cardigan that had fallen open and the blouse half-tucked into the skirt band that gaped open above her navel, revealing white flesh. Natalie's eyes grazed the multicoloured beaded bracelets on the woman's wrists and the thin-strapped watch that had stopped at seven fifty; there was a fissure running across the glass on the watch. Her eyes moved to Hattie's long, white throat and finally rested on the woman's face, which in death looked peaceful, dark eyelashes sweeping onto the tops of her delicate cheeks. Her deep auburn hair had fallen loose around her head, and close to her right temple it was matted with a dark substance.

Pinkney crouched down and attempted to lift one of the young woman's hands. There was little to no movement. Full rigor had taken place. Hattie had probably been dead for over twenty-four hours. He checked her eyes and confirmed the optic fluid had dried and the irises had changed shape. He checked the skin on the exposed parts of her limbs, face, eyelids and her mouth, and examined the side of her skull, where her hair was thick with brown blood. 'Cranial blunt force trauma,' he said. 'The skull cracked here.'

Natalie focused on the depression close to the woman's temple, where blood had congealed. It appeared as if she'd either fallen badly and hit her head, or been struck by a heavy object. One way suggested an accident, the other an act of violence, and right now, Natalie was convinced it was deliberate. She took a step backwards – allowing Pinkney to move about unimpeded by her presence – and moved outside, where she spotted Mike standing with Lucy and Murray on a grassy bank beside the road that traversed the campus. She made her way across to them. From where they stood, they had a clear view of the front of the drama studio, which resembled a large wooden cube; the only opening, a black door.

Natalie joined them, mindful of the emergency services vehicles lining the road, their blue lights flashing brightly in the darkened sky. 'She's got a serious head injury which could be the cause of death. Mike, have you had a chance to look around in there?'

'Not yet, although the photographer's been in already. We're waiting for Pinkney to finish and then we'll move in.'

Murray and Lucy went to look at the body and she remained behind with Mike. An ambulance had arrived at the scene and forensic officers milled about in front of their vans awaiting instructions. This was a brief hiatus before the activity began.

She kept her voice low. 'Another victim, Mike! This is getting out of hand. People will believe there's a crazed killer on the loose.'

'If this was the work of a random killer, they'd have chosen victims from all parts of campus, not selected three girls from the same house. There's something or someone connecting the victims.'

His words echoed her own suspicions. She mentally chastised herself. She ought to be focusing her energy on finding more connections between the three young women, or at least investigating those they were already aware of more thoroughly. 'There has to be. I have to establish what or who it is. You will run David's DNA through as soon as possible, won't you?' It could take up to seventy-two hours to check DNA and she couldn't wait that long.

'I'll sort it.' He put a friendly hand on her shoulder and gave it a quick squeeze. She responded with a grateful smile. 'We'll catch up later, right?' he said.

'Definitely.' She turned away and headed back towards Dan, who stood alone beside the cordon, his face serious.

He spoke quietly. 'We're advising the university to shut for the time being. I couldn't keep a lid on this and I've had to mollify the press. I'm sorry but I had to give them something.'

'What do you mean?'

'I've told the media office to issue a statement that a male in his late forties is currently helping us with our enquiries.'

'Currently? We let David go. You want me to question him again, this time about Hattie?'

'I imagine that would be the natural course of action.'

'I shall be questioning him as you'd expect, but we'll be talking to other people as well – the other students who lived with the girls, and the girls' friends and families. David will be one of several people interviewed.'

Dan gave a sigh and adopted a patient tone as if explaining a difficult maths problem to a child. 'The press likes things to be uncluttered. If they learn that "a person" is helping us with our enquiries, it sounds more promising than "several people are helping us". People make assumptions – that we have found the guilty party – and it makes the public feel more reassured.'

'You're arguing semantics! Besides, I disagree. If the public think there's only one person assisting us, it might indicate we are struggling to get leverage on this case.'

Dan's eyes glittered angrily. 'I'd have thought you'd want to establish whether or not David knows the third victim.'

'I do but I certainly don't want the press to find out about it. What happens if it gets out who that "male in their late forties" you referred to is? According to your argument, they'll assume David is responsible for the deaths. I'm not going to bring personal emotion into this but have you forgotten that his daughter – our daughter – was murdered only three months ago? Yes, he might be guilty of this crime, and if he is, make no mistake, I shall ensure he is brought to justice, but if his image is tarnished because assumptions are made, what will that do to him? And… where does that place me as head of this investigation?'

'That will do! I've made this call to mitigate any panic. I've presented you and your team as well-organised and on top of this case. There is nothing further to discuss. It's pointless to speculate as to whether or not David's name will be leaked. Interview him and charge him or clear him once and for all, and if you do that, find who is responsible because once we no longer have any potential suspects, we run the risk of coming under scrutiny not only from the press and public, but also from the higher authorities. Cases like this are very high-profile.'

She didn't respond but allowed her silence to leave him in no doubt as to how she felt about the situation. She didn't appreciate being pushed about, and no matter what she thought about David, if he was innocent, she wouldn't allow his name to be dragged through the mud. She glanced at the gate, caught sight of Lucy beckoning her and excused herself to join her officer. Pinkney was on his knees, his case by his side. As she strode through the gate accompanied by Lucy, he turned his head towards her.

'The head injury that crushed part of her skull was inflicted perimortem and is likely to be the cause of death. Livor mortis suggests she was lying in position elsewhere before she was brought here. I would put time of death at some point Saturday evening, any time between six and midnight, although there is a good chance she died at the time suggested by her stopped watch, at seven fifty. Anything further will have to wait until the post-mortem. Is that sufficient?'

'It's very helpful,' Natalie replied. If Hattie had died at seven fifty, she couldn't have driven her car to Samford Railway Station. She cast about for scuff marks indicating the body had been dragged to its resting spot but could see none. Forensics would be able to confirm whether or not Hattie had been carried in.

'Unless I find any fragments embedded in the skull that might suggest what was used to strike her, I'm not going to be able to speculate. Having said that, I've not uncovered any obvious bruising to indicate she actually fell: given she has struck the right side of her head, I would also expect to see some injuries – grazing or bruising, or even minor cuts – elsewhere on that side of the body, commensurate with a fall. That doesn't mean there aren't any, only that I haven't discovered any yet.'

'Do you think she might have stumbled and hit her head?'

'You need to be mindful of that possibility. I can't do much more here. I'll head back to the lab and wait for her there. While I'm at it, I'll see if I can hurry along those toxicology reports for Fran Ditton.'

'Thanks, Pinkney. I'll talk to you later.'

'You will. I doubt I'll be returning home for some time, if at all tonight.' He got to his feet with a little groan and rubbed his knees.

'You okay?' asked Lucy.

'Too much time in the saddle – bicycle not horse.'

Lucy lifted an eyebrow. 'Really? Since when?'

'Since I decided to get into shape.' He caught the look on Murray's face. 'Pooh-pooh all you like. I can take the ridicule.'

'There'll be none from me. Nothing wrong with looking after your health. Murray could do with dropping a few pounds himself. Maybe he should join you,' said Lucy.

Murray grimaced at the thought. 'Might pass on that, thanks,' he replied.

'If you change your mind, you'd be welcome to join myself and a few fellow enthusiasts on a twenty-five-mile ride next Sunday.'

Lucy's eyebrows shot up. 'Twenty-five miles! I'm impressed.'

Pinkney smiled his thanks.

'I'll speak to you later, Natalie,' he said again, reaching for his pathologist's case.

She returned a nod and gave Hattie one last look. Three dead young women, all students and all from the same house on Eastview Avenue; the latter was a fact that couldn't be ignored.

'I'll head across to break the bad news to Hattie's father. He might be able to shed some light on what's going on although I'm not holding out much hope. He didn't even know she'd disappeared,' said Natalie to Murray.

'I'll come with you,' he said.

'Yes. Good. Let's clear off and let Forensics get on with it.'

They left the yard and stood outside. The late evening sky was a dark navy rather than black, lit by pinpricks of stars, and as she looked up the road that led through campus, Natalie could make out a variety of green-roofed buildings. According to the plan she'd seen of the site, they were part of the arts and design centre and also housed the students' union, bar and cafeteria. Behind them stood tall, glass-fronted buildings, housing other humanities departments. Her attention was dragged back to the green roofs of the students' union, and her thoughts turned to the night of Gemma's attack. 'Fran had a meeting on Friday night, didn't she?'

Lucy replied, 'That's right.'

'It took place in the students' union.' It was more a statement than a question but Lucy responded all the same.

'Her alibi checked out. She was definitely at the meeting. It took place in one of the rooms off the main social area. She went into the bar after that.'

Natalie kept her focus on that area. It was a mere two-minute walk away from where she stood. Fran hadn't been far from where Gemma had been attacked and could have slipped out for a while unnoticed. The bar was busy; she might have claimed to be going to the toilet – anything was possible. Fran, who shared a house with the other victims, had been on campus Friday evening, as had Lennox for that matter. He too had been only minutes away from the library. Now they had a second victim who'd been uncovered on university land. It was perplexing.

Natalie shook her head. 'Three young women, all students and all from the same house. This is no coincidence. This has to link to the house on Eastview Avenue.'

Murray pointed out the facts. 'But that suggests either Ryan or Lennox are responsible for their deaths. What possible motive could either of them have for killing the girls?'

'That's what we need to find out.'

'They'd have to be either pretty confident we wouldn't catch them, or incredibly stupid to think they'd get away with it,' scoffed Lucy. 'Surely, they'd have realised they'd come under scrutiny?'

'As you say, either supremely confident or incredibly dense,' said Murray. 'On the other hand, they might not be responsible for the deaths and it could be somebody else altogether, someone else who knew all the victims.'

'What makes you say that, Murray?' asked Natalie, curious to understand his reasoning.

'Ryan is in the clear because he can account for his movements on both Friday evening, and Sunday, which only leaves Lennox who claims to have been in the lab. We can't prove he was actually there when he said he was. Anybody could have swiped his pass for him or he could even have swiped it but not gone into the lab. If he attacked and killed them all, wouldn't he have given himself a better alibi than that? It's so wishy-washy it almost points at his involvement.'

'Maybe he stuck to a flimsy alibi because he couldn't come up with a more concrete one,' said Lucy with a shrug.

Natalie put a halt to the conversation. 'It's no good us speculating and given all the victims have come from the same address, those two young men need to be interviewed again. Our backs are against the wall here. The press is going to be watching our every move. We have to jump on this quickly. Lucy, you deal with Ryan and Lennox, and ask Ian to go through all CCTV at the entrances to the university. We'll need to talk to the drivers of every vehicle that passed through campus after 4.25 p.m., which is when she rang me to arrange to meet me. Murray and I will speak to Hattie's father and join you afterwards. Can you also get the tech team to go through all social media accounts and phone records of all three women? There has to be some other connection that we haven't yet uncovered.'

Natalie made for her car. White-suited forensic officers had moved into the area surrounding the drama studio, a ghostly squad, silently searching for clues. Were these incidents university-related or was there something else that connected these victims? The answers, like pieces of a puzzle, were in front of her but she could make no sense of them.

CHAPTER TWENTY-ONE

MONDAY, 19 NOVEMBER – NIGHT

Gemma,
> *Look at what you've done!*
> *This needn't have happened.*
> *I hold you responsible for all of this.*
> *You're to blame, Gemma. You.*
> *If only you'd been nicer to me.*
> *An Ex-Admirer*

*

Mr Caldwell's face looked pained. 'Is this about Hattie? Is she all right?' He dropped lightly onto a chair and rested his elbows on his knees. His stripy blue-and-purple dressing gown was wrapped tightly around his slim frame, held together by a knotted belt. His pale blue pyjamas had been washed so frequently that the colour was completely faded in patches, and the sole of one of his red checked carpet slippers, peeling away from the material, flapped open like a gaping wound whenever he lifted his foot. He raised a hand and dragged elegant fingers through his beard as he waited for an answer. A clock chimed – a melancholy sound that seemed to echo – and Natalie spoke before it could chime again.

Natalie shook her head. 'I'm truly sorry, sir. Hattie was found dead only a few hours ago.'

The man squeezed his eyelids tightly together and tilted his head to the ceiling. The clock's mechanism whirred and clicked like a mechanical heart and it rang out again in defiance at the news. No sooner had one chime's lengthy echo finished than another began, and only after the eleventh time, when silence had finally fallen, did Mr Caldwell open his eyes and speak.

'How did she die?'

'She sustained a head wound which we believe might be responsible for her death but we haven't had official confirmation of that yet.'

'Do you think it was an accident?'

'We don't have sufficient information at this stage, but we are considering the possibility that she died under suspicious circumstances.'

'I see.' He dropped his head so he was looking directly at Natalie. 'Her mother passed away when she was eleven and Hattie was all I had.'

'Once again, I am very sorry to bring you this terrible news.'

'I know you are, DI Ward, and I've read about your own recent personal tragedy. I thank you sincerely for your kind words. You will understand how I feel right now.'

'Yes, sir.'

He blinked back tears that leaked from the corners of his eyes.

'I know I spoke to you before about this but I really need your help. Did Hattie mention anything about any of her housemates to you? No matter how small a detail, I'd like to know.'

'We talked about many things: her future, life, politics, religion and culture, but not her private life. Naturally, I asked her about her course and time at university and enquired about her fellow students, and she told me that this year, she was sharing with a bunch of really nice students and they got along well, but she didn't divulge more than that.'

'Has she ever been in any trouble or mixed with people who got into trouble?'

'No. She had a heart of gold and wanted to help those less fortunate than herself. She did volunteer work for the homeless. The most rebellious thing Hattie ever did was run off to join the commune and get married. As for trouble? No. Not Hattie.' He pressed his clenched fists to his mouth and bit back tears. 'I'm sorry.'

'There's no need to apologise. Can we get you anything or contact anyone?'

'No, thank you. There will be plenty of support once this gets out. We're a very tight-knit community. I will undoubtedly be smothered in sympathy.' The humour was feeble and failed to prevent the emotion which suddenly overwhelmed him. His eyes shone with tears and his face screwed up again. He managed to stutter, 'I think… I'd like to be… alone… if you don't mind.'

There was nothing further he could help them with. She'd ensure he received the emotional and practical help he needed. 'We're very sorry for your loss. I can assure you that we will do everything in our power to discover what happened to Hattie and bring to justice the person, or persons, responsible.' The man couldn't answer. He pressed his lips tightly together and nodded several times. They headed into the hall to let themselves out, pursued by keening that seemed to emanate from the very walls of the house.

CHAPTER TWENTY-TWO

On the way back to Samford from Little Beansfield, Natalie and Murray took a detour to Castergate. It was a few minutes past midnight, but she had no other option than to talk to David and didn't want to wait. If he knew all three women, he had some serious explaining to do.

Murray pulled up onto the driveway where she'd often parked behind David's Volvo. He killed the engine and glanced in her direction. 'You want me to stay in the car?'

'I'd rather you came too. This is official business and I'd like you to hear what he has to say.'

'If you're sure about it?'

'I'm sure.'

He flung open the car door. Cold air rushed in to rapidly replace the warmth of the interior. She mimicked his movements and stepped outside, the soles of her sturdy shoes slipping on the moss-covered slabs. She sighed inwardly. The house would never sell if David let it fall into a state of neglect. She hoped the interior was more appealing. A blue glow flickered in a thin gap where the heavy sitting room curtains had not been drawn together – light from a television screen. At least she wouldn't have to raise him from slumber. It felt alien to be pressing the doorbell to what had been her home for many years. She knew the tune by heart – a cheerful melody that was one of several programmed into the device that Eric, David's father, had fitted for them back when they'd been a happy family. She knew it would sound loudest in the kitchen – the room furthest from the front door – and that if the television was on in the sitting room, the tune would be muffled and blend in with whatever programme was on. Her ears were more attuned to it than David's and he often didn't hear it, consequently, it came as no surprise when he didn't answer the door.

She moved towards the window, rapped on it and waited until the curtain twitched. She called out, 'I need to talk to you, David.' The curtains were pulled to once more and the glow disappeared. She returned to the step to stand next to Murray and was rewarded when the door opened.

'I'm sorry for the late intrusion but we have to speak to you again,' said Natalie.

David's shoulders sagged, the effect making him seem even smaller than he had looked at the station. Before her stood a shrunken, wizened man whose eyes had lost their light. What had she done to him?

'Can we come in?'

He nodded but only moved back enough to allow them space to step over the threshold and remain in the hallway. The house was silent and Natalie felt icy fingers run over her scalp then down her neck and back. This no longer felt like a family home or a place in which they had shared many happy memories. It was familiar yet strange, filled with the ghosts of a life she'd lost. She fixed her eyes on David rather than look about. She didn't want to be distracted by memories.

'I'd like to know if you've ever met or had any contact with this woman,' she said, passing David a photograph of a smiling Hattie Caldwell, in a bright strappy top and waving a straw sunhat at the camera.

He shook his head.

'Please look again, carefully,' she said.

He did as she told him. 'I don't know her.'

'Does the name Hattie Caldwell mean anything to you?'

'No.'

She searched for signs of lying but saw nothing but sorrow.

'She's dead, isn't she?' he said, and without waiting for a reply continued, 'You wouldn't ask me otherwise. I don't know her. I've never met her. I've never seen her. That's all I can tell you.'

'Did Gemma or Fran ever mention her?' Her eyes held David's as if tethered.

'If they had, I would have come clean and told you, but I swear, I don't know her. Is that everything?'

'Can you tell me where you were Saturday evening?'

He raised his hand to the back of his neck, left it there. 'I was at home.'

'At home again?'

'Is there a problem with that?'

'Was anyone with you?'

'I was *alone*.'

'Did you leave the house at all that evening?'

'I don't think so?'

'You don't remember?'

David's fingers roughed his hair. Natalie knew the tell-tale sign. He was holding back.

'I don't think I went out.'

'David, it's really important you tell me the truth. I can't help if I don't have all the facts. You want me to prove you're innocent but you're keeping something from us.'

His mouth turned downwards and his brows lowered, closing his face. 'I'd have thought you'd have enough faith in me to clear my name.'

'I want to but you're not making this easy for me.'

'I didn't kill anyone. Is that not clear enough for you? Now, I'd like you both to leave. I was about to go to bed. I have an early start. Somebody is coming to view the house tomorrow at eight thirty. Obviously, if you need to talk to me again, I'll oblige, but I honestly have nothing more to add to what I've already told you. I have nothing to do with your investigation. It's unfortunate I knew two of your victims but it's no more than coincidence –and, DI Ward, I know you don't believe in coincidences, but they do exist. Please bear that in mind.'

She nodded abruptly, determined to maintain a level of professionalism. Silence fell again, followed by an audible soft cough. There was somebody in the sitting room. She threw David a sharp look but he would no longer meet her eye.

'Is there somebody else here?' she asked.

'I don't see how that has any bearing on your questions.'

'Is there?'

'Goodnight, DI Ward,' he said.

For a second, she considered entering the sitting room and ascertaining who the mystery guest was, but Murray opened the door and a draught of cool air snapped at her ankles. She retreated towards it without a word.

It was well after one thirty by the time Natalie and Murray had returned to the station. She wasn't tired or hungry and was keen to press on. Her colleagues seemed to be of the same frame of mind.

'What's the situation with Ryan and Lennox?' she asked Lucy.

'Couldn't raise either of them. They didn't answer the door or their phones.'

Natalie massaged her temples. Could something untoward have happened to the boys? 'You tried the friends who live three doors away, didn't you?'

'Stuart and William. I did, but no joy. They'd left to go to William's house in Bournemouth for a few days until lectures start again. I'll try again later when it's light. Maybe Ryan and Lennox nipped off to a friend's house or to Lennox's for a few days because the university is shut.'

Natalie kneaded the tender spots by her eyes and asked, 'We need to track them down. Murray, check out Lennox's house in case he or both of them are there. While we're waiting for DNA results, post-mortem reports and for the technical team to come back to us about vehicles entering the university campus on Saturday afternoon after 4.25 p.m., I'd like to return to the start of this investigation. We still don't know who attacked Gemma. Let's go back over all the statements and alibis and see if there are any holes. I'm pretty sure these deaths are connected, so if you have any ideas about what you think happened, I'm all ears.'

'You know my theory,' said Murray. 'Fran was responsible for the attack on Gemma, Hattie found out about it and threatened to give Fran up to the police, or Fran overheard her on the phone to you, panicked and killed her; then, overcome with guilt or afraid of the consequences, she took her own life. It has a logic, after all: she lived with the other victims and she was jealous of Gemma.'

Ian waved a pen in Murray's direction. 'What if there's some-body else who knew all three of them – maybe somebody who didn't live with them?'

Natalie wrote David's name on a notepad and circled it. He'd denied knowing Hattie but they hadn't yet established if that was really the case, and he had exhibited signs of hiding some informa-tion from her. 'I'd like to go through Hattie's emails and phone call log – see who she was in contact with.' She sincerely hoped it wasn't with David. It seemed odd to think she was investigating the man she'd been married to for more years than she cared to remember. She waited for more thoughts. Ian had another.

'All the victims were female students. Maybe they all knew or dated the same person,' said Ian.

'You mean a housemate?' Murray replied.

'No, I was thinking more another student who is on one of their courses, or a tutor, or even somebody they met online.'

'What about Professor Young?' said Lucy.

'He denied any involvement with Gemma and was having an affair with his wife's best friend. I doubt he'd have time to be having an affair with all three students, as well,' said Murray.

Lucy made a tutting noise. 'Don't be too sure. He struck me as pretty arrogant. I wouldn't put anything past him, and what about all that bullshit he gave us about being "paternal" towards his students – the creep!'

'True,' said Murray. 'There's one problem with that, though – he didn't lecture either Fran or Hattie.'

'He might still have been seeing them.'

'Bit odd though that he'd choose them – two other girls living the same house as Gemma – from all the possible other choices at the university. Besides, it'd be a risky move. They could have easily found out about each other. It would be madness to string along three girls from the same street, let alone the same house.'

'Yeah, okay. I'm tired. Not thinking straight. Go back to the online idea,' said Lucy.

Natalie shrugged. 'Not sure about that. We've examined Fran's and Gemma's devices. Neither girl was using any dating apps, were they?'

'We've only looked at social media sites. Want me to dig deeper?' Ian asked.

Natalie didn't want to waste time but there was a chance an outsider was involved. 'Okay, but let's go back through statements and evidence we gathered for all three victims. We could be missing something important,' she said. 'If any of you want to grab some shut-eye, I don't have a problem with that. We can restart this first thing.'

'All good here. I'll try to track down Ryan and Lennox,' Murray said.

Ian raised a hand but kept his head lowered as he studied his computer screen.

'I'm fine to stay too. Anyone fancy a coffee or grub? I'll make a trip to the all-night café,' said Lucy.

Natalie stared into space. What the hell was she missing? Murray peered over Ian's shoulder and stared at a couple of photos of young women on Ian's screen. His voice was low when he said, 'Mate, that's really a long shot. There's no evidence to suggest these victims were dating. Get on with something more productive.'

Ian grunted but continued to scroll, and Murray scowled. 'Fucking waste of time.'

Natalie could sense the frustration. This was laborious and Murray had a point. They had no reason to assume the students had been on a dating website or met up with anyone. 'Ian, try the girls' browsing history on their computers again. See what that turns up.'

The office fell silent and each of them settled into a rhythm. Natalie became oblivious to the world around her, concentrating on statements and trying to fathom who was responsible for harming Gemma. The deaths had begun with Gemma's, and the more Natalie thought about it, the surer she was that the others were related to it. Lucy returned. Food was consumed at desks, only the rustle of packets interrupted the industrious silence. The ringing of the internal phone made them all look up simultaneously. Murray, the nearest to it, answered.

'Really? Okay, I'll put you on loudspeaker, Mike.' He pressed a button and Mike's amplified voice was transported into the room.

'I've got some information for you. First off, there were some grey-white particles of dust on the tips of Hattie's boots, which we've now matched to a patch of dry cement by the road, directly outside the drama studio. I'd suggest whoever moved her drove to that point by the cement, as close to the back of the drama studio as possible, and then hauled her out of the car, but instead of dragging her along the ground, they lifted her up high enough that her feet would make no contact and leave a trace. They probably didn't allow for her feet falling forward and the tips of her boots trailing as they did.'

'They lifted her up,' Natalie repeated, trying to create a picture in her mind of how the killer had transported Hattie, who was about five foot seven. Had they held the woman up, holding her under her armpits, and waddled forward that way? It seemed a difficult way to carry somebody. Why not cradle her in both arms – one arm under her upper body, the other under her knees?

'We're trying to work out the logic of that, unless the perpetrator propped her up so they could shut the car door or something.' Mike said. That made more sense to Natalie.

'She's a good five foot nine in her boots and weighs a fraction over sixty kilos, so you're looking for somebody quite tall – certainly taller than her. Secondly, we examined the smartphone found in the glove box of Hattie's car. It's definitely her mobile, and although there's apparently nothing suspicious on it with regards to contacts, texts or applications, we checked the websites she'd visited and one stood out. It's an online adult-only dating website.'

Ian sat up straight and threw a meaningful look at Murray, who deflected it with a casual lift of his eyebrows.

'What's the name of the website, Mike?' asked Natalie.

'Special Ones dot com,' he replied.

'Could be significant. We could do with accessing it. Do you know anyone on the hi-tech crime team who can help out?'

There was some hesitation in his voice. 'Tricky at the moment. There's a big child porn investigation going on and they're up to their eyeballs examining seized machines. We've only got limited skills up here. I'll see if I can beg a favour for you.'

'I'd appreciate that.'

'I'll try Ralph. He's pretty good at this sort of thing and used to work with the hi-tech boys.'

Mike rang off and Natalie looked thoughtfully ahead. Ian had already swivelled back to his screen and was bringing up details of the website. Could this be a lead or a dead end? She didn't need to instruct her officers. They were already looking into it.

Ian spoke up. 'It's only showing the home screen and a few featured profiles. It won't allow us complete access unless we sign up.'

Lucy was on her mobile during the activity and said, 'I've downloaded the app and checked the site out. It's quite a simple process to register.'

'Do you have to pay a joining fee?' Natalie asked.

'No. It's free.'

'Well, we'll create a profile then and see if we can find Hattie on the site.'

Natalie reached for her mobile, which was vibrating in her pocket, expecting it to be Mike. It was David.

'You're making this personal, aren't you?' he said. His voice sounded peevish and his words slurred. She considered the possible retorts and settled for saying nothing. David continued to babble. 'I asked you to help clear my name because I'm innocent – you of all people should know that – yet all you've done is persecute me. I've got embroiled in this shit and I shouldn't be. I only wanted to earn some money. I only put up a fucking card on the board at the university to try and make a living. And now, I'm some sort of person of interest. I don't deserve this crap. I don't deserve it!' His voice had risen and anger had replaced the irritation.

'I'm not prepared to discuss this on the phone.'

He sighed, a long dramatic sigh. 'No surprises there, then. That's your problem, Natalie. You do everything by the fucking book. Oh… and for your information, yes, there was somebody in the house. She was very charming and delightful and the evening was going well until you showed up. I wish you'd stop fucking up my life!' He slammed down the phone.

CHAPTER TWENTY-THREE

TUESDAY, 20 NOVEMBER – EARLY MORNING

'Lennox isn't at the Walsh home in Shropshire,' said Murray, rubbing his hands over his head. 'The housekeeper never normally claps eyes on him until the holidays. I'm stumped.'

Natalie looked at the clock. 'Try Eastview Avenue one more time. They might be home by now. We can't ignore the fact the boys aren't answering their phones, especially given what's happened to their housemates.'

'I'll give their mobiles one last go before I leave.'

Ian was attempting to register on the Special Ones website when Ralph, a moon-faced man in his thirties, with a bald head so shiny it looked like it had been freshly waxed and eyes that were full of merriment, appeared. He carried a black bag of equipment in one hand and a Samsung mobile phone in a plastic bag in the other.

'I hear you need to get onto a dating website,' he said. His voice was chirpy and bright.

'Hi, Ralph. Thanks for coming along to sort this,' said Natalie, rising to her feet.

Ian moved away from his terminal, allowing Ralph to take his place. 'Cheers, mate. Saves me uploading all my personal information to gain access. It all takes ages.'

'And it'd be a waste of time. I doubt the site would be able to find you a match,' Murray replied, straight-faced.

'Fuck off, not-so-pretty boy!' Ian growled.

Ralph set to work, punching in codes at a frightening speed.

'How do you even work out how to do this?' Lucy asked.

'It's a knack,' Ralph replied without taking his eyes off the lines of code that covered the screen. He moved to the second screen, and several minutes later, he had gained access to SpecialOnes. com and had the site up on both screens. 'All done. Who are you looking for?'

'Hattie Caldwell.'

Ralph punched the name in and pursed his lips. 'Nothing.' He tried various other combinations to no avail. 'I don't think she's signed up.'

'If she wasn't signed up, why was she looking at the website then?' asked Ian.

Murray stood up and shoved his mobile into his pocket. 'Maybe she was looking to see what was available.'

'That seems a bit weird, though, doesn't it? There are loads of blokes at university for her to meet.'

'They're mostly younger than her,' Murray replied in a matter-of-fact tone.

'I didn't get the impression she was bothered about finding a man in her life. She was into charity work and her degree,' said Ian.

'I don't know then, mate. I can't see any reason to go on the site unless you're looking for love or a relationship.' With that, Murray took his leave.

Natalie was wondering the same thing. Why had Hattie looked at the site several times, not the once? 'If you don't register, what access do you have to the site?'

'Only to the featured profiles.'

'Then she must have been looking at those. Can we find out?' Natalie asked Ralph.

'There is a way. Hang on,' said Ralph, rummaging in his bag and pulling out a lead, which he attached to the mobile he'd brought in. Within a matter of minutes, he'd found the profile Hattie had been looking at. There was only one: a featured profile of a young woman, Maisie Simpson.

'Lucy was first to speak. 'That looks like Gemma.'

'That's definitely Gemma's photo,' said Natalie. Even from where she stood, there was no mistaking the girl in the profile picture.

'Okay, let's see what we've got,' Lucy said, picking up her chair and placing it next to Ralph's. Maisie's details were written in bold font under her photograph. Natalie moved closer and watched as they scrolled down. Lucy read aloud what Gemma, AKA Maisie, had written as her introduction: '"Don't be shy… Ask away and I'll tell you everything. I'm a genuine, fun-loving girl, hoping to meet a man who enjoys travelling, laughter and good times." Not very original, is it?'

'Don't ask me. I've never used a dating app or website. There's more,' said Ralph, clicking on a green arrow, and Lucy continued.

'"My friends say I'm warm, compassionate and very sexy. I'm looking for somebody who doesn't take life too seriously and who is willing to be adventurous. I'm an independent woman with a small business. I work hard and I like to play hard. What about you? Message me your details and maybe we can hook up and get to know each other better. I'd like that."'

'That it?' asked Ian.

'That's all, apart from stats: age, height, hair and eye colour, which match Gemma's description.'

'What about location?'

'Only shows she's from Staffordshire. Doesn't mention any towns or villages.'

'But that's clearly not Gemma. Somebody is pretending to be her,' said Natalie.

'Hattie?' said Lucy.

'Possibly, although if it were her, she'd have logged into the site as this Maisie person and she didn't do that. Hattie only looked at

Maisie's profile as an unregistered user. You're looking for somebody else who created this profile, and I'm afraid I can't help you with that. I'd need that person's computer or smartphone,' said Ralph, packing away his leads. 'Sorry, that's all I can do for the moment. I'll leave you to it. Ring upstairs if you need anything else.'

'Thanks, Ralph. We appreciate it,' said Natalie as the man headed towards the door.

Lucy slipped into the vacated seat and immediately began hunting for Gemma's matches.

Natalie fell into thought. 'Why didn't Hattie tell somebody about this?'

'She was somehow involved,' suggested Lucy.

Natalie folded her arms, her eyes screwed in concentration. 'That's likely… I can't get a handle on it. This person – this Maisie – isn't likely to be Gemma herself, is it? After all, it doesn't add up to what we know about the girl.'

'Could be. She might have had an agenda. Usually when people do this sort of thing, they're catfishing.'

'I can't see Gemma doing that, can you?' said Ian.

Natalie kept quiet. Maybe there was something they didn't know about Gemma. 'Get hold of her financial records and we'll talk to Sasha and see what she has to say.'

'What about the other students in the house?' Lucy asked.

Natalie nodded. 'Definitely ask them about this website. Hattie knew about it and maybe the others did too. Look out for any profiles that look like Fran. Maybe she was on the site too. She checked her watch. It was coming up 3 a.m. and she felt energised and keen to continue.

Lucy shifted out of the way to let Ian use the computer she'd been looking at and joined him to scrutinise Gemma/Maisie's matches. A hush fell over the office. Lucy jotted down names and headed to the far side of the office to search on the police general database for contact details and information about each of Gemma/Maisie's potential matches. Ian punched in Fran's name and finding nothing, began pulling up profile after profile, none of which looked like either Fran or Hattie. Natalie drummed a silent beat on her thigh and puzzled over why Gemma would use an alias yet put up her real photograph. This didn't marry with what she'd discovered about the girl thus far. She couldn't believe it of her although she knew people kept secrets – spouses, lovers and children. Even her own daughter had kept secrets from her. *If she hadn't, she'd be alive today.* A sharp pain pierced her ribcage at the reminder. She couldn't discount the possibility Gemma had been up to something, however distasteful that seemed. She hoped for Sasha's sake that this wasn't the case.

'It looks like she had three matches,' Ian said to Natalie, interrupting her thoughts. Lucy's checking them out now. There are other men Gemma/Maisie's connected with on the site, but it doesn't seem as if they communicated beyond the on-site messaging service. When a "Special One" match is made, a symbol appears by each name involved and indicates the couple have contacted each other via telephone or by private email.'

Natalie understood the way it worked. It allowed people to retain a level of anonymity until they were ready to take the relationship one step further and find out more about the person they'd been chatting to.

'Do you have access to her online chats with men?'

'Yes, and there's nothing weird going on. It's mainly flirty chitchat.'

'Does she mention she's a student at all in them?'

'Not that I have spotted. She talks about running a small shop in a couple of them.'

'What sort of shop?'

'Jewellery. She makes and sells jewellery.'

'Really? Not clothes?'

Ian scrolled through a series of messages. 'Definitely jewellery. According to this conversation, she's into design and crafts and claims to have some sort of qualification from a business school in Cardiff.'

Natalie stared at the wall clock, watching the second hand move silently five times. The internal phone rang, breaking into her thoughts. Murray had found the boys, who were back at the house and safe. He'd grilled them about their whereabouts and also broken the news about Hattie.

'Where the hell were they?'

'At a friend's house. They're still very drunk. Might even have been smoking a bit of dope too.'

'And they switched off their phones while they were out?'

'They weren't switched off. They put them on silent mode.'

'You believe them?'

'Yeah. I think they're telling the truth. Ryan said they needed to get out of the house after what happened to Gemma and Fran. They've been drinking for hours. Smell like they have too.'

Natalie told him what they'd discovered about Maisie. 'Are they able to answer questions?'

'I think so. I'll make them drink water to help them sober up.'

'Can you establish what they know, if anything, about the website and Maisie?'

'Will do.'

'If you have any doubts at all, bring them in.'

'Defo.'

'Hang on a sec, Murray.'

She called across to Ian, 'You mentioned she'd probably had three dates. Who are these guys?'

'Scott Vidal, Felix Conway and Henry Warburton,' said Lucy. 'They all check out as real people not fakes. I've got contact details for all three.'

'You got any photos of them?'

'Yes.'

'Murray, you still there?'

'I am.'

'We're emailing you pictures of three men who matched with Maisie online. See if the boys recognise any of them. It's unlikely, especially if this is a fake profile, but double-check all the same.'

'Roger that.'

Murray rang off and Ian arranged for the photos to be sent. Natalie was satisfied they were making progress. 'Let's go through their conversations on the website and then take a couple of hours off to get some rest before we interview each of them.'

*

Murray stood in the kitchen at 53 Eastview Avenue with Lennox and Ryan. Both were undeniably subdued, and even stone-faced Ryan was slumped over the table, head in his hands.

'I don't understand what is happening,' he said, his voice flat.

Grey-faced Lennox hadn't moved from beside the sink since Murray had told them Hattie had been found dead. He'd clawed at the side of the Formica top to steady himself and been unable to move away, in spite of Murray suggesting he sit down.

'We've discovered Gemma might have been using a dating website and an alias, "Maisie". Do you know anything at all about that, Ryan?'

He rubbed his knuckles against his cheeks. The shock seemed to have sobered him up. 'Nothing at all. She certainly never mentioned it to me. Why would she do that? She didn't need to join a dating website.' He pushed himself back in his seat. 'That's crazy. She had blokes eating out of her hands, on campus and at Chancer's Bar. She wasn't short of male attention. Why would she go online to find a date?'

Murray had wondered the very same thing, but instead of answering, he turned his attention to a glassy-eyed Lennox, who'd released the kitchen top and had clamped his hands under his armpits.

'Lennox?'

He shook himself back to reality. His speech was slightly slurred. 'Erm… no. She never said a word to me about it.'

'What about either of the other girls? Did they say anything to you about a dating website?'

'No.'

'Does the name Maisie Simpson mean anything to either of you?'

'No,' said Ryan. 'Never heard of her.'

'Me neither,' said Lennox.

'What about strangers? Have there been any visitors to the house or anyone suspicious hanging about outside over the last couple of weeks?'

There were further denials and head shaking.

'Do you recognise any of these men?' he asked, pulling out pictures of the three men they thought Gemma/Maisie might have dated.

Ryan lifted each picture slowly and scrutinised them, his eyes covering every detail of each man's features, but returned them with a shrug. 'No.'

Lennox was less thorough with his examination but equally sure he hadn't seen any of the men.

'I'm going to ask you to remain here. I understand the university is shut temporarily but I'd still like you to stay in the house and leave your phones on.'

'We're not in any danger, are we?' asked Ryan.

Although only girls had been targeted up to this point, Murray couldn't answer with any certainty. 'I'd suggest you keep the front door locked and don't allow strangers to enter.'

Ryan's jaw jutted. 'I can handle myself.'

'It would be wiser to remain inside for now, and if you go out, make sure you are not alone.'

Lennox kept his hands tucked in place. His voice held a tremor as he spoke and Murray realised he was actually frightened. 'You sure we're not going to be targeted next?'

'Keep the doors locked and ring us if you are concerned about anything.'

*

Back in the office, Lucy had gathered information on the three men who had matched with Gemma/Maisie and met up for a date. Natalie was keen to know if any of them could throw some light on who this person actually was.

Lucy read out what she'd uncovered. 'Scott Vidal, aged twenty-two, lives in Newcastle-under-Lyme. He's a sales rep for a heating company. Felix Conway, aged thirty-three, lives in Burslem, Stoke-on-Trent, and works at CRV Commercials as a yard shunter.'

'What's that?' asked Natalie.

'I think it's to do with loading and offloading vehicles,' said Ian, dragging his attention from the singles website, where he was still searching for any profiles using Fran's or Hattie's faces or details.

Lucy continued, 'Henry Warburton is forty-five, lives in Sutton Coldfield and is an accountant at an engineering company in Birmingham. One thing though, he's married. It seems he has a wife of ten years and three children. Naughty Henry being on a dating website when he isn't actually single, although I bet he isn't the only person to do that.'

After a while, Ian gave a weary sigh. 'I can't find photos of Hattie or Fran.'

Natalie glanced across at Lucy, leaning on her elbows, staring at the screen and Ian, head back against his chair. They both looked totally drained. She was reminded that both were not only police officers but parents, and recalled what it had been like for her with young children at home. She'd hated missing a moment with them. She ordered them home for some sleep. Ian wouldn't get the chance to see his daughter today, but baby Aurora might be up soon for a feed, and no doubt Lucy would like a little time with her daughter. She knew she'd give anything to have a few minutes with hers again.

CHAPTER TWENTY-FOUR

TUESDAY, 20 NOVEMBER – MORNING

Natalie only managed a short nap, but combined with a long, hot shower, it was sufficient to revive her for the day ahead. Josh was still asleep when she was ready to leave the flat to return to HQ, and rather than disturb him, she left a note propped up against the cereal box, telling him that she'd definitely be home that evening and would text him later in the day. She reflected it was no life for a child – even one who'd turned seventeen. She couldn't be out all hours and leave him alone, yet what was the alternative? She could no longer rely on David, who'd always been there for both Leigh and Josh, or Eric, who'd babysat them when they were younger.

For the second time in only a few hours, she drove to Castergate, following lorries and vans along the main A-road past retail parks and estates that gradually thinned out and gave way to meadows through which meandered brown rivers, swollen by the recent rain. Small flocks of sheep grazed in undulating fields that were topped by farms and numerous outbuildings. Natalie paid no attention to the cows that watched from their lengthy byre and chewed methodically as she sped by, her mind on David. She turned off the main road and headed though the village of Brighterly, where a small group of children wearing school uniform were gathered under a bus shelter. Her eyes searched them hungrily although she knew her daughter wasn't among them. It was an itch waiting to be scratched. They attended Leigh's school and no doubt some of them had known her daughter.

It was only three miles to Castergate but she eased off on the accelerator. Seeing the schoolchildren had knocked her for six. She didn't want to return to the house where they'd lived as a family, or have to confront David again. She was tired of the hostility. She wanted a chance to heal but these reminders of the past tugged at her and prevented her from moving on. She reasoned that she could have let one of the team speak to David and that she didn't have to punish herself this way. Yet she knew she would. Just like she had to look at the schoolchildren who were waiting for the bus to go to the school that Leigh and Zoe had attended. She had to see this through. Her stomach lifted and sank, as if on a rollercoaster ride, as she drove over the hump-backed bridge that crossed over a muddy canal. She passed several cream-coloured cottages that fronted the road and had, over the years, turned charcoal from the ground upwards to mid-point, thanks to the passing traffic. She rounded the bend and came across the place-name sign for Castergate, twinned with a village in France she'd never visited, and turned onto the road where she had lived. Once more she parked behind David's Volvo. She turned off the engine, picked up the file and opened the door. This was going to be very difficult but she'd be fine. She'd lived through worse – far worse – the last few months.

David answered the door only after she pressed the doorbell continuously for several minutes. He didn't invite her in or speak; his lips pressed together so hard they turned white. Natalie asked if she could speak to him inside but he refused.

'David, I haven't come to fight. I've come to tell you I believe you aren't involved in any of this. You asked me to help clear your name and I am. I want this to end.'

He stared at her briefly, then with a quiet, 'Come in,' he opened the door and shuffled ahead of her. The house smelt lemon-fresh. The kitchen was spick and span, tops clear of clutter and the floor shining. David, or somebody, had been cleaning. He reached for the kettle. 'You want a cup of tea?'

'Please.'

She took a seat at the table covered by a yellow checked table-cloth – a present from Eric and his girlfriend, Pam – and tried hard not to look around the familiar surroundings as he ran the water and hunted for the teapot. He moved deliberately and slowly as if it was all a huge effort. Once he'd set up, he spoke. 'I lied.'

'Lied about what?'

'The woman last night. It was Rowena who was here. She came over to tell me she'd seen you at the cemetery and that you're the person who's been laying flowers on Zoe's and Leigh's graves. We had a glass of wine. We talked about the girls. We cried. We drank some more. She went home soon after you left. There's absolutely nothing going on between us. She's having as much difficulty as me, processing what's happened. I was angry with you. I was pissed off you didn't believe me after all these years. I shouldn't have said what I did on the phone.'

She opened the folder that lay on the table. 'I had your DNA processed quickly and there's no trace of it on either victim.'

'It's not conclusive proof though, is it? People manage to commit murders and not leave DNA behind.' He poured the boiled water into the pot and swilled it around then emptied it down the sink.

'If you give me the keys to your car, we might be able to prove once and for all that you were nowhere near the crime scenes.'

'How?'

'We'll examine the satnav. It'll show when the car moved and where you travelled.'

He spooned in loose tea and then filled the pot with water. David had always been the tea maker. There was something comforting about watching him perform the practised actions. He brought it across and placed it on the table.

'Thank you.' His words carried more than gratitude. They indicated a truce had been made. Whether or not it would stay in place was another matter. He brought mugs and a jug of milk and set them down before sitting to join her. He hesitated, opened his mouth and shut it again.

'You want to tell me something.'

His squeezed his eyelids to prevent tears spilling and uttered a low, 'Yes. No.'

'What is it? What aren't you telling me?'

'I… nothing.' He opened his eyes again. 'There's nothing. I'm sorry. You'll uncover the truth.'

'What truth?' She searched for an answer but he was already retreating into himself. He had a secret and he wasn't going to divulge it no matter what she said.

'That I'm not responsible for the deaths. I'm not. You'll see. That's all that matters, isn't it?' He lowered his gaze again. There was more but he wasn't sharing it. He blinked several times and mumbled, 'I'm so fucking unhappy.'

'I know. I am too.'

'I don't know where to go from here, Natalie. I can't find my feet.'

She couldn't think of a suitable response, and when he inhaled deeply and set about pouring the tea, she was relieved. The moment had passed and she wouldn't have to offer any advice or words of comfort.

David continued talking. 'I think it's best if Josh stays with you for the time being. Once we sell the house and I move, maybe he can reconsider.'

'That sounds okay to me.'

'Then that's how we'll leave it for the moment.' He raised his mug and sipped the steaming liquid. It was a beginning. That was all she needed for now.

*

Murray sat on one of the hard chairs next to the angular desk. Opposite him was Scott Vidal, one of the men who'd met Gemma/Maisie online. He was a tiny, pencil-thin man with a long face, cropped straw-coloured hair and one blue and one brown eye. None of the men Gemma/Maisie had matched with looked alike, but Scott seemed an unlikely choice for the young woman. His stutter was light, brought on by the anxiety of the situation. Murray tried not to intimidate him too much.

'You're a sales rep?'

'That's c-c-correct. I sell heating components to businesses, not individuals.'

'I understand you actually attended Samford University in 2016 to study Electronics. Why did you drop out?'

'Pressure. I wasn't up to the c-c-course. I failed my first-year exams.'

'Did you live on campus?'

'Yes. I was in one of the b-blocks.'

'Did you ever meet anyone called Fran Ditton?'

'I-I don't know the name.'

Murray passed over a photograph. Scott shook his head. Murray passed across another, this one of Hattie. Scott squinted at it.

'I know her face. I've seen her somewhere.'

'Hattie Caldwell. Does the name ring a bell?'

Scott shook his head.

'You joined the dating website three months ago. Did you get many matches?'

'A couple.'

'I'm interested in this person – Maisie Simpson.' Murray handed him the photo of Gemma.

Scott's eyes narrowed. 'She's a fake.'

'What do you mean?'

'She's a c-c-catfisher.'

'Can you elaborate?'

'She wanted money.'

'Can you tell me about what happened?'

Scott released a sigh and prepared to unburden himself. 'I thought Maisie really liked me. I'd recently come out of a long-term relationship and my c-confidence was shot to hell. A friend suggested I sign up to the site and meet somebody to bring me out of my shell. She was my first match. We got on well. She suggested we swap emails.' He paused to conjure up the right explanation. 'To send photos of each other, talk more freely.'

'Did you exchange telephone numbers?'

'No and I admit I was suspicious about that, but she was really lovely and understood what I was going through – I didn't want it to stop. I continued to email her. She kept answering. Eventually, I suggested we meet up. She was going to drive to Newcastle, and we agreed if the date went well, we'd swap phone numbers. I sorted out a pub in the centre of town and sent her details of how to get there, and she seemed excited about it all. The day before we were due to get together, she emailed saying she was feeling really low and couldn't meet up. Her grandmother was being kicked out of her care home, where she'd been living for the last year, because the money had run out and Maisie hadn't got enough income to keep her there. She'd talked a lot about her grandmother. The old lady had brought her up after her parents were killed. That was when I became suspicious it was all a scam. I wrote back and said how sorry I was. She replied, asking if I could loan her the money to help keep her grandmother in the home. She promised she'd pay me back every month. I saw through it. She was only after money. She was never going to meet me. I told her I couldn't help.'

It rang alarm bells for Murray. Fran had a grandmother who was in a home, and he wondered if Fran had set up the profile. 'What happened next?'

'She stopped emailing me immediately. I didn't try to contact her again.'

'Did you report this to the dating website?'

He dropped his head. 'I figured the website organisers would get other complaints about her and would deal with her – if it was even a woman. It could have been some bloke emailing me from a foreign country. I felt such a prize wanker. Fancy getting taken in like that!'

'You didn't message her again?'

'No.'

'Did she ever call herself anything other than Maisie?'

'No.'

'Does the name Gemma Barnes mean anything to you?'

Murray watched the man's face closely but saw only confusion. 'Gemma? No.'

'I don't suppose you have her contact details, do you?'

'I might still have her email address but I deleted the emails.' He checked though, his brows furrowed. 'No, sorry, I deleted it too.'

'Can you recall the email address?'

'I don't remember it.'

'Would you mind granting us access to your email account in case our technicians can retrieve it?'

'Sure.'

'Thank you. A few final questions. Can you tell me your whereabouts for Friday evening at about seven?'

'I was at home with my mother.'

'You live with your mother?'

'Yes.'

'And she can vouch for you?'

'Definitely.'

'How about Saturday evening?'

'I was at a friend's birthday party at his house.'

'From what time?'

'Seven until gone midnight.'

'And you have people there who can vouch for you?'

'Yes. I can give you names. I was one of the last to leave.'

'And Sunday afternoon?'

'Cycling. I'm a member of ZippyFit cycling club. We were out most of the afternoon.'

Murray made a note and thanked the man. It appeared Gemma, or more likely the person using her photo, was a catfisher as they'd suspected. It was now a question of finding out who it was.

*

Natalie had swapped cars with David and driven his Volvo to work. The keys were with Ralph, who'd assured her he'd be able to download and examine all the routes David had driven over the last few days. She was fairly confident that the perpetrator was to be found elsewhere, and that should the media decide to press further, they'd be unlikely to hound her ex. If she could speak to the men who'd contacted Gemma/Maisie, she might be able to offer the journalists more information that would appease them and move the focus away from Dan's announcement that a man in his late forties was helping them with their enquiries. The office was very quiet with only Ian at his desk.

'Where are Murray and Lucy?' she asked.

'Murray's interviewing Scott Vidal, one of the guys who might have dated Gemma, and Lucy's popped into town on a personal errand. Henry Warburton, one of the other guys Gemma/Maisie matched with, is waiting in interview room D, and Felix Conway should be here shortly.'

'Right. I'll talk to Henry then.'

'Here are his notes. He isn't on our system for any misdemeanours or offences. There's some basic information and transcripts of conversations between him and Gemma/Maisie before they took their activities off-site. Looked like they were getting along famously and were planning to meet up,' he replied, waving a manila file.

Natalie took it and glanced through the highlighted sections of text. 'Definitely reads that way. Maybe they did. I'll see what he has to say for himself.' She bounded out of the office with renewed energy.

Dan was at the top of the stairs, eyes trained on her as she approached. 'Morning, Natalie. Any updates for me?'

'Hopefully later. I'm about to interview somebody in connection with the attack on Gemma.'

'And what about the person helping you with your enquiries?' he asked cautiously.

'I think we can say he is in the clear, sir, although we are waiting on one last piece of evidence to prove he was not involved in any way.'

He gave a reptilian blink and replied with, 'As we suspected then. Make sure you give me a progress report as soon as possible. I want to keep the media placated.'

He turned lightly on his toes and disappeared up the stairs, the backs of his shining brogues flashing briefly in the morning light streaming through the full-length windows that made the building unbearably warm in summer months. She muttered under her breath. The sodding man was getting on her nerves, and she wondered how far he'd go and who else he'd throw to the press to keep them happy.

Henry Warburton wore an expression of concern and bounced up as if on a coiled spring when Natalie appeared, his hand extended. His fingers barely brushed against her flesh but left behind a moist residue. She resisted the urge to wipe her palm dry and instead sat down to conduct the interview. Henry perched on his seat, vulture-like, regarding her intently down a prominent hooked nose.

'Mr Warburton, thank you for coming in. You do know why you're here, don't you?'

'Yes, it's about the woman I met online. She called herself Maisie.'

'That's right but we're certain that wasn't her real name. I have some transcripts here. They're messages between the pair of you on Special Ones dot com. You stopped using the site for communicating. Is that correct?'

'Yes. The site is a neutral ground and a safe place, if you like, but she felt confident enough in our relationship to move on.'

Natalie laid out her notes, the transcripts visible. She ran a finger down them. 'So I see. In fact, I note she says in one of her last messages to you, "I think we're ready to take the next step, aren't we?" and you reply, "I'm up for it. What do you suggest? Swap phone numbers?" Did you exchange numbers?'

'No. She wasn't keen on that idea. She suggested email addresses.'

'Why was that? That's not much different to messaging on the site.'

'She felt it was a step forward. She was extremely cautious about who she gave her number to. She'd had a stalker in the past. At the time, I thought that seemed logical and I didn't press her for it. We emailed each other.'

Natalie read through the last messages. It did appear that this person, *Maisie*, was reluctant to hand out any personal information other than an email address. In fact, she'd asked for Henry's address and said she'd email him, rather than message it to him on the dating website, consequently Natalie had no note of it. 'I'd like to see any emails you have from her.'

'Ah, that's a bit difficult because I deleted them.'

'Why?'

He tapped his fingertips together gently before speaking. 'Can I be completely honest with you?'

'I'd rather you were.'

'At the time I signed up with the site, I was looking for some fun. My wife and I were going through a difficult patch and having a trial separation. I joined out of… well, I don't need to explain. I wanted to meet somebody carefree with no ties, someone who wasn't into having a serious relationship. Maisie fitted the bill perfectly. She was bright, cheerful and made me laugh. Soon after we swapped email addresses, we arranged to meet in Birmingham for a day together and see where it would lead.'

He sucked in a deep breath and released it noisily. 'We emailed each other constantly every day for a week. She was giving off all the right signals – keen to meet me, had a lot in common, looking for a fun relationship – but then the day before the date, she emailed me to say she couldn't make it. Her business was struggling and she had import duty to pay on some goods she'd purchased on a recent trip to Dubai. She needed cash to get them out of customs and asked if I could lend her £3,000 to pay for them to be released. She promised she'd pay me back once the stuff was sold and assured me it was worth far more than that, but I refused. I couldn't lend her that amount. I simply didn't have it. Although we were separated, I still had a wife and three children to support. And, since then, we've got back together. Anyway, after that, she didn't reply to any of my emails and didn't contact me again. We hadn't exchanged phone numbers so I couldn't ring her. I dodged a bullet. It was clearly a scam. She'd only been after me for money. I'd made an idiot of myself, but luckily, I hadn't handed over any cash.'

'Did you report her to the dating website?'

'No, I'd stopped visiting the site by then and was in talks with my wife to try and rebuild our relationship. I figured it was best to walk away. She didn't get anything out of me.'

'But you might have saved somebody else from falling for it.'

'I honestly didn't think about that. I wanted to forget the whole sorry situation. It was embarrassing and I felt such an idiot.'

'Did she send you any photos of herself?'

'I deleted them. I want my marriage to work. I don't think hanging on to photos of a young woman would have been the best decision.'

'What sort of photos were they? Selfies? Taken at work? Holiday snaps? Sexy pictures?'

He cleared his throat before saying, 'Mostly sexy ones.'

'Did you send her any of you?'

'A few but nothing outrageous that would incriminate me.'

'What about pictures of her with other people? Was there anybody else in any of the photos?'

'No. Only her. I confess I feel really stupid about the whole thing and I haven't told my wife about it. I deleted everything on my phone and put it all behind me. We're all entitled to make the odd mistake, aren't we? In the end, I only got up to some harmless flirting, nothing more than that.'

'Can you tell me where you were on Friday last week, between seven and seven thirty in the evening?'

'At home with my wife and children.'

'And you were at home all evening?'

'Yes.'

'At your house in Sutton Coldfield?'

'That's right.'

'We'd like to examine your mobile phone if possible.'

'Certainly, but I've deleted all the emails between us.'

'Our technicians are very good at finding lost details,' she replied.

He slid a black iPhone across the table. 'When can I get it back? I need it for work.'

'As soon as we've finished with it. We'll be as quick as we can.' She took it from him and thanked him for his time.

*

'Scott was pretty sure she was trying to scam him. She came up with some cock-and-bull story about her gran being kicked out of a care home. He told her to bugger off,' said Murray. 'I couldn't find out any more but that story about the care home raised a red flag for me; Fran's grandmother's in a care home, and of course, Fran lived with Gemma. She might have set up the scam.'

'I agree. That definitely warrants our attention,' said Natalie. She told both Murray and Ian what she'd learnt from Henry. 'Definitely sounds like this person – whoever they are – was catfishing. Ian, have you got details of Gemma's bank account yet?'

'Not yet. Want me to speed things up?'

'Definitely. We need to establish if she was in debt or if any significant deposits were made into her account. Gemma might be our catfisher, but I find it really hard to believe she'd use a fake name and details but still put up her own photo. She was clearly an intelligent girl and that isn't what somebody like her would do. Run checks on Fran's account, and while you're at it, Hattie's too. Whoever was trying to scam these men might have succeeded with others. I'm going to talk to Gemma's mother. Keep me posted and let me know if there are any developments whatsoever.'

She was about to leave when she got a call from Ralph. 'I've downloaded the information from David's satnav. He wasn't any-where near the university on any occasion or even in Samford. He drove to exactly the same spot each time in Little Harding.' Little Harding was about ten minutes from Castergate. It was a small place with little to offer by way of facilities. 'The car was parked on Gower Street from six until nine thirty Friday night, from four ten to eight thirty Saturday evening, and again on Sunday from ten thirty until three thirty.'

Natalie felt her heart sink. She knew where David had been. Gower Street was home to two bookmakers and three pubs. David had undoubtedly been drinking and gambling. *Old habits die hard.*

CHAPTER TWENTY-FIVE

TUESDAY, 20 NOVEMBER – LATE MORNING

Natalie sat on the sofa next to Sasha. The woman had scooped her unwashed hair up onto the top of her head and twisted it into a tightly coiled bun. Her skin, devoid of make-up, showed signs of age, and tiny feathery lines appeared around her eyes as she read through the dialogue on the sheet.

'This doesn't sound like Gemma at all,' she said in a hushed voice. 'She was never openly flirtatious – the sexual innuendos, the suggestive tone. She didn't use language like this. She wasn't a prude but she didn't talk like this. These messages were not written by her. This isn't Gemma.'

'We suspected that was the case but I wanted to make sure by talking to you. You knew her better than anyone.'

'She wasn't interested in any of this online *rubbish*. She was better than this...' She waved a hand impotently over the printout, unable to find the correct words. She got to her feet and strode to the window. A flat waterfall of rain was sheeting against the glass, distorting the view beyond, such as it was – rooftops and fences surrounding neighbouring gardens, from which poked the odd leafless tree.

'Thank you, Sasha. You've confirmed our suspicions. We think somebody stole her photograph.'

Downloading photographs of attractive people or screenshotting them for scamming purposes was becoming increasingly popular, and talking to Sasha had convinced her that Gemma had been a victim of identity fraud. She was ready to wind up the interview when she received a message from Ian:

Gemma's account is £468 in credit. No debts. No unusual payments made into account. Still waiting for info on other accounts.

It was further proof that somebody else was behind the scam – possibly Fran. Natalie got to her feet to leave. She halted in her tracks. Sasha had turned around and was doubled over, crying silent tears. Little by little, her legs gave way and she folded slowly onto her haunches, back against the wall, face raised to Natalie. A pain ripped through Natalie's chest at the sight of the woman in such agony, and she crossed the room to comfort her. She couldn't leave her to suffer alone.

*

Gemma,

I've been checking out your selfies on Instagram again, not that you'd know I've been looking at them because I don't actually follow you, but since you haven't set your profile to private, anyone can stare at them, and I'm sure they do because no matter what you wear, you look like some sort of celebrity or pop star or model. No wonder you get hundreds of likes for every picture you post.

It was while I was looking at your latest post that I had 'the idea' and took screenshots of a few of them. I chose the one I liked best as a profile picture for the Special Ones dating website. It seemed an appropriate site. You think you're special, don't you? Oh so fucking special that you can't even give me the time of day.

I'd really like to use your actual name on this site, not a fake, but this isn't about getting my own back on a shallow bitchface who can't see what is under a person's skin. This scam is about getting money from love-struck idiots who think they're talking to you online.

I'm going to give them all the chat, and when their tongues are hanging out and they're desperate to meet you, I'm going to give them a reason to hand over money, then let them down.

Ha! They'll all end up hating you as much as I do.

An Ex-Admirer

*

On Natalie's return to headquarters, she discovered Mike in the office, talking to Murray, Ian and Lucy. His team had managed to retrieve deleted emails from Henry's account and not one of them had been sent to Maisie.

'Not only that, but there were no photographs of her, deleted or hidden, on his mobile either,' said Mike.

'He lied to us,' said Natalie as she removed her jacket and rolled up her sleeves. It was warm and stuffy in the room which now stank of bergamot, rosemary and cedar wood. Someone had liberally doused themselves in body spray and it wasn't Mike. Mike used more subtle aftershaves. It wasn't unpleasant although it irritated the back of Natalie's throat, forcing her to clear it several times.

Mike continued, 'I agree because if they'd been on that device as you know, we have the technology to retrieve them. In addition to that, we found no evidence to prove he'd logged on to the Special Ones website from his phone.' He raised his eyebrows at Natalie.

'Which suggests he accessed it from a different device,' she said.

'Exactly.'

'He's a lying sod. Drag his arse back in,' said Natalie. She leant over her desk and picked up some paperwork. The tickling in her throat proved too great and she lapsed into a rapid coughing fit. When she'd recovered, red-eyed, she demanded, 'Who's sprayed the office with Lynx or whatever it is?'

Ian apologised. 'That was me. I thought the place smelt a bit...
niffy.'

'Couldn't you have opened a window?'

'It was bucketing down with rain.'

'For crying out loud, open it for a few minutes and let some air
in. I'm choking here. Who interviewed the third man Maisie was in
contact with... Felix Conway?' she added, reading from her notes.

'I did,' said Murray, unlatching one of the windows.

'What did you get out of him?'

'Same as the others. He got chatting to Maisie on the website.
They clicked, exchanged email addresses and were going to meet
up for a weekend away, but at the eleventh hour she emailed to say
she couldn't make it. She told him some nonsense about her bank
account being hacked and frozen and how she had no money for
the train fare or to pay her rent that month. Needless to say, he
didn't fall for it and broke off contact with her.'

'Did he email her?' asked Natalie.

'Yes. Same as the other guys.'

'Weren't they even the slightest bit suspicious from the off?
Everyone's on messaging apps or texts. Why didn't they think it was
odd she wanted to keep it anonymous? It screams "scam" to me.'

'Some people are too trusting,' said Lucy.

'More like *foolish*!' Natalie cleared her throat again even though the
smell was evaporating. She despaired at the naivety of those duped by
fraudsters even though online scams had become very sophisticated
and it was often difficult to distinguish truth from fiction. It happened to numerous individuals, including those who considered
themselves savvy, and then she reflected that her outburst and sour
mood were not because of the stench in the office, or Henry's lies, but
because of Gemma. The possibility that somebody had used this girl
in fraudulent activity had angered her. Watching Sasha crushed and
sobbing had brought back her own loss. She'd bonded with Gemma's

mother, and although she was supposed to remain impartial, she couldn't help but feel empathy. She had to get to the bottom of this to help Sasha come to terms with what had happened.

'Did nobody at all report this "Maisie" to the dating website?'

'No.'

'I find that really strange. If it happened to me, I'd want to protect others from being ripped off. I'd report them to the police as well. Why didn't they do that?'

'Scott was embarrassed and thought the dating site organisers would get wind of it sooner or later, and Felix said he felt humiliated. He'd told Maisie a whole load of personal stuff about himself. He was really upset when he realised she was faking it, and part of him didn't want to accept it. I've got his statement here if you want to read it,' said Murray.

Natalie took it and glanced at it. The words 'humiliated' and 'depressed' stood out. Successful scammers, or catfishers, mostly prayed on people who were vulnerable: the elderly, widows or widowers, and those who were reeling from a recent split from loved ones. David was one such person but he hadn't been contacted by Maisie, nor was he any longer a suspect in this investigation – but Henry Warburton was.

'Why did Henry tell me he received photos and deleted them, when clearly he didn't? And why didn't he use that mobile to access the Special Ones website or download their app? And… why haven't we been able to find any emails that were sent to her?'

'Burner phone,' said Ian.

'Exactly!' Natalie had been sure of that possibility. 'I wonder if he used a burner to communicate with this person or anyone else he found on the dating website. What do you think, Mike?'

'It would explain why we can find nothing on the mobile we have. Or he might have used a separate SIM card.'

'We don't have the email address that this person used, do we?'

Murray spoke up. 'I passed it on to Mike.'

Mike took over. 'It was a disposable email address used to store emails temporarily and linked to the original email, but we've been unable to trace it or the email address it was linked to. It's disappeared. Professional scammers have various sophisticated methods to disguise their IP address but this is more basic. Looks like that's what happened here.'

'It's not complex?' Natalie asked Mike.

'Not at all. DEAs are used a lot these days to divert spam. It's easy enough to obtain one. You don't need great computer skills.'

'There's still an outside chance Gemma set up the fake profile using her own image and a fake email account to correspond with strangers and con money out of them,' said Ian.

Natalie didn't buy it. 'I don't think so. To start with, she wasn't in any debt, she had a decent part-time job and was focused on her studies, as far as we can tell. Besides, if she'd gone to all the trouble to get a DEA and make up all this crap about jewellery shops and grandmothers in homes, then surely she'd have used a different profile picture. This definitely looks as if somebody else set it up and used a photo of her to attract their prey, and at the moment, thanks to her story about the grandmother, Fran is in the frame. I'd like Forensics to send a unit to check Fran's room and see if we can find anything to prove she was behind this. Can you arrange that, Mike?'

'Definitely.'

They couldn't trace the disposable email address, and as far as Natalie was concerned, Gemma was definitely not behind the scam, yet there could still be a link between the acid attack and the scam. She threw her thoughts out there for her team to consider.

Murray shook his head. 'I can't see how this scam is related to the attack. This catfisher didn't succeed. The three men we interviewed all saw through her ploy and didn't give her any money. The only thing I can come up with is that Gemma found out about it and was attacked to keep quiet.'

Natalie considered his theory but it seemed woolly to her. 'She'd have reported the person.'

'Maybe not if it was somebody she knew, a friend even – somebody like Fran.'

'Sorry to rain on your parade, mate, but I got financial records back for Fran and Hattie and neither are in debt. Admittedly Fran only has ninety pounds in her account, but looking at her expenditure, she doesn't spend a lot. Hattie gets regular payments of a couple of hundred pounds from her father every month. He's set up a direct debit for her,' said Ian.

'So, the girls might not be behind the scam, but I still want Fran's room checked out, Mike, okay?'

'Yes.'

Ian lifted up a hand like a schoolboy in class hoping to answer a question. 'We haven't checked out the men who Maisie tried to scam, have we? What they told us might not be true.'

'It feels like we're clutching at straws,' said Natalie. She was going to dismiss the idea then decided they had no other options, and her gut told her there was some link between the scam and the attack on Gemma. 'Get hold of their financial details and see if any large amounts left their accounts. If any of them made significant cash withdrawals, that might give us a new angle to work on. We have to find a clue somewhere.' Her most likely suspect at the moment was Henry, but even he had no link to Hattie or Fran that she knew about. 'Okay, let's get on with what we have, and somebody ring Henry – I want to talk to him.'

Mike waited until everyone was occupied then tipped her a nod, indicating he wanted to speak to her more privately, and slid out into the corridor. Natalie joined him on the large multicoloured settee that was a fixture outside her office.

'Did you visit David?'

'Yes, and I told him about the DNA results although I've not yet spoken to him about his whereabouts over the last few days. Sure as eggs are eggs, he'll have been in one or both of the bookies when his car was parked on Gower Street. He'll have guessed as soon as I explained about the satnav that I'd find out where he actually went, but he didn't stop me taking it or say anything. The stupid thing is, it actually doesn't bother me. He could have told me where he was from the off and had his name cleared much sooner, but no, he kept it secret, and it doesn't annoy me. I can't even say I'm surprised by it. I've grown to expect he'll lie, especially about gambling, and I don't care. What he does with his life isn't my concern any more.'

His dark brows drew together, and he tilted his head. He clearly still cared about his friend. 'Did he seem okay to you?'

'He didn't rant at me which was a start, and we managed a civilised, albeit brief, conversation, along with a mug of tea. And the house was tidy – really clean and neat. That surprised me. I expected it to be a tip.'

'He's always had high standards. Even back in our university days, his room was always way tidier than mine,' said Mike softly. Had it not been for his relationship with Natalie, Mike would undoubtedly be there now in his friend's hour of need. David had cut both of them out of his life and tried to go it alone.

'It's been a few months. He might be more open to a reconciliation. Why don't you ring him?' she asked.

'That's highly unlikely and you know it. I've stolen his wife, and David is still a proud guy. Got to leave him a smidgeon of self-esteem. I can't go around begging for forgiveness. It's not my style. I knew what I was getting into when we made this decision, and what I was giving up.' He gave a tired smile then said, 'I'd better get back to the lab. We've got a stack of work to get through too.'

He got to his feet in one strong movement, leaving an emptiness where his solid presence had been.

She watched his retreating form, aware she was drawn to Mike more and more each day, but there was no denying Mike felt guilt at hurting one of his closest friends. Her thoughts were scattered as she overheard Lucy calling out to Ian.

'Have you requested Henry Warburton's financial details?'

'Done it.'

Murray interrupted them with, 'I've got Henry on the line, Natalie. You want to talk to him?'

Natalie scooted across. 'Mr Warburton, it's DI Ward.'

The reply was very hesitant. 'Yes.'

'We need you to come back to HQ as soon as possible.'

'I'm at work at the moment.'

'Would you prefer for us to come to you?'

'No. No. I'll see if I can get time off.'

'We can send an officer over to pick you up if that would be more helpful.'

'No. I'll drive myself. Can I ask what you want to talk to me about?'

'It's in connection with Maisie. I'd prefer to discuss the matter at the station.'

'Okay. I'll be about an hour.'

She replaced the receiver. If he didn't confess to owning a second phone, she'd require a search warrant to hunt for one, and given his home address was out of their jurisdiction, she'd need to inform colleagues at West Midlands Police. Murray had returned to his chair and had donned his spectacles to wade through paperwork. She remained in position, reflecting on how best to proceed. She wished they had more than a man who might or might not have been scammed by someone who might or might not have pretended to be Gemma, but she didn't. She could only follow the evidence, and at present there was bugger all to pursue. She moved across to her desk and made a discreet phone call to the bookies on Gower Street in Little Harding. She might not be able to charge anyone with the crimes, but she was determined to clear David's name, once and for all. Dan would have to find another scapegoat to throw to the press. For all David's faults, she wasn't going to allow him to suffer any more than he already had.

CHAPTER TWENTY-SIX

Henry was true to his word and arrived exactly one hour later at 3.40 p.m. He entered the interview room with a slight swagger, hands in his trouser pockets, his casual affectation betrayed by his forehead, which was shiny with perspiration. The officer who'd shown him to the room departed silently, the door shutting with an ominous click.

Facing Natalie and Murray, he yapped a nervous laugh as he took his seat. 'This looks serious. I don't need a solicitor, do I?'

'That depends on your answers to our questions,' said Natalie.

Henry shuffled uncomfortably before adopting a suitable position, hands on his lap, feet firmly planted on the ground. His shoulders rounded automatically. The vulture was back.

'We've checked your mobile.' Murray pushed the device in a plastic bag towards the centre of the table as he spoke.

'And you found nothing on it,' said Henry quickly.

'That's right,' Murray replied.

'Then why have you asked me to return?'

Natalie spoke. 'Because there was nothing.'

'Then I should be allowed to leave.' He made to stand.

Murray growled, 'Sit down, Mr Warburton.'

Natalie took up where she'd left off. 'When I say there is nothing, that doesn't suggest you told us the truth. In fact, quite the contrary, because our technicians are the best in the UK and can recover almost anything that has been deleted. When I say almost, I mean the only things they can't recover are those destroyed due to the destruction of the phone, or its SIM card. Did you replace the SIM card in your phone with a new one?'

'No. I didn't. This is my phone. If it's been checked as you say, then you'll know I've had it for eighteen months. The original SIM card is still in it.'

Natalie's lips twitched. The man had shifted again in his seat and his hands were now clamped tightly between his thighs. She was on to something.

'Not only were there no pictures, we couldn't find any evidence of email exchange between the pair of you.'

'I deleted all correspondence between us.'

'As I just explained. If you had done that, we would have been able to retrieve it.' She opened the file in front of her and ran a finger down a list. 'In fact, we retrieved 1,271 emails that had been deleted, dating back a year, but none were to Maisie, as she was known to you. How did you communicate with her once you and she stopped messaging on the website?'

'We emailed each other. I told you.'

'But we know that wasn't the case.'

'I used a different email address to the one you have.'

'And why didn't you tell me that sooner?'

'I forgot.' The lie was so obvious he winced as soon as it had been spoken.

'That's bollocks and you know it,' said Murray.

As Henry opened his mouth to protest, Natalie halted him with a cold look. 'Which actually makes matters even more complicated because you are clearly hiding something, Mr Warburton. You have lied, withheld information and wasted our time, which as you may know gives us reason enough to charge you.'

'Now wait a minute—'

She didn't let him finish. 'I suggest you think very carefully before answering my next question. It is the difference between you going to the cells this afternoon or walking away, and I'm not in the mood to negotiate or listen to any more lies. This is a murder investigation. Three young women are dead and it started when somebody threw acid at a girl whose photo was on that dating website. Do you understand how serious this is?'

An invisible force sucked the bravado from him and he bent further forward. 'Yes.' She almost couldn't hear his quietly spoken response. Henry was unravelling fast.

'We can get search warrants and raid your family home and your workplace and generally disrupt your life, because we believe you used either a second device to communicate with Maisie or a replacement SIM card. You did not receive any photos of her on that phone, but you did receive photos of her, didn't you?'

'Yes.'

'On another phone?'

He didn't respond.

'Mr Warburton, answer the question, please. Did you speak to or communicate with Maisie by phone?'

'I would like a lawyer before we continue.'

Murray popped his knuckles as they waited in the office for Henry's lawyer to appear. They were on to something at last and the atmosphere wasn't euphoric but certainly positive. Ian, however, changed all that in an instant.

'I've received financial records for all three men and none of them have withdrawn or transferred large amounts of money. There's nothing untoward on either Scott's or Felix's account but Henry's is in the red. Not only has he got a mortgage and the usual outgoings but he's maxed out two credit cards and has three short-term loans outstanding. He has no money to loan, let alone pay his mortgage. The man is crippled with debt.'

'Then he's not likely to have given Maisie any money.' Lucy's words hung in the air.

'If Henry didn't lend her any money, why would he harm her? And what connection does he have to Fran and Hattie?'

Ian's questions were on all of their lips. Natalie couldn't give him any answers but she recalled the look on Henry's face, the damp brow and the hands crushed between his thighs. His reactions were down to guilt. She needed him to talk and soon.

'He couldn't give Maisie what he didn't have. Funny that. An accountant with no money. That's ironic, isn't it?' Ian mused.

There was a sense of irony to it. None of the men had handed over money to the scammer. Who was this person? Was it Fran? Were they on the wrong trail, hunting for a scammer when really they should be searching for a murderer? Or were they one and the same person?

Natalie watched white clouds rush past the windows. The first looked vaguely like an elephant, its trunk raised to sound the alarm. It merged rapidly with another cloud into something unidentifiable. Natalie had never been much good at identifying shapes and patterns. Leigh, on the other hand, had been expert at making out shapes or faces in pieces of toast, in vegetables or in clouds...

'Mum, look... It's a horse stampeding away from the cloud! It's beautiful.'

Natalie opens her eyes. The sun has warmed her through and her body is heavy with laziness. Leigh is flat on her back on the blanket. She points to the sky and Natalie shields her eyes with her hand. The white horse is emerging from the top of the cloud, front hooves raised, ready to gallop to the sun. The remainder of the body is swirled together with the cloud from which it is escaping.

Escaping… like the bird on Fran's arm. Why had Fran been so reluctant to return to her home town, and why had she been antagonistic towards Gemma? Was it purely over Ryan? She hunted out details about the girl, her mind taken off cloud formations and her daughter for the moment. Fran hadn't had an easy upbringing. Her father was a criminal, attacked and killed by an inmate while he served time. Her mother had remarried a loser with a string of minor offences to his name including theft, and Fran too had been in trouble with the local police on several occasions when she was a kid. She'd run away from home twice and after the second attempt been taken in by her grandparents. Her grandfather had died four years later and her grandmother had looked after her, right through to college; only a few weeks after Fran had finished her studies, her grandmother had been admitted to a care home. She read the last sentence again. Maisie had tried to extract money using a ploy about a grandmother who'd been ejected from a care home. Had somebody used that information to make up the scam or was it Fran herself? Others who knew Fran would have known about her past and her grandmother. Had one of them created the profile?

'Mike's on the line for you, Natalie,' said Murray. Natalie hadn't registered the internal phone ringing.

Mike sounded upbeat. 'My unit found two thousand pounds in fifty-pound notes stuffed in a shoebox at the bottom of Fran's wardrobe. They're bringing it in once they've finished checking the rest of the room.'

Natalie ought to be jubilant yet there were still unanswered questions. This was, however, a step forward. 'That's great. Thanks very much.' She looked up at Lucy, perched on the desk beside her, who rubbed at the scar across the bridge of her nose as she often did when puzzling over a problem.

'I hope it helps move things on,' said Mike.

'Definitely.'

'Thought maybe we could manage a mini-celebratory drink later.'

'That would be great.'

'Good. I'll catch you later.'

Natalie ended the call. 'Forensics found a couple of grand in a shoebox in Fran's room.'

Murray whistled. 'Wow! That's a lot of cash to hide. Now we need to work out where it came from.'

'It's another mystery for us to solve, but I'm sure there's a link between this scam and the murders. We're getting closer,' Natalie replied.

Lucy rubbed at her nose again. 'The money must have come from a scam.'

'Maisie, or should I say Fran, didn't match up with any other men, and those guys we interviewed all say they saw through her scam in time, which begs the question, where did the two thousand pounds come from?' asked Murray.

Natalie stared at an angel-shaped cloud passing the window. The thought appeared from nowhere, brought to life by Ian's earlier statement regarding an accountant with no money. It was a long shot but worth a try. 'Henry handles the books at an engineering company, doesn't he? Find out if he signs cheques on behalf of the company. If he does, ask if any cheques or withdrawals have been made over the last few weeks.'

Ian scurried away, and as she tried to make sense of what she'd discovered, her mobile buzzed. David was trying to reach her and she went into the corridor to answer it.

'I'm sorry. Truly sorry. You know the truth now, don't you?'

'Know about where you were the last few days? You were in Gower Street.'

'I couldn't tell you. I couldn't look you in the eye and tell you that I'd let you and Josh and my dad down yet again. I'm fucked up in so many ways I can't even look at myself in the mirror. Every time I try to take a step forward, I fail. I am a failure. I couldn't even get a student to pay me. I frightened off a decent woman who showed me some kindness, and I screwed up again by not telling you where I was when the attack on Gemma took place. I don't even understand why I couldn't. I read the newspapers earlier. They state you were questioning a man in his late forties. That's me they're talking about, isn't it?'

'It is but that wasn't my doing. I didn't want that information to get out.'

He sighed. 'I couldn't tumble much lower, could I? A fucking suspect in a murder case. All I need now is for the press to bang on the door and question me.'

'They won't.'

'They might. You know how persistent journalists can be and my car is at HQ—'

'They won't find out.'

The sigh went on for what seemed an eternity. 'It doesn't matter any more if they do. I had to call to explain that I couldn't tell you where I was. I simply couldn't.'

'It would have been much easier if you had. There'd have been no mention in the papers. You pissed me about when I could have cleared your name instantly. You only had to tell one of us on the team where you really were. Why the hell couldn't you have been open with us? Better to admit to being in a betting shop than having people think you murdered somebody.'

'I know. I know. I'm totally pathetic and I despise myself for being this way.' His words lacked inflection.

'Anyway, we've found out where you were now, and as far as I'm concerned we won't be troubling you again about this. I won't even press charges about perverting the course of justice. I want you to get a fucking grip on your life. Maybe consider therapy. You have to break out of this self-destructive cycle. Josh needs you.' She hoped her words would hit home and galvanise him into a slightly more positive frame of mind, but his response was flat.

'No, Natalie. He needs somebody who can be a good father. Someone he can look up to. I'm no longer that person. He has you. You're a far better person than I'll ever be. You can handle it all. I can't. I'm too weak. I'm tired of all of this. I'm done.'

A prickling feeling ran up her spine. David sounded sober but odd – distant, as if he didn't care any more about anything. It struck her why. He'd given up once and for all. He was going to end it all. 'Where are you, David?'

'It doesn't matter where I am.'

That clinched it for her. She listened for any background noise, heard nothing. 'David, whatever you're thinking of doing, don't… please—'

'I still love you. I love you, Josh and Leigh more than you'll ever know. Goodbye, Natalie.'

The phone went dead. Why had he said goodbye like that? The way he'd intoned the goodbye gave it a deeper meaning than usual. He'd meant a definitive goodbye. He was going to end his life! She dialled him back but it went directly to answerphone. Natalie spun on her heel. *Shit!* Who could get to David in time? Ought she to ring an ambulance? It would take her twenty minutes to reach Castergate. That might be too late. And what if he wasn't at home, and what if she was overreacting? The questions wouldn't stop as she belted back downstairs. She halted on the first landing, charged down the corridor and banged on the pane of glass to the forensic lab. Darshan looked up and opened the door using the button by the counter.

She called out Mike's name. 'Where is he?' she demanded.

'Out. Can I hel—?'

'I'll ring him.' She dialled his number and tore downstairs towards the entrance, phone clamped to her ear.

'Hey, Natalie!'

Her heartbeat hammered in her ears. 'Mike, I've had a really weird call from David. I'm sure he's about to commit suicide.'

'Fuck!'

'How far are you from Castergate?'

'Ten minutes tops. You?'

'At HQ and his Volvo is still in the compound. I can't get there quickly. I'm not even sure he's at home. He's turned off his phone.'

She heard his breath quicken as he started to run. 'I'm on my way. Stay there. I'll try his phone too.'

'I'll get a vehicle.'

'No! Stay there. I'll handle it.'

She stood in reception and raised her face to the sky. Clouds of all shapes and sizes scudded across the roof of the glass atrium above her. She watched a dragon, smoke issuing from its nostrils, surge forwards and then she closed her eyes. For all his faults and in spite of everything, she didn't want anything bad to happen to David. She couldn't allow that. A voice brought her back to her senses. Murray was calling to her.

'The lawyer's turned up at last.'

She drew on her reserves. Mike would deal with David. He might even be on a wild goose chase, and she had an important investigation to lead. There was no choice. She powered towards Murray. 'Let's find out what the fuck Henry Warburton is keeping from us.'

CHAPTER TWENTY-SEVEN

TUESDAY, 20 NOVEMBER – LATE AFTERNOON

With a lawyer by his side, Henry had acquired a confidence not shown before, an impression tarnished by the yellowing sweat marks under his armpits, visible when he placed his hands behind his head.

Natalie made the introductions for the benefit of the recording device and they began.

'The last time we spoke, I asked you if Maisie had sent you any photographs of herself. I'd like to ask the same question again. Did she send you any photographs?'

His whole upper body, rather than just his head, bounced up and down, eager to please. 'Maisie and I decided to correspond via email rather than the website messaging service. It allowed her to send attachments and she sent me a couple of photographs of herself posing in underwear, swimsuits… nice photos, not disgusting – tasteful pictures. They weren't pornographic at all.'

'Did you download these to your phone?'

'Yes, I did.'

'And you deleted them?'

'Yes.'

'We couldn't find the deleted photographs on the mobile you gave us. Why is that?'

He glanced at the lawyer, who indicated he should continue.

'I bought a pay-as-you-go phone to keep any relationships from my wife.'

'I thought you were separated at the time you joined the dating website.'

'That wasn't the case. I was looking for some extramarital fun. I had tried other websites prior to Special Ones and had some success, but those relationships fizzled out. I love my wife, but sometimes I need more than what she can offer me. Bringing up three kids takes its toll on her. I appreciated a little company from time to time. I used the phone to keep that part of my life separate.' His eyes, like dark insects, burrowed into hers.

'Do you still have the phone?'

'No. I disposed of it after the whole scam affair. It made me realise how stupid I had been and that I could get into serious trouble if I kept up this behaviour. I smashed it up and threw it away. I haven't been on any dating site since.'

'Why did you lie to us about your email address?'

'I have no answer for that. I can only apologise. I was scared you'd accuse me of attacking that unfortunate girl. I panicked.'

'Which email address did you use to contact Maisie?'

'A disposable one,' he replied.

Has he spent the last hour thinking up this crap? She'd have found it more plausible if he'd come out with it in the first instance. The inner voices that guided her instincts bayed like wild animals. This man was lying through his teeth and she couldn't do a damn thing to prove otherwise. The knock on the door startled her. Her thoughts jumped immediately to David and she excused herself to answer it. She stepped into the corridor and closed the door behind her. Ian couldn't prevent his lips from twitching as he held out a sheet of A4.

'Henry has access to the engineering company accounts. At my request, they examined the most recent transactions and have discovered he transferred £3,000 into a PayPal account on October the nineteenth. I haven't been able to find out who the account belongs to. Ralph says it's out of his sphere of expertise and we've passed it over to the tech team in the first instance.'

Natalie took the paper with thanks. This was proof he'd lied about what had happened. *More lies.* He'd given Maisie the money she'd requested, and once he'd discovered he'd been duped, he had reason to be angry with her, or even a motive to harm her. Natalie had found him out at last. 'We need to look into his alibi for Friday night. He claims he was at home with his wife and kids. Contact his wife and see if their accounts tally.'

'You think the account was linked to Fran's?' asked Ian.

'Maybe. If that was the case, she'd already spent £1,000 of it. We'll have to wait and see if the PayPal account is linked to her bank account. You check out that alibi, and in the meantime, we'll make him squirm and hopefully confess.'

Ian acted quickly, a light-footed sprint to the staircase and out of view within seconds. She glanced at her mobile. There was nothing from Mike. *No news is good news.* That wasn't always the case as she'd found to her cost when all her hopes had been pinned on finding Leigh and Zoe alive. She couldn't bear to go through losing another person who'd been dear to her. She pocketed the mobile. She had complete faith in Mike. He'd ring when he could. She opened the door with renewed purpose.

*

Mike sped around the Vauxhall Cavalier that was holding him up, foot flat to the floor. He didn't care if he got a speeding ticket. If Natalie thought David was likely to harm himself, then he most likely was, because Natalie wasn't somebody who was prone to dramatic outbursts. David's mental state had been bothering Mike. He'd spotted him walking into HQ on Sunday and been shocked by his old friend's appearance.

Although Mike had recently become involved with Natalie, it hadn't been behind his friend's back. Natalie had been firm about that. She'd ensured her relationship with David was over before starting afresh with Mike, and he respected her for that. He'd fancied her for years but had never intended having an affair with his best friend's wife. The one-off brief affair a few years earlier had been a mistake – a thoroughly enjoyable mistake – and both he and Natalie had agreed it would go no further. She'd fallen into his bed only because David had screwed up big time. If David had resisted the urge to gamble again, Natalie would never have left him. He pushed such thoughts aside. What was done was done. Ultimately, David was his friend and he wasn't going to lose him.

Ahead the sky was black, the blackest he'd seen it in months, and branches whipped at the BMW as it hugged the tight bends. The road was clear and he opened up the growling engine, taking the hump-backed bridge at such speed he was suspended momentarily in the air until the car crashed, suspension groaning, onto the tarmac and surged forwards. A cloud of dried leaves blew up from the verge, covering the windscreen, skeletal shapes sticking to the glass, and all the while he powered on, aware that every second counted.

He barked commands at his voice-activated control to dial David's number again. 'Pick up, you stupid bastard. Pick up!' When a voice answered, it was that of the automatic answering service, and he slammed his palms against the steering wheel. 'For fuck's sake!'

David had been his best friend for decades. Mike had always believed David was the blessed one: he had an intelligent, good-looking wife, and a family – two super kids, and a respectable job with a law firm. Meanwhile, Mike had never found what he was looking for, had chased after numerous women, had far too many casual relationships, got married, only to split up, and lost a daughter in the bargain. His job had been his life but it was nothing like David's secure nine-to-five. Then everything had changed and David's life had crumbled. He'd watched his friend make mistake after mistake, and although he'd tried to help the man he considered a brother, David hadn't listened to Mike. He'd continued to mess up everything and now…

He screeched to a halt behind Natalie's car, parked on the driveway, flung open the car door and thundered up the path to David's house. Curtains were drawn at all the windows and Mike pounded first on the sitting room window then the front door, opening the mail slot and yelling, 'David! Open up… now!'

The house returned nothing but ominous silence. The first heavy drops of rain plopped onto the flagstones around him, marking them with splodges that resembled the Winnie-the-Pooh jelly shapes his daughter, Thea, loved. He cast about, looking for something to help him break in, then remembered the spare key. David had always kept one hidden outside in case either child was locked out. It was secreted under a loose brick in the wall that ran beside the house. Four strides and he was feeling for the correct brick, hunting high and low, bending and straightening, hunting for a giveaway gap. *Where the fuck are the keys?* The dark cloud burst and water cascaded over him, drenching his hair and running down his forehead, blinding him. He wiped it away and ran strong fingers over the bricks, their rough edges grazing his fingertips until, at last, one shifted slightly when he pressed it and he teased it out. The key was still there.

Ignoring the water sliding past his collar and down his neck, he unlocked the front door. The silence hit him first, then the gloom. The house no longer gave off the happy family vibes he'd always envied when he'd visited the Ward family in the past. It was as if it had absorbed all the sadness of recent months and now resonated grief. The familiar sights of children's shoes by the door, and coats tossed over the banister, or schoolbags at the bottom of the stairs, had vanished, along with the general family chaos that had made the place homely. Photographs of the family that had always been on display next to a vase of regularly replenished flowers on the hall table had been removed, leaving the table bereft.

'David! Are you here?'

There was no reply and he steeled himself for what he might find.

*

The interview room was at an ambient temperature but Henry tugged furiously at a primrose tie, fumbled with the top button of his shirt and exposed a deepening rash that covered his throat.

'I didn't mean for any of this to happen.' The blubbing started again. His lawyer looked away, shark nose in the air at the emotional display.

It hadn't been difficult to extract a confession. Henry had been willing to unburden himself, pleaded with Natalie to listen to what he had to say.

'Start again with the emails,' she said.

He blew his nose and swiped at his damp eyes with the same soggy tissue before speaking. 'I opened a second email account to communicate with women without my wife finding out.'

'And the email address you used is the one you gave me earlier in the interview?'

'Yes.'

Natalie had sent it, along with the password that Henry had supplied, to Ralph with instructions to examine it for deleted emails to Maisie.

'And how long did you correspond via email?'

'Only a few days. We were getting along so well, I suggested we swap phone numbers and meet up. She was keen to meet up but not to exchange numbers. She preferred to do that on our date, and at the time, that didn't seem strange to me. We arranged to meet at lunchtime on Saturday, October the twentieth at Birmingham

New Street Station, and the plan was to go for a drink and meal and then spend the night together. She was completely candid about it and told me what she intended doing to me when we were alone. Our relationship had… grown quickly. There was a lot of sex talk and I was looking forward to meeting her.'

The lawyer had lowered his head so only his scalp was visible, and although he appeared to be asleep, he was listening to his client repeat his confession, his fingers writing spidery notes from time to time across a spiral-bound notepad.

Henry waved his arms ineffectually as he spoke. 'On the Friday morning, the day before we were due to meet up, I was in my office and received an email from her…'

Henry can't concentrate on the accounts. In the background, there's a constant banging as somebody works on a piece of equipment with a large hammer, the clang, clang, clang jarring his nerves. Even with the office door closed, he always hears the whistles and constant shouting from below. If he wishes to, he can watch the labourers at their worksta-tions through the tiny window which overlooks the factory floor. It's only a small engineering company but the turnover is good and there's enough work to keep him in full-time employment.

His mobile bleeps an alert and he pulls out the pay-as-you-go phone from his inside jacket pocket, hands suddenly slippery with the sweat of anticipation. He can't wait to meet this exciting creature who seems to understand his sexual needs perfectly. He has already fantasised several times this morning about what they'll get up to in bed tomorrow evening. She has a vivid imagination and a gorgeous figure and he can't wait to explore every part of her. His fingers hover over the screen as he wonders what suggestive message she has sent him this time, and a small groan is released from his plump lips at the prospect of the night of passion they'll enjoy.

He opens the email, which doesn't begin in the usual flirtatious manner. Maisie is upset.

I am really sorry, Henry. I can't meet you tomorrow. I am completely up shit creek. The bastards at HMRC have impounded my jewellery I need for my exhibition on Monday, and won't release it until I pay them an outrageous amount. I don't have the cash and I need those items. Most of them are already promised to customers, and I was due to make an absolute killing on them. It's so fucking unfair. I'm completely stuffed. Sorry, lover, but I'm not in the mood for our raunchy weekend. I'll only be miserable and we won't enjoy ourselves as I had hoped. Maybe when this is all sorted, we can rearrange.

Henry can't catch his breath. He hadn't expected this. Every waking minute over the past few days has been spent looking forward to the meeting. He knows all about the jewellery. Just over a week earlier, Maisie went on a three-day shopping trip to Dubai to purchase some pieces for her business. She emailed Henry photographs of the city and a couple of selfies, but none, as he had requested, of her in a belly dancer's outfit. She also sent photos of some of the necklaces, ornate pieces set with brilliant gems that would sell well to the bohemian crowd – her target market. This was her big chance – an exhibition of custom-made pieces and these. She poured all her earnings into the big opening night at her new boutique, due to take place on Monday. And now, she doesn't want to meet up. Never has he experienced such bitter disappointment.

He hasn't got the funds to help her, and even if he did have them, he couldn't. His wife, Samira, would find out and there'd be hell to pay. He's drawn to the file on the desk and an idea is born. He is the only person who deals with the accounts and has eyes on the transactions that take place daily. Mr Winthrop, the seventy-year-old owner, hasn't been as hands-on the last three years, and he trusts Henry implicitly. Could he? He bashes out a quick email suggesting he might be able to assist Maisie. The reply pings back in an instant, full of gratitude but telling him she can't take his money. She'll have to find another way to solve the problem. He sends another message, insisting he can help. The response is more than he could hope for. The date is back on and she is eternally grateful to him. He is to send £3,000 via PayPal to her account, and she'll pay the fine to release her goods and see him the following day at 12.15 p.m. A smile plays on his lips as he types, 'What will you give me as reward for my generosity?'

The reply she sends back causes his trousers to bulge.

It is simple enough to transfer the money, and, once completed, he takes an early lunchbreak. He sits in the works canteen and types an email on his phone, asking if the money has arrived. She doesn't reply. She is no doubt trying to deal with the release of her goods. He gives it fifteen minutes before sending a second email. This is unlike her. She normally responds immediately. The canteen is filling up and he finishes his coffee and ham sandwich, checks one more time. There's still no reply. He sends a third email and heads back to the office and the clamouring of machines.

By the end of the afternoon he fingers the phone for the umpteenth time. He has stopped sending emails. He tries the dating website but she doesn't respond. He tidies away his books and locks the drawers they are kept in, then leaves the office. He feels sick to his stomach. He has been played for a fool. Maisie isn't going to reply.

Henry broke down in tears yet again. It was too much to hope he'd be able to continue without a short interlude, so Natalie organised a glass of water for him and left Murray in the interview room until Henry was recovered. She checked her phone as she headed upstairs. There was still nothing from Mike. She had to hope that was because everything was all right. Ian put down the phone the second she entered the room.

'I was speaking to Henry's wife, Samira. She can't confirm Henry's whereabouts Friday night. He didn't come home after work. They've been going through marital difficulties and she imagined he'd gone to the pub, or out with a friend. He's been going out a lot without telling her his whereabouts recently. He also asked her to tell the police he was at home if we rang.'

'What excuse did he give her?'

'He didn't. He told her he was being victimised by the police and needed her support. Said he had done nothing, he'd only sat alone in a pub in town, trying to figure out how best to mend their relationship, but he couldn't prove it or his whereabouts to us and needed her to back him up.'

'She believed him?'

'No. She said he's been lying to her face for months. She didn't want to perjure herself and said whatever he's got himself into, he can extricate himself without her help.'

'Sounds like that's a marriage that's definitely on the rocks,' muttered Lucy, who'd been listening.

Natalie agreed. 'Fortunately, it's worked in our favour. Henry's at breaking point. This should tip him over. Anything else?'

'That's it.'

Natalie left them, mind on Henry. She was sure he was responsible for harming Gemma. She had little idea why he'd target Fran or Hattie, but now was the time to find out exactly what had happened. She wished she knew what was going on with David and Mike.

CHAPTER TWENTY-EIGHT

TUESDAY, 20 NOVEMBER – EARLY EVENING

'What's this private investigator's surname?' Natalie asked.

'I don't know.'

'Oh, come on! You don't expect me to believe that, do you?'

Henry turned to his lawyer. 'I honestly don't know. I met him in the pub and he said he could help me track down Maisie. I was pissed and went along with it. I didn't ask for credentials…'

Henry opens the folder he's been given. The semi-retired private investigator, Keith, only took forty-eight hours to track down Maisie. The girl had used an alias. Her real name is Gemma Barnes and she's a language student at Samford University.

'How did you find her so easily?'

The PI wipes beer foam from his moustache and rests his hands across his wide girth. If his beard was white, not jet black, he'd pass for a friendly Santa Claus with his twinkling eyes behind frameless glasses. Henry half expects a hearty laugh but instead the man taps the side of his bulbous nose and says, 'The Internet. Everything is online these days.'

Henry gives the man five crisp ten-pound notes that he stole from the petty cash tin at work. He's been dipping into it on and off for a while. He doesn't take too much at any one time, that way he doesn't raise suspicions. The investigator came cheap, a chance encounter in the pub when Henry had consumed too many Southern Comforts and had complained bitterly to the stranger at the bar about being scammed. He reads through the handwritten notes – cloak and dagger style, with clandestine meetings in dark corners of pubs and cash-in-hand payments. The girl had played him for a fool. She hadn't been abroad to buy jewellery. The photos she'd sent him of Dubai had been screenshots taken from a tourism website.

'This her address?'

Santa Keith nods. 'It's student accommodation and she shares it with two other girls and two lads.'

Henry flicks through the notes. He's not sure how to use this information yet although he has an idea brewing, one that will prevent this girl from ever duping anyone again.

Natalie's fists balled and she hit the desk with sufficient force to make Henry stop bleating. 'That'll do. You don't know this private investigator's surname or where his office is or anything about him except he's called Keith and you first met him in the Wild Duck pub in Sutton Coldfield on October the twentieth?'

'Yes.'

'You met him again on October the twenty-second at the same place?'

'Yes.'

'How did he arrange that meeting?'

'He rang me at the office.'

'What time?'

'In the morning. Mid-morning.'

Natalie would have to get details of incoming calls to the engineering company for 22 October at around that time to try and trace this elusive PI. Henry had admitted to planning to attack Gemma. He'd stolen the sulphuric acid from work, where it was used as a pickling agent to remove impurities on metals.

'Okay. Tell me what happened on Friday the sixteenth.'

Henry scrubbed at his face with both hands. A bubble of snot appeared under his left nostril. Natalie had to look away as he spoke.

He waits for the number 34 bus. He's checked the timetable and she might be on the one due in a few minutes. The jar of acid is in his left-hand pocket and he is wearing two pairs of latex gloves to protect his hands while removing the lid. He can't afford to get any on him. He is pumped and ready to do this. He was going to shout at her so she'd know who was responsible for maiming her but decided against it. He doesn't want to be identified. He's drunk four pints of beer and a whisky chaser. There's no going back now. Gemma's going to get what she deserves. She won't be able to flirt with any other poor sods like him.

Gemma has no idea who he is. He told the engineering company he had personal problems and they gave him time off, which means he's been able to drive to Samford every day, hoping to find the right moment to exact his revenge. The first day, he walked about campus with a dog lead in his hand as if hunting for a lost hound, and no one had glanced his way. He located the language department and waited outside. His patience was rewarded and he finally saw her in the flesh. She was as beautiful as her photos had led him to believe and his chest constricted knowing she'd been leading him on. The more he thought about it, the angrier he became. He watched her laughing with a tall, blond-haired lad who wheeled his bike beside her and who couldn't tear his eyes away from her.

The following day, he found a bench close to the bus stop near the library, from which he could observe the comings and goings, and watched her get off the number 34 bus. She bussed in every day at around the same time, but the campus, filled with students, wasn't the best place to strike. He waited until she caught the bus home and boarded it, in the hope of attacking her in the street outside her house. Sitting directly behind her on the bus, breathing in the faint scent of almond shampoo she'd used on her glossy hair, he overheard her telephone conversation and learnt she

*was going to work in the library on Friday evening, after seven when it
was quieter. That would be perfect. It would be dark and he knew where
she would get off. He let her alight and carried on to the next stop, where
he got off and waited for a return bus. Friday would be the day.*

*Five minutes pass and the number 34 bus draws up to the stop
bang on time. He squints, heart thumping solidly in his chest. Is she
on it? He creeps forward towards it, hidden in the shadows and the
darkness of the evening. The doors open with a wheeze like somebody
sneezing, and Gemma descends, eyes on her mobile as she reads and
replies to a text message. He wonders if it's from a man, maybe another
sap reeled in by this unscrupulous bitch. She is alone. He looks left
and right and turns around. There isn't another soul – only Henry
and Gemma. Henry and Gemma on their date at last! The corners
of his mouth twitch at the thought, and hunched over, he loosens
the jar lid between his gloved hands. He looks back up, checks the area
is clear and takes one last look at Gemma. Her hair is swinging as she
walks and a smile plays on her lips as if she's laughing at him. Now!
He rushes towards her, freezing her to the spot. The last look he sees is
wide-eyed confusion as he hurls the jar's contents at her.*

*The scream is ear-splitting and she collapses to the ground, writh-
ing, hands scrabbling at her face. He turns and flees. As he corners the
building, out of sight once more, he glances back. A woman jumps from
an old-fashioned bicycle and, flinging it aside, crouches beside Gemma.*

Henry has had his payback.

'Never, not for one second, did I consider the possibility she would
die. I know what I did was wrong but I never, ever intended to
kill the girl. Believe me.' Henry spoke to his lawyer rather than
Natalie. The tears had dried as the realisation of what was to come
finally dawned on him.

'Wrong? It was abhorrent!' Natalie stopped herself before she
launched into a tirade fuelled by disgust at his actions and lack

of remorse. 'You are responsible for the death of Gemma Barnes.' She let the words sink in but he only looked startled and tearful. Could this man have also killed Fran and Hattie? She had seen similar looks before on the faces of cruel and clever killers, capable of great deception. Henry could be one such person, prepared only to confess to what he had to. She said sharply, 'Fran Ditton and Hattie Caldwell.'

Henry's long face stared mournfully at her. 'I don't know them.'

'But you did. They were Gemma's housemates. The private investigator gave you their details.' Her voice grew with the anger she felt towards this man, who'd felt he was justified in throwing acid in Gemma's face.

'He only gave me Gemma's identity. I swear on my children's lives, I had nothing to do with those deaths.'

Murray gave a low threatening growl but Natalie maintained a poker face. 'You expect us to believe a word of what you say after all the lies you fed us earlier?'

'I swear. I didn't do anything to them. I didn't. No.' He turned again to his lawyer, hands together in prayer. 'I'll confess to the acid attack but I didn't intend to kill Gemma and I definitely didn't harm anyone else. Please, tell them.'

The lawyer lifted one hand to calm the man. 'I think we'll leave it here, DI Ward. My client and I need to discuss this matter, and as you can hear, he is not accepting blame for the other deaths. We'll talk again should you find evidence to the contrary.'

Natalie couldn't press any further. If he wasn't going to confess, they'd have to uncover evidence to prove he was their perpetrator. For the moment, she wanted to get out of the interview room and find out what had happened to David.

'DS Anderson will read you your rights, and your lawyer will explain what will happen next.' She'd found Gemma's killer but the investigation was still wide open. It was possible somebody else had murdered Fran and Hattie, and she had no idea why.

*

Gemma,

I ought to say how sorry I am that you were attacked. I should feel guilty and be in tears, but I'm not. In many ways you got what you deserved. My main regret is that you died. If you'd lived, you'd have discovered what it's like to be ostracised. You'd have seen that look of disgust in people's eyes that I see most days. You'd have been the butt of cruel jokes, as I have been. Had I not shed several stone, I'd still be receiving jibes and caustic comments. You see, people are quick to make judgements. They don't understand why that person might be overweight or disadvantaged in some way, through no fault of their own. You'd have found out what it is like to live on the other side – the darker side. It's a shame you didn't experience that.

An Ex-Admirer

*

Mike shoved open the sitting room door, took a step inside, pulled back out. 'David!'

He took the stairs two at a time. All the bedroom doors were shut. He began with what had been David and Natalie's room. The bed was neatly made, duvet straight, cushions plumped and positioned.

'David!' His voice boomed and bounced off the light green wallpapered walls and shook the tassels hanging from the matching lampshade.

He crashed into Josh's room, with its gaming posters attached to the plain blue walls, bed made and desk empty of the computer and games console that were usually in situ.

The bathroom was next but no sign of David. That only left Leigh's room. He swallowed hard and turned the handle. The sight caused him to momentarily shut his eyes tightly.

CHAPTER TWENTY-NINE

Murray hurled his notepad onto the desk. 'The bastard's got an alibi. He was at the animal park with his kids and wife on Saturday afternoon, and Sunday he was at home.'

Natalie chewed at her thumbnail. Henry wasn't behind the other murders, so who was? She paced the floor, her nervousness not solely down to the investigation. If Mike was this long in getting back to her, something dreadful had happened. No sooner had she had the thought than her phone buzzed and Mike's name came up on the screen. She snatched it from her desk and marched into the corridor, eyes fastened on the leather settee.

'Tell me.'

'He's alive. He's been taken to Samford General.'

'Do you think he'll make it?'

'I honestly don't know.'

The news was a physical blow to her stomach, causing her to bend over involuntarily as if she was going to be sick. Lucy caught sight of her and walked to the door.

'You okay, Natalie?'

Natalie waved her away.

'I'll come to the hospital.'

'I don't think you should yet. He was unconscious when I found him and I don't know how oxygen-deprived he was. I don't know if I got to him in time.'

Natalie understood the subtext of his words. David might live but be permanently brain-damaged. This was no cry for help. David had intended on dying. 'Oh, fuck! What have I done to him?'

'It wasn't you, Natalie. It was many things that mounted up and eventually overwhelmed him. I let him down more than you did. I'll stay at the hospital for a while and see what the doctors have to say.'

Her mind shouted a hundred questions at once but one more loudly than the others. 'Josh! What do I tell him?'

'The truth. You can't keep this from him but let's give it an hour and see what the prognosis is before we tell him.'

We. She drew a shuddering breath. *We.* She wasn't alone. Mike would be by her side. There was some comfort to be drawn from that even though her heart was clattering against her ribs. She'd be of no use by David's bedside or sitting in the hospital waiting room for news. After being tugged in both directions – relationship and duty, back and forth – for what felt like minutes but was only seconds, sense prevailed. 'All right, I'll wait to hear from you… and thank you.'

The voice was heavy with sadness. 'Don't thank me yet. I'm not even sure I've done the right thing by rescuing him.'

'You have. Believe me, you have.' Mobile in hand, she took several sharp breaths and then counted to ten – inhaling on each number and exhaling slowly. The rattle in her chest lessened. *Seven. Eight.* David was safe now. *Nine.* There was nothing more she could do. *Ten.*

Lucy, now at her desk facing the door, watched Natalie's every move, her body poised to react, ready to surge forward and comfort if needed. Her shoulders relaxed when Natalie walked in and lifted her hand.

'It's okay. Everything's fine now.' She wasn't willing to discuss the matter with her team. She didn't want to give a single indication she was unfit to lead the investigation.

Murray, who'd had his back to the glass and not noticed any-thing untoward, slapped his hands against his thighs. 'Yes! We've got a trace on the PayPal account that Henry sent money to. Oh!'

'Oh, what?' said Lucy quickly, her chair sliding back across the carpet as she scrambled to her feet to join him.

'Fuck me! The account belongs to Lennox Walsh.'

'Please tell me you're joking,' said Lucy.

'See for yourself.'

'That little fucker! We've spoken to him loads of times.' Lucy stomped around in a wide circle.

Natalie wasn't wasting any time. 'Pull him in immediately.'

Lucy was halfway out of the door before Murray had stood up. He pounded after her, both flying down the corridor at speed. Natalie watched them turn left at the top of the stairs and disappear. She needed to update Dan. She wanted to see David and find out if he was going to be okay. Most of all she wanted to hold her son and assure him his father was going to be all right.

Lennox pulled at his whiskery chin, tugging at individual hairs. His demeanour had swung from outrage to rage and now truculence. His lawyer, Carolyn Pickerton, a woman in her forties, in a three-piece trouser suit and with sleek black hair swept into a clip, had advised him to calm down, so with one arm clamped under the other, and his free hand twisting hair follicles, he smouldered silently.

'The money Mr Warburton transferred was sent to a PayPal account linked to your bank account. Can you explain it?' Natalie asked for the third time.

'He made a mistake with the name of the account. Must have got the wrong one,' he mumbled, his hand partly shielding his mouth.

'Stop fucking me about!' Natalie's voice filled the room. 'We've got your bank account details. You knew that money was sitting in your account. You were over £1,000 in the red until that money arrived in your account on October the twentieth, and on the twenty-first, you spent £520' – she glanced at the notes in front of her – 'in Go-Go Games in Samford, where you purchased the Sony PlayStation 4 Pro and several games. On Monday, November the nineteenth, three days after Gemma was attacked, you withdrew £2,000 in cash, putting yourself back in the red. Was that the money we found in Fran's room?'

'No. I owed people money. I paid them back. I gave them the money I took out of my account. I don't know anything about any money in Fran's room.'

'Who did you owe money to?'

'Some guys… for drugs.'

'You owed drug dealers money?' Natalie's eyes narrowed as she spoke.

'Yes. I've been getting credit from them for a long while.'

'What drugs?'

'All sorts.'

'Be more specific!'

'Smack, snow, Billy. Crystal meth.'

The boy was confessing to taking heroin, cocaine, amphetamines and methamphetamine. The most expensive was the crystal meth at about £200 per gram. It was possible he had owed drug dealers, but Natalie didn't believe him.

'I need to know more about these so-called dealers. I want names, dates, where you met them and what you really bought, if anything.' When the boy looked away and didn't reply, she continued, 'We've confiscated your computer. We will be able to prove you were behind this scam and we will be charging you. I'm giving you one last chance to explain yourself. Tell us what happened to Hattie and Fran. Were they involved in the scam too? Make this easier on yourself, Lennox. If you remain unwilling to assist, we'll add perversion of the course of justice to the list. Your lawyer will go through the charges we'll be making against you. You'll be looking at intellectual property infringement, identity theft, criminal fraud and accessory to murder.'

'What? That's madness! I can't be guilty of all of that.'

Carolyn Pickerton gave a low cough. 'Lennox, I advise you to tell the police everything you know. These are pretty serious charges. You need to make this easier on yourself.'

'But, Carolyn—'

'No buts. Your mother hired me to sort this out. Now, tell them.' Her words were enough for Lennox to finally drop the hard-man act and speak.

'Oh, shit! I don't know what to say. Okay. I began crapping myself after Gemma was killed. I thought if you looked into her death, you'd uncover the scam. As soon as I found out Fran had been murdered, I thought it was a chance to get myself out of trouble. I took money out of my account and hid it in her room. I figured it would be found, and if you knew about the catfishing, you'd think Fran was behind it not me.'

'How did you get into her room?'

'She'd left the door unlocked.'

'You were responsible for the scam?'

He nodded. 'I admit I set up the profile on Special Ones. I didn't think I'd be hurting anyone, only a few wealthy blokes who could spare some money. I borrowed Gemma's photographs off her Instagram page. I screenshotted them and created a profile. She was pretty and I thought blokes would fall for her. It started out as a way to get extra cash.'

'But you knew it was illegal?'

He screwed up his eyes then released a lengthy, 'Ye-es. It was just a daft idea that I tried out, thinking nothing would come of it, but within hours there were matches and I thought it might be possible to squeeze a few quid out of these guys. It's rubbish having no money all the time. I'm not going to be able to clear my student debts for years, if at all. It costs a fortune to study, and if you don't land a decent job after graduation, you're fucked.'

'According to your statements, you've been receiving money every three months – £1,000 from your mother. How come you never have enough money? I'd have thought that would be enough for you to live on. She pays your accommodation and university fees too,' Murray said.

Lennox shrugged. 'She's recently stopped my allowance because I've been burning through it too quickly. She's refusing to give me any more money until I "pull up my socks". She told me to get a job but I couldn't get one. I tried but there's nothing going in town. I had to think outside the box. That's all I was doing. I was being entrepreneurial.'

'What you did was deceitful and illegal. You were stealing money from people through deception.'

'I don't see it that way. The government does that sort of thing all the time in the form of taxes. They take money from the workers to pay for all sorts of shit – weapons, wars, their wages – and we pay up thinking it's going into the NHS or road repairs or education. It's all bullshit. The BBC takes licence money from everyone, and for what? Most people pay for television channels and yet they still have to hand money to the BBC corporation to waste. Don't you read the newspapers? What I was doing wasn't that different. Besides, I was giving these guys what they wanted – a bit of fun, some flirty chitchat. I made them feel good about themselves. That deserved some reward, and they had the money.'

Murray scowled. 'You're trying to justify what you did by coming out with half-arsed political nonsense?'

Lennox shrugged. 'It's true. We're all being duped by the government and powers that be.'

'You stupid little twat. A girl died because of you!' Murray unfolded his arms and pushed himself off his chair, his face inches from Lennox's. His hand snaked towards him.

Lennox's chair screeched and his feet scrabbled against the floor as he tried to edge away.

'DS Anderson!'

Natalie's sharp reprimand stopped Murray mid-movement and he sat back down. Lennox remained at a distance.

'I think it might be best if we replace DS Anderson with another officer,' said the lawyer.

'DS Anderson stays. Lennox, the man you duped hired a private investigator to uncover Maisie's true identity. He then went after Gemma, who he believed to be this fake character, Maisie, and threw acid in her face. You are responsible for that.'

'I only made up a profile. None of that is my fault.'

'Of course it's your fault!' Murray bellowed, making Lennox jump. 'You used Gemma's photographs. You wrote on the profile that *Maisie* lived in Samford. You even gave out Gemma's real statistics – her height, weight, eye colour – you total prick.'

'I... I didn't say she was a student.'

Murray snorted. 'Are you a fucking idiot? Gemma actually lived in Samford. She had photographs of herself all over Facebook and Instagram. Anyone with half-decent computer skills could have tracked her down.'

'DS Anderson, maybe you should change your tone, please.' Carolyn regarded Murray coolly.

His response was little more than a low guttural sound.

Natalie took over. Murray was doing a good job of unnerving Lennox. She stood a chance of uncovering the truth. 'Lennox, what happened to Fran and Hattie?'

'I don't know.' His hand was back in front of his mouth, fingers stroking his facial hair.

'Did they know about your scam?'

'No. It was my plan.'

Murray, head lowered like a bull about to charge, continued to glower at Lennox. 'Your *plan*? Was it your *plan* to put Gemma in danger?'

'No.' Lennox's Adam's apple lifted and dropped. Murray's nostrils flared.

Natalie tried again. 'Have you any idea what happened to Fran and Hattie?'

'I don't.' Again, his hand covered his mouth.

'Did you kill Fran?'

'Absolutely not!'

'Hattie?'

'No!'

'Do you know who did?'

'No.' He moved his hand to completely cover his mouth, a gesture that Natalie noted.

'Who else knew about your scam?'

'Nobody.'

'None of your friends?'

'I didn't tell anyone else about it. I don't know anything about Fran or Hattie. I don't even know how they died.'

Natalie decided to call a halt to the interview. They were going around in circles and they couldn't squeeze any more information from Lennox at the moment. A night in the cells might help soften him up. 'We'll continue to hold you overnight. Your mother will have to be notified once we charge you.'

He shook his head. 'She's in New York, designing a penthouse for a client.'

'Who would you like us to call?'

'Not got anybody else.' It was the first time any sign of unhappiness had crept into his voice.

'Your mother will still have to be notified.'

He gave a weary, 'Whatever.'

'Is there anyone else you'd like us to contact?'

'No.'

Natalie ended the interview and turned off the recording device.

Carolyn sat upright. 'I'd like a few minutes alone with my client before he goes to the cells.'

'Certainly. Knock on the door when you're finished,' said Natalie.

Lennox mumbled, 'I don't know anything.'

Murray stared hard at the young man. His voice oozed menace. 'You'd better be telling the truth.'

'I am.'

Natalie watched the unconscious gesture, the hand covering his lips, a tell when people were lying. Lennox knew more than he was willing to impart, but what exactly was it?

CHAPTER THIRTY

TUESDAY, 20 NOVEMBER – LATE EVENING

'Sorry, Nat. I've got no news yet. They're still assessing him,' said
Mike.

'You should come back to work. I'll take over.'

'I've rung the lab. They know I'm out of contact for a few hours.
I don't want to leave yet. I need to be here.'

'I'll join you.'

'I know you want to but it's best if you don't. Apart from
anything else, you don't want the media to catch wind of what's
happened. He circled the article about the case that was in today's
newspapers.'

'Oh, shit! He talked to me about that. I told him the press
wouldn't guess he'd been a suspect.'

'I don't think he believed you. He left a note too.'

Her heart sank.

'Do you want me to read it to you?'

'I... I guess so.'

He cleared his throat then began, '"To everyone I love. I love
you all, and because I love you deeply, I've had no choice but to
leave you. I am not who I want to be and I'm afraid of who I've
become. I always prided myself on being the one person you could
all depend upon, but you can no longer count on me. I've become

weak and I hate myself for that. I don't want you to grow to despise me too.'" He stopped briefly.

'You don't have to do this,' she said.

'No, it's fine.' He paused again then continued, '"Please don't mourn me. Remember me as I once was. I hope there is an afterlife, and in some shape or form, I'll join Leigh. What I fear is eternal darkness alone, yet that is what I have already."' His voice cracked for a second but he continued, '"If you love somebody enough, you should let them go. I am releasing you all to live your lives, enjoy your moments. I wish I could share them with you. David." And he ends the note with a kiss.'

Natalie couldn't speak. She had known David was struggling but this was too painful. She ought to have pushed through his barriers, listened to him and been gentler with him. He'd needed professional help and guidance and she'd failed him.

Mike's voice cut through the build-up of emotion and guilt. 'You okay?'

'Sort of. Oh, Mike! This is dreadful. I let him down.'

'It wasn't only you. We both let him down, one way or another, didn't we?'

'We did.'

'I'll ring you as soon as I hear anything, I promise.'

Mike ended the call. It was gone nine and Josh would be at the flat. She hadn't yet broken the news to him and what she'd tell him depended on the next half hour. After that, she'd wait no longer. Josh deserved to know. She stepped out of the squad car, where she'd taken the call, and joined Lucy, who was waiting for her outside 53 Eastview Avenue. A forensic van was parked on the roadside. The unit would be upstairs in Lennox's room, hunting for evidence to prove his connection to Fran's and Hattie's deaths.

'If you want to talk about anything—' Lucy began.

'Thanks, but it's all in hand.'

The front door was ajar and Natalie pushed it open. Scuffling indicated there were officers upstairs and they passed one on the first landing. A damp-faced Ryan, in jogging bottoms, T-shirt and trainers, was inside his room. The exercise mat on the floor, a set of weights beside the bed and the strong smell of perspiration suggested he'd been working out.

'What's going on with Lennox?' he asked. His biceps rippled as he wiped his face with a hand towel.

'He's helping us with our enquiries.'

'Why are the white-suited guys going through his stuff?'

'As I said, he's helping us with our enquiries.'

Ryan looked blankly at Natalie. 'That's crazy. He's just a chemistry nerd. He won't be able to tell you much.'

'What can you tell us?'

'About what?'

'Let's start with the day Hattie disappeared. You went to the gym and when you came back you worked in this room and went to sleep for a while. Is that right?'

'That's right.' He dropped onto the edge of his bed, towel resting over one thigh. He glanced at the photograph of Gemma still by his bedside. His eyelids flickered momentarily. Floorboards creaked as officers continued searching Lennox's room, and a drawer clattered shut. The house was not soundproof. Lucy stood closest to the door, leaving Natalie room to stand in front of the bed and ask her questions.

'What can you remember about Saturday afternoon? Any detail at all.'

He blinked. 'I can't think of anything. I didn't see Hattie or Fran. I was busy up here. I had a snooze, grabbed a shower. There was some noise going on. You can't miss it: toilets flushing, taps running, people running up and downstairs, that sort of thing. If somebody is playing music or talking loudly, it travels in this building and I usually work with headphones on. I was wearing them that afternoon.'

'Then you didn't hear anything unusual.'

'Not unusual. There was television noise and somebody was playing AC/DC for a while, which is why I put the headphones on. There was some shouting later on but that was about eight o'clock when I was getting ready to go out.'

'Who was shouting?'

'Rhiannon and Fran, I think. It was coming from directly below me in Fran's room. I definitely heard Fran's voice.'

'What did she say?'

'"You stupid fucking bitch," was all I heard.'

'Did they normally argue?'

'Not like that. Fran was pretty het up though. I turned up my CD player to drown out the screeching.'

'They were screeching?'

His words were clipped, his accent strong. 'Yes, it sounded like a catfight.'

'Did you see either of them?'

'No. I went out about half an hour later and it was dead quiet so I thought Rhiannon had gone back to her place.'

'Where did you go?'

'Students' union. I couldn't face sitting alone in my room. I kept thinking about Gemma and everything in the house reminded me of her. I played pool and had a few drinks, chatted to friends, then went into town for a kebab after the bar closed at two in the morning.'

'Did you see Lennox at all?'

'He was at the students' union as well, with a crowd. Don't know where they went after the bar closed.'

'I know this is inconvenient, but we're going to have to ask you to move out for a few days while the forensic team is here. I believe the university authorities will be able to provide temporary accommodation.'

He scratched the side of his face but gave nothing away. 'Okay. I don't suppose there's any choice in the matter.'

'There isn't.'

'Will they go through my room too?'

'It's likely.'

'Oh, right. Do I leave it as it is, then?'

'Yes.'

'Can I take anything with me?'

'Check with the team downstairs. They'll advise you.'

He merely nodded, as if all of this was not unusual, and Natalie couldn't help but wonder if it was because of his upbringing or because he was masking his emotions expertly.

Given Rhiannon only lived a few steps down the road, Natalie decided to talk to her about the argument. They didn't have to walk as far as the house. Rhiannon was outside, sitting on the pavement, head lowered and cradled in her arms, so only two pink pompoms stuck on top of a woollen hat that resembled a child's bonnet rather than a grown woman's accessory were visible. The knitted earflaps drooped like long rabbit ears.

'Rhiannon? Are you okay?' Lucy asked. When there was no reply she crouched down next to her and murmured, 'Come on, Rhiannon. You can't stay out here. It's miserably cold. Let's take you back home.'

The girl unfurled. Her face, a bleached clown mask of horror with crimson cheeks and thick smudges of sooty mascara under eyes that dripped tears. 'I wanted to feel near Fran. I went to her room, but the officers won't let me inside.'

'I'm sorry, but that isn't possible.'

'Why are they checking her room?'

'They're examining a couple of rooms, not solely hers. You won't be able to go inside. You should return to your place.'

'I can't stand being there alone.'

'Do you want to go back home to your parents for a few days?'

The pompoms waggled. 'I don't get along too well with my ma, and Da is away in Saudi Arabia. I'd rather stay here.'

'Maybe the university could arrange for you to move into a different accommodation to be closer to your other friends.'

'Fran was my only true friend.'

'Come on. We'll talk in your room.' Lucy straightened up and caught Natalie's eye. Natalie indicated she should continue taking the lead and talk to the girl. Accompanied by snuffling noises, Rhiannon struggled to her feet and mooched alongside Lucy, head lowered, arms held out at a forty-five-degree angle, suspended by volumes of goose feathers. The bulky puffa jacket resembled a sleeping bag with arms and did nothing to flatter Rhiannon's figure.

Natalie fell into place behind them, aware of the bitterly cold wind that swept down the road, carrying a supermarket plastic bag, swirling it high over the cars until it became impaled on a low hawthorn bush and flapped to free itself to no avail. Cars lined the street, bumper to bumper. She walked past the old red Saab she knew belonged to Lennox, wedged in between a Honda Civic, littered with cuddly toys on the parcel shelf, and a Kia. She was the last to enter the old house where Rhiannon lived. The light from an energy-saving bulb barely illuminated the hallway, and Natalie picked her way cautiously around three rubbish bags and a traffic cone discarded in the passage, to the kitchen.

Every surface was invisible, covered by a mountain of waste and unwashed crockery that made Natalie cringe. The boys had left without any thought to cleaning up after themselves. Somebody had built an impressive pyramid out of the empty beer cans that reached Natalie's chest, with more cans in a pile next to it on the floor. Dirty plates, one stacked haphazardly on top of another like a bizarre variation of Jenga, jostled with cooking utensils for space. Her eyes were drawn to a frying pan still glistening with oil, and the wooden spatula, blackened by neglect, that remained in it on the table. Next to it, a fat, black fly gorged on the remnants of a curried meal, squatting first on one glued-on rice grain then another, each hop accompanied by a low drone of satisfaction. Natalie swatted at it and it flew off only to land lazily on a cup at the top of an eruption of plates and cutlery in the sink.

Rhiannon appeared oblivious to the tip and rested her back against the fridge, where magnetic letters only served to make up obscene words. She folded her arms across her chest and the room filled with a noise akin to crinkling a large packet of crisps. The puffa was noisy but Rhiannon didn't seem to be bothered by its creaks. 'I might leave university altogether. I can't imagine staying in Samford after what has happened.'

Lucy hunted for somewhere to sit down but didn't fancy the plastic chairs, stained with a sticky substance that resembled ketchup. 'I wouldn't make any rash decisions. You're in your second year. You don't want to throw away what you've already achieved.'

'I don't care about that. I can get a job.'

'You could always transfer to another university and keep on studying.'

Rhiannon didn't answer. The woollen bonnet ears lengthened her face, adding to the sorrowful demeanour, the epitome of a hang-dog expression. Natalie had been puzzling over something since passing the cars on the street.

'You own a car, don't you? A Dacia Sandero?'

'Yes.'

'Is it parked on the street? I couldn't see it.'

'There are several spaces behind the accountants' house at number 74. They don't mind if anyone uses them as long as it's out of hours.'

'Would that include the weekend?'

'Yes. They don't open Saturdays or Sundays. If there are no spaces on the road we usually try there.'

'Did you happen to park there Saturday or Sunday?'

'No, I had a spot right outside the house.'

A thought bubbled. Hattie's car had appeared at the railway car park at 10.17 p.m. but where had it been beforehand? The tech team had been unable to locate it, prior to that. If it had been parked in the accountants' car park, it would have been out of sight. She nodded to indicate she had nothing more to ask, and Lucy took over.

'We wanted to ask you about the argument you had with Fran.'

'What argument?'

'The one you had Saturday night in her room.'

Rhiannon's forehead creased lightly. 'There wasn't any argument.'

'That's not what we were told.'

'Who told you?'

'It doesn't matter who told us. We'd like to hear what happened.'

'Nothing. Fran and I were tight. We didn't row or fall out. Ever.'

'Were you in her room on Saturday night?'

'Yes. After you took our phones, I went back to her place and we sat in her room and talked about stuff.'

'What exactly did you talk about?'

'What happened to Gemma and how we'd got caught up in it because of what we'd said on Facebook. We talked about Hattie and where she might have gone and other stuff – uni stuff.'

'You deny shouting or quarrelling with her?'

'Yes, I do.'

'Raised voices were heard and Fran was clearly heard saying, "You stupid fucking bitch." Do you remember that? Maybe she was talking to somebody else.'

'There was no one else in her room while I was there. I left at about nine. Maybe it happened afterwards. We definitely didn't have any argument. Whoever said we did was wrong or lying.'

Natalie studied the girl's posture. She kept her hands deep in her pockets and her back was slightly bowed. Liars often hid their palms by keeping their hands palm down or in pockets. It was warm enough in the house to remove the hat and padded coat but Rhiannon had chosen to stay wrapped up and buried within the huge coat. She might be hiding something but it was equally likely she felt coddled inside the puffa that cocooned her. Her face showed undeniable anguish yet one thing bothered Natalie: in order for Rhiannon to be telling the truth, it meant Ryan was either wrong or lying. Natalie was being batted backwards and forwards in this investigation. When would it all end?

CHAPTER THIRTY-ONE

TUESDAY, 20 NOVEMBER – NIGHT

Fatigue was eating into Natalie, weakening her ability to think properly and affecting her movements. As much as she wished to pursue every avenue, her team – equally frayed and weary – needed time off. She and Lucy had once again left Rhiannon in Katherine's hands. The university counsellor had also assured them the kitchen would be cleaned. Libby, the student who'd been away on a field trip, was due back the following afternoon, and Katherine was certain the other girl's presence would help Rhiannon.

Coats were dragged on in haste, goodnights called out and the office emptied in no time, leaving Natalie staring at her mobile phone. Mike hadn't rung and she hadn't told Josh that his father was in hospital. It was time to face the music.

She put on her waterproof jacket and bent to untangle her shoulder bag strap from under the chair leg, where it had got caught. As she lifted the chair to free it, a familiar marimba tune rang out. She yanked her strap free and leapt to her feet, heart in her mouth.

'Mike?' Her voice was wary.

'It's going to be a while before they determine how much damage has been caused but he's going to make it. He's in intensive care.'

'Thank goodness!' The wave of relief threatened to knock her over. 'I'll collect Josh and we'll come to the hospital. Will you still be there?'

'No. I'm going to head home now. The doctors want to keep him under observation. I wasn't allowed to see him. They might allow you to visit him but I'm not family.'

'You saved his life, Mike. You're as good as family.'

'Let's see how he recovers first before we become too jubilant. There could be all sorts of damage and complications yet.'

The reality of his words punched home. If David needed care, how would they cope? She couldn't look after him. The relief was replaced by anxiety. She didn't want to be tethered to David. She needed him to make a full recovery.

'I don't want to do this on the phone but we need to talk this through properly. It could become... complicated,' he said.

'I think I know what you're saying but it needn't be.' Even as she spoke, she knew Mike was right. David's recovery might be long-term, with him reliant on loved ones and an army of professionals to guide and nurse him back to full health. He might even resent those who had saved him.

'I know this investigation is taking up every single minute of your day, and you have Josh and now this added pressure, but can we make time?' Mike asked.

'Sure. I'll ring you later, after I've been to the hospital, and we'll work something out.'

'Okay. We'll talk later.'

She ended the call and looked up to see Dan standing by the open door. 'I couldn't help but overhear. You have to go to the hospital?'

Unsure of how much of her conversation he'd eavesdropped on, and annoyed he'd caught any of it, she replied sharply, 'David's in hospital.'

'An accident?'

'No. Not an accident.' She hauled her handbag onto her shoulder. 'If you'll excuse me, sir. I need to get on my way.'

He moved aside to let her pass. 'I was going to ask for a quick update on the investigation. It can wait until the morning.'

'I'll make sure there's a report on your desk first thing.' She swept past him down the corridor before he could say anything further.

'Who rescued him?' Josh didn't seem shocked by the news of his father's attempted suicide, or curious about what had happened.

'Mike. Your dad rang me before he… Well, I rang Mike. He was closer to Castergate than me. He got to him in time.'

Although his jaw jutted, he made no comment.

'Do you want to come to the hospital with me?'

He crossed his arms. 'Uh-uh. I don't want to see him.'

Natalie wasn't going to force the boy to accompany her. She understood he wouldn't want to see his father under such circumstances. 'Think about visiting him tomorrow then. It would help him to know we care about him.'

'But I don't care about him.'

There was no anger. Josh was being factual. 'The same as he hasn't cared about me the last few months. I know it sounds cruel and I ought to feel differently, but I can't help it.'

'He does care about you.'

'You keep saying he does, but he didn't demonstrate that. He sat in his own bubble of misery. He pushed me away every single day, little by little. That's why I came to you.'

'I'm really sorry, Josh. We've put you through hell.'

'It's okay. I'm okay. I simply can't handle any more shit. It seems like I've been dealing with it forever. Leigh being murdered was the worst thing ever, but then instead of us all sticking together and helping each other through it, you and Dad split up, and then he tries to top himself! What the fuck's the matter with our family? I only want to be part of a normal family!'

She fought maternal instincts that demanded she hold him as she had done when he was a baby, soothe him and allay his fears. Her son was a young adult with a fierce determination who'd constructed a protective layer around his heart and emotions to shield him from any more upset. She understood that perfectly. She'd reacted similarly following the major fallout with her sister Frances. She'd withdrawn emotionally, buried her feelings and created a tough shell to prevent any further bruising. Those events had fashioned her as these would fashion Josh. 'If I could turn back the clock, I would. I didn't want any of this for us… especially not for you, but life is never easy and relationships can be complicated. Whatever happened between me and your dad, neither of us stopped loving you, not for one second.'

Josh swallowed hard. 'He didn't want to live, Mum. He'd given up on life… on you and on me. He wanted to die. You and Mike, you shouldn't have stopped him.'

His words clawed at her heart. She badly wanted to make him understand why she couldn't let David die, but she was unable to articulate her thoughts now enveloped in an invisible mist of confusion. His voice reached her. 'If you want to go and visit him, then go ahead, but I'm not. Not today or tomorrow or at all.'

The hospital visit was proving futile. Although she was granted permission to see David, he was unconscious and attached to drips to keep him replenished and to machines that monitored heart and brain activity. Standing by his bedside, looking at the man who'd been her lover and soulmate for the best part of two decades, she felt only sorrow. Josh's words rang in her ears. She detected a rustle and felt a sturdy presence beside her. She knew at once who it was. She'd rung him on her way over. David's father, Eric, had been a constant in their lives. He didn't speak, and when she turned her head to face him, she saw only what was reflected in her own eyes.

The old man had changed too. He'd shrunk so his skin seemed too large for his body and cheek flaps hung over what had been a plump, cheerful face. The aftermath of losing Leigh had been more than psychological; it had taken a physical toll on them all.

Eric rested rheumy eyes on her. 'Thank you.'

'I should have seen the signs…' she began.

'Difficult when he wouldn't speak to you or have any contact with you.' There was a long pause before he said, 'I saw the signs and I did nothing about them.'

Natalie didn't believe that. Eric had always been there for his son.

'He came by yesterday. He was in his usual self-pitying state and I lost my rag with him. I was tired of listening to him complain or point the finger of blame at everyone but himself. I love him but he has really tested my patience over the last few months. I told him to pull himself together and sent him packing. You see, we are both at fault, but there's only so much you can do for a person. At least your intervention has given me the chance to try again and make amends. I haven't lost my boy.' He held out a hand and she took it. It was toughened by age and hard work but felt strangely comfortable. He squeezed it, bit back tears, and then squeezed again before releasing her. 'We've been through too much tragedy. I can't face any more.'

They stood once more in silence, looking at the man who they'd both loved in their different ways, and when they left, Eric placed an arm across her shoulder and gently guided her out into the corridor, where his girlfriend, Pam, stood with open arms for them both. Natalie had been forgiven, and although she was unsure what the future would hold for David, she was once more on terra firma with support from those she loved.

CHAPTER THIRTY-TWO

WEDNESDAY, 21 NOVEMBER – MORNING

The day was brighter than it had been for a while. Weak rays of sunshine fell across Natalie's kitchen table, capturing dust particles that danced and soared in their rays like tiny fairies. A robin, perched on the fence outside, emitted a throaty warble. Natalie watched as its chest inflated and it shook its feathers. It reminded her that they were entering the festive period. It was going to be tough this year. She ought to book a holiday for her and Josh, somewhere warm, where they could escape Christmas and its reminders of what they were now lacking. Maybe Mike could join them. She'd rung him after the visit to the hospital and they'd arranged to talk at lunchtime in Samford Park, close enough to headquarters to reach on foot, but far enough to be distant from prying eyes.

The sound of running water ceased, accompanied by a clattering in the pipes and a clunk as Josh switched off the tap. The flat wasn't ideal for the pair of them. Noise readily passed through the thinly partitioned walls, and overnight she'd been subjected to noisy lovemaking coming from the flat above her. They needed their house in Castergate to sell soon, but where would that leave David?

Josh appeared, a towel wrapped around his lower body, his hair damp. 'Hairdryer's knackered,' he said, holding up the aged appliance.

'I'll buy a replacement if I find time today.'

'I'll get it for you.'

'When?'

'I've got a couple of free periods before lunch. I can walk into town and buy one.'

'Okay. Here, take this.' She reached for her purse, handed over forty pounds. 'Don't get a really expensive one. I don't need anything fancy.'

'You can count on me.' He seemed unaffected by what had happened to his father or the conversation they'd had the night before, and Natalie wondered if he was truly fine about everything. He might be putting on a brave face or front. *Like you?* He popped his head back around the door. 'Pippa's mum has invited me to stay over tonight. Is that okay with you?'

She wasn't keen. It was a college night but he needed freedom and certainly didn't need his style cramped. Maybe he also needed some of the 'normality' that Pippa and her mother offered, with their dogs and horses, and less complicated lives in the country. 'It's fine by me but promise me something.'

'What's that?'

'You won't keep secrets from me.'

'I don't.'

She tried to explain her reasoning. It wasn't that she didn't trust Josh. 'If Leigh had been open about where she was going—'

'I get it but you don't need to worry. I'm definitely going to Pippa's house. You can ring me there if you want to make sure.'

'I trust you. Promise me you'll always be open with me. I need that from you. I couldn't bear anything to happen to you.'

He gave her an affectionate look that made her want to hold him, tightly. He was still her boy. 'You got it. Can you manage without the hairdryer until tomorrow?'

'Yes, and thank you.'

'No probs.'

'Josh!'

'Yes?'

She wanted to ask him if he'd changed his mind about David but she already knew the answer. Josh hadn't asked after David. 'Nothing… I've got to scoot. Have a good day.'

'Cheers. I'll text you later.'

The robin trilled loudly as she navigated the icy puddles on the uneven path, its song lifting to the pastel blue skies. It trained bright eyes on her and followed her cautious movements as she picked her way towards the pavement. Natalie inhaled the crisp air, and on exhaling, she made a conscious effort to extinguish all thoughts of David, Josh and Mike. Her mind drifted back to the cars on Eastview Avenue and the conversation about the car park behind the accountants' house, and she wondered if there was any CCTV overlooking it. A motorbike passed her, accelerating loudly, but she paid no heed.

She was first into the office and picked up a note that had been left on her desk. It was written in Darshan's decorative handwriting, letters topped with swirls and flourishes. Forensics had found no traces of oxalic acid in any of the empty bottles found near Fran's body. Fran had consumed the acid elsewhere, not while sitting in the doorway where the homeless man, Evan Robertson, had slept. There was now little doubt in her mind that Fran had been poisoned. She hunted for the number for the firm of accountants working at 74 Eastview Avenue and then carefully prepared the report she'd promised Dan. She gave as much information as she could and sat back, satisfied with what she'd typed. At least she had some leads she could now follow.

The office, warmed by the sun streaming through the floor-to-ceiling glass window, had heated up to uncomfortable levels. 'Can't we turn off the sodding heating?' Murray grumbled, wiping his forehead.

'The thermostat's stuck,' Ian replied.

'I'm going to melt at this rate.'

'Male menopause,' whispered Lucy, who dodged to miss the notepad Murray hurled at her.

Mike and Natalie were next to her desk, heads bent over a specimen jar containing white crystals. She thanked him and he left her to brief her team.

'Listen up, people. We've got some new information.' She lifted up the jar. 'These are oxalic acid crystals, readily available in DIY stores and online. As you're aware, the forensic team were examining Lennox's room last night. They discovered traces of a white substance, which has now been identified as oxalic acid, on a pair of rubber gloves in a box at the bottom of his wardrobe. They are now examining the entire house, starting with the communal areas. The university has been notified and Ryan Hausmann has been moved to a flat on campus for the time being while Forensics conduct a thorough search. Obviously, we'll talk to Lennox immediately but we might need to establish where the substance came from. The most obvious place is the chemistry laboratory. Ian, can you check, please? Lucy, speak to the accountancy firm working at 74 Eastview Avenue. I want to know if Hattie's car was stationed in their car park on Saturday afternoon, any time after 4.25 p.m. and before 10 p.m. That means find out if there are any surveillance cameras on the property or overlooking the car park, and do a house-to-house in the area. I'd like you to talk to those people whose houses overlook that car park. Murray, you can help me persuade Lennox to open up. Make sure his lawyer, Carolyn Pickerton, gets here pronto. I'm not waiting around for her. If she can't make it, grab hold of the station lawyer. I want answers.'

The uncomfortable temperature forgotten, the team burst into action like a well-rehearsed dance routine, each member breaking away to perform their own task.

*

Carolyn happened to already be at HQ, waiting for charges to be pressed against Lennox, and was installed in an interview room. Natalie decided to share the latest discovery with her in the hope she might be able to get a confession from Lennox rather than them sitting through a lengthy interview.

The lawyer, in a tight grey skirt, white blouse and blood-red tie, looked like she ought to be dispensing financial advice or on a stock exchange trading floor. Her briefcase was open on the desk, and as she sorted through paperwork, she spoke aloud, her Bluetooth in her ear. 'Tell them we aren't willing to deal. They know what we want and we're prepared to sit it out. No. That's my final response. They want to play hardball, so can we. Get back to me when they come around to our way of thinking.' She ended the call and stood to shake Natalie's hand.

'Can I ask you, are you Jocelyn Walsh's lawyer?'

'That's correct. I'm the family lawyer.'

'Is Jocelyn coming back to the UK?'

'I'm keeping her in the loop regarding Lennox. She'll return if it's necessary. As soon as he's charged, I'll be requesting bail.'

Natalie understood. Lennox's mother would ensure her son was kept out of prison. She wasn't as uncaring as Lennox had led them to believe.

Carolyn looked up briefly. 'I've got a busy schedule today. I hope this won't take long.'

'It might take longer than you thought. We've uncovered new evidence that points to his involvement in a second murder.'

Carolyn's poker face didn't register any surprise at the revelation. 'Can I speak to him about it before you interview him? It might speed things up a bit.'

'We found oxalic acid on a pair of rubber gloves in his wardrobe. One of the victims was poisoned with oxalic acid.'

'Okay! I'll see what he has to say about that.'

Natalie headed back upstairs to allow Carolyn time with Lennox and hoped she'd be able to get him to confess.

In the office, Ian had been busy on the phone. 'Lennox didn't get any oxalic acid from the chemistry laboratory, or use it in experiments.'

'Bugger!'

'Ah, but…' said Ian, with a half-smile playing on his lips, 'I spoke to a lab technician, Jason Wight, who admitted *he* signed out a small quantity of oxalic acid to use for a rust patch on his car. He was working on it in the car park in front of the science department when Lennox pulled up and expressed interest. Apparently, his Saab was also rusting and he asked if he could obtain a small amount of oxalic acid to work on it. Jason had some left over and he gave it to Lennox.'

'When was this?'

'Monday, November the first.'

'Good work, Ian.'

'Yeah, good work, mate,' Murray repeated.

Ian grinned. 'You taking the piss?'

'No. I mean it. It saves me having to flatten the little turd when we interview him next to get the answers out of him.'

'Whoa, Rocky! Watch those fists of yours. They're lethal weapons. Not sure about the rest of you though,' said Ian.

'Fuck you. Last time I compliment you!' Murray shouted after him as Ian disappeared with a wave.

'Where's he going?' asked Natalie.

'Examine some CCTV footage. The accountancy firm has a camera that overlooks the car park.'

'That's good. I hope he finds Hattie's car on it. I can't think where else it would have been between 4.25 p.m. and 10 p.m. If we're really lucky, we might even see who drove it away.' She turned at a light tap. An officer stood in the doorway.

'I've been asked to let you know Lennox Walsh and his lawyer are ready for you, ma'am.'

'Thank you.'

Murray was on his feet in an instant. Natalie joined him. It was time to reel in Lennox.

The lilac bruises under his eyes indicated Lennox had slept badly. His head was lowered and he picked at the nail bed on his right thumb, already red raw. Carolyn Pickerton did the talking.

'My client is willing to assist you. We'd like you to take this cooperation into account of any charges you are considering levelling at him and remind you that whilst he admitted to using Gemma Barnes's photograph to create a dating profile, he did not steal her identity. My client did not attack Gemma nor was he directly or indirectly responsible for her subsequent death, and I shall strongly contest any charges that suggest he was. Lennox has now informed me that a third party was involved and he wishes to retract his initial confession.'

Once Carolyn had finished, Natalie looked across at Lennox. 'What do you have to tell us, Lennox?'

He dropped his hands onto his lap and wet his lips. 'I didn't tell you the truth yesterday. I didn't want to say anything bad about her because she's dead but I didn't come up with the plan to catfish. Fran thought up the whole idea. She and I got drunk together one night and were sympathising with each other about having no money. I told her about my debts and how my mum wouldn't help me get out of the crap, and she understood because she got no help from her mother either – only regular grief. Then we got on to Gemma and Sasha. Fran had issues with Gemma. She didn't hide the fact that she didn't get on with her, but that night she laid into her, said she was "up herself" and went on about the way Gemma and Sasha behaved together. She thought it was insane that they should be hanging out all the time like mates or sisters. The drunker she got, the more she ranted about Gemma, and then she had this wacky idea of how to make some money. She thought it would be funny to use Gemma's picture to try and catfish a few guys. I didn't take it seriously. It was purely drunk-talk so I rolled with it. We drank some more and ended up in bed together. The next morning, when I woke up, Fran was at my desk on my laptop. She'd already set up the dating profile and screenshotted a photograph from Instagram. I remember her laughing and saying if a photo of Gemma couldn't attract blokes, then there was no hope for her.' He stared ahead blankly for a few seconds before continuing.

'For me, it was all about the money. It was something else for Fran. She was jealous of both Gemma and Sasha. She never admitted it but it was obvious to me. I thought I'd see what happened. Where was the harm in making a few pounds? Fran got a real buzz when we got a match. Scott was our first match. She answered his message, got a few kicks out of egging him on. It was around that time she suggested I set up the false email and PayPal account, in case he was willing to donate money to us. That's what she called it, a "donation" to the "poor student fund". He didn't bite but we had another match by then and she tried again. Finally, she hooked Henry. He fell for it all and sent the money. It was dead easy to block him after that and we thought we'd got away with it. Neither of us could have guessed what would happen to Gemma. If we had, we'd never have done it.'

'Why didn't you split the money fifty-fifty?'

'We were going to. Fran was going to set up a building society account this week, one her mum knew nothing about, so she and Rhiannon could look to rent a place together after uni, and I was going to transfer the money into it. If you look at my bank account, you'll see I only spent some of what we took. The rest was for Fran. After I found out she was killed, I panicked. I didn't want her money, and I withdrew as much as I could from my account – I really wanted to take out £3,000 but the bank wouldn't let me – and I put it in her room.'

'Why didn't you tell us this when we spoke to you soon after Gemma's death?'

'Hand on heart, I wanted to, but Fran made me promise to say nothing. I was scared about going to prison, I listened to her.' His voice juddered and lurched. 'It was wrong of me. I'm sorry. I should have come clean immediately and then maybe Fran would still be alive.'

'What do you mean by that?' Did Lennox mean he thought somebody they'd tried to scam had killed her?

His brow knitted together. 'She'd have been here in custody, and nobody could have harmed her.'

'To summarise, you are telling me that Fran Ditton came up with the entire plan to catfish for money, using Gemma's photographs to entice men?' Natalie said.

'That's what happened and I went along with it even though I knew it was wrong. Fran could be very persuasive.'

'Did she threaten you?'

He worried his thumbnail for a brief moment and gave an embarrassed, 'Yes.'

Murray gawked at the boy. 'You were afraid of Fran?'

'Not of Fran! Of her hard-nut friends. She knew some pretty nasty characters who'd think nothing of knifing me. She warned me that if I pointed the finger of blame at her, she'd make sure they found me and gave me payback.'

Murray scoffed. 'You believed all that bull?'

'It wasn't bull. She was a member of a proper street gang. They were heavily into violence.'

'She ran with a crowd of pre-teens when she was a kid. They got into some trouble – shoplifted, graffitied walls and got into a few scuffles – but she left and moved in with her grandmother and stayed out of trouble after that. Didn't it cross your mind that she wouldn't be likely to have sat A-levels if she was in a street gang?'

Lennox shook his head like a dog worrying a lead. 'That's not true. She *was* a street gang member. She told me about it and about her time in a remand centre for GBH.'

'She never spent any time in a remand centre. She was winding you up,' said Murray.

Lennox's voice lifted in indignation. 'No! She wouldn't have done that. Why did she fuck me about like that? I believed her!'

Natalie spoke to him again. 'What happened to Fran?'

'Honestly, I don't know.'

'Can you explain why we found oxalic acid dust on a pair of rubber gloves in your room?'

'I used the acid for Sabina – my car. I got it from one of the lab technicians, Jason Wight. He'd been removing some rust on his car with it and had some left over. Sabina had a few patches that needed attention and I couldn't afford to take her into a garage to get them seen to, so I took it and worked on them myself. If you examine the car, you'll see where I used it.'

'Fran was poisoned with oxalic acid.'

'I didn't give it to her. I definitely didn't give her any.'

'Did you have any crystals left over?'

He wetted his lips again. 'There were a few teaspoons. I kept them to use at a later date.'

'Where did you put it?'

'On the top shelf in the cupboard under the stairs, in a box with other stuff I use on my car.'

'Who had access to it?'

'I guess anyone in the house.'

'Do you know what happened to Hattie?'

'No. I didn't clap eyes on her again after Friday night when you visited us and told us about Gemma.'

Carolyn tapped her paperwork together on the desk, a sharp *rat-a-tat* that signalled the end of the interview. 'My client accepts he was an accessory to fraud but denies any involvement in the deaths of Gemma Barnes, Fran Ditton or Hattie Caldwell. Unless you have any further questions or evidence to prove contrary, I suggest we wind this up. I have another meeting to attend.'

Murray stretched his legs out as far as he could, the entire width of the desk, and placed his hands behind his head. 'Where do we go from here?'

Natalie stood by the door, pondering that very question. Lennox's admission that Fran was behind the scheme made sense, but it didn't explain how she'd died or what had happened to Hattie.

'I suppose we could reconsider our earlier theory that Fran killed Hattie because she found out about the scam, and then killed herself.'

Natalie dismissed the idea. 'Why go to a doorway in a semi-abandoned street to do that, and what did she use drink from – a glass, a bottle, a cup? And, if that were the case, why couldn't Forensics find it? No, I think she swallowed that poison somewhere else and her body was moved. What we need is hard evidence, and we'll find it. Forensics are still at the house. Make sure they also examine Lennox's car.'

'To check he removed rust patches with oxalic acid?'

She opened the door. 'No, for evidence Fran was inside his vehicle. He might have transported her to the doorway.'

Murray sprang to his feet, face set. 'You know that little bastard shouldn't get away with what he did.'

'I know he shouldn't, but he has a top lawyer defending him, and if she can prove Fran was behind the whole scam, he'll get off.'

'Pin the blame on the dead girl because she can't deny it. I think he's covering his arse. He's involved deeper than he says he is.'

'We've got to find something that proves his guilt and that his lawyer can't dispute. I ran some background checks on her, and Carolyn Pickerton is one of the best. Jocelyn Walsh isn't going to let her boy go to jail.'

Murray blew out his cheeks as he pounded up the stairs behind her. 'Money can buy you anything, including freedom.'

'Not if we can find evidence to prove he is more involved in all of this than he admits.'

CHAPTER THIRTY-THREE

Natalie hadn't been back in the office five minutes before she got a call from Ian at the accountancy firm that sent her racing to Eastview Avenue.

The house, identical to others on the same side of the street, differed to those opposite, where the students lived, by having a wide driveway. She understood how they'd not found it sooner. It was only once she turned into the approach and followed a blue arrow to the rear of the building that the car park, a tarmac area large enough for ten cars, became visible.

Natalie entered via the rear entrance next to which was a discreet bronze plaque with the names of the accountants who worked there. She rang the button marked reception and the door opened with a click.

She found herself in a pale grey reception area. A piercing whistle attracted her immediate attention. The onscreen noise had come from a dog trainer attempting to control a disobedient terrier that chased after some ducks that raced about quacking, wings flapping wildly to the accompaniment of raucous canned laughter. The television was snapped off. Natalie faced the receptionist, who laid down the remote control.

'You must be DI Ward. Your colleague's in the room on the right, past the seating area. It's marked private. Can I get you anything?'

'I'm fine, thank you,' Natalie replied, sliding between the dark green chairs, which reminded her of the hospital waiting room, and the coffee table, overrun with dog-eared magazines.

Ian was staring up at the black-and-white monitor, chin resting on the flats of his hands. He sat up as soon as Natalie spoke.

'What have we got?' said Natalie, without any preamble. She glanced at the notes Ian had made of times and movements. The cursor hovered on the timestamp in the left-hand corner of the screen.

'Hattie's car arrives in the car park at eleven thirty-six on Saturday morning. It doesn't move until between ten and two minutes past ten that same night.'

'So it was there, pretty much all afternoon.'

'That's right.'

'Fran said she'd spoken to her in the kitchen late morning. It seems that was right but Hattie didn't go out, not even after she rang me to arrange to meet at Chancer's Bar, well, not in her car.'

'It would appear not.'

'Remind me, what time did the vehicle arrive at the station?'

'Ten seventeen that night.'

'How long would it take to get from Eastview Avenue to the station?'

'About a quarter of an hour.'

'Hattie can't have driven it that night. If her broken watch was any indicator, she died at seven fifty. She was already dead by the time the car left.'

'I've gone over and over this footage but there's nothing to indicate who actually drove her car. The camera shifts position every two minutes. It picked the car up at nine o'clock, but when it next moved back into that position, the car was gone.'

Natalie watched with him, but there was nothing to indicate who had driven the car out of the accountants' car park. 'Okay, show me the other thing.'

The other thing was the reason she'd come to Eastview Avenue. Ian rewound the footage to Saturday afternoon at twenty past four. 'There he is.' Natalie watched as Lennox's Saab appeared in sight and parked opposite Hattie's car.

'What time does he leave?'

'A couple of minutes after five.'

'Why didn't he mention seeing her car parked there when we asked him if he knew her whereabouts? That young man has definitely been lying to us. I'll see what Forensics have found. Any news from Lucy?'

'She's still talking to people whose properties overlook this car park to see if anyone saw anything unusual over the weekend. Some of the houses have been converted into flats and there are more people to question than we first thought.'

'Wind up here then and head back, and take that footage back with you. We'll need it for evidence.'

Natalie left the building. It was only a quick saunter up the road to the house where Gemma, Fran and Hattie had lived. The search had intensified and more white vans had appeared, parked close to number 53. Natalie also caught sight of a bent figure in a pink woollen hat, arranging a large bunch of red flowers beside the front wall. She headed across the road to Rhiannon.

'Oh, hi. I was leaving these for Fran. That's okay, isn't it?' Rhiannon's face was ghostly pale. Several angry red pimples were scattered like freckles over and around her nose. Without make-up, Rhiannon was a very plain-faced girl with sparse eyelashes and even sparser eyebrows. She propped the bunch of deep-red carnations against the wall. Natalie saw there was a card, a simple card with Fran's name on it and a heart underneath. There was nothing for either Gemma or Hattie. The girl stood up, eyes trained on the flowers. 'I want to tell you something.'

'About Fran?'

'No, it's about Hattie. It might not be important but I still think you should know about it.' She heaved a long sigh and faced Natalie.

'What do you want to tell me?'

'Saturday evening, I was driving through campus and saw her outside the science department block with Lennox.'

'What time would this have been?'

'It was about half past five.'

'When I asked you if you knew where Hattie was, you didn't tell me about this.'

'It didn't seem important, and you asked if I knew where she was, and I didn't.'

'What were they doing? Talking? Arguing?'

Her face scrunched up as she thought. 'I can't be sure but it looked intense... They were facing each other... and Hattie looked like she might have been shouting at him...' She let out a rush of air. 'I'm sorry. I really don't know.'

It was something. They now knew where Hattie had been instead of at her arranged meeting with Natalie. Had Lennox found out about it and prevented her from divulging the scam? 'Did Fran talk to you about a dating website – Special Ones?'

'No.' A cloud flittered across the girl's face.

'I need you to be completely honest with me. I understand she was your friend but you can't keep any secrets. Did Fran tell you anything about a catfishing scam?'

Rhiannon looked left and right before she spoke. 'You mean the thing Lennox was up to?'

'What do you know about it?'

'He and Fran got drunk one night and he told her he'd come up with a stupid scheme to make some money. That was to do with a dating website. Is that what you meant? He thought Fran would find it funny that he'd used Gemma's photo on the fake profile.

Fran didn't find it funny at all. She told him what he was doing was illegal and he should drop it before he got into trouble.'

Natalie hoped there'd be more but there wasn't. 'Did Fran ever mention sleeping with Lennox?'

Rhiannon made a gagging sound. 'No way! She wouldn't ever have slept with him.'

'But she got drunk with him.'

'That's different. I drink with my housemates but I wouldn't sleep with any of them. Fran didn't fancy Lennox at all.'

The girl's version of events conflicted with what Natalie had been told in the interview room. 'Rhiannon, did Fran discuss her past with you?'

'Absolutely.'

'What did she tell you?'

'About how much she hated growing up in a rough area and how she wanted to get away.'

'She ever mention being part of a street gang?'

'Like a drug-dealing violent gang?'

'Something along those lines.'

'No. She was a member of a local gang of girls when she was younger but left before she got into too much trouble. That was one of the reasons she didn't want to go back home. A lot of her old friends had become tied up with proper street gangs and she didn't want to find herself dragged into anything.'

'Did she discuss her time in a remand centre?'

Rhiannon waved hands in front of her face like Natalie was an annoying fly. 'She never went to any remand centre. That's crazy talk. You're not telling me she was sent to a remand centre, are you?'

'No, but she told others she had been, and I wondered why she'd do that.'

'No-oh! That doesn't sound like Fran at all. She didn't discuss her old life with anyone apart from me. She had that bird tattoo done to remind her of what she'd escaped. She wouldn't brag about a thing like that, even if it had happened. She really hated her old life and her mum. That's why she wanted to stay around here and not go back in the holidays. Maybe she told somebody that as a joke.'

'Yes. Maybe she did.' A forensic van drew up and Mike disembarked.

'I'd like to talk to you some more, maybe later at your house. Would that be possible?'

The girl agreed and trundled down the street, head bowed, reluctant to leave the place where her best friend had lived. Mike was already in protective clothing. He reached into the van to retrieve a metal case containing equipment.

'What's going on?' she asked.

'Progress. We were sifting through evidence brought in from Eastview Avenue, among which was an empty gin bottle found in the recycling box outside the back door. We've found Hattie's DNA on the bottle label and a trace of her blood, but the bottle's been wiped clean of prints. I think we might have found the murder weapon.'

'We always suspected she'd been killed elsewhere and transported to the drama studio.'

'We're checking the house. We've done a thorough examination of her bedroom and Lennox's room but there's nothing to suggest she was killed in either room so we're moving through the house. I'm going to try the kitchen and sitting room.'

'Can I join you?'

'Suit up and come in.'

She took a paper outfit from one of his colleagues and, once dressed, entered the house again. She edged past officers in the hallway and headed for the kitchen. Mike and another officer were examining the area with trained eyes, scouring surfaces and knocks and dents in worn cupboards for traces of blood. Mike's speciality had been blood spatter analysis before he'd become head of Forensics, and he would often help out in an investigation if there was no other bloodstain pattern expert available.

He crouched in front of a narrow gap between the units and a free-standing cupboard and ran a torch beam between them, picking up every knock and dent. 'Here!' A female officer shot forward to examine the minuscule red dots caught in a notch on the side of the pine cupboard. She placed a marker by them.

'There's more, down by the side of the cupboard on the floor.' Natalie came forward and squinted at tiny reddish-brown stains that had sprayed down the side of the cupboard and onto the floor. Mike hunted for more, and when he found none, he asked for the curtains to be closed. Natalie pulled down the kitchen blinds and the room was plunged into gloom. Once her eyes had become accustomed to the darkness, she moved against the wall.

'Okay, everyone, stand back,' he said. She heard rather than saw the efficient puffs of luminol reagent. The luminescence revealed what they'd suspected: a large patch highlighted on the floor near the door that spilt towards the cupboard and units. The attempt to clean up was apparent.

'Let the light back in.'

Natalie opened the blinds. Without the luminol, it would have been impossible to have guessed what had happened. Somebody had lost a lot of blood in here. Mike was staring at the cupboard and the gap. He took a step backwards and another then came to a halt. He raised and lowered his arm, as if wielding an object, then moved slightly to his left and repeated the action. 'How tall was Hattie?' he asked.

'About five foot seven.'

'Can you stand there for me?' he asked Natalie.

She obliged.

'Face the door.'

'She was struck on the right-hand side of her head, wasn't she?'

'That's correct.'

Natalie did as she'd been asked. Mike practised his imaginary assault on her.

'It's not an exact science, and much depends on whether or not that blood is Hattie's, but given the extent of damage to Hattie's head and the size and position of those droplets, I'd say it's possible she was attacked around about here. The blood would have sprayed out in an arc, largest spots here and tiniest spots further away. The far walls weren't washed down, so the killer must have concentrated on cleaning up only where they thought all the blood was. I'll need to perform some detailed measurements to determine blood spatter, run checks on the blood and do a follow-up presumptive test to make sure luminescence was due to the presence of haemoglobin and not down to other oxidising agents.'

'Hattie could have been killed in this room,' said Natalie.

Mike looked over at his fellow forensic officer. 'Run an urgent check on that blood to confirm it belongs to Hattie.'

As the woman collected a sample to test, Mike faced Natalie. 'If the blood is Hattie's, your killer either gained entry to this house or lives here.'

'Excuse me, ma'am. Mike, we found fingerprints in Lennox's car that match Hattie Caldwell's and strands of hair. We've sent them for analysis.'

'What colour is the hair?' asked Natalie.

'Auburn, ma'am.'

She thought of auburn-haired Hattie in her long skirt and green boots.

'How soon before you can match the blood and hair to her?'

'An hour, or maybe less if we rush it,' said Mike.

'Rush it, please. I'm going to get Lennox back into the station and I want every scrap of evidence you've got to help me nail him.'

CHAPTER THIRTY-FOUR

Carolyn sat with lips pressed together and her arms folded. Lennox's mouth was agape. Natalie asked him again.

'Can you explain why we found DNA and hair belonging to Hattie Caldwell in your Saab?'

His response was a spluttering, 'Yes… yes, I can. I gave Hattie a lift to the students' union, last week sometime…Wednesday, I think.'

'She had her own car. Why would she need a lift from you?'

'We were both going to the same place. Sometimes we shared lifts. It saves petrol.'

'You're telling me that her hair and DNA were found in your car because you gave her a lift to the students' union?'

'That's exactly what I'm saying.' He turned his head sharply to his left and snapped at Carolyn. 'Can you do anything about this? My mother's paying you to clear my name and all you're doing is sitting there.'

Carolyn took a sharp breath and replied quietly, 'Answer their questions, Lennox, and tell the truth, and I'll do my job.'

His face turned red. 'I *am* telling the truth. I didn't hurt or kill Hattie.'

Carolyn ignored his outburst and glanced at her wristwatch. 'DI Ward, please continue.'

Natalie didn't need asking twice. 'Do you recognise this bottle?' The empty gin bottle was in a plastic evidence bag, and Natalie held it with the label facing him.

'For the recorder, DI Ward is showing Lennox Walsh an empty bottle of gin, item LC127.'

'It's a gin bottle.'

'Have you seen it before?'

'I don't think I have.'

'It was found in the recycling box at your house.'

He glanced at his lawyer again. 'Everyone in the house chucks stuff in that box. That bottle doesn't belong to me. Besides, I don't drink gin. It makes me throw up. I can't even stand the smell of it. Ask my mother.'

'Then tell me, who out of your housemates drinks gin?'

'All of them, I guess, apart from me.'

'Is there any evidence to prove the bottle was handled by my client?' asked Carolyn smoothly.

'No. The prints have been wiped.'

Carolyn unfolded her arms and picked up a silver fountain pen. 'My client's fingerprints are not on the bottle?' She removed the top of her pen slowly and wrote something on her spiral notepad.

'No, they aren't.'

'I see, and have you asked the other member of the house if they recognise the bottle?'

'We'll be doing that.'

Carolyn gave a half-smile and wrote something else then said, 'Okay. You can carry on.'

Natalie turned her attention back to Lennox. 'I'd like to ask you about Saturday afternoon. Where were you around five thirty?'

'In the science department.'

'You can prove that?'

'I was alone in one of the laboratories, working on my experiment. I used my pass to get in. You can probably find out the exact time from the departmental record.'

'What time did you finish?'

'I don't know exactly. Possibly around seven or eight.'

'You didn't check to see what time it was?'

'I didn't. I went to the students' union bar for a while and had a drink with some friends but I hadn't eaten, so I headed into town for a meal and a pint at Wetherspoons.'

'What did you do afterwards?'

'I… I went for a couple of drinks.'

'Alone?'

'I wasn't feeling very sociable.'

'Where did you go?'

'Random pubs in Samford.'

'You expect me to believe you headed alone into town, to pubs you can't name, and that you didn't know what time it was?'

'I didn't much care what time it was and I didn't want to talk to anyone.'

'Why not?'

'Why do you think? Gemma was dead. I was… I don't know… really low. I needed some space. I needed time out.'

Natalie's voice dropped to a hiss. 'Do not – I repeat, do *not* – mess me about here!'

Lennox dropped his head immediately.

Murray's voice broke the silence that ensued. 'I don't buy any of this. I don't think you went to any pubs. Where were you? What were the names of these pubs? You've been living in Samford long enough to know the names of all of the pubs so stop being a prick.'

'DS Anderson, I don't want to have to remind you to watch your language again,' said Carolyn.

Murray returned her a grimace.

Lennox was rattled. 'I *did* go to a couple of pubs and I don't know their names. The one opposite the chip shop on Windrush Street and another, further along.'

Natalie jumped in with, 'Okay, let's say you were in those pubs, and we can try and determine that, what time did you leave them?'

'Late.'

Natalie wanted to shake the young man to get answers. She'd unconsciously clenched her fists and had to concentrate to relax her fingers and unball them. 'Let's go back to the chemistry lab, where you were working on your experiment at or around five thirty. Did you step outside at all?'

'Not that I remember.'

'Did you speak to Hattie outside the science block?'

'No.'

'That's strange because we have a witness who saw you with Hattie around that time. They think you might have been having some sort of disagreement.'

Lennox held up his hands, palms facing her. 'I don't know what you're talking about. I didn't see or speak to Hattie. I swear.'

Carolyn finished making notes and replaced the top of her pen. It made a sharp click as it slotted into position. 'As you've heard, my client has given you answers to your questions. He does not recognise the gin bottle. He denies speaking to, or seeing, Hattie Caldwell, and undoubtedly you will be able to place him inside the chemistry laboratory at the time he was supposedly talking to Hattie Caldwell. His pass will prove he was in the laboratory at the time he said he was. Now, I'd like to make myself quite clear on this matter: I don't expect you to recall my client unless you have concrete proof he was involved in these crimes. You are wasting our time and yours.' She picked up her notebook and tucked it and her pen into a large leather bag, then, stooping to lift up her briefcase, she rose from her chair, summoning Lennox as she left.

Natalie let them go. She'd not got a shred of concrete evidence and had been pinning all her hopes on a confession. Lennox was giving them the runaround and had slipped away because she had no admissible evidence to prove he was responsible for killing Hattie in the kitchen on Saturday evening. She resisted the urge to swear loudly.

Murray walloped the desk – a solid, satisfying thump. 'I'm convinced he's lying. That's a load of crap about going to the pubs alone.'

'I'm with you on this, but it means we have to prove the contrary.'

'I'll check out the pubs on that street. We could try asking the mobile provider to track his phone's movement for that night.'

'Thanks. I hate all this dicking about but what choice do we have?'

There was a knock at the door and Ian came into the interview room. 'I was told I'd find you here. I've brought Ryan in for interview.'

'Okay, wheel him in.'

A few minutes later there was a second knock and Ryan marched in ahead of Ian.

'Thanks for coming in, Ryan,' said Natalie.

His head moved like a robot's as he took in his surroundings before sitting down. 'When can I return to my room?'

'We're not sure yet. Forensics are still examining the house.'

'Including my room?'

'Yes, including yours.'

'They won't mess it up, will they? I don't like mess.'

'They won't cause too much disruption.'

'I might need some more clothes and my books. I only took a sports bag of stuff with me. I didn't think it would be for too long.'

'We'll arrange for more clothes if you need them.'

He appeared satisfied with her response. 'Why have you brought me here?'

'We've made an important discovery. Hattie was killed in the kitchen at your house.'

'Shit! For real?'

'I'm afraid so, and whoever killed her cleaned up the kitchen afterwards and removed her body.'

'Fuck, man! That's pretty sick shit. For the record, it wasn't me.'

'Well, we have to find out who was responsible, and to do that, I need to ask you a few questions.'

He sat up tall, unperturbed by the situation. 'Fire away. If I can help in any way, I will.'

'Firstly, do you recognise this bottle?' Natalie pointed to the bottle on the table.

Ryan stared at it for the longest moment and read the label, 'Chase GB Gin. I'm pretty certain Fran had a bottle exactly like this one in her room.'

There were no bottles of gin or any other bottle in Fran's room. Natalie had already asked Forensics. 'You actually remember seeing it in her room?'

'I'm sure there was a bottle like this on the floor by her bed.'

'When would this have been?'

'Last Thursday. I was doing a presentation that morning but it was raining hard and I didn't want to get soaked cycling onto campus. Nobody else was around and she was about to leave for a lecture, so I asked her for a lift. The bottle was definitely on the floor.'

'Fran had a car?'

'Yes. A Vauxhall Corsa.'

'Have you any idea where it is?'

'Probably somewhere along the street.'

How had they missed this? That was a gross oversight on their part. 'What colour is it?'

'Silver.'

'I don't suppose you know the registration?'

'No, sorry.'

Murray disappeared to get some information about the vehicle, leaving Natalie alone with the young man.

'We think Hattie died Saturday evening. Remind me where you were at that time.'

'I was upstairs in my room. I went out about eight thirty.'

'Did you see anything unusual at all?'

'Nothing. I heard Fran and Rhiannon shouting the odds, but I told you about that.'

'That was about eight?'

'I think it was about then.'

The timing corresponded with Hattie's death, but according to Ryan, the shouting had come from below him, in Fran's room, and Rhiannon had denied any argument. She studied his deadpan face. Was Ryan lying to her? She wished she could penetrate whatever invisible protective covering he wore and establish the truth once and for all.

CHAPTER THIRTY-FIVE

WEDNESDAY, 21 NOVEMBER – MID-AFTERNOON

Lucy had spent all day trying to establish if anyone had seen anything unusual on Eastview Avenue. The area wasn't vast but door-to-door enquiries were time-consuming, especially when most of the properties had been converted into flats and every individual had to be consulted. Many had been out on her first attempt and she'd made repeated efforts to speak to householders. Those who lived in the flats overlooking the accountants' car park were the most elusive, and although she'd managed to contact some of them thanks to helpful neighbours and friends who'd supplied phone numbers and contact details, there were still many she had yet to speak to. She was jaded and deflated and had walked miles back and forth.

It had been made longer thanks to the midday interruption when Bethany had phoned her, insisting she meet her and baby Aurora at Samford Park.

'It's a good thing we came along today. You wouldn't have eaten all day. I got you a vegan sausage roll,' says Bethany, passing Lucy a paper bag. The bottom of the bag is shiny brown with grease and the aroma of warm pastry turns her stomach to acid. She's instantly put off eating, not because of the bag and the food inside it, but because

of the schoolmarm tone Bethany has adopted. She smiles thanks but sets the bag aside on the bench, and instead of eating, she lifts the murmuring Aurora from her buggy. The baby has a smell all of her own – fresh like new sheets or warm bread – and she lowers the baby's furry hood and strokes the child's downy hair, soft and pale, unlike either hers or Bethany's.

'I would,' she mumbles, her attention on Aurora, passive and weighty in her arms, blue eyes on her, like she's the most important human in the universe. The baby is growing quickly. It only seems like yesterday she weighed next to nothing.

'You know what you're like. You'd have gone all day without a break or food. You're fading away.' Bethany's voice is mock-stern but rankles all the same. Lucy lets it go. She isn't too pleased that Bethany rang her while she was on duty and asked where she was, then arranged for this impromptu picnic lunch.

'I'm worried about you, Luce. You're worn out all the time. It was better when you moved to vice for those few months while Natalie was off,' says Bethany, voice syrupy, wheedling, irritating.

'I'll be fine once this case is over and I can catch up on some rest.' Lucy lifts Aurora up under her armpits. 'Hey, beautiful girl. You don't think I look worn out, do you?'

Aurora's lips make a semblance of a smile and she produces a spit bubble that bursts, causing dribble to run down her chin. Lucy laughs and wipes it with the bib tied around the child's neck. It's one of a set of zoo animal bibs Lucy bought in an expensive baby boutique. This one is of a beaming giraffe. Aurora gets through several bibs a day.

Bethany isn't going to be swayed. 'Why don't you ask for some leave as soon as the investigation is over? We could all go on holiday. It would do us all good.'

Lucy's heart sinks. It's not that she doesn't want to go away with Bethany and Aurora. She loves spending time with them, but she's saddened. This is the first time Bethany has put any pressure on her. She, more than anybody, ought to understand what this job means to Lucy. It isn't a mere job; it's Lucy's career. She's hoping to make DI one day in the near future, and she needs to rack up the hours and prove her dedication to the force. She'll take some holiday when it's due. Obviously, she'll take time off. She just doesn't want to be told to.

'What do you say, Luce? A few days in Cornwall with the little one or maybe even head off to the Canaries. That'd be better than the cold weather here.' Bethany prattles on, unaware that Lucy is becoming increasingly irked by the conversation.

'Aurora is invariably asleep when you get in each day and you never get enough time together. A trip away would give you a chance to bond with her, give you more than snatched moments.'

This is exactly what happened to Ian and his partner, Scarlett. Scarlett had been happy with Ian, his hours and choice of career until after baby Ruby had been born, and then she'd gradually put pressure on him to spend more time with them. Lucy wipes the baby's face again and says quietly, 'No.'

'What do you mean "no"?' Bethany gives a light laugh although her heavy brows draw together.

'I'll take leave when I want to not when I'm ordered to.'

'I wasn't ordering you to.' Bethany's face has turned ugly, her mouth drawn down. 'I only thought you'd like to see some more of our daughter… and me.'

'Don't, Bethany.'

'Don't what? Why are you getting het up?' Her intonation rises with each word.

'Don't get all needy and demanding. It's not like you.'

Bethany's hand snakes out, grabs the paper bag and she huffs. 'I think it's better if Aurora and I go. We don't want to disturb your busy work, do we, honey?'

Lucy stares at the beautiful child who shares none of her DNA but is, nevertheless, her daughter. 'I don't want us to fall out over this.'

Bethany sniffs. 'We aren't. I was only concerned about you and I wanted to see you. I haven't seen much of you since the investigation began.'

'It's been a few days.'

'But it feels longer. I haven't seen you at all since last Friday – only brief snatches before you race off again. I go to bed alone. I get up alone. I want to share the things Aurora does with you, all the experiences, so you feel part of our lives, but you're invariably out of contact. I'm sorry,' she says suddenly, tears springing to her eyes. 'I know I shouldn't behave this way, I can't help myself. I don't like being like this.'

Bethany rubs her eyes then stands up, arms outstretched to take Aurora from Lucy. 'Come on, little one. Let's get you home for a nap. Say bye-bye to Mummy Lucy.'

Lucy passes the baby over, her arms suddenly lighter and colder, already missing the baby's presence. Bethany fusses over the child, replacing her hood and tucking her back under the snuggly blanket in the buggy. This is merely a blip in their otherwise great relationship. Bethany hands over the paper bag containing Lucy's lunch. 'Make sure you eat.' She kisses her goodbye on the cheek and pushes the buggy down the path. Lucy watches the two loves of her life as they disappear from view. The pastry bag is greasy in her hand and she tosses it into the bin next to the bench they were sitting on and wipes her hands on her thighs. She hopes it is only a blip.

Lucy pressed on the doorbell to flat 1A, 216 Turner Street. She'd spoken to all the other residents in the converted mansion and been assured the occupant of the remaining flat would be home mid-afternoon. Kirsty Tungsten worked from 6 a.m. until 2 p.m. and was, according to her neighbour, as regular as clockwork when it came to routine, stopping off at the local express grocery store before coming home and usually arriving back at 2.45 p.m. It was bang on three o'clock when Lucy tried her and was in luck.

'Don't mind Ziggy. He's harmless. He doesn't often fall down,' Kirsty said. The large chameleon, a shade in between vanilla and a dusty pink which matched the patterned wallpaper, remained suspended on the ceiling, its monocular eyes rotated in opposite directions as it surveyed its surroundings, searching for prey, before it padded slowly towards the curtains, its zygodactylous feet enabling him to perform the act. The room was a testament to Kirsty's love of animals: toy mice, a scratching post, animal beds, rugs covered in squeaky toys, a hutch inside which sat a floppy-eared black rabbit, nose twitching as it chewed on fresh greens. Lucy wiped sweat from the back of her neck. The room was hot and stuffy, almost tropical. Kirsty reappeared from the kitchen, a moustachioed, black Affenpinscher terrier in a crocheted green coat under her arm. The dog wriggled to get free, keen to greet the newcomer.

'You okay with dogs?'

'Yes.'

'He's a little feisty at the moment and full of energy. I was about to walk him. Ignore him and he'll not bother you. Pat him and you'll be stuck with him for life.' She tapped the dog lightly on his nose and said, 'No jumping!'

She placed the animal on the ground and he bounded towards Lucy, racing around her ankles and sniffing, tail wagging. She took Kirsty's advice and paid him no attention. 'I wanted to talk to you about the cars in the car park opposite. I see you have a good view over it.'

'Bit of an eyesore, isn't it? Still, it could be worse.'

'I wondered if you'd seen any unusual activity in the car park: anyone arguing, a fight, people lurking about?'

'No, I haven't seen a thing. The curtains are usually drawn, especially this time of the year when I'm out most of the daylight hours. It gets dark very early this time of the year. I sometimes don't even bother to open them when I get home.'

Lucy had drawn another blank. She prepared to leave but Kirsty was chatty. 'I didn't see anything over the road but I did observe quite a commotion on Saturday night. It wasn't here though. It was along Eastview Avenue. I was walking Bailey at the time.'

'What did you see?'

'Three drunken young women. Out of their skulls, they were. Well, one of the girls was. She was so drunk she couldn't even walk. They staggered to the car, carrying her between them, and one of them kept her propped up while the other opened the door, then they pushed her into the back seat.'

'Can you describe any of them?'

'It was very dark but I did catch sight of them when the car door opened. The one they were carrying was tall, wearing a long skirt. One had piercings in her face, I think, dark-haired girl, and I can't remember much about the other woman. She was in dark clothing.'

'Any idea of height?'

'No.'

'Hair colour?'

Kirsty shook her head. 'I'm terribly sorry. To be honest, I assumed it was a young woman. It might have been a young man for all I know. I find it difficult to tell the difference some days, especially in the dark.'

'Did the dark-haired woman look anything like this?' said Lucy, drawing out a photograph of Fran.

Kirsty's head bounced slowly up and down. 'Yes. She looked like her. She got into the passenger seat. That was her. I'm sure of it.'

'Can you be more specific about the time?'

'Eight fifteen. Eight thirty? Does that help?'

'Yes, it does. I don't suppose you saw what make the car was?'

'No. I don't recognise car makes or models.'

'Any idea where the women had come from?'

'Yes, that I do know. I walk that road most days. It was number 53.'

Ian looked like he'd won first prize in a grinning contest. 'The Vauxhall Corsa was registered in March 2007 to her grandmother, Marie Bennett, who is currently residing in a care home. Fran doesn't own it but her mother confirmed she drives it, which would explain why we weren't aware of any vehicle beforehand.'

'Get Forensics onto it immediately. If Lucy's witness, Kirsty Tungsten, is correct, then Fran and an unknown person put a drunk or unconscious Hattie into the car. We have to establish who the third person was. The person who drove the car.' She glanced at Lucy, who nodded.

'Lennox,' said Murray.

A line creased Natalie's forehead as she thought about the possibility. 'Wasn't he in the students' union at around that time?'

'He was either there or in town having a drink and a meal. I passed his photo around Wetherspoons and none of the staff remember him being there, and there's no surveillance footage to confirm he was.'

'I daren't interview him again, not without something concrete. His lawyer will probably press charges of harassment. She's not your biggest fan either, Murray.'

'Like I give a shit.'

Natalie slipped off the edge of the desk where she was sitting and stared out of the window into the corridor. As usual it was empty of human traffic, their office being almost at the end of the corridor. She pinched her nose. 'No, we have to wait. Let's see what Forensics uncover first. Can we try and locate that silver Corsa on Saturday evening? Get hold of CCTV footage. I want to know where it went. Start with all the roads between Eastview Avenue and the campus road where Hattie's body was dumped.'

She was going to use the time to chase up loose ends, but a call from Eric prevented her from getting too involved. She left the work to her team and returned to the hospital. She didn't have a pathological dislike of hospitals like many people did, even though she'd had her fair share of bad news in them. Her parents, victims of a hit-and-run, had both been taken to hospital for their final hours, and she'd sat watching the life support machines breathe air into their broken bodies until she had made the decision that there was no point in prolonging the inevitable, and requested they be switched off. Two other occasions had happier connotations: when both her children had been born. Her heels clattered as she marched along the corridor, past the X-ray department where several patients in wheelchairs were lined up. Her mind was lost in the past...

'Oh my goodness! He has the tiniest hands. And look at those fingers. He's going to be a musician with fingers like that, or a tennis player, or... whatever he wants to be.' David's face is a picture of utter joy as he gazes at their firstborn child, a mini David, with dark hair, bright eyes and a grumpy frown.

'He's the spit of you,' says the midwife, ensuring the newborn is wrapped tightly in the blue blanket and can't fall from his father's arms.

David's mouth is open in amazement and happiness, and in spite of all the pain and effort, Natalie watches his reaction with such warmth in her heart she wants to cry.

'We have to clean up Mum now. If you'd like to wait in the next room, you can bring him back in a minute.'

'Come on, little chap. Let's have some "man time",' says David.

The midwife turns her attention back to Natalie. 'He's beautiful. I think all babies are beautiful, but he really is. What are you going to call him?'

'Josh.'

'That's a lovely name. Josh Ward.'

'Josh David Ward,' says Natalie. She hasn't discussed the choice of a middle name with David, but she knows it's the right one. Her heart soars. She couldn't be happier.

Natalie pressed the lift button and waited for it to descend. She was joined by a porter in a blue gown, paper cap covering his hair, who wheeled an unwieldy trolley. The grey-faced patient was elderly. His veiny hand protruded from underneath the blanket. She read his name on his wristband and gave him a comforting smile. He didn't return it, too far gone on pre-med to know what was happening. The lift arrived with a hefty clunk and the doors opened. She motioned for the porter to take it. She'd wait for it to return. He stamped on the brake, releasing it, and heaved the wheeled stretcher into the lift.

'Plenty of room for us all,' he said. She followed them in. The man on the gurney groaned.

'It's all right, Tony, soon be over,' said the porter. He lifted up the notes at the foot of the bed and read them silently as the lift ascended.

The doors opened at the first floor and he juggled to manoeuvre the patient out, trolley wheels clattering as he hauled it into the corridor and thrust it in the direction of the operating theatre. Natalie pressed the button for the second floor and rubbed her hands on her thighs to remove the sweat. The doors opened with a swish and she found herself where she needed to be. A pile of plastic bags containing paper suits, much like the forensic team wore, were piled on a table next to a bin, along with a sign telling her to ensure all footwear was wrapped in protective covers. She dressed in one of the outfits then pressed the buzzer. Peering through the square window in the door, she could see nothing but doors. A nurse in green scrubs appeared and granted her entry onto the ward, heavy with silence apart from the beeping of machines.

'I've come to see David Ward. I'm his wife.'

The name badge indicated the woman was Staff Nurse Ursula Leifer.

'He's this way,' said the nurse, taking her to a door halfway down.

Natalie made no move to enter the room. 'How bad is he?'

'His vitals are acceptable. His ECG was fine and he has been conscious. The consultant will be along later to decide what will happen next. Obviously, they will have to assess what damage has been done, but initial signs are quite good. His father is with him at the moment.' She opened the door and Natalie entered the white room, with white walls, white blinds at the window and a white locker beside a bed with white sheets. David looked pitifully small lying there, attached to machines. The oxygen mask was still in place. Eric was on chair beside the bed, head back, eyes shut. His blue-and-red striped jumper the only colours in the sterile room.

'Eric?'

His eyes snapped open and he struggled to his feet.

'No, you stay there.'

'If it's all the same to you, I'd rather have a walk to the canteen and get a cup of tea.'

'Has he said anything more?' Eric had told her David had spoken only one word – "why?"

'Nothing apart from asking for you. He's been drifting in and out of consciousness. You might have to wait a while before he comes round and speaks again.'

'Take your time.'

'I'll be about half an hour at the most. I might ring Pam.'

'You do that. I'll have to go back to HQ, but I'll stay here for as long as I can.'

Eric shuffled away silently. The sprightly elderly man had become old. The loss of his granddaughter and his son's attempt to commit suicide had added years to his face and whole demeanour. It was only a short while ago he'd been stripped off to the waist, working in their garden, mowing grass, digging out new borders and raking up moss, beads of sweat dripping from his face.

'Hard work never killed anyone,' he'd said when Natalie had tried to get him to slow down. He was right. It would be sadness that would do it for Eric.

Natalie made for the chair at the side of the bed and was about to sit down when David mumbled something. She moved closer to hear him.

'David?'

His eyelids fluttered but didn't open.

'David, it's Natalie. You're in hospital but you're okay.'

The eyelids fluttered again and one opened. His eye was glazed, and pink. 'Nat.'

'You're okay.'

'Nat. Why?' He couldn't say any more and she was reluctant to remove the oxygen mask so that he could speak more clearly. His eyelid closed and she thought he'd drifted off but then both eyes opened and he attempted to sit up, held back by the lines and tubes.

'No, don't move. Stay still. The doctor needs to examine you before you try to sit up.'

He flopped back onto the pillow, either because of her words or lack of energy. 'Why... am... I here?'

'You don't remember?'

His fingers moved, searching for her hand. He was vulnerable and confused so she took his hand, cool in her own. It seemed to calm him. He stared at the ceiling. A minute passed and he tried again.

'I was... with Leigh. Did we... have... an accident? Is she... okay?'

Natalie couldn't speak for the thickening in her throat. His eyes fluttered again and shut, and this time he lost consciousness. She released his hand and stood up quietly. She had to report this to the nurses. One thing was certain, she couldn't tell him the truth. That would have to come from the doctors and at a later stage.

CHAPTER THIRTY-SIX

Natalie tumbled into the office to find enthusiastic faces huddled around a screen.

'What have you found?'

'You won't believe it,' said Lucy.

Natalie chucked her bag onto the floor, folded her arms, efficient again. Murray pressed the cursor and the footage ran. A silver Corsa drove up to traffic lights close to the campus entrance. The time-stamp showed it was Saturday night at 8.46 p.m. The car was held in position waiting for the lights to turn green and the driver's face was visible. It wasn't Lennox at the wheel; it was the shaven-headed Rhiannon, staring sternly ahead. Natalie didn't need to say a word. Lucy was already searching for her car keys under a pile of paperwork. The internal phone halted proceedings as Natalie took the call.

'DI Ward.'

'Nat, we have a match. We've uncovered evidence of Hattie's blood and her DNA in the back seat of the silver Corsa.' Mike's discovery had come at exactly the right time for the team.

'Thank you. You've just made our job a lot easier.'

'You got a suspect?'

'We have. Lucy and Murray are about to get her.' Her words sent the pair scurrying at high speed down the corridor and helter-skelter towards the stairs.

'Been a tough one.'

'Not over yet but we're a lot closer to a result.'

'You'd better tell Dan that. He was prowling around here earlier hoping for new information. I'm under the distinct impression he's under considerable pressure from his superiors. Wouldn't harm your reputation to let him know.'

Natalie caught his drift. He wanted her to get credit for a job well done. He believed in her abilities. 'I'll talk to him.'

'Break a leg.'

She gave a satisfied smile. This time she had facts and proof. She always preferred it when she had something substantial to back up her theories.

'Want me to prepare the evidence and stills for the interview?' asked Ian.

'Yes, please. I have to speak to the superintendent.'

Rhiannon's round face was as expressionless as Ryan's had been. The tears had long dried and she listened to what Natalie had to say and glanced at the stills taken from the traffic camera without saying a word. She was trapped, with a great deal of evidence to prove her involvement. The duty solicitor had advised her to come clean. Withholding facts would only result in further charges. All that remained was for her to tell her version of events. She heaved a deep sigh.

'Look, I know this looks bad, but I didn't kill Gemma or Hattie. The whole thing got out of hand. If Hattie had been half as nice as she pretended to be, none of this would have happened.'

'What do you mean by that?' asked Natalie.

'Gemma is starting to get right on my tits and so's Sasha. I'm sick of her coming around all the time, sitting about the house. She's never out

of the place. It's like having a permanent, useless lodger, and if Gemma asks me one more time if I'm feeling okay in that girly voice and with that fucking bright smile on her face, I swear I'll hit her,' says Hattie, downing her vodka in one.

'I second that. Miss Popular is an irritating cow,' says Fran. 'Here, Rhiannon, tell Hattie about what you're up to.'

'Shh!'

'No, go on. She won't say anything, will you, Hattie?'

'Scout's honour,' says Hattie and makes the sign of the cross on her chest then giggles.

'Well, if you don't tell her, I will,' says Fran. She grabs the vodka bottle and refills everyone's glasses. They've been drinking solidly for over an hour and Rhiannon is feeling woozy. Hattie has confessed to spitting in Gemma's coffee and stealing her favourite lipstick. Rhiannon can't believe it. She thought Hattie was one of the good ones, but it turns out she's as miserable and insecure as her and Fran. It's all on account of her mother dying and her father being a vicar. She's sick of being expected to be good and kind like him. Rhiannon belches sour breath. She ought to have eaten but she's been starving herself to try and lose weight. None of the diets work. Starvation is the only way. The problem is, the less she eats the worse her complexion gets. She's had another heavy outbreak of spots and there's a whopper on the end of her nose that is still obvious, even with thick concealer covering it. She slugs the vodka.

'Go on then,' she says.

Fran laughs. 'Rhiannon's had a brilliant idea. She's running a catfishing scam and using Gemma's picture as bait. It's working too, isn't it, Rhi?'

Rhiannon smiles. Fran's called her idea brilliant. It warms her insides and Hattie is staring at her open-mouthed.

'Fucking brilliant,' says Hattie, and Rhiannon is filled with a sudden happiness she rarely experiences.

*

'Hattie thought the scam was a great idea, but after what happened to Gemma, she flipped. She blackmailed me to keep quiet even though I hadn't got any money. My share of the £3,000 was in Lennox's account. The idea had been to move it to a building society account, but after what happened to Gemma, I didn't want anything else to do with it. I told him to keep it.'

'How come Lennox got involved in this?'

'Money. Lennox needed money. He's been moaning about his mother stopping his allowance for ages and he was desperate for some cash. I proposed we went halves on anything we got if he set up the PayPal link to his account.'

'Why? Why didn't you set up a link to your account?'

'I didn't want the whole thing to blow up in my face and thought if it got traced, Lennox would take the blame.'

'And he accepted that?'

'Lennox is a spoilt rich kid. He isn't used to having nothing to live on. He's been struggling the last month, even cadging food and beer money off friends and housemates. He'd pretty much do anything for money.'

'He had no part in setting up the dating profile?'

'He only set up the PayPal link. I set up the profile.'

'Tell me what happened after Hattie "flipped",' said Natalie.

'Fran and I were in the kitchen. It was after you'd confiscated our phones and we were pretty low. Fran brought down a bottle of gin and we drank it. Hattie came in just as we were finishing the last of it. She said she'd phoned you and had been going to meet you to tell you about the scam but changed her mind at the last minute. She wanted £1,000 to keep quiet. I told her to get screwed. I hadn't got it.'

Hattie's skirt is so long it almost sweeps across the floor. She looks like an extra in a television period drama.

'If you don't give me the money, I'll go to the police. I mean it,'
says Hattie.

'You fucking bitch!' shouts Fran. 'I thought you were our friend.'

'That was before you got Gemma killed.'

'We didn't get her killed.'

'You did.'

'Then go to the police. Tell them. We'll deny it and say you've been
trying to blackmail us.'

Hattie sneers. 'Don't say I didn't give you a chance.'

She turns away, and in that instant, Fran utters an animal-like
sound and rushes at her, bottle raised. It smashes against Hattie's head
and she topples.

'Hattie! Hattie!' Fran's on her knees. 'Hattie, I didn't mean it. Wake
up.' She doubles over in tears.

'Fran was crazy and I couldn't calm her down. I wanted to take
Hattie to the woods and bury her but Fran was having some sort
of breakdown, and in the end I drove to the back of the old drama
studio. It never gets used any more so I didn't think she'd be found
for a while.'

'That wasn't very well thought through, was it?'

'No. I panicked. Fran was yelling about telling the police, and
I knew if she did, she'd end up going to jail and I didn't want that.
She was my friend. I wanted to save her. I bought us some time.
I suggested we drop our courses, move away, get a place together,
maybe even ask for a transfer to another university.'

'And what did she think about that idea?'

'She was considering it.'

'You say Hattie tried to blackmail you. Why didn't she try to
do the same to Lennox?'

'She didn't know about my arrangement with him. She thought
I was behind the whole scam.'

'And what happened to Fran?'

Rhiannon rubbed her lips together, back and forth, then decided to speak.

'She died.'

'But how, Rhiannon? How did she die?'

Rhiannon looked away and wouldn't answer. Her lawyer urged her to talk but she shook her head.

'Did you poison Fran with oxalic acid crystals?'

'No comment.'

'Don't start that with me!'

Rhiannon shifted position, interlaced her fingers, her look far away as if lost in time. She cleared her throat. 'Vodka. I poured her a glass of vodka to calm her down. Right up until that moment, I hadn't really planned on going through with it.'

'But you had oxalic acid crystals.'

'Sort of. That's to say, I didn't have them on me. I knew where I'd find them. There's a difference. I didn't decide to use them until Fran forced me to. If she'd kept her cool or been a true friend, I'd never have been tempted to poison her. It was a crime of passion. The French justice system recognises it. It's not like I actually set out to kill her... It happened. It was a spur-of-the-moment decision. I didn't plan it. There's a difference, surely?' She faced her lawyer. 'There *is* a difference, right?'

The young man representing Rhiannon brushed her off with a cool stare and Natalie urged, 'Tell us what happened.'

Rhiannon stared straight ahead and began...

Fran is marching up and down the small kitchen, her face crimson with anger. 'It's your fucking fault we're in this mess.'

'Mine?'

'You and that stupid scam.'

'You killed Hattie, not me!'

'*Fuck off! It was an accident, and if I'd dialled 999 and called it in, I wouldn't be in this shitty mess. It was your idea to drive her to campus and dump her. I was out of my mind and scared and you manipulated me.*'

'*I didn't!*'

'*You fucking well did. You used the fact I was scared and drunk and set me up. You even used my car to do it, you bitch! I'm going to tell the police everything. I might even be able to make some sort of deal with them to get off.*'

Rhiannon can't believe what she's hearing. She's tried to save her friend from prison and this is the gratitude she gets. She spies the yellow Marigold gloves hanging over the tap from when they were last used. Hattie, no doubt. She always used gloves. Fran is still hurling abuse at her.

'*Stop it. We're friends, Fran.*'

'*You're not my friend. You're a fucking leech. You hang around all the time and are so thick-skinned you don't know when you are not wanted. I'm sick to death of you coming around every single day, but even after I tell you to leave me alone to work, you text or reappear later, and now you've dragged me into this. I wish I'd never met you…*'

Rhiannon doesn't hear the rest of her words for the buzzing in her ears. Fran is her one true friend. How could she say such things?

'*You're just upset. I'm going to get a drink for us and then we can sort this out. We'll go to the police, confess, and I'll explain it was my fault Hattie was taken to the drama studio. I'll tell them what happened was an accident and that she attacked you first. We'll fix this,*' she says with a calm she doesn't feel.

The fight whooshes out of Fran, who slumps onto a chair and doesn't notice Rhiannon pick up the gloves. Rhiannon heads to the sitting room, where she checks the shelf and lifts a miniature bottle of vodka, one of a few bottles that still has alcohol in it, and pours the contents into a tumbler. Then she heads for the cupboard. Lennox's car-washing kit is in a box on the shelf, and donning the gloves, she pulls it down and hunts for the acid crystals. It's in the hands of the fates now. If he's used *up the oxalic acid crystals, she'll return to Fran, have a drink and then discuss what to tell the police. That's not how she wants to play this. She doesn't want to spend any time in jail, and if she's honest, she knows they'll both be charged with numerous offences – at best, manslaughter, which carries a prison sentence with it. She gives a smile as she spies a small jar. The fates have decided, and she tips a few of the crystals into the tumbler, swilling until they dissolve.*

'Fran only had one sip. The poison took no time at all to act. I carried her to my car, got her into the passenger seat and drove. At first, I was going to leave her in the same place as Hattie, but I spotted the blankets in the abandoned doorway and stopped there. It was more convenient. I didn't think anyone would find her straight away and I'd have time to return with a suicide note to leave with her body. I typed a note saying she'd killed herself because she was responsible for the whole scam and Hattie's death and was on my way back when I saw the police vehicles. You'd already found her.'

'You typed a note on your laptop?'

'No, I used one of the computers in the library and printed it off there.'

'You killed your friend – you murdered your best friend,' said Natalie.

Rhiannon looked straight through her. 'She wasn't a true friend. I don't have any friends.'

The girl's confession went further than accounting for what had happened to Hattie and Fran. Natalie was reminded of the typed note found in Gemma's diary and suddenly, pieces shifted more firmly into position. 'But you wanted to be friends with people, didn't you? You wanted to be friends with Gemma. You sent Gemma that anonymous note we found in her room. You were her admirer.'

'That was a mistake. I sent her the note because I thought she'd be flattered and pleased and would be happy to have me as a friend, but she didn't even mention it to anyone; not to Fran, Hattie or even Ryan. She did tell her mother though because I overheard them laughing and joking about her admirer. They thought I was a crackpot! I assumed she'd thrown the letter away and I was hurt. Really hurt. If somebody told you that you were special or amazing, you'd be pleased, right? She wasn't. She was too big-headed and full of herself. I knew after I'd sent it that I should have kept my letter secret like I did after the incidents with Gwen and Nora.'

'Who's Gwen?'

'She was in my class at my old school.' She sighed again. 'She freaked out when I told her I'd sent them and wouldn't talk to me again. I also wrote to Nora, who was in the year above me, but she told her friends, who found out I'd sent the letters and took the piss out of me. They made my life truly miserable. I don't know why they were horrible to me. I was only being friendly. I didn't write any more until I left home and came to Samford, then I wrote to Fran but I didn't send them to her. I kept all those letters hidden in my room, and after we became good friends, I ripped them up in case she ever found them. I shouldn't have ever sent that one to Gemma. She didn't appreciate it. She was exactly the same as the others.'

'What do you mean "as the others"?'

'She was a two-faced bitch, just like Gwen and Nora were. She didn't deserve to be admired…'

Nora's nostrils are flaring and her two friends are blocking the exit to the shower block. Naked and dripping with water, Rhiannon begins to shake. She's always last to shower after PE lessons. She hates anyone seeing her undressed in the communal showers and waits until the last girl sprints out before she goes in. Her towel is out of reach, high in Nora's hand.

Rhiannon tries to cover her stomach and chest with her arms and ignore Nora's friends, who stare openly at her, jeering at her plump body.

'You fancy me then, do you?' says Nora.

'No.'

'Yes, you do. What about, "You're so beautiful and I love your hair. It looks incredibly soft." Sounds like you fancy me.' Nora stares again.

Rhiannon can hear laughter from the changing room. Her classmates are listening to the conversation. She knows what she wrote in the letter, but the way Nora says it makes it sound stupid and childish when all she wanted to do was make Nora realise she was admired.

Nora continues in a silly girly voice, "'I think your friends are really lucky to have you as a friend.'" She pretends to stick two fingers into her mouth to make herself sick then continues, 'And who the fuck says they "admire" anybody these days?' There's more giggling in the changing room and a couple of faces peer in at the scene taking place in the shower.

'I only wanted to be friendly—'

The dark-haired girl throws her head back as she laughs then spits out, 'Who'd want you as a friend? Look at you!'

In spite of the burning embarrassment she's experiencing, Rhiannon begins to shiver. She's ashamed of her body and how vulnerable she feels with these pretty sixteen-year-old girls looking at her. 'Can I… have… my towel?'

'You are fucking weird,' says Nora, hanging on to the massive blue towel that Rhiannon uses to hide in when she gets out of the shower. It's large enough for her to dress under it. Rhiannon could step forward and try to grab it, but she knows the girls will make sure she doesn't get it. She spies Gwen, the girl in her class who she also once sent letters to. Her face oozes disdain.

'She's fucking weird,' says Gwen. 'She wrote something like that to me too.'

Nora's eyebrows shoot upwards. 'Really? You got a thing for girls, then?' she asks.

'No. I was only being nice—'

The girl with black hair points a finger at her. 'Shut up.'

'You want me, do you?' says Nora, running her hands over her shapely hips.

'No!'

'Yes, she does,' says her friend.

'You want to be my special bitch, don't you?' Nora taunts.

'I don't!' wails Rhiannon. They don't understand. This isn't sexual. She only wanted to be friends.

'She's got the hots for you,' says Gwen. 'Sad cow.' She gives Rhiannon a cold look and turns away to join her classmates, leaving Rhiannon alone with Nora and her friends.

Tears fill her eyes. She doesn't deserve this.

'What shall we do to her?' asks the other girl, who's been staring the entire time, a sneer across her face.

'Make her regret it,' says Nora. 'Hide her clothes in a classroom then she'll have to walk around school like that.'

'NO!' Rhiannon is horrified. She often has nightmares about being stark naked and people laughing at her. 'No... please,' she begs.

'Do it,' says Nora.

Rhiannon can hardly breathe for fear then the door flies open and Gwen reappears.

'Teacher's coming,' she hisses.

Nora tosses Rhiannon the towel.

'Better watch your back. Next time you won't be as lucky.'

'Why did Lennox tell us Fran was behind the scam? Why didn't he tell us you were?'

For the first time since she sat down, Rhiannon permitted herself a small smile. 'Ask Lennox.'

'I'm asking you.'

Her eyebrows danced on her forehead and she dropped her voice to a conspiratorial whisper. 'A couple of weeks ago, I caught Lennox giving his tutor a blow job at the back of the science department.'

'And you used that information to keep him quiet?'

She nodded. 'He was more ashamed of being found out about that than stealing money from a stranger. I told him I'd tell everyone about it if he dropped me in it, and I explained it was better to frame Fran and to tell you she was behind the scam. I even went through what he'd tell you – about them going to bed together and her threatening him to remain silent.' It went some way to explaining his loyalty to Rhiannon but not completely.

'Did he know who had killed Fran?'

'Maybe, maybe not. I didn't tell him.'

Natalie would have to ask Lennox that question herself. 'Doesn't matter though, does it? His rich mummy will hire a fantastic team of defence lawyers and get him off any charges. Mine won't.' Rhiannon heaved a sigh of acceptance and stared at her yellow nails.

Dear Gemma,

I lost my cool today with somebody I thought was a good friend but who proved she was exactly the same as everyone else – shallow and self-centred.

Fran wanted to confess to everything that's happened, including hitting Hattie over the head and dumping her body on campus.

'It was an accident!' she cried.

You see, Gemma, no matter what Fran said, there was no getting away from it; Fran whacked Hattie over the head with the gin bottle and Hattie crumpled like a sack of potatoes. If it hadn't been for my quick thinking, we'd have been in serious shit. I saved us, not Fran. Not the girl who claimed to be hard and dangerous. Not the tattooed, tough Fran with her 'fuck you' attitude. She burst into tears at the sight of Hattie lying on the floor. I fixed everything, from cleaning up the blood to moving Hattie's body, and then the stupid, ungrateful cow was going to confess to the police and drag me into the mess with her.

It's a good thing I listen. It's one of the advantages of people not noticing me. You, being Miss Popular, wouldn't know about that, but I am the opposite – Miss Unpopular – and I knew all about Lennox's precious car and its rust patches. It's amazing how boring that boy can be. He droned on about his damn car, and everybody at the lunch table switched off, but I listened and I remembered the oxalic acid crystals and I'd seen where he kept his car cleaning equipment.

Fran was in a dreadful state. She needed a glass of vodka – a glass of vodka with a little added something special.

I wasn't as upset as I expected I'd be. I'd been pissed off at her for a while. I'd gone to all this trouble to get some money together to rent a flat for us both when term ends and she'd been coming up with excuses not to look at potential flats, on top of which, she'd begun to avoid me – making excuses not to hang out together, going out with other girls without me and pretending to be out when she was actually in her room. She thought I was too dumb to work out what was happening but I am not dumb, Gemma. I don't handle rejection well. It was better to get rid of her before she decided it was time to dump me.

I'm hopeful the police will think she committed suicide and will put two and two together and believe Fran was behind the scam and Hattie's death. I can sort out Lennox. He won't dare breathe a word, not with what I know about the dirty little sod. He's scared witless his mother will find out he's been blowing off his tutor to get better grades.

All of this means I now have no friends at all. Not one.

See what you started, Gemma? This is your fault. If you'd been nice to me, none of this would have happened.

An Ex-Admirer

CHAPTER THIRTY-SEVEN

WEDNESDAY, 21 NOVEMBER – NIGHT

'I'd like to thank you all for your efforts. You excelled during this investigation,' said Natalie. She looked around at the tired faces. It was almost midnight but they'd all pulled their weight and Rhiannon had been charged for her part in the scam, for acting as an accomplice in Hattie's death, and for the murder of Fran Ditton. Lennox had been given a lesser charge for assisting with the catfish scam but had also been charged with perverting the course of justice, although his lawyer had applied for bail.

They'd established that Rhiannon had driven Hattie's car to the station and parked it up after she and Fran had dumped Hattie's body. The last piece of evidence had come in via Forensics, who'd uncovered a collection of letters printed on A4 paper and kept in a folder hidden among lecture notes. At first glance, they'd thought they were part of Rhiannon's coursework, but one of the eagle-eyed team had spotted the name Gemma several times and the letters had been brought back to the station for further examination. There was no doubt Rhiannon had typed and printed them, and each one revealed the truth behind the scam and the deaths of Hattie and Fran. It was another vital piece of the jigsaw explaining why Rhiannon had drummed up the idea of the scam – jealousy at Gemma's popularity and upset at being rejected by somebody she admired.

Lennox had been shocked to discover Rhiannon had been behind Fran's death, and whether or not that shock was genuine, Natalie would never know. His lawyer had been quick to point out that Rhiannon had been emotionally blackmailing Lennox, and Natalie knew that with Carolyn acting on his behalf, once the case went to trial, he was likely to get away with minimum sentencing. Natalie and her team could only find those responsible for acts, not give out the punishments. They'd played their role. Now it was up to the justice system.

Dan, who'd been standing by the door next to Mike, took a step forward. 'I'd like to add my thanks to DI Ward's. Great job, everyone.'

The team disbanded but Dan wanted a word with Natalie. Mike murmured, 'I'll wait in my car for you.'

With the office empty, Dan unfolded his hands from behind his back and, lifting his trousers slightly at the knees so he didn't ruin the creases in them, sat down carefully. He motioned for her to join him and she dropped down on her own chair.

'I've only known you a short while but you've impressed me. More importantly, you've impressed upstairs.' Upstairs referred to the senior level staff who shared the same floor as Dan. 'What I'm going to tell you is highly confidential and mustn't leave this room.' He waited for a gesture of acknowledgement before carrying on. 'There's going to be some restructuring over the next few months. Samford was built as a centre of excellence but is already outgrowing its purpose, and I have been informed that certain units are to be moved into another purpose-built building which will be situated not far from HQ. Your unit will be amalgamated with several others to form a special crimes unit and be one of three units relocated to the new premises. How you have handled high-profile investigations, especially while under personal stress, has not gone unnoticed, and I've been tasked with asking you if you would consider overseeing the new unit. Naturally, that responsibility will carry promotion, and there'll be an opportunity for one of your team to step into your shoes as DI of the unit. I'd also like you to put forward a recommendation for whoever you think would be best suited to that job.'

'I see.' Her mind seesawed between the pros and cons. The pros would be leaving HQ, promotion, an increase in salary, and against that, the facts that the team's dynamics would change and she would no longer work in the same building as Mike; moreover, the big question – could she take on any more responsibility? She had Josh to consider and of course, David. She couldn't completely walk away from him.

'You'll need time to think about this. How about I give you until the end of the month. That's just over a week. I'll expect your answer by then.'

She couldn't formulate a response, caught up in a blizzard of thoughts. She settled on a simple, 'Thank you, sir.'

He placed both hands on his knees and stood up effortlessly. 'As I said, good job today. Oh, by the way, how's your ex-husband doing?'

'He's recovering.'

'Excellent. Right-ho!' He moved off, halting by the door to say, 'Give it serious thought, Natalie. I think you'd be perfect for the job… and not a word to anyone at all. This news is not to leave this room.'

She waited until he was out of sight before rubbing her forehead with both hands, massaging away the confusion. Did she really want this opportunity? It wasn't so much an opportunity as something being forced on her. Her unit would be moved regardless of her decision and would grow in size. How would her team feel about that? She'd been ordered not to say anything to anyone, but she had to at least discuss it with Mike. *Shit!* Mike was waiting for her. She scrambled to her feet.

*

True to his word, Mike was waiting for her in his warm car, the interior a mixture of woody aftershave and spearmint gum. Coldplay crooned about a sky full of stars and he gave her a tired smile. 'Home?'

She flopped back into the soft leather seat. 'Please. Do you want to stay the night – or what's left of it? It'll give us a chance to talk, seeing as we missed out on our meeting in the park.'

'One of the drawbacks of our jobs – at times, we get no bloody personal life! I'd love to but I am properly done in, and besides, it feels a bit wrong with David in hospital. When he's recovered—'

'David can't remember what's happened to him. He thinks Leigh's still alive.'

'Fuck!'

'I couldn't tell him, not about Leigh and not about me and him splitting up, or about you. I'm hoping the doctors will, or his memory will come back.'

'Oh, fucking hell, Nat!' He reached for his cigarettes, started to tap one out, changed his mind and replaced the packet in the door pocket.

Natalie understood. David had to go through the whole pain again of finding out that his daughter was dead and that his wife had left him.

They arrived at the flat and she turned towards him. 'Look, I won't hold it against you if you want to step back, call it off – us, I mean.' She couldn't articulate what she truly wanted to say, that she wanted Mike, and to see what the future held for them both, but it had all suddenly become messy, and if David was somehow back in her life, even on the periphery, requiring her attention and assistance, that complicated everything further, not to mention the promotion.

She ought to tell Mike about what she'd been told. He hadn't yet mentioned it, but he'd undoubtedly be curious as to why Dan had wanted to talk to her. She couldn't bear deceit and lies, and if it meant losing the promotion on account of the news getting out, then so be it. She wasn't going to lose Mike by hiding anything from him.

'There's something else I have to tell you. I've been offered a promotion – new unit, near HQ.'

Mike said nothing. She hunted for a sign and saw nothing but deliberation as he chewed over what she'd said. Mike didn't rush into anything. He was weighing up the options as she had done. She stared ahead rather than watch him struggle. If this changed everything between them, then it did. They weren't meant to be together.

'It would mean we wouldn't bump into each other at work any more, and we see precious little of each other as it is,' she said. Ahead of them a driver on a motorcycle accelerated then performed a wheelie past the car, followed by another, copying their actions. *Bored youngsters.*

His hands caressed the leather steering wheel, rubbing up and down. 'It's fine. You should take it. We need to sort out what we're going to do as a couple, and if we can get our act together and move in together, then it won't hurt if we work in different places. It might be better for us both.'

Her voice lifted in surprise. 'Move in together?'

'Yes, I was going to ask you about it when we met up in the park. My house is plenty big enough for you, me, Thea, when she visits, and Josh. He'd be very welcome too – more than welcome. You can't remain in that poky flat and heaven knows when you'll sell your house. It'd work out. I'm sure of it.'

'What about David?'

'That's the million-dollar question. Only you can decide if or how much he still fits into your life.'

She searched her soul for the answer and it was as clear as the sky Chris Martin sang about. No matter how little David remembered, or how much support he'd require, the fact remained that his and Natalie's relationship and marriage were over. She'd left him to start again with Mike. 'Josh is out tonight. Why don't you come in?'

'Yeah, I'd like that.'

CHAPTER THIRTY-EIGHT

Natalie and her team had spent the day writing up reports and ensuring every piece of evidence was logged in preparation for the trials that Henry, Lennox and Rhiannon would face. At 3 p.m. she left and drove across town to visit Sasha.

Sasha had been busy. Photographs of Gemma that had been in albums were now artistically displayed as montages in frames – a timeline of her daughter's life from infant to a nineteen-year-old, stretched across the sitting room wall. Everywhere Natalie looked, she saw Gemma's smiling face.

'I don't ever want to forget her. I'm returning everything to her room and setting it up as it was before she left home,' said Sasha with a heavy sadness. She lifted the pink jumper she'd been clutching and held it to her nose. Natalie recognised the garment. It was in front of her in the most recent montage of photos where Gemma, with arms out to her side, swirled and twirled for the camera, in that very garment and ripped jeans. 'What do I do when the smell goes?' The voice had weakened and Natalie understood her anxiety.

'By then, you'll be ready to move forward. One step at a time,' said Natalie, who still slept with Leigh's teddy bear for exactly the same reason. She ought to embrace Leigh's life not hide it away in boxes as she had been doing. She should make collages and montages, like these on the wall, from photos of her own beautiful child. Sasha's grief was as palpable as her own but she was already ahead of Natalie in terms of progress. She talked about her child, rather than hiding from the truth.

'Will you be at the funeral?'

'Yes.' Natalie wasn't going to allow this woman to sit alone in a church while she buried her only child. She would be there for her as would the others on her team as a mark of respect.

'Thank you. And will you still come and visit me afterwards when it's all over? Just for a cup of tea or a glass of wine?'

'Yes.' She meant it.

Sasha gave a brave smile. 'I've got something to show you. I finished it last night.' She disappeared for a minute and returned with an emerald-green bibbed dress hanging from a wooden coat hanger. 'It's the first in a collection of clothes especially designed for students. I've named the collection after her. This was her favourite colour. I'm going to keep on with the sewing. There's a boutique in town that's expressed some interest in selling my clothes. I'm going to prove Gemma right.'

'She'd have been very proud of you.'

'Yes, she would, wouldn't she?' She looked up at the collages of photos on the wall.

'For you, my baby girl. I love you so much.' Silver tears trickled down her cheeks and Natalie moved towards her, putting arms around her to comfort her, and they stood, sharing the pain that only they could understand existed.

The phone call had come as she was on her way back to the flat. David was conscious and this time his memory was working. The consultant was encouraged. David was showing no signs of brain damage, and appointments to see a psychiatrist had been arranged. David wanted to see her again if she could find time to come by. She opened the door to her flat and caught the smell of Italian herbs. David's signature dish was lasagne, and for one fleeting moment, she imagined he was here. It wasn't David who shouted hello but Josh.

'Hi, Mum. I thought I'd cook for us tonight – it's only a ready meal. Is that okay?'

She beamed at her son. A box sat on the kitchen table. It was the hairdryer he'd promised to buy. She couldn't help herself and wrapped her arms around him and kissed him on the cheek. He didn't push her away. When she broke off, he said, 'I was talking to Pippa about Dad and she made me understand a couple of things. I think I'd like to go and see him, if that's okay.'

'That's definitely okay. He'll be glad. We can go after we've eaten, if you like.'

'Yeah, that'd be good.'

She headed into the bedroom to get changed then crouched down to pull out a box. She lifted the lid and pulled out the top few photographs. Leigh's face brightened the room. Her hair blown by the sea breeze was soft and light and framed her sweet face. The top that Eric had bought her on holiday had wrapped itself around her slim frame. Her right arm was balanced across her brother's shoulders and Josh smiled proudly at the camera. Natalie pressed the picture to her lips and placed it on the bed. It would go into a frame much like the ones Sasha had put up on her walls. She was going to fill frames with photos of her children, and when she finally moved in with Mike, she'd make up frames of Thea and him and hopefully more montages of them with her and Josh. She had to stop hiding away her memories. It was time to move on.

A LETTER FROM CAROL

Hello, dear reader,

My sincere thanks to you for buying and reading *The Secret Admirer*. I really hope you enjoyed reading it as much as I did writing it. There's more to come in this series, and if you'd like to keep up to date with all my latest releases, just sign up at the following link. Your email address will never be shared and you can unsubscribe at any time.

www.bookouture.com/carol-wyer

Wow! Book six in the series already and I find myself fully enmeshed in Natalie's life and wondering what will happen next. Actually, I already know… but that would be telling.

I am aware that many of my readers have found David to be somebody they love to hate. I hope after reading *The Secret Admirer* you will feel more sympathy towards him and have an understanding of what he has been through. Of course, Natalie has had her own fair share of troubles and difficulties, and I'm afraid there are more problems and shocks to come in the next book.

If you enjoyed reading *The Secret Admirer*, please write a review, no matter how brief it is. You have no idea how much they mean to me and I would be hugely grateful if you would spare a few minutes to write one.

I hope you'll join me for the next book in the DI Natalie Ward series, which will be out Summer 2020.

Thank you,
Carol

AuthorCarolEWyer

@carolewyer

www.carolwyer.co.uk

ACKNOWLEDGEMENTS

The Secret Admirer would not have been possible without a huge amount of help from my outstanding editor Lydia Vassar-Smith, who not only came up with the brilliant title but helped dig me out of a few plot holes.

As always, I owe a debt of gratitude to the entire dynamic production team at Bookouture. You would be surprised at how many people work on each book before it is published, and I have many eagle-eyed editors, including DeAndra Lupu, who not only copy edits my work but leaves me entertaining messages throughout the script that keep me going, and Liz, who proofreads the final text and always manages to catch errant punctuation marks.

Huge thanks to my readers, who message me regularly and stay in contact on social media. You are my constant support and see me through many a sleepless night of writing or editing. Heartfelt thanks for that.

Sincerest thanks to my incredible Street Team, who offer endless support and help promote my books. I love you guys!

Thanks too to Jenny O'Brien aka @ScribblerJB on Twitter, for providing me with valuable information on brain injuries.

And finally, thanks to my other half, Mr Grumpy, for all the cups of tea and chocolate biscuits and for putting up with constant neglect. I couldn't do any of this without you.

Made in the USA
Coppell, TX
06 April 2020

19178280R00215